THINK INC. MYSTERIES Vol. I

LAST BREATH

By H.P. BARNETT

Join the most beautiful and seductive Egyptian woman since Cleopatra as she, her lover and her friends save the world from certain destruction.

Cover Photo "Rainy Nights at Tijuana" by Christian Javan

DEDICATION

To my sister Michelle. Losing you so early in your life gave me that extra resolve to follow my dreams. To live each day doing what I want to do.

ACKNOWLEDGMENTS

I want to thank my wife, Linda, for her untiring assistance with my first writing endeavor. I also want to thank my children who have offered constructive criticism, enthusiasm for my efforts, encouragement to follow my passion, and some very valuable advice. Without the support of my family, this book would not have been possible.

PREFACE

Corporate survival, through recessionary times, is a difficult challenge for any management team. Some of the most prestigious corporations and investment firms have failed to achieve success in their endeavors to survive. Millions, in fact tens-of-millions of investors, globally, have lost everything. Rich or poor, privileged or middle-class, the financial consequence of the global recession affects everyone.

Chemico International, its board of directors and its shareholders, were facing this same challenge; how to survive in a shrinking and increasingly competitive global market. There weren't going to be any, high-profile, politically-motivated, government bail-outs as seen in the automotive and financial sectors. Chemico, and hundreds-of-thousands of other companies, had been set adrift to navigate their own course through these tough times.

With their corporate backs against the wall, many companies made decisions for short-term survival without consideration of the long-term consequences. In a few cases, these potential consequences were of epic proportion; sufficient to threaten global security; sufficient to tip the global balance-of-power, both financially and militarily.

These were frightening times, for those in-the-know.

Chemico International manufactured products commonly referred to as blasting media. Explosives used primarily by mining companies to blast rock, aggregate mainly, sand and gravel for asphalt paving, and also for hard-rock mining of precious metals, gold, silver and the like. In comparison to their competitors, Chemico was a small-fish in a very large pond, due mainly to a dramatic loss in sales; sales lost to their competition. With the shortfall in revenue, the company found it necessary to shut-down two of its three manufacturing plants; one in Butte Montana and the second in Stavanger, Norway. Their remaining sales represented only fifteen-percent of the available mining business in the geographic area they still serviced from their one remaining plant in Canada. Chemico desperately needed to increase sales and grow the business back to its former level if they were to remain a viable company. And they were willing to try anything.

CHAPTER ONE

March 15, 11:00 am EDT
Offices of Chemico International - Ottawa, Canada

John Bentley, Manager of Product Development for Chemico International, had summoned his newest employee, Edward Milton, to his office. Bentley had received a phone call earlier that morning from William Playfield, head of security for the company, concerning a security breach in the corporate computer system. It was reported that Edward had gained access to several computer files; files containing information for which he didn't have sufficient security clearance to access. As Edward walked along the corridor towards Bentley's office, he stopped at the desk of Monica Chilling.

"Good...morning beautiful."

Monica was startled by Edward's sudden appearance. She calmly covered several sheets of paper on her desk and clicked her computer to her wallpaper screen. "Good morning yourself, Edward."

Despite her valiant effort to retain a very business-like expression and demeanor, these three simple words brought a rose-colored hew to Monica's cheeks. Edward was a flirt, and although she enjoyed the attention, Monica was the Office Manager and as such she was required to maintain proper office decorum.

Edward was a new employee in the Product Development Department having recently been transferred from his previous position in Product Service. His last position responsibility was largely shot design; working directly with customers to assist them in the most cost-effective shot pattern. The pattern of holes to drill in the rock and fill with blasting media, so it could be blasted. He had been with Chemico for two years, recruited straight out of university. He had only met John Bentley once when he was first interviewed for this new position. A position for which he hadn't applied. His name somehow appeared on the list of potential internal candidates. Edward never did find out how that occurred.

Monica Chilling was in her mid-thirties. Her auburn-hair was short, a change from the shoulder-length style she wore before she went on maternity leave with her most recent child. She was married with two young children, both boys, and had recently returned from her maternity leave. She had worked very hard to lose the weight she gained with her pregnancy, and was almost back to her normal figure, although she still felt she needed to shed a few more pounds. Neither an uncommon goal nor feeling for many women at her stage in life, especially, immediately after a pregnancy.

Monica and Edward had known each other and had a friendly relationship since Edward first joined the company. Edward was a tease and a flirt but always in a nice way. He was an all-round nice guy to know. Most everyone in the office liked him. It wasn't very long before Monica gave into his charm and cracked a smile in response to his current antics.

Edward returned a smile. "See, I knew there was a smile behind those pretty brown eyes," he whispered.

"One of these days, you're going to get into trouble with your forward behavior," she scolded, trying to recover the business-like expression she had mustered only a few seconds earlier.

"I know, but that's just me," he admitted. He sat in the visitor chair at the side of her desk. "I've been summoned by my commander-and-chief, and to be honest with you, I've forgotten where his office is. I don't get into this area of the plant very often and it all looks the same to me."

"Someone as smart as you is lost? How can that be?"

"I'm a mining Engineer, not an explorer. What can I say?" Edward shrugged.

"It's down the hall and to the right, third door on the outside wall, to the left. His name is on the door."

"I thought so. I wanted to stop and welcome you back. How's little Chad doing? I thought you were going to call him Edward," he mused as he stood.

"The baby's name was always going to be Chad. It's his father's middle name. You know, the man I'm married to," she quipped, holding out her ring hand for him to see. "You do know I'm very happily married, don't you?"

"Yeah, but I'm waiting in the wings if things ever change."

"They won't and you need to get to your meeting before you get into more trouble."

"Why do you always assume I'm in trouble?"

"Because you *are* always in trouble. Now scoot," Monica whispered while she swished him in the direction of his bosses' office.

******

Edward proceeded down the hallway towards Bentley's office, noting the vanilla office décor everywhere he looked. Every office he walked past was the same. Almost exactly the same size; the same desks stained that awful non-distinct light oak color; the same matching credenza behind the desk adding to the oh-hum. The same three cookie-cutter visitors' chairs and the same whiteboard hanging on the side wall. Pictures of various mine-sites around the country graced the wall of every office. The pictures were the only feature in the offices that were unique. Edward noted that the more important your management position the better your view, or so it appeared. The more senior level managers' offices were positioned along the outside walls of the building which meant they had a window and a panoramic view of... the parking lot.

"This is career hell," Edward thought to himself as he viewed the scene. "*No way am I getting stuck in this world, forever.*

Edward reached Bentley's office; poked his head in the door; and knocked softly. Bentley had his back to the door and hadn't heard his knock. As he spoke on the phone, he gazed out his window at a massive truck backing up to the loading dock. The beeping of the vehicle's backup alarm caused him to pause his phone conversation. He noticed Edward out of the corner of his eye, waved him in and motioned for him to take a seat. He ended his telephone conversation and turned his attention towards Edward.

John Bentley appeared to be in his mid-forties; slightly balding but he still had most of his dark-brown hair, slicked down with hair-product. He was the one and only person Edward knew who still used hair cream to plaster his doo into place. Bentley topped off his unique style with a pair of black, owl-like framed glasses. A framed picture of his wife and two teenage children, a girl and a boy, sat on the credenza behind his desk next to the bowling trophy he won in last year's company bowling league. He stood and shook Edward's hand then settled back into his mock-leather, high back, Office Depot, executive chair.

"I must apologize," he announced in his booming voice. "I haven't had time to get down among the troops and welcome you properly to the team."

Edward guessed he used his big voice so he would be heard over the ambient noise coming from the parking lot outside his window. He motioned for Edward to close the office door, which he did.

"Welcome to the Product Development department. I like to think of us as the backbone of the company. I trust your office is to your liking."

"Thanks. Everything is fine," Edward replied. He wasn't sure what Bentley meant by office. Edward had a fabric-walled cubical in the corner of the department. It gave him zero incentive to work his way up through the ranks, and maybe one day have an office as fine as this one. If he was lucky, maybe his view would overlook the executive parking lot. At least he'd be staring at a higher quality vehicle. A Volvo, or Subaru, or perhaps that magnificent, "day-glow-caution-yellow, Hummer the president of the company drove. An improvement for certain over the dirty truck he viewed and heard outside Bentley's window.

"We have a potential problem, Edward," Bentley stated. "Seems William Playfield; do you know Playfield? He's head of security. Seems Bill has been tipped off by the computer geeks in IT about a breach in the security of the company computer system. You, my friend, were apparently into some files you weren't supposed to be in. I'm scheduled to have a discussion about that with the big guy, Martin Stanley, at one this afternoon. I need to have the details on exactly how that happened."

"I don't know how it happened. I assume you're referring to some files I was into the other day, or actually the night before last. I was in late, working on a project the team leader assigned me, and all of a sudden I started to see data scrolling across my screen. I read a little bit of it as it sped by. It was pretty clear that it was kind of secretive stuff - not intended for my eyes at least; so I shut it down. The only thing that really stuck in my head was the acronym O.D.D.; I assume it's an acronym for something. That's the only thing I recall from the brief encounter with the files."

"Why were you in late? You just started in the department."

"I have a conference to attend in a few days. I felt, being new to the department maybe I should cancel; but I was told by my supervisor to attend the conference. I wanted to make sure I left things in good order before I left."

"What's the conference? I don't recall approving a travel and expense request."

"It was set up before I came to the department. It's the Mensa International Annual Conference."

"What's Mensa International?"

"I belong to an organization called Mensa. Mensa is a group of people with high IQs." Edward explained. He was trying to explain what the organization was about without going into too much detail. Edward had always been modest about his level of intelligence and preferred to keep it to himself.

"Is this an engineering group or professional membership of some kind?" Bentley inquired.

"No. Membership eligibility is not dependent on your vocation or your level of academic achievement. It's based solely on your IQ score. Only the scores in the top two percentile qualify for membership."

"Top two percentile of...?"

"Of people in the world. Or at least the world where IQ is measured."

"I'm impressed. Why would someone as smart as you choose to work here?" Bentley questioned.

"Having a high IQ doesn't mean that you're relegated to academia, if that's what you mean. I'm here because I was interested in mining and decided that was going to be my career goal. Chemico is big in supplying the mining industry; I'm pursuing my goal."

"I see. Good for you, Edward. By all means attend the conference. It sounds very interesting. From what you're telling me about the other incident, it was clearly an error on the part of IT. They gave you too high a clearance level. I am curious why I haven't been included in what appears to be a new product development. That's a question for Mr. Stanley.

I'm good with your explanation. Thanks for coming in and explaining the situation. I'll see you when you get back. Where is the conference by the way?"

"Mexico City."

"Nice... Enjoy," Bentley finished. He smiled and escorted Edward to the door while shaking his hand.

Edward left the meeting feeling confident that his explanation of the security breach was sufficient for Bentley. Edward made certain to wink at Monica as he passed her desk on his way back to his cubicle. He didn't take the time to stop and chat. She simply waved and smiled as she continued with her phone conversation.

CHAPTER TWO

March 15, 11:30 am EDT
Office of Martin Stanley - CEO of Chemico International
Ottawa, Canada

"I'm telling you Martin, there's been a breach of security in the system. Like I explained earlier this morning, whether it was unintentional or not, someone has accessed files they had no business seeing," Playfield said.

William Playfield was security-chief at Chemico International. He had called the meeting with the President and C.E.O. of the company, Martin Stanley, to discuss a breach in the security of the corporate computer system. It had been reported to him that an employee had opened computer files he didn't have sufficient security clearance to see. Files that contained detailed information concerning a new explosive the company was developing for a customer in the U.S. Playfield had already informed the employee's boss about the situation, but according to procedure, he was also required to notify the CEO immediately if there was a breach in security such as this.

"Bill, I'm telling you, our I.T. people assure me the system is foolproof. No one can break in," Stanley replied.

"It's no more sinister than IT assigning too high a security clearance for this guy."

"I'm not saying anyone broke in. I'm telling you this new guy, Milton, has been into some high- security sections in the system, snooping around," Playfield argued.

"Alright. Alright. I already spoke to his boss and he's scheduled in here after lunch. I'll talk to John Bentley first and see what kind of guy this Milton is. I'm not sure I've ever met him. I think he's one of our new top picks from the University highest achievers' list. He has recently been moved to Product Development."

"I'm available if you want me to be here for your discussion with Bentley," Playfield offered. "I have notified you of the incident. That's what the policy requires. But from this point on, the ball is in your court as far as how you want to handle it. I'm here if you want my take on it, or not. Your choice, Martin."

"I prefer to deal with this myself, Bill. I'll call on you if I feel it's anything other than an error by the I.T. folks," Stanley assured.

William Playfield returned to his office. He wasn't convinced that Stanley was taking him seriously enough. He was the President and he made the final decisions. He had done what policy dictated he do in reporting the incident to the CEO. If Stanley didn't feel it was serious enough a situation to take further steps, then so-be-it.

Stanley dialed John Bentley's extension to remind his secretary that John had a meeting with him immediately after lunch.

"Mr. Bentley is currently reviewing budget information in the Finance Manager's office. Did you want me to interrupt and have him come to see you sooner?" the secretary asked.

"No. Just remind him of the one o'clock, sharp, meeting."

******

"John, I had Bill Playfield in here before lunch, all in a flap about our computer system security being compromised. Apparently your new man, Milton, was into something he shouldn't have been," Stanley said.

It was clear that John Bentley was uncomfortable with being summoned by the top executive in the company. Fortunately for him, he had done some homework and was somewhat prepared to discuss the situation.

"Mr. Stanley, as a matter of fact, I do know a little about the situation. Edward is new to my division. I only met him once during the interview process, however he comes highly recommended from his previous department head. He has a good feel for product development, I'm told. I spoke with him this morning about the incident."

"What did he say when he spoke with you, John?" Stanley asked in an impatient tone.

"All he said was that he was in working after hours and inadvertently accessed some files he felt he shouldn't have once he glanced at them for a short time. He guessed, and I concur, that I.T. likely gave him too high a security clearance in the system. I don't even have clearance to access the files he was describing and I'm the head of the department."

"I thought you said he only glanced at them. What did he tell you he saw in the files? How much did he only *glance at* before he got out of the file?"

"He assured me he shut it down immediately after he realized he maybe shouldn't have been there. As soon as I was informed of what had happened, I instructed the I.T. department to reset his security access to the appropriate level for his position. From what he saw in the brief period of time he was in the file, it appeared to be referencing a new product. Something for use in what was described as an "ODD". That was all it said. No explanation. It looked to Edward, like it was some type of a new explosive that has some kind of a special additive. He seems like a bright kid. Did you know he was a Mensa member?"

"This product is something one of our customers has asked me to look into. It's not for general knowledge, John. I do know that we have an employee who is a Mensa member but I wasn't certain it was Milton. Good for him. That's a prestigious organization."

"Mr. Stanley, I was just in the finance department going over some cost overruns in my department. If this new product development cost is being charged to my accounts, isn't it only fair that I know what it is?"

"John, I'll arrange to have the accounting corrected on this. It'll all be charged to my budget but for now please stay out of it. It's not something we're likely to pursue. It's a waste of your time. Thanks for coming in so quickly. I hear that you and your staff are doing some good work. Keep it up." Stanley stood and shook John's hand, signifying that as far as he was concerned, the meeting was over and the issue was closed.

As soon as John left, Stanley picked up the phone and dialed.

"Dennis, I need to advise you that we have had a slight slip-up here."

He was speaking to Dennis Wirth, CEO of Airtec Engineering. Wirth was one of the customers for this new explosive product and a key investor. He was also one of the three men mainly responsible for getting many of the other current investors in on the project. There had been a significant amount of money invested into the project by a short list of very wealthy and powerful individuals. Jason Being, Assistant Deputy for Homeland Security in the U.S., and Maxwell Wesley, Under Secretary of Defense were the other two people who had managed to secure a considerable amount of investment in this new product. Wirth was really spearheading the entire project, using his company's expertise in aeronautics to provide equipment for a key component of the total package.

"What kind of a slip-up?" Wirth asked.

"One of our new people, in the Product Development department, accessed some computer files he shouldn't have. The O.D.D. files to be specific. He asked his boss a number of questions about it. I just finished a meeting with his boss and told him to let it go. He got the message," Stanley assured.

"I hope he got the message. Are you sure we don't need to do anything further?"

"No, I think we're good."

"You think? I have, we have our necks on the line on this, not to mention a lot of money invested by some very important people. I'll talk this over with Jason, but I'm certain he's going to tell you the same thing I am. We have too much riding on this project to allow any slip-ups. If there's any doubt, we need to do what's necessary to keep this a secret," Wirth warned.

"Yes, sir," Stanley replied as he ended the call.

CHAPTER THREE

March 25, 9:00 am CST-Mensa International Annual Conference Matador Resort Hotel - Mexico City

"Ladies and gentlemen, if we could please bring this meeting to order."

The sound of a gavel, repeatedly striking the podium, was faintly heard over the noise of 500 people all speaking at the same time.

"If I could ask the meeting to please come to order; we can begin."

The gavel struck the podium twice more. The audience noise, from individual conversations, began to decrease. The meeting room was in relative silence.

"Ladies and gentlemen, I would like to begin the 65 Annual Mensa International Conference by welcoming all of our members to this marvelous meeting hall in the Matador Resort Hotel and to the very vibrant and exciting Mexico City. This is the first time that our Mexican membership has hosted this annual event, and we expect there will be much to enjoy over the next four days of the conference. A sincere thank you to their organizing team."

There was a round of applause to acknowledge everyone's appreciation. A few people, seated throughout the venue, stood to identify themselves as members of the local organizing committee and took a modest bow. The sound system squealed slightly. The emcee tapped on the microphone as a test.

"My name is Rolland Berill, Jr. As I'm certain many of you are already aware, my father and Dr. Lancelot Ware founded this society in 1946. This association was, and continues to be, the premier association within the global community whose membership requirements are based solely on an individual's I.Q. I am proud to say that membership to this organization continues to be without regard to gender, nationality, political, or religious beliefs. Our members are all in the top two percentile of the intellectual elite of this world, and we are proud of it."

There was an outpouring of cheers and applause from the floor. It continued for some time, until a strike of the gavel brought the members back to order.

"I am pleased to report that our global membership now exceeds one hundred thousand, and we are represented in more than one hundred countries. The membership from Mexico has risen to more than one hundred and fifty, and we couldn't be more pleased. Membership continues to increase from many of our member countries. In addition to our gains in Mexico, we are pleased to announce that China now totals over eighty members; South Africa has just broken the one- thousand mark, and we have recently welcomed our first member from Egypt. This is all evidence that the Mensa organization is strong and remains relevant in this ever-changing world."

The emcee's voice became louder as he progressed through his comments.

There was another burst of applause. As the speaker waited for the audience to return to order, he took the opportunity to make a visual overview of the audience. The room was configured as a lecture theater. In addition to the theater seating, there was a large balcony that ran the entire width of the room. The brightly upholstered seats were an indication of how new this facility was. It had recently been totally refurbished after, what was considered a small fire, left considerable smoke damage throughout the facility. It was necessary to replace everything on the first three floors of the entire complex. In an attempt to recapture some of the convention business the hotel had lost during the restoration, the hotel had offered very competitive pricing to the Mensa organizing committee; not to mention a few kick-backs to key members of the committee, which is necessary when doing business in Mexico. The hotel also took the opportunity during the restoration to improve on the security of the facility.

Security had become a key stumbling-block to growing the convention business in Mexico City. The tourist business, in general, suffered due to the never-ending wars between the Mexican drug-lords. Many innocent tourists had been killed or injured, and despite the efforts of the government to cover up that information, word was out that Mexico could be a hostile place to visit. A twelve-foot wire fence around the perimeter of the entire hotel complex was now in place, including appropriate coils of barbed and razor wire and several electrified sections, in some of the critical sections. All intended to keep the guests secure. Mexico City's reputation of being a dangerous destination was costing the hotel a significant amount and they had to improve their image.

In addition to the erection of the fence, the hotel also invested in more security staff to patrol the buildings and the grounds on a 24/7 basis. This was more a perception of security than a reality of security, as most of the new guards were on-the-take. They would often turn a blind eye to a pick-pocket, petty criminal, and certainly to prostitutes working the hotel. They received a piece of the action for their cooperation. In some cases, they were paid in trade rather than money when it came to the hookers doing business. A nice bonus for a man making a few dollars an hour as a security guard.

"As I look around this room, I am pleased to see that one of our long standing traditions appears to remain. As many of you know, the M.I. executive committee has requested that each attending member dress as would be the custom in their homeland. Before the assembly convened, I had an opportunity to greet many of our membership from the far corners of the globe. Most of them were wearing their national dress, and this is very gratifying to see. This is requested only for the duration of the opening ceremonies and the first day of the conference, however, if anyone wishes to retain their traditional dress throughout the entire conference, by all means do so. This tradition has been maintained to further reinforce one of our primary objectives: to recognize, encourage, and welcome cultural differences within our membership. It's a pleasure to see so many varied and colorful garments throughout the auditorium. Thank you for keeping this tradition alive, and I hope that you will continue to wear your traditional wardrobe for the duration of this conference."

There was a buzz in the audience as members took special note of each other's attire. In particular, some of the garments from the South African delegation were spectacular and drew a great deal of attention from other members. Several of the middle-eastern delegates had created some concern and attention earlier in the day. Most of their traditional forms of dress included ceremonial weapons of various types; mostly swords and daggers but this proved to be disconcerting to some in the audience. There had actually been quite a scene when security prevented some of these early-arriving delegates from entering the facility. The metal detectors, set up at every doorway in and out of the building, easily detected their weapons. It was only after considerable discussion with the individuals in question that they were allowed to retain their ceremonial weapons. Security was advised to keep a close-eye on the situation.

"It is also gratifying to hear of the varied occupations held by our membership. We have captains of industry, science, and politics among our members; doctors, lawyers, company executives and the-like. We also have a myriad of other occupations represented in our group. I met several police officers, elementary school teachers and an actor," he said as he smiled. "What a great organization to have such a wealth of true diversity among our members."

There was brief applause.

"The first order of business will be to break away into our discussion groups. The group membership selection process has been quite simple. This year, and for the first time, we have decided to retain the same group members for the duration of the conference. In past years, group membership changed daily, but it was felt that a more permanent team membership would provide more topic-review time. If at any time, however, anyone feels that they must leave a particular group, please let one of our committee members know. We will try to accommodate your request, if at all possible. With a group as large as this one, there can be differences that would best be resolved by an adjustment in group membership. We have assigned each attending member with a specific number. This is purely random as we feel that is the best way to ensure healthy dialog within each group. Your team number is located on the front of the document package you were handed upon registration."

There was the sound of paper shuffling as the membership looked through their documents for the all-important number.

"Your objective, for the next thirty minutes or so, is to move into the large conference center located across the hall from where we are now seated and find the table with your corresponding number. There will be a total of six people per table."

There was a rush of noise from the floor as people began to leave the room. In a louder than normal voice, so as to be heard, the speaker finished his instructions.

"Once you have found your tables and your group partners, please take an additional thirty minutes to get acquainted before we begin the discussion segment of this conference. I would expect that within one hour, or by 10 am, we will be ready to go. Thanks again and one more thing: we have assistance available for you at the tables located towards the front of the discussion hall should you need help finding your group or have any other general questions. Enjoy."

The audience exited the lecture theater and moved towards the large conference room across the hall. There was a general flurry of activity, within the room, as individuals located their respective tables. The conference room, itself, was very large and was broken into three sections by movable wall partitions, suspended from the ceiling. These fabric-covered panels acted as both a visual and a sound break for the room. The walls had been pulled back to provide one very large, open room.

At table 74, there was a group of people in the early stages of greeting each other.

CHAPTER FOUR

March 25, 9:15 am CST- Mensa International Conference
Matador Resort Hotel - Mexico City

Two young delegates approached the table as the man, already seated, stood to greet them.

"Nice to meet you," he said, as he extended his hand to both men, "my name is Jack Daniels."

"Glad to meet you, Jack. My name is Edward Milton," one of the men stated while shaking hands.

"And my name is Reggie Viscusi," said the second young man. "It looks like we have three more yet to come to make this team. Hopefully it won't be too long."

As the three young men engaged in small-talk, a young woman approached the group. She appeared to either be lost or extremely shy by her posture and demeanor. She seemed quite hesitant about approaching the table.

"Hi and you are?" Jack inquired of the young woman as he extended his hand.

"My name is Rachel Wi," she replied and greeted all three men with a soft handshake. She quickly moved to take a seat on the far side of the table. It was clear that she was uncomfortable meeting three young men without the accompaniment of another woman. She sighed in relief, almost audibly, as she spotted the next team member approaching the table. Another woman.

"Two more to go and we have a six pack," Edward joked. Everyone smiled at his attempt to break the ice.

The next to arrive was a young woman dressed in the traditional hijab. Her body was completely covered, including her hair. All that could be seen was her strikingly-beautiful face. Her high cheek bones and light bronze skin-tone confirmed her Middle-Eastern heritage. Her eyes were a bewitching emerald green; they appeared almost liquid they were so beautiful. Rachel noticed immediately that this woman wore no makeup and yet she appeared to be off the pages of a beauty magazine. The newcomer greeted the group.

"It's a pleasure to meet you. My name is Angelina Evangeline," she said. She moved close enough to the group to be heard over the muffled noise in the room and extended her hand in greeting.

"That's a bit of a mouthful," Edward quipped. The others smile politely.

"Yes it is," she replied while smiling and looking directly into Edward's eyes. "I get that a lot."

Angelina took a seat next to Rachel and reintroduced herself to the young woman.

"I love your suit," Angelina said in an attempt to break the ice with this, obviously shy, young woman.

"Thank you. It was really difficult to decide what to wear to a meeting such as this. I opted for business attire. I designed it myself."

"Did you do your own sewing?"

"No... I have a lady in Chinatown, in New York, who does the sewing. I'm not very talented in sewing. That's a skill of its own and Mrs. Chuen, my seamstress, is very good at it."

"You clearly have a talent for design. You chose well," Angelina complimented.

"While we wait for our last teammate, why don't we get to know each other?" Reggie suggested. "Let's give the group a few details about ourselves; who we are and where we come from. If no one objects, I'll go first."

Reggie was about six foot two in height. He had a heavy build but appeared to be in good physical shape. He had a full head of thick curly-black hair, no doubt a result of his Italian ancestry, and a very mischievous and bewitching smile. The most striking feature of his smile, besides his bright-white teeth, were his dimples. Combined with his five-o'clock shadow, facial stubble he was a handsome young man. His eyes were brown and he had a twinkle in his eye that complemented his mischievous smile. He was a good looking Italian-American man and his demeanor seemed to indicate he was self-assured and comfortable meeting people. He wore a dark suit, blue almost black, with a white chest-hugging golf shirt underneath; no tie. In fact, from his appearance, it was unlikely that he was a tie kind of guy. His shoes were a more formal style of running shoes or perhaps deck shoe might best have described them. He was a casual-looking young man with an obvious quick wit and a wicked sense of humor.

"My name is Reginald Viscusi; I prefer to be called Reggie. I grew up in Connecticut, and I am currently working and living in New York City. I have a Masters Degree in mathematics, from Harvard University. I work for a company called Statco doing statistical probability and evaluation work, and as an aside, I really really hate what I'm doing." He smiled slightly as he took a breath. "If anyone has a lead on any other kind of job that requires math skills, please let me know. I'm willing to relocate." The group looked at each other and smiled at his last remark. They were not sure what kind of response was appropriate to that statement, so they remained silent. "My father is a business man, with offices in Manhattan, and my mother is a stay at home mom."

Reggie always described his father's vocation as a *business man*. He really had no idea, or more correctly, *never wanted to admit to having an idea,* of what his father did for a living. He knew he had an office in Manhattan, although Reggie had never been there. And he knew there were some pretty strong hints that his father, and his grandfather for that matter, were in some way connected to organized crime. The mafia as described by most law enforcement types. That was likely the case. One had only to look at their surroundings and the people his father associated with to make the connection. It made the Godfather look like a Disney film. What he did know for certain, was that his father dealt with multimillion dollar transactions and was never willing to discuss his business. His father's business was something Reggie had recently shown an interest in but he hadn't discussed it with either of his parents, as yet. He was obviously good in mathematics, however, finance specifically was not necessarily his forte. There had never been any attempt by his mother or Reggie to delve any deeper into the details of his father's business. Some things were best left unsaid.

"I don't really play sports with any degree of regularity; however, I'm a big baseball and hockey fan. I do try to take in as many games as I can each year. I don't currently have a girlfriend but I'm always looking. If either of you young ladies would be interested, we can talk," he added as he smiled.

He looked at the young women as they both slowly and discreetly moved their heads from side to side while maintaining courteous smiles. Rachel's face revealed a pinkish glow as she was perhaps a little embarrassed by his forwardness. Angelina's face showed no expression. He knew, at this point, Angelina was going to be a tough one to get to know. He wondered what she really looked like once she revealed more than her eyes to the world. Her eyes and her face were gorgeous, to be sure. He had difficulty not staring at her eyes.

"I'm simply a normal kind of guy, I guess."

As he finished his statement, a smile appeared on Rachel's, now rose-cheeked, face as she thought about this guy who was always on the lookout for a girlfriend. He was very good looking. *I wonder what his problem is.* She thought to herself.

Angelina had noticed his periodic stare. She was no stranger to men's fascination with her eyes; to her entire body for that matter. She chose not to acknowledge anything this early in the relationships with her team members.

"Thanks Reggie for that update," Jack said. "It appears that we have a mathematician in the group. That should come in handy. We'll keep our eyes peeled for the woman of your dreams," he said as he smiled. He looked next to Rachel for her story.

"Oh, my turn," she said, and she blushed even more.

Rachel was very attractive and obviously very shy. She was of Chinese descent with coal-black, curly, shoulder-length hair. Curling her hair appeared to be the only attention she paid to her looks. She didn't seem to be wearing any makeup. She had a tiny face; her dark brown eyes sparkled when she spoke. Her eyes were complemented by her, extraordinarily long eyelashes. They appeared almost unreal. It was clear that her thoughts could be understood from her facial expressions. Her current pink glow indicated that she was not comfortable meeting people. The more she spoke the deeper red she became. She was wearing a dark-blue suit jacket with a matching skirt that was cut slightly above the knee. Angelina was already aware that her clothes were her own design and she was very impressed. Rachel's suit was of the quality that might be available in any of the high-end clothing store in Paris or New York. It was interesting to Angelina. Rachel appeared to be very professional. If you looked closely, you would surmise that she had a pretty nice figure under that suit jacket; petite, for certain, but better than what her five foot nothing in height might indicate.

"My name is Rachel Wi and I was born in China. I have a Masters Degree in Mechanical Engineering from the University of Hong Kong and I hold a Ph.D. in Aeronautical Engineering from the University of Southern California. I came to America with my masters and earned my Doctorate here."

As she continued, the group glanced at each other. This tiny woman, with an almost nonexistent volume to her voice, had a Masters Degree and a Doctorate. The manner in which she divulged this information to complete strangers was so matter-of-fact. She didn't seem to be boastful of her academic accomplishments in any way. They were all impressed.

"Um..., I am currently working for a company called Airtec Engineering out of its New York office, and like Mr. Viscusi, I don't really like what I do." She glanced at Reggie with a smile before she continued. "I am *not,* however, currently looking for a boyfriend. I don't have a boyfriend at this time nor am I looking for one." she confirmed.

As she finished she sat down politely and waited for the next team member to speak.

"That's interesting," Angelina said. "I work for Airtec as well but out of the California office. How odd is this?" She looked at Rachel who seemed to be surprised and delighted at this latest revelation. Rachel had come to this conference with the assumption that she would have very little in common with anyone, other than their IQ score. She was very pleased that she had already found someone with some common circumstance. "What would you rather be doing Rachel?" Angelina asked.

"I'm sorry?" Rachel asked. She wasn't sure why she was being asked a question about what she assumed was a routine description of herself to these strangers. Usually people simply nod politely when you tell them about yourself.

"You said you don't really like what you do. What would you rather be doing?" Angelina repeated.

Reggie's face showed slight disappointment that Angelina was asking Rachel a question about her aspirations and had said nothing to him about his opening remarks. Angelina noticed his facial expression but ignored it.

"I've always dreamed of being a fashion designer," Rachel replied. She was really pleased that someone had been interested enough in her story to ask a simple question. "However, being from China limited my educational options. Being a female further restricted my choices. Fashion design is not considered a worthwhile discipline. Engineering was the most viable option. Once I received my master's, it was prudent for me to move to the U.S. for my Doctorate. People who exceed the master's level of education are not always permitted to immigrate," she finished solemnly.

"I'm sure you're a fine engineer and it's a real coincidence that we both work for the same company," Angelina responded as her hand covered Rachel's hand on the table. It was her way of showing support. "As far as pursuing design, you should all know gentlemen that what Rachel is currently wearing is her own design. She is already demonstrating her fashion talents. Maybe you should think again about a change from your current vocation, Rachel."

Rachel's face turned rose-red with all the attention being paid to her. She smiled but found it unnerving to be the center of attention. She was accustomed to blending into the surroundings not being put at center stage.

"Angelina, it makes sense for you to go next. We seem to have some commonality forming here," Jack said. He motioned to Angelina to take the floor.

"By all means; my name is Angelina Evangeline and I was born in Cairo," she said as she stood up.

"So you're... the one and only member from Egypt, I guess," Reggie interrupted.

"You would be correct in that assumption, Mr. Viscusi," she replied, trying to continue with her statement. Angelina found it annoying that he had interrupted her so soon after her first statement of disclosure.

"I believe we have almost fifty-thousand members in the U.S.," he interrupted, for the second time.

"I believe your observation is correct in this regard as well. The United States has by far the most members in Mensa."

She hesitated before she made her next assertion. It was obvious she was willing to get into it with this stranger with twenty questions.

"That would make you one of a great many and me unique then, wouldn't it?" Angelina replied, with a challenging tone to her voice. She glanced at the others and saw a slight smile appear on everyone's face. Except Reggie. She had struck a verbal blow in the joust of words.

"Why only one?" he responded.

He either hadn't caught her sarcastic comment or he was ignoring it. In either case, it was annoying. All eyes turned on Angelina. It was like watching a tennis match. The spectator's heads moved from side to side with each verbal volley. Angelina paused before responding.

"It could be that there is less of a desire in my country for one possessing special talents or attributes to belong to a group sharing similar traits. Or perhaps it's a cultural issue. The same question could be asked of China. Why does this country of over a billion in population have only eighty Mensa members? Most likely, as highlighted by Dr. Wi, there are internal political or perhaps some human rights aspects to the decision to become a member. There are many reasons why things are as they are. The United States is a very large participant in the Mensa organization, however, bigger is not always better in every situation, Mr. Viscusi."

"You sound offended. No offense intended."

"None taken," Angelina replied instantly, then paused again. "Would it be all right with you if I continue?"

"By all means."

"Thank you."

Angelina turned her attention to the rest of the group; intentionally ignoring her inquisitive team member, Mr. Viscusi. The remaining members of the team had been listening to the banter between these two strong personalities. None of them chose to jump in on the discussion. A good decision on their part. Angelina appeared to be right on the edge of an explosive response to any additional questions from their Italian team member.

"I have an MBA from the University of International Studies in Paris. As I said, I am currently working for Airtec Engineering out of the California office." She glanced again at Rachel trying to recall if she had ever heard of her before. "I'm also in the midst of setting up an unofficial office in Cairo; but I'm primarily working out of the California office. I sell airplanes."

She knew this piece of information would prompt another round of questions from Mr. Viscusi. She was ready. It actually surprised all of the men in the group that she sold airplanes but only Reggie dared to comment. They were all curious how Angelina, who appeared to be a traditional Muslim woman, got into selling airplanes? Both Jack and Edward smiled slightly; they knew round two in the verbal duel was on.

"What kind of airplanes?" Reggie asked. It was like he had no idea that Angelina was getting pissed-off with him. He was oblivious to her growing annoyance.

"You sound surprised by that, Mr. Viscusi." She was glaring at Reggie with raised eyebrows as she spoke. "You have a very inquisitive mind. To answer your most recent question, I sell mostly small private and commuter-size jets; the kind that would carry from four to twenty-four passengers. I'm trying to move most of my work from California to Cairo because the world economy isn't the best right now. It seems that the only money remaining is oil-money out of the Middle-East. Working from Cairo makes more sense. I like my job very much but the travel is sometimes tiring. I would also like to expand my product offering to include some of the other products our company sells; some of the larger units and the military side as well."

"You mean like fighter jets?" Reggie inquired. He asked the question like it was the first one he has asked and not the tenth. This was even more infuriating to Angelina. She grits her teeth as she responded.

"Yes, fighter jets, surveillance aircraft, helicopters, that kind of product. Why do you look so surprised?" The volume of her voice, although not to the point of yelling, had become quite loud as she fought to control her displeasure with this stranger's endless questions and comments about her life. "Is there some reason why a woman can't sell airplanes?"

"No, not at all. I'm just surprised that someone so young would want to sell fighter jets."

"So young, or so female?"

"So young. There's no reason why a female can't sell airplanes. Is there?" Reggie knew that was one point for his side of the discussion.

"As I was saying..., I want to get into some of our other product offerings but I am presently restricted to selling smaller aircraft. I am a pilot and have been since I was sixteen. I'm licensed to operate most of the aircraft in the size range I currently sell. I am also currently working towards my accreditation for the larger passenger aircraft and for one final surprise for Mr. Viscusi." She looked deep into Reggie's eyes, "I am also an expert markswoman. I hold two titles from my country in long range rifle. Does that piece of information trigger any more questions, Mr. Viscusi? Would my age or gender also hamper my ability to be a good shot?"

Reggie slightly shrugged his shoulders. Angelina had completed her information and she sat back down next to Rachel. It's very obvious to everyone that Angelina was not pleased with Mr. Viscusi. It showed in her face.

"Do you have any concerns about setting up a new office in Cairo, Angelina?" Edward asked. "Haven't there been security issues in that region?"

"You are correct. There are security issues almost anywhere in the Middle-East. Cairo or even most of Egypt itself are no exceptions, however, Cairo is the hub of the region. When you want to sell airplanes you're pretty much committed to having a presence in the region. Otherwise, you're just another outsider. It helps that I'm from the region, however we will still have to be careful where we locate and take the appropriate security measures. At this point in time, I'm less concerned with security than I am with being successful in securing the best location for the office. Thanks for asking an intelligent question, Edward." She looked first at Edward and then to Reggie as she took her seat.

"Hey, my questions were intelligent," Reggie complained, almost under his breath but it was heard by all, including Angelina.

"Thanks Angelina," Jack interjected before Angelina had a chance to respond. "Let's move on to Edward, if we can." *And before we get into a donnybrook* he thought to himself. He sensed at one point during the latest altercation that they were going to come to blows. From Angelina's perspective, anyway. Reggie seemed to be unscathed by her obvious disapproval. He actually seems amused by it. This added more fuel to the fire under Angelina.

"Hello, my name is Edward Milton; I prefer Eddy, and I come from Canada. I have a degree in Mining Engineering from Queens University, and I currently work for a company that manufactures blasting media out of its Ottawa offices, Chemico International. I was doing blast-hole design, working with our customers to aid them in efficient drill-blast techniques. I have recently been moved to Product Development; a promotion according to the company; but I'm not so sure. It's too early to tell if I'm going to like it in the new department. This new position does seem to provide access to, and hopefully some participation in, some of the more interesting divisions in the company. I didn't realize for instance, that we had a military side to the company," he said as he looked at Angelina. She had mentioned she wanted to expand into the military equipment her company offered. He thought this might be some common ground for them. He noticed that her eyebrows moved slightly as he spoke. It appeared that she made the connection.

"I have already seen preliminary details on some of their products and they appear interesting. Not sure where that's going, but I'll follow up when I get back to the office on Monday. Um... My father passed away when I was sixteen, so it's just my mother, kid-sister and me. They still live in my hometown of Kingston, Ontario. Kingston is about two-hours from where I live, still fairly close to them. I like, but don't love, my new job. It will do for now. I currently don't have a girlfriend either, however, I think I have fallen in love..." His voice lowered and tapered off as his eyes moved focus towards a young woman approaching the table. "This could be the woman of my dreams," he stated as he moved towards the young woman and extended his hand in greeting. He was in a different space. "How are you? My name is Edward."

Angelina looked at Rachel as they watched Edward make his move on the newest member of the team. "Really?" Rachel whispered under her breath; an obvious reference to this guy hitting on everyone in a skirt.

"Nice to meet you," was the newcomer's short response as she shook his hand. "My name is Candice Bergen."

"Like the actress?" Edward asked.

"Yes, like the actress." She paused slightly and smiled at the group while extending her hand to the remaining members. "I get that a lot."

Everyone welcomed their newest team member with handshakes. There were head-to-toe visual inspections from the men in the group and no wonder. Candice was best described as a knock- out. She was tall, perhaps five foot ten or eleven, slim and very blonde. She was wearing a business suit with a matching skirt, cut short but not too short. It was obvious she had very large breasts and her legs seem to go on forever. She was dressed appropriately for this type of meeting but her body's considerable attributes were difficult to conceal. Her sky-blue eyes were breathtaking.

"Welcome, Ms. Bergen," Jack said. "We were just getting to know each other with a short rundown of our personal histories. Kind of a *get acquainted* session and we have finished up with Edward. I think. If everyone will introduce themselves, we will ask our newest member to give us her statistics, or rather history." He realized he had perhaps made an inappropriate slip. As he looked at Angelina, he could see that she hadn't missed the obvious reference to this woman's physical attributes, even if everyone else had. It showed in her facial expression towards Jack.

"Sorry," he whispered in the lowest volume possible to Angelina. "I didn't mean to say that."

Angelina looked at him with her already familiar, *I-don't-approve-of-you* raised eyebrow. He was caught and the best he could do was to do nothing. He wondered if anyone else caught his subtle error in vocabulary selection. At that point, Angelina was thinking to herself that she had been placed on a team with at least two, and likely three, Neanderthals. She hadn't realized there were still young men out there living with social skills and attitudes towards women that were stuck in the fifties. At least not in North America. It was going to be a challenge for her to get through the next four days without doing serious harm to at least one of them. Most likely the inquisitive and extremely annoying Mr. Viscusi

"Sure," Candice volunteered, "I would be pleased to go next but first let me apologize for being late. My plane from Chicago was delayed. I came directly from the airport; so sorry about that. Hi to all, my name is Candice Bergen; yes like the actress as has been so kindly pointed out," she said as she glanced at Edward. "I was born in Stockholm, Sweden. I have a Ph.D. in Marine Biology from the University of Stockholm. I'm currently not working in my field of study; I am pursuing a career as a model, more specifically, a Playboy Centerfold."

You could have heard a pin drop at table 74. Rachel emitted a very low but audible, "Oh my." The guys were heard saying, "Wow", under their breath as they gave Candice another head to toe scan with their eyes. They were clearly undressing her with their eyes; trying to picture what she might look like on the pages of Playboy. Angelina said nothing; a slight smile appeared on her face. She had three so-called-normal young men in her group and they had been introduced to a real-live Playboy model. "*It's going to be fun to see where this goes,*" she thought.

"Dr. Bergen, how close are you to achieving your career goal?"Angelina inquired, putting emphasis on *Doctor*. She could sense a new round of questions from the inquisitive Mr. Viscusi, and she was ready for it. She looked at Candice as she replied. She could tell Candice knew where she was going with this and she got a definite go-ahead sign from her to have some fun; even if it was at her expense. Candice was accustomed to this type of attention from men. It really didn't bother her. She actually found it rather amusing as long as it didn't become inappropriate. This level of enthusiasm when meeting a Playboy model was a very common and predictable reaction for young guys. Older men as well.

"I'm very close as of these past few days and the reason I was late getting here this morning. I was in Chicago, meeting with the *Playboy* people about possibly doing a shoot for next year. Once that happens, then I would be included in next year's calendar; hopefully as Miss January."

There was no response from the group to her statement. The guys were almost drooling as the conversation continued. They didn't know what to say or do. They wanted the conversation to continue while they visualized the January page of next year's Playboy calendar. All three women were now beginning to have fun with their male team members. Even straight-laced Rachel was seeing the humor in the situation.

"I seem to recall, there was a previous Mensa member who was a *Playboy* Bunny," Angelina stated. She was attempting to keep the conversation moving, and have some more fun.

All three of the men's heads turned to Candice for her response to that unexpected piece of information. Their eyes opened even wider.

"You're good," Candice replied as she smiled at Angelina. "Yes, Dr. Julie Peterson was and still is a Mensa member. She was also a Playboy Bunny and appeared on the calendar in February 1987. She serves as my validation that my aspirations are achievable. Most people think, because I have a degree, I should be working in my field. I will no doubt, because I love the work; but that's for a later time. Others who focus on physical appearance," she added as she outlined her body from head to toe with her hands, "find it hard to believe I have a brain at all. They think I should be a stripper or a porn actress. Do you get that as well?" she asked, as she looked at Angelina. "You're a woman of success and yet you are very beautiful. Just look at her face. She's gorgeous and I bet there is a body to match under that clothing." She was speaking to the group as much as Angelina. Candice could spot hidden beauty and this woman, sitting across from her, was a natural beauty.

That was the first time the group saw Angelina taken off guard. She had not expected to be drawn into this topic of discussion. She wasn't offended by the statements Candice was making, but she was slightly embarrassed by bringing her appearance into a discussion about strippers and nude models. Down deep she knew she had the body and the looks to do this kind of modeling, and she certainly wasn't shy or self conscious about her body; however it's wasn't what she had in mind as a career goal.

"Well, I don't want to dwell on me forever. To finish up, I also did a Victoria's Secret Christmas special last year and some other modeling. I think I have a pretty good chance at the *Playboy* shoot; at least I hope so."

"I saw that last year. Which one were you?" Reggie asked. You could see the look of regret on his face the moment the words left his lips. He hadn't thought about the every-willing-to-challenge Angelina. He knew she would push this one back in his face.

Candice was surprised that someone recalled her latest show. Even more surprised that he recalled seeing her. She knew it wasn't true. There are very few men who watch a Victoria's Secret show and remember the model's faces. Almost none, actually. She was willing to play along.

"I had several runway walks. One with the black panties with the uplift bra and the second with the sheer white negligee. Do you recall seeing me?"

"Yes," Reggie lied. "You looked great."

"Thanks, I was proud of that shoot. If you all will excuse me, I have to visit the ladies room. Please continue and I'll be back as soon as possible. By the way, please call me Candy. I'm not big on the whole *Doctor* thing."

There was silence as Candice removed her suit jacket and placed it on the back of her chair. She turned towards the restrooms which were located along the back wall of the room, and started to walk away. It was all the men could do not to make a motion or a sound. Candice had one beautiful body, and although she was certainly tastefully dressed, it was not difficult to notice that she was very well endowed. She was making a conscious effort to contain all her womanly attributes. Her blouse was buttoned almost to the neck; but there was still plenty to see, or more correctly to imagine. As she turned, she noticed that her blouse was very similar to the one that Rachel was wearing.

"Look at that, we're wearing almost the same blouse; very pretty."

Candice left the table to find the rest rooms. The men watched her walk until she disappeared through the conference room door. All eyes turned to Rachel to see what similarities there were in the blouses they were wearing. Rachel peered down at her chest and the blouse covering her small frame.

"It is the same blouse alright. We could be twins." A big smile came across her face.

"This girl has a sense of humor," Jack thought to himself.

Angelina had something to say. She considered, only briefly not following her first impulse but she was ready for another joist and Reggie was her opponent.

"Mr. Viscusi seems to have remembered *Dr.* Bergen's last Victoria's Secret shoot. Do you really expect us to believe you were looking at the models' faces and that you recall seeing *Dr.* Bergen?" She was directing her question directly at Reggie.

"Here.... we go," Jack whispered under his breath. He was hoping there wouldn't be another round between these two so early in the day. He was about to be disappointed.

"She prefers Candy, if you don't mind, and I do look at faces not just breasts and butts."

"I bet you do." Angelina knew it wasn't true but she let it go. He hadn't taken the bait to debate the matter but she knew there would be a next time. They had work to do and there was one more team member yet to tell his story.

"Well that was Dr. Bergen," Jack stated, wanting to keep things moving. "I guess I'm the last one, so I'll make this simple."

Angelina cleared her throat to indicate she was about to speak. She had noticed that there were two very dim glimmers of light coming from under the table in the vicinity of Reggie and Edward. She knew what it was, and she did not hesitate to call them on it.

"I apologize for interrupting you Jack; however before you tell us about yourself, I would hope that the other two gentlemen in the group will have the courtesy to turn off their blackberry devices. My guess would be, and I hope I'm wrong on this, that there has been a quick Goggle search by one or both of you gentlemen for either Dr. Julie Peterson's calendar shot from the 1987 *Playboy* magazine or perhaps the Victoria's Secret Christmas lingerie special as was seen on ABC. A special in which *Dr.* Bergen was a model, complete with her angel wings. My other hope is that the three numbers that were just jotted down on your napkin, Mr. Viscusi, 38-24-36 and slid to your partner-in-mischief next to you, is the combination to your high school locker. 38-24-36 looks like a combination to a locker; at least I hope it's a not any physical measurement you may have obtained from what you were viewing. Would I be incorrect in these assumptions?" she asked while she looked critically at the two men who were clearly engrossed in what they were viewing on their cell phone screens.

Rachel glanced towards Reggie's phone, by reflex, and quickly turned away with a soft "Oh my!" His small screen showed a picture of a scantly clothed woman wearing an almost transparent negligee and thong. Her large breasts were only slightly concealed by the fabric of the negligee. *This must have been Dr. Peterson.* She assumed.

"I'm reading a very important e-mail from the office," Reggie explained. Edward said nothing. Both lights turned off. The men place their respective cell phones on the white table cloth in plain view.

"Please continue," Angelina said. She looked away from the guilty parties and turned her attention to Jack. She was pleased with herself that she caught the two men in their boyish fascination with scantily clad women. Reggie and Edward gave a slight shrug of their shoulders. They knew they'd had been caught and they tried to re-focus on the conversation.

"As I was saying, my name is Jack Daniels, yes the same as the beverage as I'm sure you are asking yourselves. I will be short. I see Candice returning and we're running out of time. I was born in Montana and my parents run a cattle ranch. I have a Masters in Computer Software Engineering from MIT, and I work for a company called Softco Engineering in California. My current position is as software review supervisor which means I proofread other people's software designs and correct them where need be. Not a real challenge, and like many in this group, I could do with a career change but in this economy I guess any job is a good job."

With that, Candice returned and took a seat at the table.

Jack continued, "Now that we all know a little about each other, let's get to the discussion on today's agenda and see if we can put our collective brain-power to good use." He opened the envelope and read the contents to the group.

CHAPTER FIVE

March 25, 10:15 am CST - Mensa International Conference
Matador Resort Hotel - Mexico City

The purpose of the discussion groups was to engage some of the top minds in the world to provide constructive recommendations towards resolving some of the world's most significant challenges. The topics ranged from environmental matters to political and religious differences. It was very common for the summary reports, generated by each group, to be passed on to government leaders or others in places of authority as suggested resolutions to some of their collective problems. In the past, many complicated and challenging global decisions were made with consideration given to the suggested course of action as stated by a group from the Mensa organization. It was almost never reported where the input came from. The important part was that members of this elite organization were assisting in the decision-making process.

The topic for this team, as read from the package documents by Jack, had to do with encouraging all countries to recognize and take steps to curb greenhouse gas emissions. The Kyoto accord had been a dismal failure mainly because the United States did not sign on to the agreement. This left the opportunity for other countries, such as China and India, to opt out as well and they are some of the worst polluters on the planet. These countries were focused on taking over the manufacture of the majority of the world's requirement for most everything. To this end, there was little or no thought to the consequence of increased dependence on fossil fuel, primarily coal. While most other countries develop programs to improve efficiencies, China and India continued piling on the coal and cranking out the goods. The other side to the question related to the competitive advantage that countries such as China have over others. Without concern for the cost associated with responsible environmental activity, China had a huge advantage. All other countries were trying to compete in a global economy; the rules were not the same for all players. It was a predictable topic for this type of forum. As teams were getting into the discussion, the mediator made some additional announcements.

"Ladies and gentlemen, if I could have your attention for just a moment."

The room slowly lowered the level of conversation in order to hear his comments.

"Thank you. One more thing to announce or actually two, if you will bear with me. The first is to advise everyone that starting with this year's conference, the final reports from the various groups are not expected to be submitted until two months after the end of the conference. It is felt that we can provide more detailed input in our reports if more preparation time is provided. This will give team members an opportunity to continue their debate even after the conference ends. So, you have until May 31 to submit your reports."

There was a short mumble of discussion in the room about what had been said by the moderator.

"The second item of business," he continued, "is that there is a dinner being hosted each evening by the Mexican delegation in this hotel complex. In no attempt to discourage touring this fine city after conference hours, we would like to remind you to take precautions while doing so. We all expect that there are not going to be any security issues, however, precaution is always the best deterrent to these types of occurrences. Thank you for your attention, once again and carry on."

The group returned to their project. The topic of discussion was to say the least, predictable. The group of young people all participated in a healthy and often over-enthusiastic discussion. During the remainder of the day the group seemed to be developing a real connection with each other. Edward continued to crack jokes; Reggie continued to antagonize Angelina with his questions; and she continued to pretend to be the straight-laced woman in the group. It actually appeared to some that they were enjoying their verbal exchanges more than they admitted.

Rachel seemed to be loosening her conservative demeanor and joining in on more of the friendly exchange of jokes and light conversation. She even took a few verbal jabs at Jack concerning his name, Jack Daniels, and why his parents may have made the decision to name their son after a popular alcoholic beverage brand. Candice was certainly the expert on environmental issues so she often led the discussion. She was quick to point out that the issue which had most recently been identified in her field of study was the alarming number of occurrences of OD. Scientists were uncertain what caused the phenomenon but it seemed to be on the rise. She made a point to the group that they needed to include some specific dialogue concerning this issue in their dissertation. She felt the OD occurrences were one more consequence of global warming that needed to be referenced.

"I don't mean to sound stupid," Edward said. "But what exactly is an O.D. phenomenon? I have seen an acronym very similar to that and wondered what it was. The one I saw was O.D.D.; could it mean the same thing?"

"Oh, I'm sorry," Candice replied, more to the group than specifically to Edward. "I get into the science of it and forget that not everyone is a biologist. O.D. is the acronym for Oxygen Deprivation. It occurs when the oxygen is taken from the water in a certain area. When this occurs, it has a devastating effect on the marine life that depends on oxygen for survival. I'm not sure if you would have the same definition in your field Edward, so I can't say for certain what the interpretation of O.D.D. might mean to your company."

"I thought I would ask," Edward replied.

"Edward, why don't you and I team up on this specific aspect of our dissertation?" Candice suggested. She was finding Edward to be an interesting character. Behind his obvious giant sense of humor, he was a very intelligent young man. She was more accustomed to socializing with jocks at cocktail parties than academics, and it was a refreshing change.

"Absolutely," he replied, probably a little more quickly than would be the norm. It was clear that he was anxious and excited to be asked by Candice. "I would love to work more closely with you."

"Well, if no one objects," Candice stated as she looked at the others in the group and gave Angelina a subtle wink, "Edward and I will work closely on this aspect of the project."

"Call me "Eddy"," he said to Candice and to the group. "Eddy is what most everyone calls me. Edward always seems too formal."

"Eddy it is," Candice replied. She smiled and turned the meeting back to the group for continued discussion.

"Fine then," Jack confirmed, "team Eddy and Candy will be working in the area of O.D. as a sub group."

As the group was getting back to the business at hand, Eddy glanced at Angelina. He was certain she would have an opinion about him working closely with Candice. He was right. She was looking directly at him. It was clear by the expression on her face that she was not surprised by Eddy's desire to work more closely with a Playboy model.

"What?" he whispered to Angelina. He shrugged his shoulders. "It wasn't my idea, it was Candy's."

Angelina gave no reply and turned back to the others. Eddy had moved his chair closer to Candice which was also no surprise to Angelina or the rest of the group for that matter.

By lunch break the first day, the team had already formulated most of the content for their dissertation. It was clear to the group that developing countries could not be convinced to improve healthy environmental measures by simply pronouncing a global accord as was the case with Kyoto. These countries simply ignored them. The only way to prod these countries into dealing with the environmental challenges faced by everyone on this planet was to force them into it; force them through economic means and measures. It is the only approach they understand. In taking this approach, the existing responsible countries would also gain back some of their competitive edge in global markets.

"How about we break for lunch," Jack suggested while glancing at his watch. "It's slightly after twelve. Shall we meet back here by... 1:15 or 1:30?"

"Ladies, there's a nice little coffee shop I spotted, when I first came in. It appears to back onto the atrium in the center of the hotel complex. Do we want to eat as a group or on our own?" Candice asked. She was asking the question of everyone, although she felt the guys were probably going to want to eat in the bar at the back of the hotel complex. It was a steakhouse, and likely served a more substantial meal than scones and muffins. The ladies decided they would join each other and, as expected, the men headed for the rear of the hotel.

The men entered the "Double R" bar, as it stated on the front door. They waited to be seated. The room was noisy;

they could hear the noise but see almost nothing of the restaurant. It was so dark in the room, they couldn't see much more than five feet past the desk at the entrance. It was all they could do to make out the shadowed-outline of the first table. Coming from the florescent glow of the hotel hallway didn't help their eyes adjust to the almost absolute absence of light. To their surprise and pleasure, they were greeted by a very pretty young woman who showed them to their booth. She wore a western style shirt, a white Stetson hat, shorts and pink boots to complete the ensemble. Her hair was in a pony tail and bounced as she escorted the men through the maze-like establishment. By the time they reached the booth, their eyes were becoming accustomed to the shortage of available of light in the room. They took in their surroundings. It was clear the restaurant was attempting to portray the old-west in their choice of decor. The men reviewed the menu while waiting for their waitress. The selection was pretty much steak or steak and a choice of fries or hash browns. Not exactly what they thought it would be, but they were here and they were hungry.

Their luck changed when a cute little waitress appeared out of nowhere at the side of their table. As an added bonus, the uniform for the waitresses in the establishment were slightly different from the one they saw when they first came in. Same familiar Stetson hat, however the cowgirl shirt had been changed to a cotton tee shirt, tied in a knot at the waist. Apparently, undergarments were not mandatory as they could clearly see this young lady's considerable attributes through the thin fabric of her white top. Her shorts were best described as very short-shorts and her boots were the finishing touch to an otherwise perfect waitress uniform, as far as the men in the room were concerned.

"My name is Tiffany," she explained as she took out her order pad. "I'll be you're waitress. Can I get you-all a drink first?"

The guys ordered a beer and watched as Tiffany made her way back to the bar. She had a very nice body, even better on the return trip as they tried not to stare as she approached the table. They fumbled through the menu and all ordered something-beefy. It really didn't matter at this point. It was clear the food was not the drawing-card for this establishment.

It took quite a while for the food to come and they passed the time *people watching*. There were some very pretty people to watch, so they didn't mind at all. It seemed that every waitress in this establishment was pretty and petite; some more endowed than others- all were easy on the eyes. Lunch finally came and they somehow managed to get it down. It was overcooked and flavorless, but they were hungry. It was better than starving, but only slightly.

"Shit, it's ten after one," Jack said, looking at his luminescent watch. "The women are going to kill us if were late. Check please."

Tiffany was quick to present them their bill and made a point of saying goodbye at the front door. They left a considerable tip for her at the table. She had been a really fine waitress. "You-all come back now." she said as she waved them through the door."

They knew they were going to be late getting back, so they sprinted down the hallway back to the conference center. Out of breath, they made it back to table 74 at exactly 1:30. The women were waiting and apparently had begun the afternoon discussion.

"How was your lunch?" Candice asked.

"Not so good," Jack said. "It was pretty bad beef and very noisy. I don't recommend that restaurant if you're ever thinking of going. It's terrible."

"Really bad," Reggie added. "Wouldn't recommend it to my enemy."

"What's it called?"

"I don't remember. It was the double something. Maybe Double Down or Double T. I don't remember. Kind of a cowboy theme," Jack replied.

"Maybe the Double R?" she replied.

"Could be."

"There are some Double R's in California. I've heard the food is lousy there as well. Wonder why so many guys like to keep going back to these places that serves bad food."

"It's a guy thing," Edward added.

"I bet it is," Candice smiled. She knew what the draw was for men at the Double R chain of establishments. She simply smiled and turned her attention back to the group.

The afternoon session seemed to fly by. The guys were regretting their decision to eat at the Double R. Not being there, just eating there. The food was creating quite a digestive turmoil for most of them, but they forged ahead.

As it approached the time to end the day's discussion, Edward suggested that the group might like to dine somewhere other than in the hotel. Maybe take in some local entertainment at an outside venue. He would have been happy if only Candice had agreed, perhaps more happy than if the whole group had.

"So what do you say?" Eddy asked the group collectively, "are we good to go for tonight? I have a line on a supposedly hot place to go in town. What do you say?"

"Is it another Double R?" Candice joked. He knew, she knew what kind of an establishment they had been to for lunch. He was pleased that it didn't seem to bother her at all.

"Nothing like the Double R, I promise," he chuckled as he smiled back at Candice.

There was a surprisingly short discussion and they decided it was a go for everyone. Edward expected there would a lot persuading before the ladies would agree to accompany them. He was almost positive that Angelina would never choose to spend any more time than absolutely necessary with Reggie Viscusi. In the end, he was proven wrong. They were set to meet at 8:00 o'clock in the main lobby.

"I'd like to take some time to work out in the women's exercise room, if no one objects," Candice said. "Would either or both of you ladies like to join me?"

To her surprise both Angelina and Rachel replied with an enthusiastic *yes* to her invitation. Angelina was already planning to do so and Rachel thought it might be fun to be part of the ladies group.

"I'm game," Reggie said jokingly. He had expected a curt response from Angelina.

Before she could voice her opinion Rachel spoke up, "Nice try, *Mister I can't find a girlfriend.* Ladies only, if you don't mind. You will have to cast your line somewhere else for a while."

Everyone looked at Rachel. She blushed after she made the statement. It had just come out. She was feeling comfortable with the group, and so she said what she was thinking. She surprised herself.

"Oh, that's cruel." Reggie joked as he looked at her now fully rose-colored face.

CHAPTER SIX

March 25, 4:30 pm CST - Exercise Room
Matador Resort Hotel - Mexico City

The ladies had returned to their respective rooms to pick up their workout clothes. Rachel felt more comfortable changing in her room rather than in the locker room. She put on her black shorts and matching tee shirt. She pulled on a pair of slacks and a bulky top over them, and proceeded to the workout room. She maneuvered her way through the rows of exercise machines. Men and women were running; bicycling; lifting weights; doing pushups; pull ups and all forms of body-torturous moves all around her. It seemed to be busy, but not as crowded as she had anticipated it would be. As Rachel entered the ladies' change room, she could hear both Angelina and Candice laughing. It sounded like they were talking from a long distance apart; it was difficult to tell. There was an echo created by the ceramic tile that lined the floors, walls, and ceiling of the change room. As she rounded the corner past the washroom stalls, she entered the main change room and was taken aback by what she saw.

"Oh, I'm sorry." was all she could think to say when she saw Candice from the back view wearing only her sports bra and thong. Rachel turned her head slightly, trying not to be too obvious about her embarrassment. Candice was adjusting her bra in an effort to get her well endowed breasts completely covered. The thin strip of fabric of the thong covered almost nothing of her behind. As she spoke to Rachel, she turned and continued to adjust the bra into position. While this was happening, Rachel had a clear frontal view of Candice. Even with Candice partially covered, Rachel could clearly see that she had all the right parts to be a *Playboy* model.

"Don't be shy," Candice called to Rachel, "we're all girls here. We all have the same parts."

My parts look nothing like your parts, Rachel thought to herself, as she began to take off her slacks and bulky sweater to reveal the shorts and top that covered her petite, but shapely body.

"See, you have a great looking body," Candice pointed out. "I didn't expect your figure would be as shapely when we first met this morning. You need to show a little more sometime."

As Candice finished speaking, a woman came around the corner from the shower area. She was dripping wet and in the process of wrapping a towel around her hair. A second towel was wrapped loosely around her body. *Oh my god*, Rachel thought. *Is everybody naked-crazy in this country?* As she finished that thought she heard the partially-naked woman speak.

"Hey Rachel; what kept you?"

It was Angelina. The last person in the world Rachel ever expected to see nearly naked in a change room. This beautiful Muslim woman, who earlier today was completely covered from head to toe, was now standing barely covered in front of them and she didn't seem to be concerned about it at all. Not sure of where to look, Rachel concentrated on Angelina's eyes when she spoke.

"Sorry I'm late. I was trying to figure out what I was going to wear later this evening. I really didn't bring any clothes *suitable for nightclubs,*" Rachel explained.

"Hey," Candice joined the conversation, "I saw a great little dress shop just off the main lobby when I came in this morning. I'll bet you could pick up something there. It may be expensive for what you get but what the hell. If you like, I would be more than pleased to go with you. I might even find something for myself."

"I'll come too, if that's okay with you," Angelina said.

"That would be great," Rachel responded with enthusiasm. "I wasn't going to bother but if you don't mind giving me some advice it would really help. I'm not much of a dress-up kind of girl. I guess it comes from growing up in China and not having a lot of choice about what I wore. There didn't seem to be an occasion when I was required to dress up. You probably know about that kind of thing," she said while looking at Angelina.

Angelina looked slightly puzzled, as she pulled up her panties under the towel and began to put on her bra. It took her a few moments to connect the dots.

"Oh..., it's the clothing I wore earlier today that confuses you. As the speaker said at the opening ceremonies this morning, we were asked to wear traditional clothing from the country of our origin. I come from Egypt. In respect of that tradition, I wore the customary dress - the hijab, and covered my hair. It's what's worn in a lot of Middle Eastern countries. The fact of the matter is that other than when I'm actually in a city in Egypt, I wear pretty much what women wear in America. I like to think I dress more sophisticated than a lot of them; a skirt, or dress, or slacks are all part of my regular clothing, even at home."

It was obvious from the look on both Rachel and Candice's faces that neither one of them would have guessed what they were hearing from Angelina.

"Almost 95 percent of Egypt's population are Sunni Muslim," she informed. "You're correct in your understanding that most women are covered by traditional garments in my country. The reality is that the remaining six percent of the population are Coptic Christians. I happen to be one of the other six percent of the population. It's no big deal with the clothing. I sometimes prefer to wear more conservative clothing. It takes the emphasis off you when you walk through the mall or on a downtown street. You don't have every guy peering at you and undressing you with his eyes like women experience in other parts of the world. Italy is the worst; the men in Rome are plain rude."

"I don't have men undressing me with their eyes," Rachel joked.

"Let's see if we can change that. Let's pass on the workout and get shopping for that perfect dress," Candice suggested.

They agreed, changed back into their regular clothes, and headed out to the hotel lobby.

The dress shop was small, and as Candice expected, it was also very expensive, although it seemed to have a good selection. As they all looked through the various racks of clothing, Angelina began pulling dresses for Rachel to try on. Candice had two on her own arm.

"Looks like we have a few. Let's get trying them on and see if we can find a winner," Angelina said.

"I'll help you, if you don't mind," Candice said. She stepped into one of the larger change rooms with Rachel. Rachel seemed a little ill-at-ease with that but she didn't object. As Rachel began to undress, Candice noticed problem number one.

"We're never going to find you a dress if you intend to wear that kind of underwear. The panties and the bra have to go. We need to build you from the skin out."

She leaned out the door and asked Angelina to head to lingerie and pick out a proper pair of panties and a bra for Rachel. She asked Rachel what size of bra she wore and then instructed Angelina to pick her size in an undercut, push-up style.

"You don't have huge boobs but they're a good size and nice and firm from what I can see. Let's see if we can pick them up a little. You have to show what you own is my opinion."

Rachel's face burned red. She was so embarrassed by the attention being paid to her body. She had never really given much thought about her body. She knew she had a nice figure but it never dawned on her to embellish one's natural self with push-up-this and pull-over-that clothing. She knew many women were comfortable wearing that type of clothing; she preferred a simple dress and jacket or slacks and a top. She had never tried to make a statement through her clothing. Even the little bit of design work she had done in her spare time was very conservative.

The most embarrassing part of this for Rachel was changing her panties and bra for the new style. Rachel tried to cover herself from view as she shed one style for the other. She had never worn a thong before. She felt quite exposed and very self conscious. The bra felt odd. She was accustomed to full coverage. This one barely covered her nipples. The design of the new bra was to achieve maximum lift as Candice called it and exposed more flesh. It felt strange although she could understand why some women preferred this approach. She was starting to feel kind of sexy in her new under garments. After much deliberation and trial and error they finally narrowed the choice to, what is generally known as, the LBD. They should have done that from the beginning and they all laughed. This choice featured spaghetti-straps and was cut just low enough in the front to expose the top of Rachel's breasts. She wouldn't be hanging out all over as she first thought she might be asked to do. It was an acceptable compromise. The dress was a floor length style, complete with a slit up the side to reveal her leg to mid-thigh. Rachel realized now why her choice in undergarments had to be changed. She looked and felt great as she peered at the stranger in the mirror. It took quite awhile before she and the ladies made a final confirmation of the dress selection; one that Rachel felt she could wear comfortably. At one point in the process, Candice and

Angelina were both in the change room with her; helping her make the final selection. They were all having a fun time. Rachel's face never lost the deep crimson-red color. Despite the embarrassment of the situation, she was determined to stay with it until she had the dress she wanted.

"You can see my breasts jiggle when I move," Rachel said in a concerned tone. She pointed to the upper section of her breasts. She was looking at herself dressed in their final dress selection, for the tenth time.

"They're supposed to jiggle," Candice laughed. "You look great. There's not too much exposed and the important parts are covered."

"Not by much," Rachel replied. "If I jumped up and down they're likely to pop right out."

"They won't pop out," Angelina assured as she chuckled. "Just in case... don't jump up and down."

"Here," Candice offered, "this will cover them up," she said. She placed a lovely shawl over Rachel's shoulders. "This will hide the jiggling boobs."

Rachel took one final look at herself in the dressing room mirror. She turned in every direction to see what it looked like from all angles. She had to be sure.

Candice took the opportunity to leave Rachel alone in the dressing room while she retrieved a dress for herself that she had seen earlier. She had spotted the dress and fell in love with it when she was searching the racks earlier. Candice returned to the change room with her new find on her arm.

"I have to try this one," Candice said. "I saw it earlier and it's just what I need."

Candice was undressed and stepping into her new found gem within a few moments of arriving in the change room. Rachel kept her eyes on her own reflection in the mirror as her friend changed behind her. Once dressed, Candice stood beside Rachel as they shared the large mirror. It was a quick decision for Candice. The dress fit her perfect body and showed everything she wanted it to show. Rachel, seeing how the amount of flesh exposed in her dress paled by comparison to Candice's new find, decided she also had the dress she wanted. *I can do this*, Rachel thought to herself as she took one final look at her reflection. The women changed back into their sweats and met up with Angelina and her new found high heels at the till.

"One last thing," Rachel asked as the women were walking towards the elevator. "What do you think of my hair? I decided to try something different when I came to the conference. Normally my hair is straight, plain old black and straight. I curled it earlier this morning and now it's almost back to its normal boring self."

"It's a lot of work and frustration to try to change what your ethnic genes dictate," Angelina replied. "I have the same problem. My Egyptian roots prevent me from doing much more than I have now with my hair. It's pretty much natural. Chinese women, and men for that matter, normally have straight black hair. I wouldn't fight it."

"You have such a tiny face," Candice added. "The length you have it now and going back to straight will frame that pretty face perfectly."

"I'll wash it as soon as I arrive back in my room. It will dry straight," Rachel announced. She was pleased to have received reassurance from two women as beautiful as Candice and Angelina.

"Somehow, I don't think the guys are going to be looking at your hair when you show up in your new outfit," Angelina joked. Rachel's face glowed red as the elevator doors closed. "Once we are all ready we'll come down to your room, Rachel. Then we can prepare for our grand entrance. Eight o'clock ladies.

CHAPTER SEVEN

March 25, 7:45 pm CST - Main Lobby
Matador Resort Hotel - Mexico City

The plan was to meet in the lobby, at eight. The men were the first to arrive. They sat on the window seats, waiting. Waiting and watching the people pass by heading in all directions through the busy hotel lobby.

The lion's share of the hotel refurbishment budget had been spent on the lobby. The first impression a customer has about your hotel is the one that stays with them and keeps them coming back. It was critical that the lobby be nothing short of spectacular. They had achieved their objective. From the brightly-colored Mexican tile floor to the magnificent winding staircase on each side of the main foyer, elegance was the only word you could use to describe it. A massive fountain, complete with a more than life-size matador slaying a massive bull, proved that you were in one of the grandest hotels in Mexico City.

"Is it just me, or do you guys get the feeling that there are a lot of smoking hot, young women in this hotel?" Reggie said while he leaned against the glass behind the window seat.

"I noticed and thought it was just my imagination," Jack confessed.

"Take a gander at these three," Edward whispered as three very pretty young women passed by, very close to where they were sitting. They were obviously on their way to the pool. The men could clearly see their tiny bikinis through their cover-ups.

"Must be spring break. They all look like college-coeds," Reggie concluded.

"Oh... to be back in college," both Edward and Jack chimed in unison.

The ladies had collectively decided to make a grand entrance together. Rachel knew she would be eclipsed by these two buxom beauties, however, she was confident that her new dress would be something special. Angelina was anxious to see the response from the men about her complete reversal of wardrobe from earlier today, especially from Reggie and the clown of the group, Edward. Candice knew they would be drooling over her full breasts and short skirt and she enjoyed every moment of the attention.

"They're everywhere. Take a look, at the top of the stairs," Reggie said, gently elbowing his friends sitting next to him. They all looked towards the top landing for a better view.

Reggie was the first to notice the women standing on the top landing of the staircase. More specifically, he recognized Candice. She was hard not to notice. Her figure and her blonde hair were a dead giveaway. But there were two other babes standing next to her. It took a minute for him to realize who they were. He turned to the others.

"Holy shit," he said, directing their attention towards the women. "Do you believe this? Look at Angelina, no more Muslim chick and who's the China doll? Do you believe this?"

He was clearly taken by surprise, as were the other two young men. As they watched the women descend the stairs, they were speechless. They got up from their seats and stood, staring at this trio of beautiful women as they approached.

Charlie's Angels, Edward thought as he looked at them, comparing them to the lovely ladies in the popular movie. *We are going out with three angels. There is a god and this is heaven.*

The ladies stopped short of reaching the men and turned slowly to give their admirers a full 360 degree view of their dates for the evening. Rachel was hesitant at first however, this was the plan they had discussed in her room a few short minutes ago. She soon followed the others and turned slowly as well.

Rachel's dress was an obvious hit. She was feeling more comfortable with the low cut front and even allowed her shawl to open slightly, to show a little flesh. The slit in the side was something she wasn't quite comfortable with as yet. At least she knew no one could see her underwear. She really liked the new lingerie. It felt sexy; almost like she wasn't wearing anything at all. She wore high heels but not as teetering-high as the other women's. She felt good about her hair as well. She wasn't sure if the guys would even notice; they were so busy looking everywhere else.

Candice's new dress fit her like a glove. The white fabric held every curve of her ample body. Unlike Rachel, Candice was not self-conscious about a little jiggle. In fact, she was accustomed to a lot of jiggle. *Her breasts were spectacular,* Edward thought to himself. She had been somewhat covered up for most of the day in her business attire. At least as much as her considerable attributes would allow. As she turned, they all viewed her bare back. The dress plunged to stop at her tail bone. The very short skirt was accentuated even more by the length of her legs and her five inch platform high heels. Candice enjoyed playing with men's minds in her provocative choice of clothing. It was clear she came to play.

Angelina was the one that really surprised everyone. Like Rachel, everyone assumed that she always dressed in her traditional, more conservative wardrobe. No one had any idea of what her body looked like under the fabric of the clothing she wore earlier in the day. Angelina's floor length dress was jet-black and the silk fabric captured the light. Not a glossy-black but better described as a shimmering-black. The front was tied at the neck, in a collar-like design, and there was, what the guys believed they called, a peek-a-boo cut-out over the breasts. It was more than a peek-a-boo, it was more like a come-look-and-see cut out. Her breasts were incredible, from what they could see. Not as large as Candice's but full and firm. As she turned, they saw the same peek-a-boo drape in the back of the dress. Although fastened at her neck, there was nothing covering her beautiful, bronze-colored, skin. Like Candice's dress, it also stopped slightly above her behind. From what the men saw, she had as equally exquisite a behind as any of the other women. Angelina had sensuality in her appearance. Candice evoked a more sexual image, as well might be expected with a *Playboy* model, but Angelina was more like what you would find on the pages of an expensive art-magazine, rather than a news-stand publication. Angelina's appearance was sexy and exotic for certain, and at the same time very elegant. Angelina was first to speak. She had heard Reggie's comments when they first appeared at the top of the stairs. The marble in the lobby made it difficult to whisper. It magnified the volume of any words, no matter how quietly they were spoken.

"I'm not sure *Muslim chick* and *China doll* are appropriate descriptions of young ladies about to go out with you for the evening," she said directly to Reggie, as she smiled at the group and winked at Candice and Rachel.

I didn't think you'd hear me," Reggie replied.

"Well, I did hear you, and it's inappropriate to use one's ethnic origin or gender in describing them the way you did. How would you like it if I were to do the same to you? Perhaps I should describe you as the "Italian meatball."

Angelina was quite proud of herself for coming up with that witty-response off the top of her head. The others were listening to this latest discussion with interest. It was always a lively and humorous exchange when these two went at it.

"I would prefer "Italian stallion". You know, like Sly Stallone in Rocky."

Angelina stopped in her tracks. Once again, he had a smart-assed comeback and it was a pretty good one, she thought.

"I'm sure you would. I seriously doubt that's the case. I watched that movie late one night, and you look nothing like Sylvester Stallone. I recall another movie from my youth with a character named Rocky. His side-kick was Bullwinkle. How about I call you Bullwinkle?" Angelina was proud of this zinger as well. *I'm getting pretty good at this,* she thought.

"How about just Sly?" Reggie continued. He was having a tough time holding back a big smile.

"How about I not talk to you at all," Angelina replied, trying to control her annoyance with his continued pursuit of this silly conversation. "Then we can end this discussion. We will take your descriptive comments as a compliment and your approval of our wardrobe selection. Let's get this party started."

Angelina locked arms with Jack on her way out the door. There was no way she was giving Reggie the satisfaction of having her on his arm. They all proceeded to the waiting limo.

The limo driver held the door as they entered the vehicle and each took a seat. The women facing towards the back of the car and the men facing forward. They had decided to take a private vehicle rather than rely on the public taxi service. A small safety measure yet a wise one. Many unfortunate incidents in Mexico City begin in public buses and taxies.

As far as the quality of limo was concerned, this one was at the bottom of the list. It was a limo for sure, however the condition of the inside of the vehicle was a far-cry from elegant. The white seats could have used a scrub; the windows a clean; and a few repairs to some of the tears in the faux-leather upholstery were also required.

The entertainment venue the men had chosen turned out to be a short ten-minute drive from the Matador. A fortunate occurrence as it meant they spent less time in their sub-standard transportation. As they exited the vehicle and made their way through the main doors, they could hear the loud music coming from the rear of the building.

Dinner was the first item on their agenda. They located the restaurant and were seated almost immediately in a booth along the inside glass wall of the room. A location that overlooked the pool and common open area in the center of the complex. The waitress arrived quickly and took their drink orders. The men ordered beer and the women a glass of white-wine. After a lengthy review of the extensive menu, they decided to order several trays of a variety of foods. This would provide some choice for those unfamiliar with Mexican food.

"Jack," Candice said, "you had to rush through you opening remarks this morning. Why don't you pick up where you left off and fill us in on some of your life's story."

Jack was surprised by her request, but willing to start over. He didn't feel his life story was anything interesting.

"I don't recall where I was in my story, so I'll begin again. My Name is Jack Daniels, and yes, I was actually named after the popular beverage of the same name. My mother and father decided that since I was conceived after they had both consumed considerable volumes of my namesake beverage at a school dance, it might be humorous to use the name. Jack I mean; the Daniels was a given. It really doesn't bother me. It's often a conversation starter," he smiled as he looked at the group. "See it works. Here we are talking about it already. It turned out after my parents were married, because that's what was done in those days when a girl got pregnant, my grandfather passed away and left his Montana ranch to my dad. The rest of the family, his two sisters, were pretty pissed about that but it was done and my dad and mom were in the cattle business immediately after graduating high school. It turned out that dad, and mom for that matter, were pretty good at raising cattle. Didn't hurt that the ranch was a few thousand acres and the existing herd was also several thousand strong. They have done extremely well."

Jack paused to take a sip of beer before continuing. Candice looked more closely at Jack. He actually did look like he could be a cowboy. He was tall and well muscled. Likely worked out on a semi-regular basis and his sandy brown hair was never really combed in any particular style. It kind of did its own thing. He looked good with his chiseled face and scruffy hair.

"Little Jack soon blossomed into quite an academic. I blew through elementary school and high school, by the time I was fourteen, and straight into MIT. I don't think the public school system knew what to do with me so they just allowed me to push on. I even blew through MIT receiving my Masters by my twentieth birthday. There I was, a masters degree in computer software engineering, at twenty. I took the first job I was offered and got out of Dodge. I really didn't want to go back to Montana, so I headed for California and here I am." Jack smiled and he turned the conversation back to Candice.

All through Jack's story, Angelina noticed that Reggie was looking very intently at her and the other women. It seemed odd. She decided to leave it alone for now. She assumed he was still surprised and pleased with their dates' attire for the evening.

"I noted that you, Reggie, described your father's vocation as a business-man," Candice stated, turning her attention from Jack. "What business is he in?"

"He's in the investment business. Mostly real-estate acquisitions." Reggie prevaricated. He suspected his father was involved in organized crime to some degree.

"He builds houses?"

"No, not residential real estate. He buys property - office buildings, shopping malls, old factories and the like. No actual construction work, but rather the property acquisition part of these deals. He and some others he works with."

"Is that something you might decide to do?"

"There's a little more to it but yeah I wouldn't mind if the opportunity was a good one. I'm a math guy not really a finance type although I think I could wrap my head around it. Kicker is, I'm not sure dad wants me to follow in his footsteps."

"I'm sure he would," Rachel assured.

"Maybe."

"And what about you, Mr. Milton? Candice continued. "We know your father has passed away and it's only your mother, your sister and yourself. How old is your sister?"

"My sister is nineteen, I think. Maybe twenty."

"She's hardly your kid-sister, as you described earlier," Rachel added.

"Who, bug? She's still a kid as far as I'm concerned." Edward sounded very fatherly in his statement. It was clear to the women that as the only man in the house, he likely took on the father's role when it came to his sister.

"Your sister's name is bug?" Rachel quizzed.

"Her name is Anna. I just call her bug because she bugged me when we were younger. She was always trying to hang around with me and my friends. I called her carrot before that because she had red hair when she was very young. I had to stop calling her that because she would go to mom in tears all the time. I got into a lot of trouble over that. Her hair changed color as she got older."

"And she prefers bug to Anna?"

"No, but I call her that anyway. She's at college right now, planning to change to a university. I'll be bringing her to Ottawa, where I can keep an eye on her. That's where I live."

"She'll live with you?"

"Hell no, she'll have her own place but she needs to be supervised. She's starting to become all womanly and will likely be dating boys soon. She needs her big-brother to guide her, whether she thinks so or not. She's becoming quite a handful for mom and me."

"I would think at nineteen, or maybe twenty, she may have already had a date or two," Rachel guessed.

"Not that I'm aware of," he stated in his same fatherly voice.

"I'm sure you will be an excellent guide," Rachel said.

The women glanced at one another. They knew there was no way a big brother was going to be welcomed as a chaperone for a twenty-year old younger sister. Edward had some surprises in store for him.

During the conversation, everyone had consumed almost everything that was on the trays. It was getting close to ten o'clock and the party in the back room was in full swing, based on the increased level of noise.

"Let's... party..." Angelina declared. She raised her arms and stood up. She took Jack's arm once again and proceeded out of the restaurant; heading to the dance hall and to a table, hopefully at the back of the room.

As she walked out of the restaurant, she took the opportunity to make a comment to Reggie about his earlier staring. He was right ahead of her and Jack as they walked. She leaned slightly forward so he knew she was speaking to him.

"I noticed throughout dinner that you seemed to be staring at me. At us, Rachel, Candice and me. Was there something you wanted to say?"

"I wasn't staring." Reggie denied. His head turned back as he spoke.

"Yes you were, and it's not polite to stare. Particularly where you were staring," Angelina replied glaring back.

"At your beautiful faces? I was looking at all of your beautiful faces."

"No. You were focused ten inches below our faces is more like it. You need to be more subtle when gawking at a woman's chest. It's not polite."

"You all look very nice," he conceded.

"Thank you."

Reggie kept walking. Angelina smiled ever-so-slightly.

The party was already in full swing. The place was alive with music and gyrating bodies. Jack wasn't all that enthusiastic about dancing but he knew he had to at least get out there. Reggie and Edward on the other hand, were enthusiastic. They liked to party and there appeared to be an abundance of good looking women to party with. Including the three they came with. After everyone was seated at their table, the men rose and offered to buy the ladies a drink; then they headed through the maze of dancing people towards the bar. It took only a few minutes to fill their orders. With drinks in hands, they returned to their table. To their surprise none of the women were *at* the table. They were all on the dance floor dancing with complete strangers. They had left the table for only a few minutes, and in that short a period of time, the women had already been scooped up.

Rachel was obviously the shy one as she moved very cautiously with her unknown dance partner. Angelina, and more specifically Candice, were the opposite. They were enjoying themselves and working their assets to the fullest. Each of the women had removed her high heels before stepping onto the dance floor. Seeing these beautiful women dressed as they were and barefoot only added to the imaginations of all the men in the room. These three ladies had caught almost every male eye in the house. As the song ended, the three women were escorted back to the table by their dance partners. They were out of breath and looking for refreshments.

"Well, that didn't take you too long to find a friend," Reggie said to Angelina as he watched her partner return to the dance floor.

She was out of breath but managed to respond. "We didn't find anyone; they found us."

"Didn't look like they took you by force; you seemed to be enjoying yourself."

Angelina looked in the direction of her recent dance partner. "Why wouldn't I? He's one good looking guy," she said.

"What's his name?"

"I have no idea," Angelina shot back. "I never asked him his name; he never asked me mine." Now her tone turned mischievous. She could sense that there was some jealously and she was going to have some fun with it. "Is there something wrong with dancing? Or perhaps it's just with me dancing."Angelina baited.

"Here we go," Jack said, a little louder than he intended. Angelina and the others heard his comment.

"No Jack, Mr. Viscusi seems troubled by my dancing with that perfectly nice young man. I didn't hear him ask me to dance. Am I supposed to sit by and wait for the honor of being asked?"

"You don't even know his name." Reggie defended.

Angelina didn't respond. He was right. She didn't know his name but she wasn't about to admit it. She glanced out to the dance floor and saw her previous dance partner returning to their table. She had her out. The moment he reached their table, Angelina jumped into his arms and they headed for the dance floor. Reggie watched as they wormed their way through the crowd, holding hands with him leading the way. He thought that Angelina was demonstrating a little more hip movement than she normally had, as she walked away. No doubt for his benefit, he assumed.

This seemed to open the flood gate of interest in the women sitting at their table. Within a very short time the constant flow of men approaching the table, looking for an opportunity to dance with the ladies, was almost comical. It was like someone put up a sign; *come dance with three beautiful women, come one, come all.*

The guys watched the crowd dance to the wild music. The women had all been asked to dance by strangers and were out there, somewhere. Reggie kept a close eye on Angelina. She knew he was watching her; she could almost feel his eyes burning into her. In response, she made every seductive dance move she knew. She ran her fingers through her dance partner's hair; ran her hands down his back; moved her body up and down the length of his. If he was going to be watching her all night, she wanted to show him what he was missing. The only thing she didn't do was knock her partner to the floor and tear off his clothes. At least that's what Reggie thought. The music stopped and she was escorted back to the table. She sat down and took a sip from her drink without saying a word. After a few moments, Angelina leaned over and whispered into Reggie's ear. She was very quiet but made certain she inflected as much sexual suggestiveness as she could muster.

"Demetrious."

"What?" Reggie asked.

"His name is Demetrious and he's Greek. It seemed important to you that I know his name, so I asked him. It's Demetrious."

"You were talking a lot; what did he say to you?" Reggie countered.

"You're not content with me knowing his name before he presses his gorgeous body against me? He has a very nice body, don't you agree." She was now glancing at the others in the group, as she pulled Reggie's chain. "Now you want the details of our conversation. Maybe he was whispering sweet-nothings in my ear. I have no idea what he was saying. He doesn't speak English. I just like his accent. Greek is a very sexy language." She sat back to finish her drink. Angelina knew she had him on the ropes and she was enjoying it.

While this was playing out, Candice and Edward had spent almost all of the time on the dance floor. Fast, slow, any kind of music was good with them. They seemed to be infatuated with each other. Angelina hadn't noticed the vibe between them before but it was definitely there. On several occasions men would tap on Edward's shoulder in an effort to cut in on him. Candice had a killer body and every man in the room would give his week's pay to be as close to her as the man she was currently dancing with. All requests to cut in were rejected. It was clear they were partners for the night.

Angelina watched a less defined scenario happening between Jack and Rachel, as well. Although Rachel was far less seductive in her dance moves, she appeared to be a pretty good dancer. On several occasions, Jack was also tapped on the shoulder by other men but never for slow dances. Rachel seemed comfortable dancing with a stranger if it was a fast dance. She was more selective when it came to the slow dances and being held close against a strange man. During slow dances, Rachel took the opportunity to move as close to Jack as her shyness would allow. She seemed quite comfortable with that arrangement. Coupled with her new dress and her newfound zest for fun, she was enjoying the party immensely. Rachel seemed surprised that so many men would ask her to dance. She had hardly sat out one dance because she lacked a partner. She was unaccustomed to the attention.

A few more minutes passed and two young women approached the table. It was between dances and both Jack and Reggie were sipping their beers. These women were tall, blonde and had very large, exposed breasts. They appeared to be twins, and very young. This added to their allure.

As they reached the table, one young woman leaned into Reggie and whispered in his ear. This resulted in Reggie tapping Jack on the shoulder and motioning him to join them on the dance floor. Angelina watched from the table as they danced. Rachel kept an eye on Jack from the dance floor. She was dancing with a very attractive young man, a few couples away. This was her third dance with the same man, and although he seemed a bit forward for Rachel's taste, she was having fun. She did have to pay close attention to his hand placement. She was unaccustomed to having a strange man's hands on her bare back and had to reposition them slightly higher, more than once. The young blonde women bounced and flaunted their bodies as close to Jack and Reggie as possible. Neither Jack nor Reggie were really dancing; they were standing relatively still and watching the girls put on a show. These girls were hot. Partway through the dance, two other young men came along and tapped the girls on the shoulder. The women turned and danced away with their new partners, as if Jack and Reggie never existed. They had been replaced. Reggie and Jack returned to the table, looking a little disappointed.

"What happen with Miss Bounce and Miss Flounce?" Angelina asked. She was trying to hold back a large smile.

"It's Mindy and Molly if you don't mind; they're twins," Reggie replied. "I take the time to ask for names."

"I see that." Angelina looked out to the dance floor at the two blondes. They were still bouncing from man to man. "Did you take any time to ask for ID? They can't be any older than 18. Did you even look at how young their faces were? Did you look anywhere above their neckline or were you fixated on staring at their breasts? You have a habit of doing that. A girl 18 and built like that is a very dangerous thing for a young man these days." She had him again, and she knew it. It was true. These women were very young. They were likely part of the crowd of scantily clad college coeds, she noticed earlier, putting on a show by the pool; all around the hotel, for that matter.

"I don't always stare at women's breasts," he protested. "They were blonde. I live for danger." He knew she was right about the staring. He didn't remember anything about the women, except their hair color. He never looked at their eyes or even their faces. His gaze was about ten inches below their eyes and he liked what he saw. That's what he remembered.

The band ended one song and it was clear that the next would be a slow dance. Reggie could see the Greek guy starting to head their way. He reached over and took Angelina's hand and pulled her towards the dance floor. She was startled by his sudden move but delighted as she rose and followed him onto the dance floor.

"Are you asking me or *telling* me to dance?" she teased as they reached the dance floor.

"I'm sorry. Would you like to dance?"

"I would be delighted. Thank you for asking."

As they came together on the floor, their bodies seemed to melt into each other. It was the most familiar and natural feeling when they were in a tight embrace. Both of their minds were racing as they tried to decipher what it was they were feeling. Angelina was unnerved by this new sense of attachment. She had spent most of the day chastising this caveman and now she felt herself strangely attracted to him. It was more than an attraction; stronger than an attraction; it was almost a lusting for this guy she was feeling. She shook her head discretely, trying to shake the thoughts out of her mind, but they wouldn't go away. As the dance ended, they returned to the table and sat silent. They were both confused by what had just happened, and they needed time to figure it out.

Angelina took the opportunity to visit the ladies room. More correctly, she took the opportunity to leave the table to meet someone she spotted from across the room. She had made a phone call several hours earlier, and this man was here in response to her call. They had a brief conversation and Angelina returned to the table. Reggie had been watching her. He thought it was odd that she would be speaking to some stranger, but the conversation was very short so he let it go.

Nearing 12 midnight, Eddy had an urgent call on his cell. He left the dance floor so he could hear what was being said. It was Monica Chilling, the office manager from his work.

As he stepped into the hall, he noticed several tough-looking characters leaning against the wall. They moved towards him as he walked, so he quickly turned and walked through the crowd of partiers to the other end of the hall. He noticed that both Reggie and Jack had also entered the hallway and noticed the men leaning against the wall. He didn't give it much thought other than they appeared to be looking for trouble and he had side-stepped it. He turned his attention to his call. It was Monica Chilling.

"I knew you couldn't get along without me. When are you going to run away with me?" he was being his usual tease. Eddy always joked that she was going to leave it all behind and run off with him to a deserted island.

"I don't think my husband and kids would like that very much." Eddy could hear in her voice that she wasn't as jovial in her response to his antics as she normally was.

"Is there a problem?" His voice had become more serious.

"Eddy, I have some bad news. John Bentley was killed yesterday in a car accident. Actually, he was hit by a car on the sidewalk next to the bus stop. According to police, it was a hit and run. The preliminary police reports indicate some young people stole a car. They were joy riding; lost control; mounted the curb and struck John killing him almost instantly. Then they tore away from the scene of the accident. Apparently, the abandoned car was found a short time later smashed up against a guard rail on an off-ramp."

"Oh Monica, that's really sad news. I only knew him for a day or two before I left for Mexico. Only met him twice but he seemed like a nice guy. I saw the picture of his wife and kids behind his desk when I was in his office the other day. They look to be in their teens. How are they doing?"

"I hear as best they can."

"Monica, John was only my boss for a few days, and I don't really have much experience in the department, but would it help if I came back early?"

"No, the other bosses discussed that and they asked me to tell you to stay with the conference."

"Let me know if they change their minds. Can you do me a favor and send some flowers for me and extend my condolences to his wife and kids? I know what it's like to lose a father and it's not an easy time to get through."

"I would be glad to. We debated whether or not to call you, because you hardly knew John, but I'm glad we did. It's sad but it's just one of those things in life. Try not to let it ruin your time at the conference."

"I will. You know I was secretly hoping to see you down here." He was trying to end this solemn conversation on a lighter note.

"You're going to find yourself in trouble one day. One of these times, one of the women you flirt with is going to show up on your doorstep. Then what are you going to do?"

"I'll deal with it when that happens."

"Talk to you when you get back, Eddy." she said as she hung up.

Eddy felt bad about the situation. It was true that John had only been his boss for a short period of time; but he knew what it was like to lose a father and he felt sorry for his family. He did wonder, though, if his boss ever found anything out about the ODD reference they had discussed before he left for Mexico. He never spoke to John after he had his meeting with Mr. Stanley. All he remembered was John's assurance that his explanation about how he got into the secret files was accepted by him. He assumed it was also fine with Mr. Stanley or surely they would have insisted on interviewing him as well. He still wondered if there was any connection with what he saw at Chemico to what Candice had spoken about during today's Mensa session. "*The OD acronym remains a secret,*" he thought to himself.

After a few minutes, Edward returned to the group.

CHAPTER EIGHT

March 26, 2:00 am CST
Matador Resort Hotel - Mexico City

It was 2:00 am, time to head back to the hotel. The limo was called to pick them up. Everyone packed up their things and left the table. They walked through the lobby and into the waiting limo. Jack noticed two of the guys he had seen earlier in the hallway; he ignored them. They didn't appear to have noticed him so he just walked on by them. Hardly a word was spoken by any of their group during the time it took to walk to the car. Some, in the group, had a lot on their minds.

Everyone was seated in the back seat of the limo, this time the men and women sat alongside one another. Unlike the ride to the dance, they were now more comfortable with each other. The Limo was beginning to pull away from the hotel when someone stopped the car and knocked on the driver's side window. When the driver put the window down, there was a short conversation resulting in the driver getting out of the car and a stranger replacing him behind the wheel. Only two of the passengers seemed to have noticed this exchange of drivers. Reggie and Angelina. Reggie tapped on the divider window between the driver and the passengers, to ask what was happening. There was no reply and the window remained closed. The door locks were heard to engage. Reggie looked at Angelina with a questioning expression. *Why did Angelina not seem concerned in any way with what had just transpired?* He wondered. They seemed to be the only two who noticed the exchange of drivers.

The others had bounced back to their normal chatty selves, and were busy talking and laughing about their evening activities. Eddy was joining in but was slightly subdued. The others wondered about his sudden change in moods. They hadn't witnessed this before in their new friend. Reggie was still concentrating on the sudden change in drivers. His first thought was that this could be a possible kidnapping. You read about it happening in Mexico, but you never think it could happen to you. He looked to Angelina for her read on the situation but she still appeared to be unconcerned. The limo pulled out onto the main street and headed for the hotel. *So far so good,* Reggie thought, *at least we're headed in the right direction.*

"Did you not see what just happened?" Reggie asked Angelina while motioning towards the front seat of the limo.

"I saw it, and I can tell by the look on your face that you're imagining the worst."

Angelina continued to appear unaffected by the incident.

"How about we're being kidnapped for starters?" Reggie whispered, trying not to alarm the others.

"It's probably just a shift change. Shifts change at two o'clock, I understand. I read that somewhere. We're heading in the direction of our hotel. You're worrying about nothing."

"It's not nothing when you're in a place like Mexico City. There's a lot of unexplained stuff going on down here. For instance, who was that guy you were talking to earlier tonight? The big guy in the hall outside the washroom."

"You were watching me on my way to the bathroom?"

"No, I simply noticed that someone was talking to you. I was concerned that he might be bothering you."

"And if he was, would you come to my rescue? You are a true gentleman, Mr. Viscusi." Angelina smiled. She was trying to take his mind off the current situation and avoid the question asked.

This seemed to lighten the mood. Reggie appeared to be less concerned about the switch in drivers. The conversation Angelina had with the man Reggie saw earlier was about changing the limo drivers. At this point no one else needed to know why. She knew she had to keep Reggie distracted for the rest of the trip to their hotel. She was running out of ideas.

"Hey Reggie," Angelina said, in an attempt to distract him, "can you help me with my dress? I think Demetrious was fooling around with the zipper. He seemed to have a problem controlling his hands when we were dancing. He was kind of a forward guy. Very sexy voice but *very* forward."

She turned her back to him for his assistance. The diversion worked; Reggie changed his focus from the earlier events and was quite intent on having a good look at her outstanding bare back. *Demetrious wasn't the only one with wandering hands* he recalled. He had also spent a lot of time running his hands up and down her back during their dancing. He had even let them venture further down towards her perfect butt, however, he had yet to look closely at her from this direction. Those moves had met no resistance from Angelina but he had decided not to push his luck in this situation and tried to keep his hands in respectable places. Even though the zipper appeared to be in good repair he tugged at it anyway.

"How's that?"

"Much better." She sat back in the seat next to him as they continued on their trip back to the hotel.

After ten or so minutes had passed, Angelina noticed that the driver was looking frequently into the rear and side mirrors. She could see a blurred image of him doing so through the window divider. The dark tint of the glass prevented a sharp image of the front seat area but she could see enough to know something was happening. She also noticed that the limo had started to speed up and then slow down. The driver kept constant watch on the car behind them. It appeared that the car was, for some reason, following the group. Angelina, still trying to distract Reggie from noticing what was occurring, reached across and held his hand. He was surprised but obviously pleased by that move.

"Do you mind?" Her heart was beating. The contact she had just made with Reggie started a flurry of strange emotions through her entire body; the same emotions she felt earlier when they were on the dance floor. She had never felt this before from a simple touch of a hand.

"Absolutely not." The move seemed to be working. He didn't appear to have picked up on what was happening. He was focused on their interaction.

The limo sped up again and began to take corners slightly faster than would normally be the case. Angelina still seemed to be the only one who recognized that there might be a problem. Reggie had been successfully distracted by her touch. In a second move to retain Reggie's attention, Angelina moved her leg tight against his leg. She also took their clasped hands and placed them on her bare knee. She said nothing this time but was certain she could feel his heart beat increase through the veins in his hands. She wondered if he could feel her heart beat as it jumped into high gear at his touch. As the limo was going through the final set of traffic lights before the hotel turn, there was a loud crash from behind. Someone had smashed broadside into the car that was following the limo. It spun out of control and landed up against a lamp post. Everyone in the car heard the accident and turned to see what had happened through the back window. As the limo sped away from the scene, everyone turned back to their earlier conversations; everyone except Reggie and Angelina who continued to focus on the accident behind them.

As they watched, two men left their car and walked to opposite sides of the vehicle they had broadsided. Three flashes of light could be seen coming from each side of the damaged car. Reggie and Angelina looked at each other. They both knew what had just happened. The two people in the damaged car had just been shot dead. Reggie's earlier focus on Angelina's activities was broken. She knew, even if she stripping down and attacking him, there was no way he was going to be distracted from what was happening outside the limo. The limo continued at an increased rate of speed. Slightly prior to the final turn into the main driveway of the hotel, the car slowed and the privacy window was lowered. The driver spoke directly to Angelina. He spoke in a language unfamiliar to Reggie. Angelina nodded to the man as the window was raised back into position and the limo came to a stop at the hotel entrance. The locks were heard to be opened and the group began to exit the vehicle. Angelina kept a straight face as she tapped on the center window, as if to say goodbye to the stranger driving the car. Angelina and Reggie were the last to exit the limo. They were still holding hands. As they entered the revolving door into the lobby, Reggie released her hand, grabbed Angelina's forearm and spoke directly into her eyes.

"What the fuck was that?" He said it louder than he intended and hoped that none of the others heard him. He also hoped that it got Angelina's attention. "Did you know that guy driving the limo? Who the hell are you anyway?"

Angelina put her finger to her lips and hushed him. She took his hand again and squeezed it tight.

"Don't hush me. Who the fuck was that and why did someone just kill two people in the car behind us, and what did the driver say to you just before we got here? I need"..."

"Calm down. Follow me back to my room and I'll tell you what you need to know." Angelina was whispering, trying not to draw attention to their discussion.

"You'll tell me everything," Reggie declared. He was still holding her hand but had moved slightly behind her. Almost like he was being led to the elevator.

As he walked behind her, he couldn't help but notice how gorgeous her ass looked in the shimmering black dress. *Who is this woman?* He thought to himself, *and why are people getting killed.* They entered the elevator, and just as the doors were closing he caught a glimpse of Candice and Eddy holding hands. They were walking away from the direction where he knew Eddy's room was; perhaps their destination was Candice's room. He had too much on his mind at this point in time to be thinking about his two new friends. He concentrated on the situation he found himself to be in.

CHAPTER NINE

March 26, 2:30 am CST - Room 407
Matador Resort Hotel - Mexico City

"Okay tell me now," Reggie demanded as soon as the hotel room door closed behind them. They had gone to Angelina's room to have their discussion. The room was fairly large with a main seating area and a separate bedroom off to one side. There were the usual lamps and dressers in the room. It was a nice room but nothing special. Reggie had flipped the lights on in the entrance way when he came through the door. Angelina reached over and turned them off. She didn't respond to his question. Instead she turned and slowly walked up and stood very close, directly in front of him. She reached up and turned his head slightly as she turned hers and kissed him full on the mouth. The kiss became more passionate as it continued and it lasted for some time. The longer it lasted the more Reggie returned the passion in what he had hoped would be foreplay. She finally released him and stood back. Her breasts were still up against his chest and she was staring directly into his eyes. Her eyes were a penetrating emerald green color. There was a mysticism to her eyes that was almost hypnotic as he gazed into them. Not a word was spoken as Reggie tried to recover from what had to be the greatest kiss of his life. After what seemed like an eternity of simply staring into his eyes, Angelina turned and with her back to Reggie, she tried to reach behind her in an attempt to undo her dress. By her slow seductive motion this was an obvious prompt for Reggie to undo her dress.

"Would you mind? You did such a great job before."

Reggie complied without hesitation. Two rhinestone buttons held the halter closed at her neck, and there was a short zipper much lower on her back. He slid the zipper down slowly, leaving the buttons fastened. With the dress zipper fully opened, he could see her entire back, below her waist to her ass. Clearly, she was not wearing a bra; he couldn't be sure if she was wearing panties. It didn't look like it. Although his hands had explored most of this area of her body while they danced, this was the first time he was cluing into the possibility that she was not wearing panties. Without turning or saying a word, Angelina took Reggie's hand and they walked slowly into the bedroom. She sat him down on the bed and stood in front of him. She reached back and unfastened the two buttons at the back of her dress. With a blink of her eye and a slight shrug of her shoulders her dress pooled on the floor. He was right, she wasn't wearing any panties. He was gazing at the most beautiful woman he had ever seen. Her breasts were magnificent, large and firm with milk chocolate-brown nipples, fully aroused. Her waist was small and her pussy was perfectly smooth, just the way he liked it. She was still wearing her sheer stockings and her very high heels.

"You weren't wearing any panties.

"I never wear panties when I go dancing. It interferes with my movement. I can put some panties on if you like." She was toying with him and he knew it. She knew there was no way he was going to ask her to put panties on. She also knew there was no way she could stop herself from having this man. It was exciting.

"No, I'm really liking what I see right now."

"You really like or kind of like what you see?"

"Really...like what I see."

"That's good. Do the stockings bother you? I keep them on to warm my legs."

Her stockings were ultra sheer and the tops were red lace. They accentuated her long sexy legs perfectly.

"Don't want you to have cold legs."

Reggie was trying to keep his cool. There was so much to look at he had trouble deciding. His eyes wandered from her face to her toes. Angelina was well aware of his dilemma and was enjoying every moment of it.

"How about my high heels? she asked. "Would you prefer if I removed my high heels? I wouldn't want to hurt you in any way with them."

"Your shoes are very nice; I like them a lot. I'll take my chances on possible injury; let's leave them on as well."

Angelina moved in closer to him. As she did, he raised his hand and held her left breast; took her nipple into his mouth; and slowly ran his tongue around the circumference. He alternated from side to side. Her response was to arch her back and press her breast against his mouth. He continued with his kisses; first between her breasts then down the length of her stomach. As he tried to continue lower, she lifted his head gently.

"Keep that thought. You will have plenty of time to explore." She knew where he was heading and was quite willing to let him explore.

"Promise?"

"I promise." She gently pushed him back onto the bed. Slowly and seductively, she unbuttoned his shirt. She eased it from his shoulders and pulled it off, and threw it over her head, out of the way. She moved lower and unfastened his belt and lowered the zipper on his pants. She stood up and pulled his pants off his legs while giving him yet another full-on gaze of her perfect body. Now that he was completely naked, she moved forward again and straddled him. She lowered her mouth onto his lips as she felt him enter her.

CHAPTER TEN

March 26, 5:30 am CST - Room 407
Matador Resort Hotel - Mexico City

It was several hours later. Reggie was lying in bed trying to comprehend his good fortune when he rolled over to face Angelina. She appeared to be sleeping but he knew better.

Several times during the past few hours, he thought she was sleeping only to find her discovering her second, third, and fourth wind and asking for more of the same. He was only too happy to oblige. He could make love to her all night long.

Her mind was racing. *What have I done? What have I done? I just had sex, I don't even remember how many times with a perfect stranger and it was the best ever. What am I doing?*

"So what was that all about last night?" he finally asked. His voice brought her back to the current situation.

"You mean the sex or the other stuff?"

"Both, but let's get the sex question out of the way." Angelina paused before she replied.

"It's no big deal. I find you very attractive. I'm comfortable with you and last night I was turned on by what had just happened so I decided to have you. Are you complaining?" It was the best she could do on short notice. *I can't very well admit I have no idea what I'm doing or why I'm doing it,* she thought.

"Absolutely not but how often does this happen to you?"

"A girl never tells, but if you must know, this is the second time I have had this kind of experience." *That's a good answer* she told herself. *Twice doesn't make me sound too easy.*

"Only two? I'm flattered."

"You should be. Now what do we need to say about the other events last evening? It was an adrenaline-creating experience."

"So it's the adrenaline rush that turns you on?" he said as he made the connection between her need for sex with the rush she must have felt being chased in the limo.

"No, you turn me on," she replied. She rolled him over and kissed him again. Her inner voice kicked in. *He was right; he knows me better than I know myself. Adrenalin makes me sleep with the guy I'm with – that can't be; I'm better than that; I'm not a slave to my adrenalin rush. Or am I?*

"Was someone chasing you and ended up dead the last time this happened?" he asked. He wasn't letting it go, like she had hoped. There was no reply. She rolled onto her back. She didn't make any attempt to cover her breasts as she lay on top of the covers. He was enjoying the view. *God she had great tits*, he thought. Reggie was gently tracing her body with his fingers. He ran them slowly between her breasts, down the length of her body and back again. He then concentrated on gently circling her, now aroused, nipples lightly with his fingers.

"You know, it's difficult to concentrate when you're doing that," she joked, glancing at his hand on her breast.

Reggie stopped.

"I didn't ask you to stop. I just said it was difficult to concentrate," she smiled, then rolled over to face her lover.

"We do need to talk," she finally said, pulling the covers over her upper body. It was clear that she needed his full attention and that wasn't going to happen with her breasts in full view. She positioned herself on her side, facing Reggie.

"My name is Angelina Evangeline and my family, or more accurately my *father,* is in the arms business."

"You mean like guns and shit?"

"Yes. Guns, tanks, aircraft, anything related to military armament. He's a major player in the Middle Eastern countries; actually in the world for that matter. What you saw last night was an attempt on my life."

Reggie couldn't believe what he was hearing, but he didn't want to interrupt. She continued.

"The man who was driving our limo is a body guard hired by my father to protect me. My father has a real concern, and a correct one as evidenced last night, that my life can be in danger from time to time. He knows his business is dangerous and he tries desperately to keep his family out of it but sometimes it can't be avoided. I knew the driver was a body guard as soon as he took the other driver's place. Actually I had a feeling at the dance that someone was following us so I called a special phone number my father set up for me. Remember when I left to go to the bathroom and was speaking to that very large man? My father has connections almost everywhere in the world so it usually doesn't take much more than a few hours to recruit some protection from some person he knows. I most often don't know who they are but I can usually tell they're there for my protection. These people are the best of the best. Most of them are trained assassins, if you really want to know the truth."

Angelina expected Reggie to react to her last statement but when he didn't appear to be upset by it; she decided to continue.

"Here's the scary part; my father has made it known to the entire global arms community that my mother and I are off limits. There is an understanding and a commitment from my father and all who work for him that should any harm befall either me or my mother the consequence will be total elimination of the perpetrator, his or her immediate family and as much of the extended family as may be living.

My father is a dangerous man, in a dangerous business. People know that his word is his bond. What happened last night is a rare occurrence. It is very unusual for anyone to chance a consequence as severe as this one."

"Were the two people in the car behind us killed?" Reggie asked. He knew the answer but he had to ask.

"Yes, they were and unfortunately as distasteful as it may sound, as we speak his or her relatives all over the world are meeting the same fate. If my father doesn't follow through with the consequence of trying to harm us then it's meaningless. My mother's and my life would be in constant danger. He is not himself a violent man but he believes it's the only way to protect his family. As gruesome as it sounds, the threat only becomes reality if someone breaks the rules. So... what do you think?"

During her explanation, Reggie had thoughts about perhaps airing his own family's dirty laundry but he felt it could wait for another day. He wasn't certain himself about what was true or false about his father's connection to organized crime.

"*What do I think* is the question?" Reggie repeated slowly in an attempt to lighten the mood in the room. "I think you have to be the most beautiful, desirable, and sensual woman in the world," he said. Angelina smiled and he placed his hand on her back side. "After saying that, I sincerely hope that making love to your father's daughter doesn't constitute a threat to her life in any way."

Angelina laughed softly at him finding humor in an otherwise serious discussion. She was pleased Reggie seemed to have taken this revelation with relative ease. "And finally, I think we need to get up; take a long hot shower, together of course, and make our way down to today's session without revealing our secret to the other four. I'm not sure they're ready for that after just one day. The shower may take some time. There are one or two areas on your body that I am yet unfamiliar with. I enjoyed most of them last night but I'm betting there are more."

Angelina made a motion as if she was going to get out of bed; hesitated and then lay back down.

"I have a question for you," she said as she rubbed his cheek softly. "Did you see where Demetrious got to last night? I lost track of him after I came back from the bathroom."

"I believe he ended up with the two blondes you so aptly dubbed Miss Bounce and Miss Flounce. Why do you ask?"

"That's strange; I expected he would be back for at least one more attempt at winning either me or Rachel over before he gave up."

Reggie hesitated slightly before responding.

"I kind of had a chat with Mr. Greek God and got a few things straight," Reggie confessed in a defiant, but mischievous tone.

"And what exactly did you chat about, and by the way, how would you have a chat with someone who only speaks Greek?"

"Oh, he speaks English, Miss Naive. That's the oldest trick in the book for a man to fake that he doesn't understand the woman's language. He understands everything you said, and what you talked about with Rachel and Candice, as well. From that he knew what he had to do to win you."

"What do you mean by *win me*? That sounds a little crass. It sounds like it's a game, and I'm no prize in some man's little game."

"It *is* a game for many men," Reggie smiled, "and this is often very successful technique to bed a beautiful woman."

"Well, it looks like he lost that game. What did you tell him to persuade him to back off?"

"I told him you and Rachel were lesbians and Candice was a transgendered male."

"And he bought that?" Angelina replied in disbelief as her eyes opened wide.

"Greeks may have a romantic sounding language, but this guy was as dumb as a post.

"He was really dumb enough to believe that tale?" Angelina asked.

"As a post," Reggie replied as he kissed her full on the lips.

Their lips remained locked in a sensual kiss until Angelina pulled back from their embrace. He expected she would want to continue their conversation and he was trying to decide if he would or would not go into some of his family history.

To his surprise, Angelina arose from the bed and walked to the bathroom. She turned on the shower and stepped in, leaving the shower door open. Reggie stretched out on the bed and enjoyed watching the water cascade over her naked body. He was about to rise and join her when she reached out of the shower and swung the bathroom door closed. Reggie was confused. He was certain the message he received from her upon leaving the shower door open, was for him to watch her shower for a time then join her to make love to her one more time. He heard the water turn off. After a few minutes, the bathroom door opened and Angelina stepped back into the bedroom wearing a fluffy-white bathrobe. Angelina cleared her throat.

"I really enjoyed our time last night and this morning, and now I think it's time for you, for us, to get ready for today's meeting. I would appreciate it if you would do so in your own room. I will meet you at the table." She spoke as if she was trying to convincing herself as much as him.

Reggie was surprised by her sudden change in attitude. Her voice sounded like she was trying to hold back her emotions, tears perhaps.

"Have I done something wrong? I'm sorry if I have..."

"You haven't done anything wrong. I enjoyed our time together however it's time to get ready and it would really be helpful to me if you would do so in your own room. I need some time on my own."

It was clear she was becoming very emotional; close to tears. Reggie put on the other bathrobe; gathered up his clothes; and slipped out into the hall. He paused outside her door, wondering what just happened. He hoped he hadn't somehow screwed up.

CHAPTER ELEVEN

March 26, 10:30 am CST - Mensa International Conference
Matador Resort Hotel - Mexico City

The group met at nine. Surprisingly, little was said about the previous evening's activities. Candice said she had fun and Rachel agreed. Angelina made no comment. The group discussion resumed about the topic at hand. Angelina participated in the group but it was clear that something was bothering her.

The group took a break at 10:30. Candice and Rachel disappeared to the washroom while Jack and Eddy headed out for a breath of fresh air, leaving Reggie and Angelina at their table, alone. Angelina appeared to be deep in thought about something. She had looked like she was a million miles away for most of the morning. Reggie was concerned.

"A penny for your thoughts. Is there anything I can help you with?" Reggie said as he moved closer to her.

"Last night," Angelina replied.

"It was great and this morning as well."

"It was a onetime lapse in judgment. I've been thinking about it all morning, and as great as it was, it can't happen again."

"I don't understand. I thought you enjoyed last night."

"I did. I did enjoy last night and this morning. That's the problem. I've only known you for a day; not even a full day; it was eighteen hours. My god, when I say it like that, eighteen hours. What was I thinking? I don't know anything about you. I had sex with a stranger. I never have sex with a stranger; I don't do one night stands." Angelina was firm in her statement.

"You did have sex with a stranger and so did I. You don't see me all worried about what happened. It just happened. It was great, but we didn't plan on it, it just happened."

"It can't happen again. I can't allow it to happen again." She was speaking to herself as much as Reggie, shaking her head from side to side. Trying to talk herself out of having sex again with this strange man.

"You didn't enjoy the sex?"

"Of course I enjoyed the sex. It was great sex, best I ever had, you're missing my point. We shouldn't be having sex when we have only known each other for a day; eighteen hours for goodness sake."

"The best you ever had. That's nice to know that it was the best ever. Remember earlier in the evening when you called me the Italian meatball. I suggested Italian Stallion, or better-still Sly, and you scoffed at me. Doubted my claim. What do you say now, Miss best-I-ever-had?"

He was trying to bring some humor into the situation. He knew if he got her laughing he might have a chance at her changing her mind about never again having sex with him.

"Stop talking. Just stop talking. I'm not having sex with you again and I'm not going to even think of you as an Italian Stallion or call you Sly," Angelina said. She was trying not to laugh at how the conversation had turned on her. Reggie's ploy may have worked, she was finding the humour in the situation. She started out with a firm no-way and now they were talking about the merits of their love making. It was kind of funny in a strange way. "And you can stop giving me your deep-dimpled look as well. I see what you're doing with your devil-dimples and it won't work. I fell for it once, but not again."

"Devil-dimples? I'm just smiling. I can't help what I look like when I smile," Reggie replied. He could see the others returning to the table and knew their conversation was over. He also knew that this was not going to be a one-night-stand. "Best ever. Remember the sex was the best ever." He whispered. He was standing very close to her as he smiled.

"Not-going-to-happen. Now, stop talking." Her attention turned to the others as they took a seat and resumed their discussion.

The remainder of the day was spent collecting more data for their dissertation. It seemed to be developing into a fine report, and they were anxious to include as much as they could about this very important topic. The discussion specifically dealing with the OD in marine life was covered extensively. Candice and Eddy never made a connection with the acronym to anything he might be involved with in his business.

Midway through the afternoon, it was announced that there was going to be a conference banquet this evening in the hotel. Everyone pretty much felt exhausted from their previous night's antics, so they all decided to remain at the hotel for the dinner. Angelina vowed to herself there wasn't going to be a repeat of last night's indiscretions. She felt comfortable that a group dinner would be a safe bet.

There was a two-hour break between the end of the day's session and dinner. Most everyone took the time to head back to their rooms for a short nap; make some calls; or just freshen up. Reggie considered paying a visit to Angelina's room but thought better of it. He knew he had a few more days to win his way back into the life.

Dinner was much like everyone expected. Choices included usual dishes, chicken, beef, and a vegetarian entrée, for the herbivores in the crowd. There were the usual speeches. Special thanks to this member and that. All-in-all a pretty boring evening. The dinner activities were over by ten and everyone drifted off in different directions, indicating they would see each other in the morning.

The guys headed down to the Double R for a drink. After the first beer was downed they called it a night. The night shift waitresses were not nearly as pretty as those on the day shift. They all headed back to their rooms for the night.

Reggie showered when he got back to his room; flipped on the television and channel surfed until he found an English speaking news channel. He laid down on his bed in his shorts and soon after drifted off to sleep.

It was a soft tapping on his door that brought Reggie out of his unsettled sleep. He sat up on the end of the bed; glanced at the bedside clock and saw that it was two-thirty. He gave his face a brisk rub and opened the door. It was Angelina. They both stood silent for a few moments until she untied the rope belt of her robe and allowed it to open slightly. Enough for Reggie to see that she was naked and for him to catch another glimpse of that perfect body he had enjoyed only twenty-four hours earlier. She placed her hands on his bare chest and pushed him gently back into his room, swinging the door closed behind her with a nudge of her foot. She backed him across the room up against his bed, and he fell backwards with her on top. Her robe had been shed halfway between the door and his bed.

"Do not say a word," was all she whispered as her lips met his.

CHAPTER TWELVE

March 27, 7:00 am CST - Main Lobby
Matador Resort Hotel - Mexico City

Jack, Rachel, Angelina and Reggie met early for breakfast at the small coffee shop in the hotel. The ladies seemed to prefer the small venue rather than the larger, more open restaurant that served the majority of the hotel guests. During last night's dinner, Candice explained that she had an early morning conference call with the Playboy people and her agent. They seemed very interested in having a second Mensa Playboy bunny and were getting close to a deal. They were going to tie it into the earlier 1987 shoot with the previous Mensa member, Dr. Julie Peterson. Kind of a now-and-then comparison. Candice seemed very excited about the possibility that her goal would soon be achieved.

Edward explained to the group what had happened to his boss, John Bentley and told them he had an early call set up with the office manager, Monica Chilling. She wanted to have their talk early to avoid the hustle and bustle of the daily office routine. Edward confessed that he felt bad that he didn't attend John's funeral, even though he was specifically asked to stay at the conference. Monica was going to fill him in on how his family was doing. Edward seemed to really feel bad about the situation back home. As jovial as Edward appeared to be on the outside, he was sensitive and sympathetic to difficult situations that families faced. He went through it when losing his father so early in his life. He knew it was tough, and he really wanted to help if he could.

The foursome had finished breakfast and were waiting for the elevator when they were ushered aside to make way for some emergency attendants. Two gurneys wheeled past them into the elevator, and the doors closed. There were a few people gathered in the lobby discussing what had just occurred. A young woman in the crowd seemed to know what was going on and was answering questions from the others gathered.

"What's the problem? " Angelina asked the young women. Reggie was at her side as they spoke. Jack and Rachel had stepped back, away from the crowded area.

"The hotel is trying to keep it quiet, but apparently two people were killed very early this morning. Both shot, they say. It's not good for business so the hotel is not saying much."

"Who were they?" Angelina asked. She was hoping they weren't anyone they may have met at the conference. Two people being killed was a terrible event, but it would bring it closer to home if they were a part of their conference group.

"All I heard was, a man and a woman," the stranger answered. "The man apparently was a Canadian or from somewhere up north. They didn't know if the woman was his wife or not. Some have said she might have even been a prostitute. Apparently she's a busty, blonde. Who knows? They're apparently here with that convention of egg-heads meeting in the big conference center. At least the man is. Again, not sure about the woman."

Angelina's heart sank. Reggie had to hold her arm to steady her on her feet. A Canadian and a busty blonde is exactly how one would describe Edward and Candice.

"What room are they in?" Reggie asked quickly. He knew that Edward's room was somewhere towards the middle of the hotel. Edward had made an earlier comment to the group about how good the view was from his balcony. Reggie couldn't remember the floor number, or even if Edward told them a floor number, but he knew it would be in the middle, somewhere.

"I think someone said 1527, fifteenth floor."

"It's Eddy and Candice," Angelina whispered to Reggie as he continued to hold her arm. Her voice was weak and trembling. She leaned more heavily against Reggie. Tears began to form in her eyes as she looked at Reggie.

"We don't know that," Reggie assured. "The people were both killed in the same room. Candice's room is a few floors below Eddy's. It's not going to be them, they wouldn't both be in the same room."

"I can feel it," Angelina said. "It's them. We need to find out if it's them, Reggie."

"She said the woman could have been a prostitute. It's not unusual for some guy's to pick up hookers when they attend conventions, you know. But I don't think Eddy is one of those guys. I don't believe he's like that," Reggie shrugged.

"I've heard what some men do when they go to conventions. Eddy isn't the type to pick up a prostitute."

"Then why would you think it's Eddy and Candice?"

"I have a feeling. Woman's intuition," Angelina said.

"Okay, okay." Reggie whispered. He held her shoulders more tightly. "It won't be them. I'll find out what's going on but it's not going to be them. Believe me when I tell you, it's not them." He was holding her shoulders, speaking directly into her eyes. He still didn't understand why she suspected it was Eddy and Candice, but he had to prove it to her.

Rachel was watching from a few yards away. She saw the reaction Angelina had to whatever it was she had been told by the unknown woman in the crowd. She tugged on Jack's arm and they made their way through the crowd. They reached Reggie and Angelina.

"What is it?" Rachel asked Reggie. She could see the tears flowing down Angelina's cheeks.

"There's been some trouble and Angelina is afraid that Eddy and Candice may be involved. There were two people killed in the hotel last night. "

"My god no. What makes her think it's them? It can't be them."

"I know, I know. Let's move over to the side. Let's get Angelina sitting down, and Jack and I will find out what's going on. It's not them. I know it."

They made their way to the front of the lobby and sat both Angelina and Rachel down on the window seat. Both women were now in tears and seemed to be consoling each other. Jack and Reggie headed for the front desk to get some answers.

The desk clerk was on the phone when they reached the desk. He was having a conversation in Spanish, completely ignoring them standing not a foot away across the counter top. Jack reached across the counter and pushed his finger down on the button on the carriage of the phone, disconnecting the call.

"I need some answers about what's going on," Reggie stated.

Jack had never seen Reggie when he was angry, and he was definitely angry. His voice was plain scary when he spoke. His face was red, sweat was on his brow and trickling down the side of his face. It was clear that any hesitation on the part of the desk clerk was going to be met with an unfortunate response from one very angry Italian.

"I'm sorry sir, but I am not at liberty to discuss hotel business," he stammered in broken English. His voice was quivering; his eyes were scanning the room for some help. Likely a security guard or manager would be his preference to dealing with this customer on his own. There was no one to come to his rescue.

Reggie reached across the counter; ripped the phone from its mounting - wires and all and flung it across the lobby. It skidded across the floor coming to rest at the feet of someone in the crowd gathered at the door of the elevator.

"What room is involved with the problem you're having here this morning?" Reggie hissed.

"1527."

Reggie flinched when he heard the room number. He knew that room would be at the midway point in the hotel. Just as Edward had described it.

"You're absolutely certain about that?"

"Yes sir."

"What rooms are Edward Milton and Dr. Candice Bergen in?"

The clerk didn't hesitate in his response, this time. He tapped his computer key-board.

"Dr. Bergen is in 1235 and Mr. Milton is in 1427, sir."

Jack could see a slight relaxation in Reggie's stance at the news.

"You're absolutely certain? 1235 and 1427," Jack asked."

The clerk glanced at the screen to confirm.

"Yes sir, 1235 and 1427,"

"I need you to call each room for me," Reggie ordered. "I want to confirm if they are in their rooms."

The desk clerk had to retrieve one of the other phones that were at the front desk. Reggie had thrown his phone across the lobby. He dialed one number and waited. It rang six times until the answering machine picked up.

"I'm sorry sir, there is no answer in Dr. Bergen's room," the young clerk advised.

Both Reggie and Jack took a deep breath. The clerk dialed 1427. Edwards's room. They waited once again. Same result, no answer.

"I'm sorry sir, but there is no answer in Mr. Milton's room, either," the clerk almost whispered.

Reggie hesitated. He glanced over at Jack and back to the desk clerk. He looked more closely at the clerk and read the name tag on the front of his, now sweat stained, shirt.

"Thank you... Ernesto. I'm sorry for the trouble. Please bill my room for any damage I may have done to your phone. Have a nice day."

Reggie and Jack turned and began to walk back to join the ladies.

"What are we going to tell them?" Jack asked.

Reggie smiled as he glanced towards the women.

"We don't have to tell them anything," he replied. He put his arm around Jack's shoulder and pointed towards the women. "Look who's here."

As they reached the window seat, Edward and Candice strolled in from the base of the stairs, on the far side of the lobby. Rachel and Angelina embraced them as they sobbed. Both Edward and Candice looked confused. They returned the hugs from the women and simultaneously looked towards Reggie and Jack for a clue as to what was going on. Angelina struck Edward across his chest with her forearm. It startled him.

"Don't ever do that again." Angelina cried and she stomped off towards the women's washroom. Candice and Rachel followed her. The men watched them disappear into the ladies room.

"What the hell was that?" Edward shrugged.

Jack and Reggie shook his hand as they all sat down on the window seat.

"Let me explain," Reggie said.

******

While the ladies got themselves under control emotionally, Reggie and Jack explained what had occurred, and why Angelina and Rachel were so upset.

"I can see why they were upset, but we had no idea what was going on. I tried to get on the elevator on my floor and it was locked-out. I decided to take the stairs, forgetting that I was on the fourteen floor. I ran into Candice a few floors down. The stairwell was full of people all doing what we were, so we never thought anything of it. We show up here and Angelina attacks me for no apparent good reason; all teary-eyed," he joked. "We didn't do it on purpose."

"We believed it was you and Candice. Angelina believed it was you and Candice." Jack further clarified.

"Why would she think that?" Edward asked almost defensively. He was certain that none of the others knew he and Candice had been together.

"It was either you and Candice or you and a prostitute in Angelina's mind," Reggie explained. "I can't explain the why, but that's what she believed."

"A Hooker. I'll have her know that I have never paid for sex in my life," Edward huffed. He knew there was validity in Angelina's suspicion about he and Candice and he wanted to shed suspicion. Actually, it was Candice who wanted to keep their relationship quiet. If it was up to Eddy, he would be flying a banner across the sky that he was with her, however it wasn't his call. He also didn't want the others to believe he hired women to sleep with him. "I'm glad we cleared that one up," Edward smiled as he sat quietly. It was best to let it go.

In the women's washroom, Angelina was finding it difficult to explain why she thought Candice and Eddy would be together and Candice wasn't making it any easier on her. Rachel was baffled that this conversation was taking place.

"I just had a feeling," Angelina finally relented. She hoped that would be the out for Candice to let it go.

"I don't know what's worse," Candice finally said with a joking inflection in her voice and gestures, "that you thought I would be mistaken for a prostitute or that Edward would hire a prostitute."

******

9:30 am

It took a good hour for the conference center to resume its daily activities. The women at table 74 were anxious to move on with the day. Angelina and Candice for other than business reasons. The group continued to gather information and work through the details of their paper. During the conversations there were periodic comments, side comments really, between Angelina and Candice about relationships and how they evolved. They skirted and flirted with the truth as they laughed and joked about various relationships they had in their pasts. Rachel hadn't experienced as much of the dating scene as Candice and to a lesser degree Angelina.

At noon, Angelina said she needed to go back to her room to make some calls. Reggie used much the same excuse and they both met in Reggie's room. They both needed to release some of the pent-up stress they experienced earlier that morning. Angelina needed to be held and comforted by Reggie.

CHAPTER THIRTEEN

March 29, 9:00 am CST - Mensa International Conference
Matador Hotel- Mexico City

Before they all realized, it was early morning on the final day of the conference. For the past four days the discussion at table 74 had varied from serious to humorous as the young people delved deeper into their topic. By the end of day two most of the groundwork for the paper had been established. All that was needed was to pull the final data together. Candice and Eddy had researched the O.D. phenomenon and this was reported prominently as a newfound consequence of global warming. They failed to make a connection between the environmental definition of O.D. and what it might possibly represent in the blasting media world. There was a great deal of their collective dissertation devoted to that matter.

Angelina had noticed that there seemed to be a bond developing between Candice and Eddy. Reggie had to pretty much be told what was happening. He still lacked the body-language skills Angelina had well honed over the years. She could guess what someone was thinking by the way they moved. Reggie had no idea what anyone was thinking unless he asked. It was another difference that made them unique.

Angelina was almost certain Candice was with Eddy. They never denied that they could have been in the same room when that other couple was tragically killed. That lack of denial, in itself, was evidence that they were together in Eddy's room. They just let it slide and everyone was so upset by the incident they never followed up on it.

Candice had noticed the relationship develop between Angelina and Reggie. She noted that they took every opportunity to make physical contact with each other. They couldn't keep their hands off each other. She kept her observations to herself.

Rachel and Jack were also showing signs of being better acquainted than they had been at the beginning of the conference. Angelina doubted that this had progressed to actual sex, but the relationship was showing signs of promise.

It was at mid-afternoon of the last day when they decided to call it quits, as far as the topic discussion was concerned.

"We're down to the last of it. We need to make a plan for one last meeting to pull this all together," Jack stated. "We could do it through an internet conference call or we could meet face to face. What is our collective pleasure?"

The group all knew they were far enough along in their research that a simple conference call would be sufficient to bring it all together. They preferred to meet again. For a number of reasons.

As everyone checked their schedules on their computers and mobile phones there were several dates suggested. After a brief discussion and verification of everyone's availability, the unanimous vote was for another face to face meeting May 1.

"How about New York City?" Reggie suggested. "Some of us live there anyway and the others have to travel regardless of where we meet, so why not the big apple?"

It didn't take much persuading to reach a consensus on New York as the place to meet.

"I'll make all the arrangements and e-mail you the details," Reggie offered. "So it's confirmed with everyone for May 1 and let's go all out and have it at the Waldorf Astoria. What the hell."

With the time and place for the follow-up meeting established, the group disbanded and went their separate ways. The two couples, who had been together during the conference, made additional plans to see each other before the next meeting date but the May 1 meeting would be the next official time for the group session.

CHAPTER FOURTEEN

April 25, 1:00 pm EDT - The Office of Martin Stanley, CEO of Chemico International- Ottawa Canada

Edward Milton had been summoned to the office of Martin Stanley, CEO of Chemico International. Edward had called Monica Chilling to see if she knew anything about the reason for this meeting.

"Why does he want to see me?" Edward whispered as he took a seat next to Monica's desk.

"I have no idea."

"Maybe you were right when you said I was going to find myself in trouble, teasing women."

"I said you were going to get into trouble flirting with women, Edward. What have you done? Who did you flirt with?"

"Everyone. I flirt with everyone. You know that." He was trying to recall who might have been offended by his actions. "That cute, little girl in shipping. The little red-head. She's new, Mary something. I saw her and I knew she was new so I welcomed her to the company. I don't remember what I said but I don't think it was anything bad."

"Cute-little-red-headed-new-girl is likely one of the issues some might have with your description of this young woman." Monica chastised. "You can't go around describing people by their physical attributes."

"I know, I know. Whatever it is, it is. I'm not that keen on this job anyway, as you know. I'll let you know. I have to get down there," he finished as he left her office.

******

It was clear from the moment Eddy shook Mr. Stanley's hand that, his meeting with Stanley was a serious matter. There was something Stanley was upset or concerned about but Eddy had no idea what it could be. That's what he was here to find out. Eddy had thought about this meeting since he was told he was summoned, earlier that morning. He had made up his mind that what was done was done. During the time he spent with his new friends at the Mensa Conference in Mexico, they had talked quite a lot about their current careers. With the exception of his beautiful Candice, everyone else admitted that they would prefer to be doing something other than what they were doing. They all felt that a change in career direction was on the short list of things to do. Eddy really like his old job, and even though he had only been in Product Development for a short time, he wasn't enjoying it. He missed the interaction with customers and working out in the field. Eddy wasn't an office kind of guy. He was prepared for whatever it was Stanley had to say and willing to tell him to shove the job where the sun don't shine, if it came to that.

"I understand you were in Mexico recently," Stanley began. "You're a Mensa member. I'm impressed."

"Thank you. The conference went very well. I think our report will be interesting to a lot of people."

"Why's that?"

"We made some detailed recommendations on how to proceed with convincing, or forcing if need be, other countries to join the rest of the world in the concern over the global environment. The time for endless debate is over.

The final report will be completed in a few weeks. I'm going to New York on the first of May to finalize the paper. The team and I are meeting there."

"Put it through on your expense account, Edward," Stanley instructed. "We like to encourage and support forward-thinkers, and you seem to be one of them."

It was sounding to Edward like Stanley maybe wasn't pissed off, or upset with him after all. Edward was curious as to where this conversation was going.

"That's great. Thank you," Edward replied.

"Edward, you know we are all very upset about John Bentley being killed. It was a tragic loss for his family and for Chemico. He was a good man."

"I leaned of his passing when I was in Mexico," Eddy replied. "I felt I should come back for the funeral however the acting department manager almost insisted I stay in Mexico for the duration of the conference. I felt badly about that."

"He was acting on my instructions, Edward," Stanley admitted. "I told him I wanted you to remain at the conference. As I said before, we like to encourage our forward thinking and the Mensa organization supports that as well. I knew you hadn't known John for very long. There didn't seem to be much point in having you come all the way back for a couple of hours for his funeral. What's done is done."

"I understand his family is doing well under the circumstances," Edward said.

"Yes. John was covered by a company insurance plan so there will be some money for his wife. The man can never be replaced but at least they will have a good start in moving on. That brings me to the reason for our meeting today, Edward. The loss of John Bentley has left a hole in our product development department. As you most likely know, Chemico has and still is going through some tough times during this recession. You saw the announcement concerning the decision to close the Norway and Montana plants. We really struggled with making that decision, but it had to be done. That being the case, it makes our product development efforts here in Ottawa even more critical to the survival of the company."

"Is this plant in danger of closing?" Edward asked.

"You can never-say-never, however there are no immediate plans to shut this plant down. We are pulling out all the stops to gain back the sales we have lost over the past two years," Stanley replied. "That's where you come in, Edward. I want you to take over for John, as Product Development Manager."

Edward was shocked. Of all the possible scenarios he had considered, it never occurred to him this would be one of them. He was speechless.

"Mr. Stanley, you've caught me by surprise. I was not expecting this. There has to be more experienced managers to take John's place," Edward replied.

"I know it's a big responsibility. If I didn't think you could handle it, I wouldn't have made the offer," Stanley added. "Do you not want the job?"

"I don't know if I do or don't at this point," Edward admitted. "I've never given it any thought."

"I thought you would jump at the chance. I must say Edward, I'm surprised by your reluctance. Most people don't have to think about accepting a promotion."

"I'm coming off as ungrateful and I'm not; not at all. I am honored that you would consider me for the position. Like I said, I've never thought about this job as a possibility for me."

"It's yours, if you want it," Stanley replied.

"New Product Development," Edward said slowly. He was trying to get his head around the offer. "Before I left for Mexico, I had a discussion with John about something I accidently saw on my computer. He said he was going to meet with you and straighten it all out. He also seemed surprised that he didn't know anything about the ODD product. Is this going to be one of the new products I'll be working on?"

He was watching Stanley's face for a reaction to his question and he got one. Stanley went from being cordial to angry in a split second. Edward knew he had hit a nerve but he had to know what it was he was going to be asked to develop.

"I told John and he was to pass it on to you that this was something he was not to be concerned about. It's not going to fly anyway and it's been a waste of everyone's time."

Ignoring the warning signs, Edward continued. "What does the acronym stand for? We discussed something similar O.D. when I was in Mexico. It had to do with lack of oxygen in an environmental situation," Edward explained. He could see that Stanley was becoming more agitated, as he spoke.

"Edward, this was a project concept that was scraped. You need to let it go," Stanley said. His emotions colored his words. He was one step away from exploding.

"Got it," Eddy replied. "Can I have some time to consider the offer? A few weeks would be great. I'll be back from New York on the fifth of May."

Stanley stood and extended his hand to Edward. It was clear the meeting was over. Stanley was walking Edward towards the door as he replied.

"Not a day longer, Edward. We are very anxious to fill this position, and you're the man we want, however, if it's not your cup-of-tea then I'll move on," Stanley stated.

Stanley closed his office door; walked to his desk and sat down as he dialed the phone.

"Dennis, you were right. We need to deal with Edward Milton. I tried to talk to him but he's not going to let it go. Do what you think best," he said and hung up the phone.

CHAPTER FIFTEEN

May 1, 2:00 pm EDT- Waldorf Astoria Hotel
New York City, New York

May 1st turned out to be a glorious day in New York City. Spring had arrived and the city was a flurry of outdoor activity. The airports were jammed with travelers including a few who shared a common destination. The legendary Waldorf Astoria Hotel. The Waldorf Astoria Hotel is a four star hotel located in the heart of New York. In recent years, there have been much larger and more opulent five-star hotels built in the city but none that rival the Waldorf in terms of class. This is the most historic hotel in the city. Countless movie stars and world leaders have graced its accommodations. The history is palpable as you enter the main lobby.

Reggie had reserved some rooms but left everyone to make their own final arrangements. In that way if some were cohabitating, it could remain their business. For the time being, that's what Angelina and he had decided regarding their relationship. They were sharing the hotel room, but it wouldn't be common knowledge. One final detail was to make restaurant reservations. He and Angelina decided it would be most convenient if they could eat in the hotel. It would be the grand kickoff for what they hoped would be a great weekend. Reggie warned her that it was unlikely they could make a reservation for Friday night at such a prestigious establishment as the Waldorf on short notice, yet he offered to try. He placed the call to the restaurant from his office.

"Hello, I would like to make a reservation for Friday evening, at 6 pm for six people."

"And your name, sir?"

"Reggie Viscusi." He continued by spelling his surname.

"Thank you, Mr. Viscusi, would you be so kind as to hold the line while I see what we have for you?"

There was a shorter than expected delay before someone returned to the phone.

"Mr. Viscusi, my name is Vincent Demarco and I am the manager of the restaurant. We look forward to your visit Friday. We have booked your father's personal table for your party. I trust this is satisfactory."

Reggie was confused; he didn't know his father had a regular table at the Waldorf or that he even frequented this establishment.

"That would be fine," was the only response Reggie could think to make. He was taken aback to hear his father had a personal table at the Waldorf.

What Reggie didn't know, or perhaps what he didn't want to acknowledge, was the Waldorf Astoria had a long history of catering to the famous and infamous elite of New York City. In its day, the hotel had been the home address for heads of state, including former President, Herbert Hoover. The legendary, General Douglas MacArthur, and even Paris Hilton who lived in the hotel during her childhood. This was not surprising the modern Waldorf was part of the Hilton chain of resort hotels. It had also been the home of several of New York's most notorious gangsters; Benjamin "Bugsy" Siegel, Charles "Lucky" Luciano and Frank Costello, to name a few. Perhaps the Viscusi private table wasn't so unusual, after all.

******

Reggie was first to arrive at the restaurant. It was approaching seven pm. He wanted to be at the table to greet his friends when they arrived. As he was taken to the reserved table, he was confused by the location within the restaurant. He had assumed that a prime location for a private table might provide a full view of the street or perhaps overlook the foyer of the hotel. His father's idea, and as he was later to discover, his grandfather's idea of a private table was closer to the back of the room, beside the kitchen. Once Reggie was seated and had an opportunity to look around the room, he realized why this particular table location had been chosen. It provided a full view of everyone entering and leaving the room and it allowed for a quick exit through the kitchen. This was a perfect table considering the type of business Reggie's family was purported to be involved in.

After Jack and Rachel arrived, it didn't take long before they were all laughing and teasing each other. As Angelina approached the table, Reggie gave her a subtle wink. This was not the first time they had seen each other. Actually they had met several times since the Mensa conference, both at Angelina's place in California and at Reggie's place in New York.

Reggie's New York apartment left something to be desired, a whole lot to be desired as Angelina described it. He had been in this space since he first started working at Statco, and even though he could afford a much larger apartment, it never really occurred to him to make a move. It was convenient and didn't involve a lot of work to keep it tidy. It was close to a multitude restaurants and bars. He liked the neighborhood and the people. It was a two-bedroom, one bath apartment with a compact kitchen opening to the living room, and it was situated above one of his favorite Pizza parlors; which also doubled as a message parlor. His decorating style was *early student.* He still had the pull-out couch and cheap chairs he had when he went to university. Angelina's reluctance to be in his neighborhood had prompted thoughts that maybe it was time for a change of address. He knew everyone in the neighborhood, including the ladies from the massage parlor below; a fact not missed by Angelina the few times she had walked with Reggie to his place. It was like men at a construction site, the cat-calls and whistling the ladies bestowed on their handsome Italian neighbor. He was accustomed to it and knew they meant nothing by it. Although, he was pretty sure if he was to pursue it with any of the ladies, they would likely follow through with their boisterous claims; an idea he never planned to act upon. He always smiled and joked with all of them. He was a frequent customer at the pizza joint. So much so, there was no need for him to place his order, they already knew.

There was little time spent sightseeing during the occasions Reggie and Angelina got together after Mexico. As far as she and Reggie knew, their romantic relationship remained a secret from the others.

Edward was last to arrive. He explained that Candice was going to be a little late as she was meeting with the *Playboy* people. She was in New York but not able to shake free for a few hours. They were still discussing the past and present playmate Mensa member theme and it looked promising for Candice. He explained he knew all of this because she had phoned him on his cell. It was a lame attempt to keep their relationship a secret, but it's what Candice wanted, for now. Angelina wondered why she hadn't informed one of the girls about her delay instead of Edward. As Edward spoke there was something in his tone that caused he to believe there was more to this. She would find out eventually. In the meantime, it gave her some satisfaction that she and Reggie may not be the only ones who hooked up in Mexico. She really liked Candice. She had briefly thought that she, herself could do a nude picture if she really wanted. The fact that she had spent most of her free time naked with Reggie likely added to the possibility of the unlikely. She had a nice body and how bad could it be to have a bunch of strange men look at your naked body and take pictures? *My father would have a heart attack*, she thought, *maybe not such a great idea.*

Edward also informed them that Candice had recently finished another Victoria's Secret shoot in Florida, and she was bringing the ladies a surprise package. Rachel's face turned a bright red as she guessed what it likely was. She was nervous about how revealing it would be. She knew Jack would approve, but he would approve of a paper bag if it showed bare skin. They weren't quite at that point in their relationship for her to be wearing provocative lingerie. They had been intimate with each other twice. Naked and low lights were sufficient for now. She lacked the confidence to prance around in skimpy lingerie.

The before dinner drinks were ordered and served. The group took some time to peruse the dinner menu. It wasn't an overly large menu, unlike the I Hop and Denny's, two of the most popular restaurant chains in America and the establishments often frequented by the men in the group. The Waldorf was everything about quality and almost nothing about quantity.

Candice arrived late and the restaurant staff made an extra effort to prepare her dinner on a rush basis. She decided she would simply have the salad, to make it easier on them. She felt badly they had to rush just because she had been a late arriving.

Angelina had ordered the Grilled Gulf Coast Shrimp with the legendary Waldorf salad. Rachel chose the Half North Carolina Hen and Waldorf salad while; both Edward and Reggie selected, no surprise to anyone, the Long Bone-Prime Dry Rib Eye steak *blood red and still kicking on the plate,* as described by Edward, and the largest portion of house salad on the menu. Despite Jack having been raised on a cattle ranch, or perhaps because of it, he ordered the Two-Pound Maine Lobster. No salad. He figured after eating two pounds of lobster he would be full.

The restaurant staff made certain their every need was met. They all knew those who sat at the Viscussi table were to receive the very best service the Waldorf had to offer. The conversation subsided in favor of eating these gastronomic delights. Stuffing ones face, as so eloquently described by Reggie.

The choice of desert was a foregone conclusion. Nothing was a better choice than the ever popular New York cheese cake. No one could visit New York without experiencing its cheese cake.

Reggie asked for the bill. When it wasn't presented after the third attempt, he went to the manager who was standing at the front desk of the restaurant.

"I'm sorry Mr. Viscusi. There will not be a bill this evening for your party. I should have explained earlier. It has taken care of," Mr. Demarco explained.

"By whom?" Reggie asked quickly followed by "Never mind." He realized that since this was his father's table, the cost was being charged to his account. He was okay with that. When he returned to the table, both Jack and Edward asked what their portion of the bill was. Reggie explained that the tab had been paid. "Welcome to New York." he smiled.

As they finished their final cup of after-dinner coffee and tea, Reggie shared what he had planned for the weekend with his friends. It was subject to their agreement, however it sounded pretty good to all. Although, there would be some time devoted to completing their dissertation on the Mensa paper the majority of their time was going to be spent on activities.

"It will likely take most of a morning to finish up the Mensa submission. I had planned on us doing that Sunday morning," he suggested. "I have planned something else for mid-afternoon Sunday if that's okay with everyone, after the report is finished. It's a surprise so you will have to wait to until then. Tomorrow, Saturday is scheduled full of sightseeing and another special treat that you will also remain a mystery."

It was close to midnight. They couldn't believe they had spent almost five hours eating and talking; the time had flown by. They decided to call it a day and head back to their rooms.

"I almost forgot," Candice said as she rushed to the hotel lobby. She picked up the two packages she had left at the front desk and handed Angelina and Rachel each a small gift bag. "I picked these out especially for you. Enjoy."

They accepted their gift and thanked Candice for her thoughtfulness. The men hung back in the lobby for awhile until the three women had entered the elevator. Once they figured it was clear to meet up with the women in their rooms, they each left the main lobby. It was a silly game; but for some reason the ladies all seemed uncomfortable divulging their romantic relationships to their new friends. It wasn't a big deal for the guys; they could wait.

Reggie tapped on the hotel room door and Angelina let him in. She was dressed in a hotel robe. He had a thought, a hope really, that maybe she had tried on what Candice had given her. He had a good idea of what it would likely be and was anxious to see it; to see her in it to be precise.

"Want to go back to my place?" he joked as he looked around the elegant room that was the standard for the Waldorf.

"Hardly." Angelina's face was scrunched up like she had chewed on a lemon.

She sat next to him on the bed. "What you got under the robe?" he whispered

"Nothing," Angelina replied. She held the front of the robe tight against her in a move of mock modesty.

"You mean nothing or nothing special?"

"I think what's under the robe is pretty special." Angelina was teasing him as she always did. Teasing and the back-and-forth pretend quibbling dialogue the others were accustomed to hearing between these two was really foreplay, or so they had discovered.

"You know what I mean."

Angelina stood and turned to Reggie. She slowly unfastened the rope belt on the robe and shrugged the robe off her shoulders, letting it puddle at her feet. "See, I told you there was nothing."

CHAPTER SIXTEEN

May 2, 8:30 am EDT - Room 524
The Waldorf Astoria Hotel - New York City, New York

It was Saturday morning and as Reggie entered the bedroom from the bathroom he noticed that the message light on his hotel room's phone was flashing. *There must have been a call come through while he and Angelina were in the shower,* he thought. *It only took us an hour this time,* he mused as he thought about how he and Angelina had just enjoyed each other, again, and no one in the group had any idea. This was fun. He picked up the receiver and punched in the required numbers to retrieve his message. To his surprise, it was his mother:

"Buongiorn. How are you, my baby-boy? Your father and I would like it very much if you and your friends would come for dinner tonight. Do you think that would be possible? We would love to meet your friends. Please call me as soon as you can. Arrivederci, sweetie." His mother's accent was very strong. He didn't know why he was always surprised by that fact when he heard her speak but it struck him as odd. Odd that after all these years, away from the New York Italian neighborhood she grew up in, she still had such a strong accent.

How did they know his friends were in town? He thought. Then he recalled the reserved table and the tab for last night's dinner, and he knew. He wouldn't respond until he had polled the group to see if they were in agreement.

"I'll see you downstairs?" he told Angelina when she came out of the bathroom drying her hair with a towel.

"I'll be right behind you." She walked over to him and kissed him on the lips. "Thanks."

"Thanks for what?"

"For earlier this morning."

"You're welcome. My pleasure. Anytime," he replied. He tapped her backside and kissed her on the lips. "When are we going to tell everyone we're together, by the way?"

"Soon." She smiled and winked at him, and went back into the bathroom to finish getting ready.

"Oh, by the way, my mother called and she's invited us all to dinner this evening," he said as the bathroom door closed. Angelina hesitated slightly before turning and going back into the bedroom. Reggie was gone.

******

Reggie was first to be seated for breakfast in the hotel restaurant. The others wandered in soon after he had arrived. Angelina delayed her arrival in an effort to dispel any suspicions. When she appeared in the doorway of the restaurant she glowed; she was drop-dead gorgeous. No other words could describe her stature, her figure and her appearance. When she saw Reggie, she waved as if they were meeting for the first time this morning and proceeded to the table. As she seated herself across the table from him, he looked closely at her face. She didn't appear to be wearing any makeup whatsoever. *"How beautiful must you be to not use any makeup and yet appear that you just stepped off the pages of Vogue?* he thought. *This woman is an extraordinary and rare natural beauty."*

The breakfast conversation picked up where they left off at dinner last evening. They really seemed to be enjoying each other's company.

Near the end of breakfast, Reggie explained that he had originally planned for the day to include several sightseeing trips to some of the more interesting attractions in the city: the Empire State building, Statue of Liberty, and a few others.

"I have scored some tickets to a ball game on Sunday afternoon. I hope that's agreeable with everyone," he explained. "We can finish the submission in the morning, as I suggested yesterday, and have the afternoon free for the game."

He paused while the group came to a consensus that those plans were acceptable to them. None of the women had ever been to a professional baseball game. It would be a fun experience, they thought.

"I have one last item of business that came up. I picked up a message earlier from my mother. She and my father would be pleased if we could visit their home later this afternoon and stay for dinner."

"What's the occasion? Why, why would your mom and dad want to meet us?" Angelina asked. She sounded panicked. It struck the others as strange that a simple idea like this would make Angelina nervous. They had never seen her this way. The ever calm, ever under control woman had disappeared with this tiny bit of news.

"It's no big deal. My mother and father heard we were all in town. I told them about you guys when I got back from Mexico and they want to meet you. They're just being friendly."

He paused again, anticipating a similar negative response to this change in plans from the others, but to his relief everyone was wholeheartedly in favor of a trip to Reggie's family home. Everyone with the possible exception of Angelina, that is.

"This will be fun to see where you came from and meet your mom and dad," Rachel said. She seemed excited.

It had been a long time since Reggie thought of his parents as "mom" and "dad" but he was pleased that his new found friends wanted to learn more about him.

Angelina was not so sure now was the time to meet someone's parents. She had mixed emotions about meeting Reggie's parents. She had to at some point, perhaps now was as good a time as any. *Having the others along would help,* she reasoned.

Reggie called his mother.

"Hi mom: I spoke with my friends about your invitation to dinner this evening, and they are all pleased to accept. I wish you and Father would have asked sooner, though. It would have made it easier to plan our other activities had we known."

His mother was pleased and seemed excited that Reggie was bringing his friends to dinner. Throughout Reggie's childhood, he had difficulty getting his friends to come over to his house. He realized later in his adolescence, it was most likely because the parents of these kids were concerned about their children spending time in a house with armed guards roaming the property. What they didn't realize was that they were probably safer at Reggie's than at the park.

The day went as planned, lots of conversation, an abundance of laughs, and a good overall bonding of the group. In particular, the ladies seemed to be picking up where they left off and were truly enjoying each other's company.

Part of the morning was spent on a cruise of the harbor. That was something none of them had ever done, including those who lived in the city. They passed the Statue of Liberty and were amazed by its grandeur. When they sailed close to Ellis Island, there was a noticeable downturn in the mood, particularly from Rachel.

"Does this upset you?" Jack asked Rachel quietly. He was standing beside her, shoulder to shoulder, as they leaned on the top of the railing of the boat.

"Not upsetting but I think about all the people who would have come to this country through what I see as this very frightening place. Being kept within these walls must have seemed like prison to some. All of us women are from other countries," she said as she pointed to her friends. "None of us had to endure any form of hardship when we arrived. Thank God for that."

Jack subtly moved closer to her as their bodies felt each other's comforting warmth. The mood picked up considerably as they passed by the large ships that were anchored in the harbor. It was an impressive sight to see such powerful war machines up close. By the time they docked, and rode the cab back to the city, their collective spirits were lifted.

Next on the agenda was a walk down Fifth Avenue. It was clear that this was not the first time Angelina had been here. She was familiar with almost all of the high-end women's shops.

"My mother used to bring me here when I was a young teen," she explained. "Here and Paris. I was always amazed by the clothing women in this country were permitted to wear. Most of my childhood, I dressed in the traditional garments of Egypt. It was only after I went to Paris for University that I had the opportunity to wear western clothing. I was almost twenty before I owned my first pair of silk stockings," she said as a statement of hardship.

"Did they have red lace at the top?" Reggie asked in a mischievous tone. The others looked at him with confusion, wondering why he would ask such a question. Angelina knew exactly why. She shot him a stern look in return.

"I was maybe twenty. Twenty-year old girls don't have red lace on the top of their stockings." she replied haughtily.

"Oh," he replied in a tone that suggested he was letting it go. "Well, look at you now," Reggie joked, drawing attention to her very stylish outfit.

"That *must* have been a hardship, Angelina. A big day for me was a trip to Hong Kong once in a while; if I had the legs to hop a bus to get there," Rachel laughed.

Angelina continued to be impressed by her new friend. There never seemed to be any jealousy over looks or position in life. Angelina was truly interested in Rachel's childhood history and interested in how it differed from hers. She had taken time when they were in Mexico to listen to Rachel explain what it was like being a female child in China and how that limited her educational opportunities. Her first choice would have been to study fashion as she had pointed out; but it was not to be. Angelina seemed quite understanding and sympathetic to the plight of young women in the Chinese culture. Women in general, struggled to be treated as equals. In some cultures, it was an intolerable situation. It saddened Angelina that her friend was not allowed to follow her passion.

It was almost three hours after Reggie spoke with his mother that his father called him on his cell. It turned out to be a call from his father's secretary.

"Reggie, it's Mary Elizabeth here. How are you this morning?"

She sounded like a teenager and the name didn't click right away with Reggie. After a moment, he realized that this was his father's secretary calling; his *new* secretary. He recalled that Mrs. Gambrony had retired after being with his father for forty years. *I bet she has some stories to tell*, he thought. *She must have been like a hundred,* he thought to himself.

"Oh hi, Mary Elizabeth. What's up?"

"Reggie, your father wanted me to tell you that there will be a car sent for you at four and to remind you that he would prefer more formal dinner attire rather than casual clothing for this evening."

Reggie was angry that he wasn't hearing this directly from his father; not giving him the opportunity to debate this with his father. Unfortunately he was used to it.

"That'll be fine, Mary Elizabeth. Tell him I got the message."

He would explain to the group about the formality of the dinner and hope they would understand. More importantly, he hoped that they had brought something suitable to wear. The men explained that they had the suits they wore to dinner the previous evening, which were fine, and the ladies had thought ahead about some of the partying they might be doing and had brought some evening wear as well.

"I have a nice dress," Rachel told Angelina. "I should be good."

"Is it that little number you wore in Mexico?" Jack piped up. "It was hot."

"Oh stop," Rachel scolded Jack for being so bold. *It was interesting that he remembered her dress*, she thought to herself.

A few moments later, Reggie cell phone rang. It was Mary Elizabeth.

"I forgot to tell you to tell the ladies not to be concerned about outfits. If they haven't brought something suitable, take them to Saks on Fifth Avenue. Your father will pick up the tab for the dresses," she explained.

"They have outfits," Reggie stated and hung up.

Reggie never passed on the offer of clothing to the ladies. It was too embarrassing, and besides they already had their own. *What was he thinking? And Mary Elizabeth. What flavor of the month is she?*

The next attraction was a special one. The group was enjoying a routine tour of the USS Franklin aircraft carrier that was anchored in the New York harbor. This World War II ship was now a permanent museum. They had joined up with other tourists on one of the daily tours of the ship. As they arrived on the deck, a helicopter was seen coming in for a landing. This, in itself, was exciting, and there was more to follow.

"Okay, let's go," Angelina said. She started to walk around the barriers towards the helicopter.

"Where are you going? Come back," they all yelled. "We can't go out there."

"Yes, we can, c'mon," she replied and motioned for the others to follow. Reggie was the only one in the group who knew about this next part of the day's events. Angelina had arranged for a helicopter tour of New York. Angelina took the seat next to the pilot: fitted her head gear and buckled herself in. The rest of the group sat behind. As they finished buckling and fitting their head gear, Angelina turned to explain. She could see a mixed excited and frightened expression on Rachel's face. She knew what kind of aircraft this was but she had never actually been in one before.

"Ladies and gentlemen," she said into the microphone. "Welcome to the newest, most technically advanced helicopter in the Airtec Engineering fleet. This is the ATT 720, eight- passenger, attack chopper. It's better known as *Panther*. This lovely lady beside me," she said motioning towards the pilot, "is Wendy Moore. Wendy and I have worked together on many occasions on more conventional aircraft sales. This is the first unit of its type that I have sold as I am just now getting into some of the other areas of the company's product offering. We have been pretty successful with planes, though," she added as she tapped her friend on the shoulder.

Wendy simply waved her hand in welcome. She wore orange coveralls with what appeared to be a vest interwoven in the front section. Her head and face were completely covered by her helmet and glass face shield.

"This particular unit is headed to the Middle East shortly to be rigged with the customer's requirements for armament. Wendy will go along and provide training for the new potential pilots for this aircraft. She is part of the package. And will likely be there for three months, or so."

"And looking forward to it," Wendy interjected through the microphone. The others could tell now that she was British. Her accent was quite strong.

"I worked on some of the guidance system for this," Rachel stated with a tone of confidence.

"Yes, you did," Angelina replied. "This is the end result of your fine engineering."

The fact was that, Rachel had headed the team that designed the entire guidance system for this and most of the other helicopters Airtec was planning to unveil over the next several years. Rachel was one of the best engineers Airtec employed. She was smart, detailed and imaginative when it came to designing aircraft of all types and the company was benefitting greatly from having Rachel on board. Rachel, being as modest as she always was, never said too much to anyone about what she did at work. Certainly not to be boastful. That simply wasn't in her nature.

"Rachel, when I took off this morning, it took a few minutes for the gyro-guidance monitor to kick in. I wasn't sure if it was working. Is there a problem with this monitor?" Wendy asked.

"Only that they bought the cheapest one they could find," Rachel replied in a disgusted tone. "When you take it back to the pad, fill out your flight report and note the problem you had. Because it's a new unit, it should prompt a flag back to us in engineering. I'll keep an eye open for it and push to see if we can convince the company to purchase a better monitor. It's things like this that make our jobs more difficult. You would think for what they sell these for, they would put more than a dime store monitor into the guidance system."

"Will do, thanks," Wendy replied. She and everyone else were impressed with Rachel's knowledge of the equipment.

"How much is one of these babies worth?" Jack asked Angelina.

"As she sits, this chopper costs about thirty-five million. In full armament, as this particular customer has specified, it will likely add twelve or thirteen million to that number so maybe close to fifty million. It's a lot of machine and a lot of money."

"How'd you manage to lay your hands on this?"

"This is a demo slash training run," Angelina explained with a smirk on her face. "I won't get into the details but she's all ours for a few hours at least."

Angelina had obviously made up a story that the company bought into. It also didn't hurt their cause that Wendy was the secret love interest of one Jeremy Jackson. Jeremy worked at Airtec and managed the testing of all new aircraft. He had a not-so-subtle crush on Wendy; pretty much anything she asked for, she got.

They flew for two hours covering almost the entire city and a great deal of the outlying areas. They took time to circle most of the major New York attractions, including Yankee Stadium.

"There's where we are heading tomorrow," Reggie explained as they circled the stadium. "Field level, behind the visitors' dugout; doesn't get much better than that."

"How did you score those tickets?" Edward asked.

"I have my connections." It was actually his father who had managed to obtain six prime tickets on short notice.

After almost two hours of breathtaking scenery and a few sudden drops and rises in altitude to make the ride more exciting courtesy of Wendy Moore, their flight was coming to an end. For the final thrill of the tour, Wendy ended the trip by landing atop the Trump Tower building. It was the ride of a lifetime. They took the elevator to the ground floor and hailed a cab.

When the group returned to the hotel, they retired to their rooms to prepare for the trip to Reggie's house. Angelina had not taken the opportunity to open the package from Candice. It wasn't hard to guess it would be the latest in sexy lingerie from the Victoria's Secret collection. She wondered what Rachel must have thought about her own gift. Rachel had become more liberal in her choice of attire since they first met in Mexico City; but was she ready for Victoria's Secret? Angelina was very pleased with her gift. She knew that Reggie would be as well.

CHAPTER SEVENTEEN

May 2, 4:00 pm EST - Viscusi Estate
New Canaan CT

It was four o'clock sharp and a long black limousine arrived at the front door of the Waldorf. Although a common occurrence for this quality of establishment, a stretch limo still drew attention as people outside the hotel watched the driver hold the door for the passengers. The five-foot eleven-inch blonde chauffeur added to the interest of the passers-by. Once the passengers were seated, the driver took her position behind the wheel and lowered the privacy window as she spoke.

"Good afternoon. My name is Sam and I will be your driver. I expect it will take about forty minutes to reach our destination, depending on traffic. Are we ready to go?" she asked. Since there was little or no response from the group Reggie quietly said, "Let's go."

With the partition window lowered, Rachel noticed a very large man sitting next to Sam. He made no effort to communicate with the passengers but rather concentrated his focus on the surrounding area ahead of the car. His job, as Reggie was well aware, was as a body guard.

"Hey, Uncle Vincent," Reggie said.

Vincent turned and gave Reggie a friendly smile. At least as friendly a smile as someone six-foot-four and three-hundred-fifty pounds could give while his eyes swept the open area ahead like a mine sweeper. He never spoke a word.

As the window was returned to the closed position, Angelina glanced at Reggie; held her finger to her nose and moved it slightly to one side. She mouthed the words *Vincent and Sam* with a questioning tone. She was clearly teasing Reggie about his uncle perhaps being a bit of a thug and this beautiful blonde woman called Sam. Reggie hushed her by placing his finger to his lips as they both smiled. It had been awhile since Reggie had a ride with Sam at the wheel; Sam, who drove Reggie and his date to their high school prom. This was the car where Reggie lost his virginity to the very lovely Mary Margaret Menotti, and Angelina was now in the same car.

Seeing Sam again also reminded him of the questions that troubled him at that same time about his father employing such a beautiful woman as a chauffeur. He wondered if perhaps his father had been unfaithful to his mother with this woman. He never got an answer to his question mainly because he chose not to pursue it. There were a lot of questions from his youth left unanswered because he chose not to pursue them. He was content to believe it was not the reason his father kept Sam on as his driver.

The first part of the ride to Connecticut was uneventful. Most of the passengers were tired from their day's activity and the energy level reflected their weariness. The traffic was stop-and-go until they reached the outer limits of the city and turned onto the Merritt Parkway, leading to Connecticut.

"I forgot you said you were from Connecticut," Angelina commented when the exit sign rushed past her window. "I think of you as a New Yorker."

"Connecticut is almost New York, although I don't think anyone who lives here would be willing to admit that," Reggie joked. "It's kind of a bedroom community."

Sam left the parkway at the New Canaan exit. The road very quickly became narrow and winding, canopied by the roadside trees. This coverage was so dense it almost entirely blocked any sun from reaching the road. Between the trees, there were glimpses of estate after estate positioned well back from the road's edge. This was clearly a neighborhood of the rich and perhaps less famous people of New York.

"I think this bedroom community is an executive suites community," Rachel whispered to Candice.

"You never told us you were a rich guy, Reggie," Jack joked.

It was clear that some in the group had begun to wonder who this Reggie guy was and why he kept this lifestyle a secret. It wasn't a secret as far as Reggie was concerned; it was simply irrelevant as far as the implications on his lifestyle today. Angelina was also somewhat surprised. She knew he came from some money, however, they had never really spoken about his childhood or his family. She made a mental note that she would find out why Reggie was so unwilling to discuss his family life.

"I'm hardly rich," Reggie replied. "This is my parents' place. I live in a tiny apartment in the city, if you recall." He wasn't indignant or harsh with his reply to Jack and the group; he was merely pointing out that this was not what or who he was as a man.

The limo glided up to a large and somewhat foreboding, iron gate. The gate was draped in shadow by the surrounding trees. Trees that perhaps needed some trimming as they had an overgrown appearance to them. Bracketing the gate, there was a pair of statuary lions each standing guard over the entrance to the property. A typical decorative element Angelina thought to herself as she recalled Reggie's Italian heritage. *What's with Italians and their statues?* she wondered. This coming from someone originating from the land of pyramids struck her as amusing when she really thought about it.

Sam could be heard on the radio asking for the gate to be opened. As it started to open, Vincent left the limo and entered a guard house that was located to the left of the entrance. Sam continued driving deeper into the property along the winding lane. The gravel driveway emitted a crushing sound as the heavy vehicle slowly rolled its way toward the house. From time to time, the passengers noticed they were passing very large men who looked a lot like Vincent. They were on the roadside or off in the short grass beside the road. A little strange perhaps, but it was what it was.

Sam stopped at the entrance to, what could only be described as a mansion- the biggest house most of the group had ever seen. It was enormous. The entrance to the house was a continuation of the design element seen at the gate. There stood a massive fountain spewing a steady stream of water from a lion's mouth. The splashing water overpowered any other sounds of nature that may have existed. The front door was guarded by two statuary winged-creatures of some sort. It was obvious, by the wear on the stone, these were ancient pieces. Most likely brought to America from an Italian villa or church.

"This is something like you would see in a movie," Rachel gasped.

Angelina was having the same thought. It reminded her of a movie she saw starring Al Pacino; it was *The Godfather*.

Reggie's mother came out to greet them at the front entrance. She was accompanied by two *Vincent-type men* who stood on either side of the massive oak filigreed door.

"Buongiorno, buongirno," she squealed as she hugged Reggie. "Welcome to our home," she said to the others.

She also hugged the visitors, even before she knew who they were. That was just her way. She was a classic example of an Italian mother. She was so pleased to see women included in Reggie's group of friends and such pretty ones as well. Sam popped the trunk and the two large men began unloading the few pieces of luggage. All of the visitors had garment bags protecting the dresses and suits they had brought for the formal dinner.

As they walked closer to the door and beyond, there were quiet gasps heard from several of the guests. The group was astounded by the opulence and sheer grandeur of the main foyer. It was a full forty feet in height. The marble floors glistened in the reflected light of the massive crystal chandelier that hung in the center of this picture of sheer elegance. A magnificent winding staircase led to the upper floor, both the railings and steps were solid Italian marble. To the left there was, what appeared to be, a private office. This room was in darkness, save a small green shaded light that outlined the massive cherry desk. To the right, there was a formal dining room and living room and beyond the staircase was what could only be described as the mother of all kitchens. They walked though the kitchen area and nodded to the two women who were busy preparing dinner. Beyond the kitchen was the covered courtyard and pool area, again in marble. Everywhere they looked there was marble. Everyone walked around the pool, marveling at the beautiful tile work. Once Reggie's mother sat, the rest of the group found a seat beside the pool.

"So tell me all about yourselves," Mrs. Viscusi invited, everyone at the same time. She was very impressed by how handsome her Reggie looked; all the men for that matter and the young women were stunning.

"Mom, there's too much to tell; it would take all afternoon. Why don't I introduce my friends and give you a short version of their stories."

She nodded her approval.

"This is Jack Daniels and he is a computer engineer. Sitting next to Jack is Rachel Wi. She's also an engineer. Actually it's Doctor Rachel Wi. Rachel holds a Doctorate in Aeronautical Engineering. Candice or Dr. Candice Bergen is next to Rachel. She is also a Ph.D. but in Marine Biology.

Candice is a very successful model as well. Next is Angelina Evangeline and she has an MBA from a University in Paris and sells airplanes. Last but not least, of course, is Edward Milton who is also an engineer. Edward comes from Canada and works for a company that blows things up."

"What kind of a company blows things up?" Mrs. Viscusi asked.

"It's a company that makes explosives for use in mining operations primarily," Edward explained.

"A model, what kind of a model? Would I have seen Candice in one of my magazines?"

As his mother finished her questions, Reggie glanced at Angelina who was smiling. She knew Reggie wasn't going to elaborate on exactly what type of a model Candice was, so she decided to have some fun with him. Candice watched the exchange of unspoken communications between Angelina and Reggie and decided to let her friend have some fun at her expense. She looked at Angelina and winked as a sign for her to carry on with her game. Candice was not surprised by his mother's questions. This was the usual response from older folks when she told them what she did.

"Yes," Angelina said as she gave Reggie her typical mischievous smile. "Our friend, Dr. Bergen, is a very beautiful model. She is in New York for a photo shoot."

"What kind of model is she?"

Reggie took the lead, "Candice is a fashion model, mother. She's doing some magazine stuff, I believe."

"Isn't that nice. You will have to let me know which magazine the pictures will be in so I can get one," his mother replied.

"I will make sure you are advised on that Mrs. Viscusi," Angelina said. "Don't worry about that."

Reggie glared at Angelina. His eyes were pleading with her not to continue with her little game. The rest of the group was amused.

"You are all so well educated and have such interesting jobs," Mrs. Viscusi stated. "I guess you all know that our

Reggie has been promoted. He's vice presidents now, aren't you my dear."

All eyes turned to Reggie as his face turned red. This was news to the entire group, including Angelina. He had in fact been promoted two weeks earlier. He was now Vice President of Statistical Analysis and Data Systems. One of the top two positions in the company and he was the youngest employee to reach the position of Vice President.

"When did this happen? I certainly didn't know about this. Did any of you know about this?" Angelina asked as she looked at their friends. They knew where Angelina was going with this and they enjoyed watching these two verbally torment each other.

"You haven't told your friends? Oh my dear, I'm sorry if I spoke out of turn. Is it a secret? I didn't think it was a secret," his mother said.

"Apparently it is a secret," Angelina whispered.

"I was planning to," Reggie said as he stared at Angelina, "I haven't had time. We have been busy doing our Mensa report and touring the city. It certainly isn't a secret, mother."

"Maybe you will find the time later to tell us all about your new job," Angelina said. She glanced at the others. "Maybe you'll also make plans to move to a slightly better apartment with your newfound wealth."

She'd gone too far and she knew it. One comment too many. She looked at the others after she made her last statement. They were clearly wondering how it was that Angelina knew what Reggie's apartment looked like. She knew she had made a mistake and her mind was scrambling for a way out. Reggie knew that she had just stepped into a mine field. He knew that, for whatever reason she had, she didn't want to make their relationship common knowledge. He also knew he could get her out of her current dilemma, however, he was willing to watch her squirm before he brought relief to the situation.

"You know what his apartment looks like. When were you at Reggie's apartment?" Candice asked. This was the proof she needed to confirm they were in a relationship. She didn't want to let the others in on it if it meant so much to Angelina not to, but she wanted Angelina to know, she knew.

Angelina's face was blank. She had no idea how to respond to the question asked.

"I showed her some pictures of a college party we had there one time," Reggie replied. He was coming to her rescue in this difficult situation. "She commented on how grungy it looked. Right Angelina? It was the pictures I showed you."

"That's it, from what I saw I wouldn't set foot in your place."

"He has promised me he will find a new place," his mother announced. "There are very bad people down in that part of town."

"What exactly does a Vice President of Statistical Analysis and Data Systems do?" Rachel asked.

"I do a lot of things. I gather statistics and manage data system," Reggie replied, almost with an uncertainty to his answer. Hearing his own explanation made him wonder exactly what he was supposed to be doing in his new position.

"It sounds like Chandler Bing, you know the guy on Friends. Everyone knows he has a really important job but no one knows what he does," Edward joked.

"Enough about me," Reggie finally said. "Why don't we make some drinks and have a short rest by the pool."

Under normal circumstances Edward would have made some additional comments about Reggie's new position but he was in a similar situation. He hadn't told Candice, or any of the others about his job offer. He wasn't sure he wanted the job but it was still under consideration.

It was a warm afternoon for this time of year; however, more seasonal weather seemed to be moving in as the sun turned cool as time passed to late afternoon. The group retired to a very comfortable living room. On their way through the kitchen, there seemed to be an increased level of activity as the dinner hour approached.

Reggie's mother was in mid-sentence about some achievement of his in his youth when his father entered the room. She stopped speaking immediately. Reggie took over with the introduction of his father to his freinds.

"Oh hello Father, I would like to introduce my friends that I told you and Mother about."

Reggie's father was also named Reginald but he was always referred to by his second name, Joseph. Joseph's mother, Reggie's grandmother, was English. She met and fell in love with his grandfather, Joseph Vincenzo Viscusi, during the first world war when he was stationed in England. She was what is described as a war bride. "War bride" was a more prevalent term used to refer to brides from the second world war but there were many that came before them.

When her first son was born she insisted that he have a proper English name. Reginald was her father's name so it was decided that Reginald Joseph Vincenzo would be the child's given name. Joseph was Mrs. Viscusi's father's name. Young Joseph had a mix of English and Italian in his blood and it was appropriate his name reflect his heritage. They only used Reginald for the first year of his life. His parents knew that being Italian in New York City required an Italian name. His mother always called him Reginald when they were alone and until the day she died, but Reginald was a name that would get his ass kicked for sure out on the streets of Little Italy, New York City.

When young Reggie was born, his grandmother was still alive and carried enough influence with her son to have their child, her only grandchild, named Reginald. Reggie's full name was Reginald Vincenzo Viscusi, although he almost never was referred to by any name other than Reggie.

Joe Viscusi was approximately 5'11" and his build could best be described as solid. He was a fine figure of an Italian-

American businessman. He had a full head of thick, curly, salt and pepper hair. He spoke slowly with a slight accent and with authority. There was an obvious effort on his part to select the proper words as he spoke. Jack seemed to be most cognizant of this. He had seen this type of effort with his own father. His father was very successful in the cattle business but lacked a formal education beyond the high school level; likely due to the need to leave school early to be the man of the house. He and his mother had Jack at a very young age.

Angelina was surprised that Reggie's dad didn't go by his first name. The name Joseph Viscusi seemed somewhat familiar to her. Not a strong familiarity as if she had met him before; but it sounded familiar – possibly through her work. As she thought more about it, perhaps she had heard his name through listening to her father in his study when he was on the phone. That seemed to be more likely. She would often, as a young girl, play in her father's study. On occasion, he would forget she was there during a business call, and have to change his tone or use of language. Usually when this occurred, she was asked to play somewhere else.

Reggie continued with the introductions and coming to Angelina, he said. "Father, this is Angelina Evangeline."

Angelina noticed that when Reggie introduced her to his father, Joseph seemed to show a little more familiarity with her name than he did with any of the others.

"Miss Evangeline," he repeated when he was introduced to her.

With the others he had repeated only their first name; in what appeared to be an effort to remember all the new names. With her it seemed to be more like recognition of a name; a name he might have been familiar with. She thought that was odd and decided that she might have to follow up a little on this during dinner conversation.

As the dinner hour approached, it was explained that it was a more formal than normal dinner in honor of his son's new friends. "I apologize for the sudden change in plans,"

Mr. Viscusi explained to the group. "I felt this was a special occasion and called for some formality. I hope you young ladies were successful in finding a nice outfit."

The women appeared confused by what he had said. They were unaware of his offer to purchase them clothing. Reggie hadn't passed that message on to them, it was embarrassing. Rachel happened to glance at Reggie's mom and wondered why she appeared to be a little confused as well. Angelina had guessed where this conversation was coming from and she simply responded on behalf of all of the women.

"We have come prepared for the formality. Thank you very much."

"Reggie if you would show your guests to their rooms to change, we can get on with the festivities," his mother instructed. "I hope you ladies don't mind but we are renovating some of the upper rooms. We have put you in the only remaining guest room to change. The young men can use Reggie's room."

The guys were shown to Reggie's room; the women to the guest bedroom. Each of the rooms had its own bathroom. Everyone wanted to take advantage of the opportunity to have a shower and clean up after a busy day in the city. As they were approaching their room, it hit Angelina; she was certain she recalled where she first heard of Joseph Viscusi. She took Reggie by the arm and held him back in the hall as the others entered their respective rooms.

"Your dad's in the Mafia," she whispered to Reggie with a tone of excitement. She had found the answer to the question she had struggled with for the past hour. Reggie's face clearly showed that she had made a very uncomfortable observation. "I'm right. I've heard his name before. Your dad's a Mafia guy. I can see it in your face."

Reggie pulled her aside and whispered back. He tried his best to maintain a stern appearance as he spoke with Angelina. "Keep your voice down. What the hell are you talking about? My dad's not a Mafia guy. Where did you come up with that?"

"I know he is; you can't deny it. I remember when I was young hearing his name. My father had some dealings with him. I was a little girl but I recall it like it was yesterday. I was hiding in my dad's office when they were talking on the phone. That was the only time my dad every slapped my behind," she said in a louder, but still muted tone. "I will prove it to you. By the end of the night you will know the truth about who your father is."

"You're wrong. Don't you think I would know who my father is?" Reggie replied.

"You tell me then, what does your father do for a living?"

"He's a business man."

"Yeah, a Mafia business man," she replied with a knowing smile. "By the end of the night, you will know for sure. I can tell by the smirk on your face you know it's true. You just won't admit it."

"I already know for sure and it's not that he's a Mafia guy. You behave yourself. You're going to land us in a whole lot of trouble."

Reggie was struggling to maintain an indignant facial expression.

"Yeah, Mafia trouble," she joked. Angelina placed her finger to her nose and moved it to the side as she entered her room.

CHAPTER EIGHTEEN

May 2, 6:00 pm EDT - Viscusi Estate
New Canaan, CT

In the guest room, Angelina showered first. She was anxious to get on with the evening and to prove her point to Reggie. She took less time in the shower than she would normally; just long enough to wash her hair and apply some cream rinse. Rachel was surprised when she opened the bathroom door so soon after she had started.

"That was quick," she said as Angelina exited the bathroom wrapping a towel around her hair and dressed in a white fluffy bathrobe.

"Kind of not my size," Angelina joked outlining the robe with the hands, showing off the bulky fabric.

Candice was next to use the shower. No surprise to Rachel, Candice was down to her panties and bra even before she entered the bathroom. Rachel had anticipated this so she made certain her eyes were elsewhere as Candice passed her on the way to the shower. Angelina paid no attention. Next it was Rachel's turn. Quite a bit had changed in her life, since they last met in Mexico. Rachel had become far more liberal in her dress. She had replaced all of her old style undergarments. Her bras were now all very modern and sheer; her panties all thongs. The thong was the most dramatic change; she found them to be far more comfortable than more conservative style panties. Although she wasn't quite ready to walk naked in a change room, she was now more comfortable with her body. In preparation for her shower, she disrobed down to her bra and thong before quickly dawning her robe. Angelina was first to notice.

"You go girl; look at you in your tiny panties. When did you choose them on your own?"

"I will have you know," Rachel replied with a modest smile and a blush on her face, "that I have replaced my entire collection with the new style."

"And the bra, that looks to me like a Secret's bra," Candice stated.

"Correct again, my friend. I have become quite a fan of Victoria. They make nice things."

Candice acknowledged her agreement, and with a nod of her head to Angelina, Rachel entered the bathroom for her shower. Rachel also made an effort to take less time than she normally would. Rachel was in the habit of taking very long showers. She believed the habit had come from her childhood when hot water wasn't plentiful. It was expensive to heat water and the Wi household needed to watch their money very closely. Any chance she had to enjoy the warmth of the water; she would try to extend her stay until her mother pounded on the door to leave some water for others. Now that she was on her won, she afforded herself the luxury of plenty of hot water. Rachel had also washed her hair but she didn't really need to wrap a towel around it due to the shorter cut. Rather, she rubbed it in the towel to dry it sufficiently to run a brush through it. She hadn't curled her hair since Candice and Angelina had convinced her to leave it natural and straight that first night they spent in Mexico City. She would use the blow dryer to finish the job. Rachel was so pleased with herself for the way she handled her pre-shower experience, she forgot about the after shower experience; the one she had witnessed in Mexico. As she left the bathroom she was caught, again, in an embarrassing moment.

"Oh, my," Rachel said softly to herself as she gazed at a nearly naked Angelina.

Angelina had discarded the bath robe and was in the process of combing her hair wearing only her panties. She had forgotten about Rachel's issues with nudity that she discovered at the spa in Mexico City. Candice had already begun to dress so her appearance was fine but Angelina was topless, again. Rachel tried to casually look the other way but Angelina had heard her soft comment.

"I'm sorry, I forgot," Angelina said. She quickly put on her bra. "I'm really sorry; I need to be more considerate in the future."

Not a lot better Rachel thought to herself. Angelina's ample breasts filled her bra to the point of overflow, but at least she was covered.

Rachel blushed. "Oh, that's okay," she replied. Even with Rachel's assurance that it was acceptable, Angelina was embarrassed that she had forgotten to consider her new friend's feelings. She wasn't embarrassed about the nudity. She was very comfortable with her body, however, she made a mental note to herself that Rachel was less than free spirited when it came to the female form. Rachel felt more at ease with Angelina more covered. She concentrated on speaking to her eyes and not letting her gaze wander to other parts of Angelina's body. How nice it would be, Angelina thought, if the men she met would look her in the eyes instead of being fixated on her chest.

"You have a very nice figure," Rachel said. She was careful to keep her gaze at Angelina's eye level.

"Thanks, you look pretty good yourself," Angelina replied while looking her friend up and down in a teasing manner.

The ladies seemed to loosen up after this encounter. They chatted freely with each other as they prepared for the dinner. Rachel had brought a different dress from the one she wore in Mexico; another sign to the other women that their friend was progressing. Angelina noticed it was a different dress but it also seemed that Rachel was having some real issues about the height of the slit up the side of her new dress. Angelina could see her through the mirror, pulling at it. Trying to close the gap. It was a beautiful dress, and Rachel had the body to wear it, but again there was her comfort level.

"Wow; pretty dress; it's new isn't it?" Angelina asked.

"It certainly is. It looks a little like the one you girls helped me choose in Mexico, but I bought it in New York."

"If I could make one suggestion about that wonderful dress you're wearing," Angelina said. "I think there are times when less is more, if you know what I mean. It's more important that one feels comfortable in one's attire than just in style. As for men, they seem to be more interested in what they can't see sometimes. That's why Victoria's Secret is so successful; it allows men to fantasize. Oh they love naked, don't get me wrong. Every woman in the world knows that, however sometimes less is more. Men are really a simple breed," she joked. "I'm not talking about your cleavage, you're showing just the right amount," she continued while looking at the side slit in Rachel's dress. "Would you mind if I make some changes to the length of the reveal in the side? I think we could improve on this part of the dress."

Rachel looked to Candice for her confirmation.

"Yes, Angelina's right; men are simple," Candice laughed. "You only need to reveal as much as makes you comfortable. If you cut low on the top, fashion dictates you cover the bottom, or vice versa."

Angelina pulled a small sewing kit from her bag and held it up for Rachel to see. "I can make a small adjustment to the length of that reveal for you, Rachel. I'm never comfortable with a lot leg showing either," she fibbed.

Rachel knew that wasn't likely true, given how comfortable her new friends seemed to be with their bodies.

It was a kind gesture. Both Angelina and Candice had the legs all women would die to have. Perfectly shaped and endless. Angelina saw a sigh of relief from Rachel as she moved beside her to allow her to measure how much additional coverage they could achieve without making it look like a patch job. Angelina looked at the adjustment that had to be made.

"You're going to have to take it off for me to do this right."

"Oh, right," was Rachel's only response. She unzipped the back and slipped out of the dress.

Rachel stood next to Angelina, watching the repair job, dressed only in her panties and bra. Her hands and arms were strategically placed to retain her modesty. She noticed that Angelina never gave her a second look. Angelina performed some magic on the dress, closing the slit about four inches before handing it back to her friend. Rachel slipped back into the dress and gazed at herself in the mirror. It was clear that she was pleased with the alterations.

"There," Angelina said. "That fixes the design problem in the dress."

That was a more appropriate comment than highlighting Rachel's obvious issues with modesty.

"That dress really compliments your shape."

So she had noticed, Rachel realized. She blushed a little. To have someone as beautiful as Angelina make a comment like that to her was a first. What a kind person her new friend seemed to be. All she said, in response to Angelina's comment, was

"Thanks."

After some hair drying and a lot of primping and preening, the women were happy with their appearance. Angelina had also realized that perhaps Rachel was less versed in makeup application, so she offered to help her.

"It's a real treat when a makeup artist applies your makeup. That's how all the models do it," she explained as she looked over to Candice for confirmation.

"I very seldom put on my own makeup," Candice confirmed.

Rachel was grateful for the assistance. She also noted that Angelina used a simple eye shadow and nothing else in her own preparation. Her friend was a true beauty and there was no need to mess with perfection. Just before the women were ready to step out the door, Candice decided to make an announcement.

"If I could have your attention, I have an announcement to make," she said.

Angelina assumed that it had to do with her *Playboy* aspirations.

"Before we head down to dinner, I want you two to know that Eddy and I are together. We are a couple. I don't want to sidetrack the evening, so try to keep it to yourselves for tonight at least, I had to tell my best friends."

The other ladies couldn't have been more pleased.

"I knew it," Angelina joked. "It shows in Eddy's eyes."

"More like the great big smile on his face," Rachel added as she and Angelina hugged Candice.

CHAPTER NINETEEN

May 2, 7:00 pm EDT - Viscusi Estate
New Canaan, CT

The men had been in the living room nursing their beers for about 20 minutes before the women arrived. Angelina and Candice made certain that Rachel stepped first onto the top landing of the magnificent winding staircase. They had done the same in Mexico and it really boosted Rachel's self esteem, so they wanted to repeat it. As Rachel stepped forward, she caught the eye of all the men seated in the living room. They were off to the side of the main foyer. As if by experience, all three of the men in the group stood up when Rachel appeared. There were a few audible sighs of approval and one clear,

"Holy cow, she's gorgeous." It seemed to have come from Jack.

Rachel's dress was perfect. It outlined her trim body and slight figure while clearly bringing out all of her femininity. The reveal in the side of the dress, which Angelina had so kindly altered for her, showed off just enough of her perfect leg. *It's just the right amount of sass but had class*, she thought to herself; sexy in a good girl kind of way. The neckline showed just enough to keep you interested without giving away the farm. It was slightly more revealing than her previous dress but she was comfortable with that. As Rachel started to descend the stairs, the other ladies purposely stayed behind her, trying to stay out of the spotlight. It was difficult to do with their figures and stature; they were clearly trying to keep the focus on Rachel. As they descended the staircase behind Rachel, Angelina made some subtle motions with her hands to prompt the men to speak up with their adoration of Rachel's appearance. She knew that this would be a great self-confidence-builder for her friend. There were a few "wows" and "holy shits". Rachel waved them off in a self conscious manner.

"Don't be so bold, you guys," she said as her smile widened.

She was clearly glowing in the attention. When they reached the bottom of the stairs, all the men came over to give the ladies a friendly kiss on the cheek as a welcome to the evening. They turned to rejoin Reggie's mother and father in the living room. As they did, Rachel and Angelina stayed back from the group. Rachel touched Angelina's arm and simply said, "Thank you."

As they joined Mr. and Mrs. Viscusi, Mrs. Viscusi leaned into her son and whispered into his ear, "These ladies are really lovely. Which one is yours?" she asked.

"We don't look at it like any of them belong to us."

"Oh, I know that, but which one is your special someone?"

"Well, they're all my friends; but if you must know, Angelina and I are dating."

He was reluctant to tell his mother that his relationship with Angelina was more than merely dating. He knew if he did, she would tell the world that her son had a girl.

"She's very bosomy," she stated as she looked at Angelina. "In fact, all these girls are showing a lot of bosom. Do they always show so much?"

"Not always, Mother. It's the fashion to show one's figure."

"Well, Angelina is a pretty one for sure. Is she Italian?"

"No...., she's Egyptian."

"Oh my, how exotic. I'll put in a good word for you during dinner," she assured her son.

"You do that," he replied with a glancing look towards Angelina. Angelina was curious as to what his mother was talking to him about and why she was looking at all the women in the room as she spoke.

It wasn't long before dinner was announced by a rather unusual looking butler. He was short and stocky and had several rather pronounced scars across his face. He spoke softly but it was clear that he was making an effort to be soft and formal. It was also clear that he was making an equal effort to mask his strong New York street-fighter accent. The guests glanced at each other without a word but a few subtle shrugs of the shoulders as to his validity as a butler. Angelina mouthed the word, *Mafia*, to Reggie as he shook his head in disbelief. Mrs. Viscusi thanked "James" as they moved into the dining room. She called him James although most likely he was known as Jimmy by everyone other than Reggie's mother. She seemed to be very concerned about keeping the image of a refined family more than her husband or son. Before they entered the room, Angelina cornered Reggie.

"What was your mother talking to you about?"

"Oh, she wanted to know which one of you I had; you know, which one belonged to me?"

"I hope you told her none," Angelina replied in her typical indignant tone.

"Yes, I told her none of you belonged to anyone," he said and then hesitated. "She also said she thought you were very exotic and showed a lot of bosom."

Angelina's was taken aback by this. She wasn't sure how to respond.

"Showed bosom? I don't show any more bosom than any of the others. Look at Candice if she wants to see bosoms."

"Well, she thought you all showed bosoms, but you showed the most. What can I say? She's my mother."

"Great," Angelina replied as she sat down at the table, "I'm trying to make a good first impression with your parents and I'm showing too much bosom as your mother so quaintly puts it. All you want to do is play with my boobs and your mother thinks I show too much of them. I can't win. This is just too much fun for you, isn't it?"

Reggie gave her a slight shrug of his shoulder and patted her softly on her back.

"She also said you were very exotic looking," Reggie added. "Or maybe it was you looked very erotic."

Angelina simply smiled.

"I don't hear any complaints from you," she grumbled as they took their places at the table.

CHAPTER TWENTY

May 2, 9:00 pm EDT - Viscusi Estate
New Canaan, CT

The meal that had been prepared was magnificent. It began with an outstanding antipasto, followed by an equally outstanding Italian soup. The main course was, the most melt-in-your-mouth, tender veal cooked to perfection in the Old Italian tradition. As a side, there was beautiful full pasta with a subtle tomato sauce; finally a homemade gelato. The wines selected by Mr. Viscusi were from his personal wine cellar located in the lower level of this magnificent estate as it was explained. It was a French wine which surprised Angelina a little. She had expected only Italian wines.

"I see you also chose a French white wine this evening," she said to Mr. Viscusi. "Do you prefer French over Italian?"

"Sometimes," he replied while he dabbed his mouth with the linen napkin. "It is clear that Ms. Evangeline has some experience with fine wines. I have what is described by some as one of the most diverse and extensive wine cellars in the eastern United States. I would be only too pleased to show you young people, if anyone wants to take a few moments after dinner."

There's that, *Ms. Evangeline* again, Angelina thought to herself. *I am right and I will prove it.*

"We would be honored," Candice answered for the group.

Jack, who was seated beside Rachel at the table, seemed to be having a great deal of difficulty keeping his attention on the entire group. He was focused on Rachel and more specifically her exposed leg and cleavage. It became obvious to everyone. It took a wink and a turn of the head from Angelina for Rachel to realize that she seemed to have an admirer. Rachel liked Jack a lot. They had been intimate a few times but she was not prepared to declare anything to the group as yet. She acknowledged Angelina's attempt to inform her with a slight nod of her own head. Now aware of his interest, Rachel made an effort to return Jack's attention and engage him in conversation. Their relationship was still evolving. Soon she glanced at Angelina who was concentrating on her conversation with Reggie. When Rachel caught her attention, Angelina flashed thumbs up. Rachel could feel the color flowing to her cheeks but she didn't mind; it felt good but she wanted to shift the focus off of herself.

"You have a lovely home, Mr. and Mrs. Viscusi. Have you been here long?" Rachel asked.

"Yes my dear, we have been in this house since we were married. It had belonged to Reggie's grandparents, Vincenzo and Elizabeth Viscusi. Our Reggie is named after his grandfather- Reginald Vincenzo Viscusi."

"Vincenzo Viscusi sounds like a fine Italian name," Angelina smiled. This was new information to her as well as the others. "I think we should all start calling you Vincenzo or maybe Vinnie."

"I don't think so," Reggie glared back at Angelina.

"How large is the house? I see much of it is under renovations," Candice asked.

"It's quite large," Joseph stated. "Too large but we like the property. We have thirty-five acres here backing onto a wooded area owned by our neighbor behind us. I believe he has one hundred acres. His property includes a small lake, or large pond depending on which way want to describe it."

In fact, the Viscusi home was enormous. There were twenty bedrooms and four different wings in the house; master, family, guest and servant. The guest wing was currently closed for significant renovations. Joseph always downplayed the actual vastness of the property. It drew too much attention to their wealth.

"Reggie used to camp out behind the property when he was in Boy Scouts," Mrs. Viscusi divulged. "He pitched his little tent and sometimes had a small fire further away from the house. He was an Eagle Scout, you know, and shot bows and arrows behind the house. I can show you all his badges he won for various skills; bow and arrows; campfire lighting; cooking, housekeeping. He had a whole arm full of badges on his scout shirt."

"I would like to see them. I'm not sure what an Eagle Scout is. We didn't have anything like that for boys in Egypt, but if he shot a bow and arrow, it must be a kind of Robin Hood club," Angelina joked.

Reggie was annoyed and embarrassed by his mother going on about his childhood accomplishments. He wanted this conversation to be over. The others were as amused as Angelina by his childhood history. He knew he needed to change the focus of the conversation.

"Father, you offered a tour of the wine cellar. I think it may be time for that."

"Yes, of course. Who would like a tour of the wine cellar?" Reggie's father inquired.

At first the entire group took Mr. Viscusi up on his offer. It was clear that Angelina was the most enthusiastic. Reggie noted her interest. After some additional consideration of what it would be like to navigate down a dark and likely damp cellar with her current attire, Rachel had second thoughts. She was also concerned about what a cold, damp basement might result in when she was dressed in such a sheer gown. She knew her bra was little more than a cover. She didn't relish the idea of having to cross her arms to keep from revealing more of herself than she cared to at this point in time. Candice was agreeable to whatever the group decided about the tour.

Rachel whispered to Jack, "I'm a little nervous about the tour and trying to navigate in these heels."

"I understand," he replied quietly. He leaned over to catch Reggie's ear. "Hey Reg, how damp and dingy are we talking about in this cellar? The girls might not be dressed appropriately for a dungeon tour. Do you think your dad would be offended if Rachel stayed above ground?"

"It may not be suitable for them, now that you mention it. Father, would it be okay if some of us took the tour at another time? It's a little damp and cool down there."

"Not a problem at all. I should have considered that."

Rachel was happy for the reprieve. By the time they had all rethought their initial enthusiasm for the tour, only Angelina and Reggie's father were left to take the tour. Angelina wanted to further the investigation into the mysterious Mr. Viscusi and nothing was going to deter her from her mission.

"I'd still like to go," she asserted, "if you don't mind a lone participant."

"Not at all, Ms. Evangeline, I would be pleased to show off my collection."

"I'll go with you," Reggie offered. He was reluctant to send her on her own with his father. Who knows what she might uncover during their tour? Angelina knew exactly what he was thinking and she would have none of it. She knew that having Reggie present would slow her down on her quest for information.

"Thanks, Reggie. Your father and I will be just fine. You stay with your other guests," Angelina replied.

Reggie knew he was beat. He also knew there was no point in continuing the discussion about accompanying her to the lower level. He was not going to win. He did think that she might be cool in the wine cellar, so he removed his suit jacket and put it around her shoulders.

"Thanks Reggie," she said as she smiled, acknowledging both his kindness in giving her his jacket and her success in getting her way.

CHAPTER TWENTY-ONE

May 2, 10:30 pm EDT - Viscusi Estate
New Canaan, CT.

As the remaining group headed for after-dinner drinks, Angelina and her newfound tour guide walked through the kitchen on their way to the very rear of the house. Joseph unlocked the cellar door and swung the heavy wooden and steel structure to one side. It appeared to Angelina that this was not likely the main entrance to the cellar as there was a considerable cloud of dust that resulted from the door being opened. She was unsure of why he would bring her into the lower level from anything other than the main entrance way. Perhaps there was something he didn't or did want her to see if they entered from the other direction. Joseph turned on the lights and led her down the wooden stairs.

"Please be very careful my dear, I don't want you falling wearing those high heels."

Angelina was an expert at managing some of the highest heels there were. There was little chance of her falling.

"Thanks, I'll be careful."

The pungent aroma of musty dampness drifted over her when she reached the bottom step. She noticed a significant drop in temperature and was thankful Reggie had the foresight to lend her his jacket. It took her a few steps before her eyes adjusted to the low lighting. The walls, she noted, were solid stone and mortar; damp with moisture; some displaying moss growing between the cracks. As they continued past the first turn in the hall, Angelina thought she heard voices coming from a room, barely visible, on the right side of the cobble-stone pathway. As they approached the darkened room, the door that was partially ajar swing closed; sealing the room from view and sound. She thought she had caught a glimpse of several men sitting at a table before the door was closed. Mr. Viscusi, realizing that she probably noticed the other people, explained.

"I will have to ask Mrs. Viscusi to speak to them about using the cellar as a place to play cards," Angelina now knew for certain there were people in the room and she had heard voices.

They proceeded a few more feet and passed a second room. This one was in total darkness and the door was fully open. Angelina noticed a strong odor coming from the room. She thought for a moment, and then realized that it was the same smell of gun oil like she used to clean her practice rifle. It was a distinct metallic scent. She peeked into the room, and as she slid her hand along the wall, she inadvertently switched on the lights. Instantly, Mr. Viscusi was standing in the open doorway. He quickly turned off the light and positioned his body in an attempt to partially block Angelina's view of the room and its contents. But not before she caught a glimpse of what she thought were gun racks. She was certain that there were weapons in that room. From the size of it, she thought perhaps a lot of weapons.

"I apologize," Mr. Viscusi said. "We normally keep this room locked. I will find out why we have not been following procedure."

"What is it that you do exactly?" she asked Joseph. It seemed like the time to begin the question period. "Reggie told us a little about his family but nothing specific."

"I am a business man."

"What kind of business, if you don't mind me asking?"

"I am in the finance business. I finance large acquisitions. Real-estate mostly, but not always."

Angelina had a feeling that Joseph wanted her to make a connection from his name and occupation. He certainly could have taken better steps to conceal the details had he wanted; it was time for a more aggressive stance to find out all she could. This man could be an enemy of her father's, for all she knew. She had to be sure. The game was on.

"Were there guns in that room?" Angelina asked. "I recognize the smell; it's like the oil I used to use to clean my practice rifle back home. I am an accomplished markswoman, in case you didn't know."

"Yes." He remained in the doorway. It seemed that he was hoping she would pursue the matter further. It was as if he wanted her to know more, but was perhaps reluctant or uncertain if he was providing too much detail.

"Can I see your collection?" she asked. "I'm interested in long guns in particular and like to see all the various types there are."

"I suppose, if you're interested." Joseph's tone was one of indifference. Angelina was confused by his apparent change in attitude.

He hesitated for a split second. Then reached in and flicked on the lights. The room lit up like a Christmas tree. There were fluorescent lights everywhere. As her eyes adjusted to the sudden jolt of light, she could see five or six rows of heavy metal shelving positioned down the center portion of the room. There was every size and type of weapon imaginable; automatic weapons, single-shot sniper weapons and hand guns. Everything she imagined her father might have sold over the years. Along the back wall, there were a number of metal cabinets. One was partially open and she could see the metal case of what was likely a rocket launcher just inside the door. Mr. Viscusi was clearly proud of his collection and all he said in response to Angelina's look of astonishment was, "Welcome to America".

"I guess, "welcome to America"," Angelina repeated. "This is an incredible collection of hardware. There are weapons here I don't recognize and I'm a gun enthusiast."

"I do pride myself on the variety of my collection. Just like the variation in my wine, there needs to be variety in every good collection."

"Variety is an understatement. Can you describe the various weapons to me?"

"Let's leave that for another day. I think we need to, at least, have a look at what we came to see, the wine cellar."

"You know my father is also a collector of guns," Angelina stated. "In fact, he sells and trades a lot in weapons of all types: It's his passion."

Joseph hesitated before replying. Angelina sensed the familiar reluctance she had detected from Joseph's body language just moments ago.

"What is your father's name?"

"Anwar Evangeline. Do you know of him?"

"I believe I do. I may have had some dealings with him many years ago."

Angelina felt, for the first time, she was getting somewhere in resolving this mystery and she had to push on. She had an admission that he at least knew of her father and had possibly done business with him. This was too much of a connection to be a coincidence.

"Have you ever purchased any weapons from him?"

"I don't recall the details of our business. I'm sure you can appreciate that I am involved with many transactions every year. I don't recall all of them?" Joseph was clearly not willing to divulge any more detail on the subject. Angelina doubted that he didn't recall the nature of the business he may have done with her father. *Where was all this going*?, she thought.

"I totally understand. I will have to inquire of my father when next we speak."

Disappointed, but not surprised by his responses, Angelina agreed to come back another day to take a closer look at his fine collection. As they viewed the wine cellar, Angelina couldn't help but ask herself. *I know who you are and Reggie is going to flip. I have a strong feeling that you and my father are somehow connected. How am I connected to these people? Where do I go from here?* Then it occurred to her that this was a game. A game of who blinks first and she was determined to win.

Game on Mr. Viscusi, she thought as they ended their tour and returned to the group.

After one final nightcap, the group was ready to be taken back to the hotel. Angelina was unusually quiet on the return drive to the hotel. Her mind was working at warp-speed. Trying to put together all the pieces of this ever growing puzzle in her head. Reggie could see that she was in one of her *thinking modes* as he described it. He had seen her like this before when they were in Mexico. She had felt that there was some connection between Eddy and Candice and the two unfortunate people who had been killed in the hotel. She felt it but she couldn't prove it, and it drove her crazy.

He knew she was going to have something to say about what was on her mind as soon as they were alone in the hotel. He was right. No sooner had they entered their room and Angelina was into it. She repeated the conversation she had with his father, detail by detail. She told Reggie what she thought it all meant and after she was done she said, "See, there I proved it. Your dad is a Mafia guy. To boot, he knows my dad. How weird is that?"

Reggie was prepared for this. He knew how smart Angelina was and he knew she was going to make the connection between her father and his father, but he couldn't allow himself to admit defeat.

"It's unusual, I'll give you that, but you haven't proved anything. Maybe they know each other, after all they have been businessmen for decades. They're bound to run into each other." Reggie was really reaching with this last comment but he was having some fun watching his beautiful girlfriend investigate and he didn't want to end it too soon.

"My dad lives in Egypt. What do you think the odds are that they're going to bump into each other on the streets of Cairo? You're in denial, my friend. This isn't over. I am going to stick to this like glue and prove it to you beyond any shadow of doubt."

"You do that," he replied. "Hey, by the way, what was it that Candice brought for you? I was thinking about it earlier."

"I bet you were. Why don't you take a seat and the show will begin shortly?" She smiled as she disappeared into the bathroom to change.

CHAPTER TWENTY-TWO

May 3, 8:30 am EDT - Waldorf Astoria Hotel
New York City, New York

The sun was shining when the group awoke Sunday morning. Everyone met in the Waldorf restaurant for breakfast. The topic of discussion for this morning was the revelation that Candice and Edward were seeing each other. Rachel and Angelina couldn't keep this big news flash a secret for very long. They had spilled the beans to Reggie and Jack very soon after arriving back at the hotel last evening. The guys were already making jokes to Eddy about dating a *Playboy* model and how did he ever manage to be so lucky. The truth was that everyone was very pleased and excited by their relationship. Eddy and Candice seemed to be well suited for each other.

They all knew there was a paper for Mensa to complete. They also knew that if they had really tried, the paper could have been completed while they were in Mexico at the conference. They had consciously chosen to meet again, purely for social reasons. The completion of the Mensa paper was simply an excuse.

Everyone got right to work immediately after breakfast. They set up in Jack's room. He had his computer all prepared to document the final paper. It took less time to complete than they had originally estimated. The dissertation was now finally finished and ready for publication. High on the list of the issues they outlined in their report, was the impact of global warming on the environment and in particular, the depletion of oxygen from the waters in the oceans – the OD effect as they called it. There had been a lot of discussion by the group about this and how it might be related to what Eddy saw at Chemico International, although they were unable to make a solid connection.

"Great," Jack stated, "we have it all finished on my computer. Did you want me to send it into Mensa? What are your thoughts?"

It was agreed that he would submit it on behalf of the team. Next on the agenda was the baseball game. It was still well before the opening pitch, however, they decided to go to the stadium early. This had been the first time any of the women had seen a professional baseball game.

At the start of the game, they were simply enjoying each other's company and not paying too much attention to the field. It was Rachel who first noticed that the crowd seemed to always be yelling at the players on the field. They would yell obscenities, and even some boo's one minute and cheers the next.

"What are they yelling about?" she asked Jack after one very loud outburst from the fans subsided.

"Didn't you see that home run hit?"

"I saw a ball go over the fence," she continued, "but I assumed it was a lost ball and they would have to find another one to continue the game. Are they supposed to hit it over the fence?"

The guys looked at each other with smiles on their faces.

"Yes," Reggie replied. "Hitting the ball over the fence is a good thing. As long as it's the guys in the white shirts," he clarified.

The afternoon was enjoyed by all. It was perfect weather and the game was full of excitement. The ladies continued to be less interested in the game and more with each other's conversation but the guys were really enjoying the ground level seats. At the end of the game, they all returned to the hotel and packed for their trip home. Sam brought the limo to take them to the airport.

CHAPTER TWENTY-THREE

May 4, 10:00 am EDT - 2302 Mulberry Street
New York City, New York

Angelina had decided to stay in New York for a few days after the others were gone. She was planning to move from the hotel to be with Reggie in his tiny apartment, although she wasn't really looking forward to being in his neighborhood. She was determined to find out everything she could about Reggie's family. She was equally determined to ask her father about his relationship to Joseph Viscusi. If her father knew him, she wanted to know when, why, and how that relationship existed. Reggie was less enthusiastic about delving into his father's business but he knew at some point in time, it was going to come up; better he be prepared than not.

They were sitting in a coffee shop across from Central Park enjoying the early morning sun and debating which one of them was going to take the first step to solving the puzzle.

"Well, who's going to make the first call?" Angelina inquired. "Do I call Cairo or do you call Connecticut?"

"Why don't you call Cairo?" Reggie replied, trying to postpone this discussion with his father for as long as possible.

"You're chicken."

"No, it's ladies first," Reggie replied as the excuse popped into his head. It was clear by her facial expression that Angelina wasn't buying that line; but someone had to make the first move.

Angelina placed the call to her father's cell phone.

"Good morning, my dear," her father answered. "I was just going to call you and here you are calling me; isn't that funny?"

"Why were you going to call me?"

"I'm in Chicago on business. I'm about to board a plane for New York and I understand from your mother that you may be in New York working on a report of some kind for your little IQ club. Are you still there?" he asked.

Her father was immensely proud of Angelina for becoming a member of Mensa; especially her being the first member from Egypt. When they had first discussed her applying for membership several years ago, he dubbed it her little IQ Club as a joke between them. The name stuck: It was their little inside joke.

"It's Mensa International, Daddy. It's a well respected organization and I am fortunate to be a member."

"It is they who are fortunate to have you my dear. *Are* you in New York and how long will you be there?"

Now she had a problem. Her father had no idea that she was cohabitating with Reggie while staying in New York. He still thought of her as his little girl and living with men was out of the question. She knew if he showed up and Reggie was in the same hotel room, it would not be good; even worse if he found out that she was staying in his apartment. Angelina and her mother had been trying for years to make her father realize that at some point in her life, she was going to be with a man. He chose not to acknowledge that fact and vowed that dire consequences would befall any man who dared to dishonor his daughter. Angelina tried to explain that being with a man is not a dishonorable thing to do but she had all but given up on the fight. What he didn't know can't hurt him, so she kept her private life to herself. She had to think quickly.

"I am in New York, Daddy, however I'm going to be boarding a plane later this afternoon and heading to California. If you arrive in New York by noon, maybe we could have lunch. How about the Waldorf?" she asked. She thought, hoped actually, the short timeline would be difficult for him to meet.

"You're staying at the Waldorf? That's pretty big stuff for my little girl."

"Daddy, we have this conversation every time we talk. I'm not your little girl. I am a grown woman and yes, I always stay at nice hotels."

"You must take precautions my dear. There are men everywhere who think nothing of taking advantage of a young girl like you."

"It's, *woman,* Daddy," she said, in as harsh a tone as she dared without scolding him.

"I understand. Yes, I can be at the Waldorf by noon my dear, see you then."

All the time Angelina was on the phone, Reggie was listening to her half of the conversation. As she hung up, she looked at the big smile on his face.

"What's so funny?"

"I was just wondering what your father would do if he knew what his little girl has been doing with this evil man last night and for the last several months."

"You can take the smirk off your face and hope he never finds out."

Reggie thought about her response; recalled the discussion they had earlier about her father protecting her; and the smile disappeared.

Angelina leaned over and kissed him on the cheek. "Not so smirky now are you?" she joked.

He pulled back from the kiss and pretended to be frightened by her advance. "Are you trying to get me killed?" he mused. "I remember what you said earlier."

"How about I head over to my father's office and you take lunch with your father when he arrives?" he suggested.

"Fine; but he won't be here for several hours. Do you want to hang out here for awhile?" she replied.

"Actually," he said, as a big smile reappeared on his face, "I was thinking we could go back to my place for a few hours."

"It's your life," she joked, "but if I show up for lunch with my hair all mussed and smelling all *sex sweaty,* it's going to be you who pays the price."

"What does 'sex sweaty' smell like?" he asked.

"Let's find out," she replied. She took his hand and pulled him out of his chair. They ran back to his apartment.

CHAPTER TWENTY-FOUR

May 4, 12:00 Noon EDT - Waldorf Astoria Restaurant
New York City, New York

Several hours had passed. Angelina was waiting at the Viscusi reserved table in the hotel and Reggie was just exiting the elevator in his father's office building. This was his first visit to his father's office since he had moved, almost ten years ago. As he entered the main office, he saw a woman whom he assumed was Mary Elizabeth. She was filing some paper in the bottom drawer of a file cabinet across from her desk. He couldn't help but notice her long legs and very short skirt. It amazed Reggie that he couldn't see more considering how far she was bending over. She looked as he had imagined she would when he spoke to her on the phone the other day. She couldn't have been any older than twenty-one, tall with long dark hair, and as she straightened up, he could see that she was extremely well endowed. Mary Elizabeth was a Candice level of endowed. It was difficult to take his eyes of her chest as he spoke.

"Hello, Mary Elizabeth; I'm Reggie. Dad knows I'm coming. Is he available?"

"Well, how nice to finally meet you," she replied, leaning over her desk and extending her hand to shake his.

She's a Candice endowed times two, he thought, trying to avoid looking directly down the front of her blouse. If Angelina had taught him anything in their short time together, it was how not to get caught when looking at women's breasts; or so he thought.

She held the front of her blouse closed and stood up straight. "Oh, I'm sorry." Mary Elizabeth remarked. It was obvious that she had realized she had just put on quite a show for her boss' son. "I forget sometimes that there are other people in the room. We don't have too many people who actually come into the office. Sometimes I just throw on what I have in my closet. Your dad always reminds me that a suit jacket might be more appropriate attire for the office."

"I bet he does," Reggie thought to himself.

His father came out of his office and shook his hand. "Alright son, let's head out. We have my table waiting," his father said. He was directing Reggie towards the door.

Reggie's head instantly started to pound as he pictured Angelina sitting at his father's private table and the arrival of her father as well. He was screwed, or more correctly, he was dead if her father made a romantic connection between him and Angelina.

"Where are we going?" Reggie asked, as if he didn't know.

"Son, *you* booked my table. We are going to the Waldorf. Vincent Demarco called me earlier and told me you had booked the table. I assumed it was for us. Then he called back and told me that Ms. Evangeline was already at my table, waiting. I assumed she is waiting for us."

"Dad, I booked the table for Angelina and her father. Her father is meeting her at noon. She wasn't sure where to go for lunch so I booked your table. I wasn't planning on all of us having lunch. I thought it would be okay."

"Of course it's fine; any friend of yours is a friend of our family. Your mother told me that she was the one you had your eye on the other night. Mr. Evangeline and I have not seen each other for many years. I look forward to seeing him once again."

"You know him?"

"A long time ago, but yes, I know him."

"Dad, you can't say anything about Angelina and me to her dad. She wants to tell him in her own way. He is really sensitive about her dating and she has a special way to speak to her dad so he doesn't become angry."

"Why would he be angry about you two getting together? She is a beautiful woman in her prime child bearing years, and you are a successful young man from a good family."

"It's not just me. It's any guy. Please, you have to take my word on this and keep our relationship to yourself; and for god sake, don't describe her as being in her prime child bearing years. That's not the way young women like to be defined in today's world."

"I will not be deceitful when dealing with people. I will not lie to him if he asks a direct question. I will, however, make every effort to comply with your request. You know she is going to have to tell him at some point if you two stay together and want to give him grandchildren." All Reggie heard was the word *grandchildren. If my dad says grandchildren, I'm a dead man,* he thought as they took their seats in the limo for the short trip to the Waldorf.

Upon entering the hotel, Reggie could see straight through to the restaurant and his father's table. Angelina and her father were already seated and having a drink. As he stood at the entrance, Angelina looked over and noticed him. Her eyes widened once she realized it was Reggie and his father no less. As they approached the table, Angelina got up and walked over to greet them. She took Reggie's arm, holding him back from his father.

"Good day Mr. Viscusi," she uttered as they passed in the aisle. She didn't wait for his reply. Reggie's father proceeded to the table and greeted Anwar as if they had just seen each other yesterday. Angelina knew she had maybe twenty seconds to talk to Reggie before her father was going to start to ask questions.

"What the hell are you doing here and why the hell is your father with you?" she whispered in a panicked voice.

"It's a long story," Reggie replied.

"It will be shorter than your life expectancy, if it slips that you're sleeping with me." She looked worriedly at the table.

"I already filled dad in on the need for discretion."

"And he agreed?"

"He kind of agreed. He said that he wouldn't make a point to bring it up. He also said he wouldn't lie if he was asked a direct question."

"That may work but what else aren't you telling me?" she asked worriedly. She could tell by the slight hesitation in his voice that he was keeping something from her.

"He said he didn't see anything wrong with you and me hooking up, you being of prime child bearing years and me being from a good family."

Angelina could do nothing but stare at Reggie after that statement. She remained still. Her mind was locked on the words *prime child bearing years*. Her brain was frozen in time.

"Tell me you're making that up," she finally said. "Tell me you're making a joke at my expense and he didn't describe me as being in my *prime child bearing years*." There was a look of sheer terror on her face. She flashed back to an earlier conversation she had with Reggie at his parents' place, and how his mother thought she looked bosomy. *I am a bosomy woman in my prime child bearing years* was all that raced through her mind.

"I'm not making a joke. Come on, we need to make our way to the table before they both say too much," he replied. He moved her towards the two older gentlemen.

"Talk business. Keep it to business. Nothing about child bearing. Keep it to business." Angelina said as a last instruction to Reggie.

The conversation started off very slowly. Angelina mentioned how she had met Reggie, purely by accident at the Mensa meeting, and how they and four other friends were all in New York for the sole purpose of completing their submission.

"Yes," Joseph said, in an attempt to be included in on the discussion, "Angelina and the whole group came to our house for a formal dinner on Saturday. You should have seen your young lady. She was dressed in a very beautiful gown and from the way she looked, she's all grown up." He had added that final part to try to demonstrate to Anwar how mature his daughter had become. He thought that might be helpful in her effort to appear mature in her father's eyes.

"Do you not wear your more traditional clothing at a formal affair?" Anwar asked Angelina.

"I have on occasion worn my traditional wardrobe and I enjoy wearing it. In America there are times through when a western style gown is more appropriate at a business function," she explained.

"Does your mother know of this?"

"Yes. Well maybe not about this specific gown. Mother and I shop in Paris. You know that and sometimes I purchase business clothes. The gown is like business clothes."

Reggie cut in, trying to change the subject.

"The reason why we wanted the four of us to meet is because we have something in common, or at least I think we do."

Reggie looked at Angelina. She appeared to be in shock. She was obviously worried about where he was taking this conversation. It was that same expression he had seen earlier when he and his father had arrived.

"What do we have in common?" Anwar asked, looking at Joseph.

"Gentlemen, your son and daughter are no longer children," Reggie continued. Angelina's face grew more solemn with each word he spoke. "We have been out in the world and we know that you both have unconventional careers. Careers that are somewhat unique as a matter of fact."

He decided to continue. He felt he was on a roll. Angelina appeared to be breathing once again. Color was returning to her face. She looked a lot better.

"We think that we know what it is that you do but you have never really talked about it. Angelina and I would like to know more. At some point, we may even have aspirations to be in the family business. We have talents that you may find useful."

Anwar was first to speak. His face showed his concern for where the discussion was heading.

"I will be frank. Angelina and Joseph both know that I sell weapons. Do you know this, Reggie?"

"I do."

"Then you also know that this is a very dangerous business; a business that is not for everyone."

"You mean not for women?" Angelina added, sensing it was what her father had meant but not expressed.

"Women or men have nothing to do with it," he continued. "It's a dangerous business for anyone."

"If I were a male, would you be more inclined to include me in your confidence?"

"My dear, I have never considered you as anything other than my most beloved child. It makes no difference to me male or female. In fact, I am the first man to boast of your achievements in academics, marksmanship, and in business. I hope that you can believe me when I say this to you."

"I suppose so."

"You need to *know* so. If you feel you wish to follow in my footsteps, I must warn you, be careful what you wish for."

"I'm not saying, take over your business but maybe we could work together on some projects. I have expertise you could use, and you have contacts that I don't have. Wouldn't it be wonderful if we could be a team from time to time? Father daughter," she asked.

"That would fulfill my deepest wish, if you were to know my true feelings. Let's work on this and see if we can also bring our other American friends into this discussion. They are worthy potential partners," he said as he turned to Joseph. "Before I end, the only provision must be that your mother is to never be made aware of our business connection. She would never approve of you working with me, under any circumstances. I would rather face ten of the most dangerous terrorists than sleep next to your mother if she found out our secret. You must all promise me."

"I promise, Daddy," she replied as she smiled, leaned in and kissed her father on the cheek.

"I guess we're next," Reggie stated. He turned to look at his father.

This was going to be a more difficult discussion and they both knew it. Anwar was in the arms business. Although some might think that was an unsavory occupation, it certainly wasn't illegal, at least most of it was legal. The same could not be said for Joseph. His investment business, although completely legal, was influenced by both his historic and perceived current involvement in organized crime. He also had the issue of Angelina finding out, for certain, that his father was a mafia guy, as she so quaintly defined it.

"Do you think you and I might be able to work together?" he asked his father.

Joseph paused before he answered.

"As Anwar has so eloquently stated, be careful what you wish for my son. My business is not always in my total control. There are others who play a role in my dealings."

"You have partners?"

"Not really partners. Strong business relationships that go back many years. It's like a family in many ways."

Reggie knew what Angelina would be thinking after that last statement. He purposely refrained from looking directly at her. His father had used the word *family*.

"As I think about it, however, I can see where your expertise with mathematics could provide an opportunity for us to work together. Perhaps you and Angelina, if you're still together."

Angelina turned her head in a flash. She was looking at her father's facial expression to see if he made a connection between them. Reggie knew he needed to clarify.

"Well, being together isn't perhaps the most accurate description. I'm certain our two families can have a long relationship going forward." Reggie stated.

"Agreed," the two older men echoed in unison.

"I look forward to further discussions in this regard but I must be going," Anwar interjected. "I have a meeting at two this afternoon and then I'm heading back to Cairo this evening."

"We have a lot to talk about. Reggie and I too look forward to the discussions. Anwar, I would be only too pleased to provide you a ride to your next meeting," Joseph offered. "I can also make my driver available to take you to the airport later today if that would be of interest to you."

"A kind offer that I will gladly accept," Anwar replied. "I always have trouble finding my way around New York. You see children, there have been benefits between us already in this relationship."

With that, both men rose from the table. Anwar kissed his daughter and Joseph shook Reggie's hand. The two older gentlemen headed out the door. Reggie and Angelina watched until they were out the front door and out of sight.

"Well," Reggie stated, "we started out trying to discover what our fathers did for a living and we ended up being partners. That's an amazing twist," he stated as he looked at Angelina.

Her face showed no emotion whatsoever. She didn't look sad but neither did she look happy.

"What's wrong?" Reggie asked.

Angelina hesitated while regaining her composure and responded.

"We're still alive. I can't believe we pulled that off."

"I think we did." Reggie replied with a smile.

"How far is your apartment from here?" Angelina asked. Reggie appeared confused by the sudden change in topic.

"Maybe ten minutes, if we took a cab."

Angelina hesitated again. It was clear that she was formulating her next statement in her head.

"That has to be the biggest rush I have ever experienced," she stated in a quiet voice. "I can feel my entire body full of adrenaline and I haven't moved an inch. We need to get to your place as quickly as possible because if we don't I am going to do you right here on this table at the Waldorf." She grinned, they both rose and rushed out the door.

CHAPTER TWENTY-FIVE

June 4, 10:00 am EET - Villa Evangeline
Cairo, Egypt

Four weeks had passed since the group meeting in New York. Angelina was now back in Cairo and concentrating her work in and around the Middle East. The downturn in the global economy was having a significant impact on sales and what money there was, mostly from the Middle East, was vigorously pursued by every competitor in the business. It was true that the oil rich countries in the Middle East were less adversely affected by these recessionary influences but not entirely. She had just recently secured both an office and an apartment for herself in the downtown area of Cairo.

She had seen Reggie only once since New York. They met in California for a weekend. Reggie was extremely busy with his new Vice President position. He was trying to define for himself exactly what his role was in the company was. His position was a new one for the firm and the position description had yet to be finalized. He often recalled, with humor, the comment made by Edward about him being like Chandler Bing. He was beginning to think he was right. It was a funny observation by Edward but it was turning out to be a correct one. In addition, Reggie was fulfilling his earlier promise to both Angelina and his mother to look for a new place. He could definitely see why Angelina wanted him to move. He had finally admitted to himself that it was a pretty bad area to be in. He had some ideas about that subject and was working with his father on a new project to change the face of the old neighborhood. Despite their busy schedule, Reggie and Angelina made time every day to call each other.

June was the hottest month of the year in Egypt. Angelina's parents were making preparations for their annual retreat to their yacht on the Mediterranean to escape the severe heat. At this point in time, Angelina's parents were not aware that she had convinced her company to allow her to set up a permanent field office in Cairo. They were certainly not aware of her leasing an apartment for herself, close to the office. The small office was expensive but it was also one of the few available spaces in the downtown core, and it was close to her new apartment. Her argument to her parents would be that the office was in a perfect location and her apartment was close to the office. Angelina did not want to live with her parents at their villa. She knew she had to have an apartment already rented before she broached the subject of her living in the downtown area of Cairo. As good as her parents were about letting her live her own life, Angelina knew they would not like her being in Cairo on her own. Now that everything was in place, she could announce the good news about her Cairo office to her mother and father, and inform them she would also be living near the office. It was too late to change the plan because she had already signed leases on both the office and apartment space.

Cairo was a vibrant city and she enjoyed the hassle-bustle in the streets. She didn't mind that her wardrobe had to be simplified to meet with the requirements of the Muslim tradition. No short skirts or high heels for the women of this Middle Eastern country, at least not in public. Angelina embraced the tradition and dressed appropriately. It was a nice change for her not to have to worry about what to wear. It would also be great to have a break from the peering looks and off-handed comments about her appearance that still occurred in the so-called "more advanced" countries of the world.

Angelina had also managed to hire a local young man, a recent University graduate, to be her assistant in the office. His name was Anton Bashandi. Angelina had very specific reasons for hiring a man over a woman. As much as she disagreed with it, she had to acknowledge that it was still an advantage to be a man in Egypt. Angelina also knew that she dealt better with men than women in the business world. She didn't like to admit her biases in this regard either, but the truth was there was no jealousy to overcome and just a whole lot less drama when dealing with men.

Anton was working out well. They had already purchased furniture and worked to get the office ready. Angelina had a small inner office with a black cherry desk and chair as well as some very modern visitors' chairs. Anton's office doubled as the reception area and consisted of his small desk and a number of visitors chairs. Anton was a hard worker. He worked on his own time to paint the entire office bright white. He had also obtained some beautiful artwork and sculptures to enhance the otherwise sparse surroundings. Anton proved to be a resourceful employee; one who knew the ropes in Cairo. He was capable of getting things done and this was just what Angelina needed.

It was the weekend and Angelina had spent it with her parents at their villa. She had taken the opportunity at breakfast to tell her parents about her new office and apartment. Her father was not pleased.

"Daddy, I want you to know I'll be just fine with my office in the city," she said. "I have Anton there and I'm well aware of the dangers. I'll take every precaution." As she anticipated, her parents' first reaction was to try to have her move back with them. Her plan had worked. It appeared like she was winning the argument to work and live in the city. "The only way my company will allow me to work from Cairo is if I have a formal office. Since it has to be in the downtown core, it only makes sense for me to locate my new apartment there as well. The commute to Cairo from here would be far too stressful," she reasoned.

She could tell that her mother was disappointed but she sensed that her father had either anticipated her maneuver, or realized they had been played. He didn't seem to be objecting enough to suit his nature. He was accepting of his daughter living in the downtown core. He knew this would require him to set up some additional security measures for her and it had to be done without her knowledge. She would never agree to this, so she couldn't know. This arrangement would be put in place by the end of the weekend.

CHAPTER TWENTY-SIX

June 4, 2:00 pm EET - Villa Evangeline
Cairo, Egypt

Angelina was taking a much needed rest by the pool after the vigorous debate with her parents earlier that morning. Her parents had left the villa to go into the city for some last minute shopping. The house maid approached her and announced that Angelina had a phone call. It was from a woman named Wi and it was from New York City, in the United States of America. Angelina had given Rachel several numbers where she could be found abroad. She was not surprised that it was Rachel. They had continued their friendship; in fact the entire group had kept in touch with each other through e-mails and such. The group seemed to mesh very well, even with their varied interests. Angelina had been advising Rachel on a personal matter. Rachel was being formally courted (as she so quaintly expressed it) by Jack Daniels, and Angelina couldn't have been more pleased. She had teased Rachel about it, and how Jack's interest was likely prompted by that fabulous dress she wore to the Viscusi's home. She reminded Rachel that Jack couldn't take his eyes off her for that entire weekend and how they had sat next to each other at the baseball game, that Sunday afternoon. There were some issues since Jack resided in California and Rachel in New York. In spite of this, it was working. Rachel felt confident asking relationship questions of Angelina. The most recent hurdle was when, Jack decided to spend a weekend in New York, to see Rachel. The question of where he would stay came up. Angelina knew that she had to be very cautious with her advice. She had to counsel Rachel, not advise her in this most delicate matter. Angelina was pleased and amused when Rachel had called her late that Sunday to announce that they had spent the weekend together in her apartment. Rachel excitedly described her entire weekend with Jack and how they seemed to be a good fit. There was a subtle hint from Rachel that perhaps they had moved to the next level in their relationship. Angelina knew her friend would be reluctant to go into detail. Angelina surmised, from the little Rachel did share with her, this was for her the first weekend away with a guy- with a really great guy.

Angelina took the call in her father's office. She closed the door. She was certain the conversation with Rachel would be about things best not overheard by the servants. When she picked up the phone she knew instantly that Rachel was very upset. She had been crying for certain and Angelina's stomach dropped when she guessed that perhaps Jack had broken up with her.

"What's wrong?" Angelina asked.

There was a delay in Rachel's response. Then in a soft voice she simply said: "They're dead; Candice and Eddy are dead."

There was silence on the line for what seemed like an eternity. Angelina's mind was racing; trying to make sense of what she had just been told. She could feel the tears welling up in her eyes. Angelina took a deep breath and haltingly replied.

"How can that be? We just saw them a few weeks ago." Angelina was having some difficulty keeping it together in order to ask the next obvious question. "What happened?"

There was another silence while Rachel took time to compose herself; enough to at least to allow her to explain the basic information. She exhaled her breath and replied.

" Apparently, Edward and Candice were vacationing in Mexico. Maybe she was working there. It's not clear. There was some kind of a robbery. It isn't clear whether their car was hijacked or it happened in their hotel. They were both shot and they're both dead. Eddy and Candice are dead."

It was all she managed to say before she burst into tears. It was a jumbled message but enough to provide some of the most basic details to Angelina. The news hit Angelina hard as well. She was trying to contain her emotions. After a lengthy pause, Angelina was able to control her own emotions and broke the silence.

"Sweetie, I know this is hard; I know we have some tough days ahead. We will get through this. We are going to find out what happened to our friends. We will make sure whoever did this, will pay for their crime. I promise you that."

Rachel took a deep breath and finished providing Angelina with all the remaining details she knew about what happened to Edward and Candice. They weren't much but Angelina knew they would find out more as time went by. Once the women had both managed to get their emotions under control sufficiently to continue the conversation, Angelina put her organizational skills in motion and began to lay out the next course of action.

"Do you know where Jack is right now?"Angelina asked.

"Jack is with me. I believe Reggie is in New York as well."

"Jack seems to be spending a lot of his time in New York these days. Is there anything I should know about you two?" she asked, trying to inject some lightness into an otherwise tragic time.

"No." was the only response from Rachel. She sounded a little embarrassed announcing that Jack was with her in her apartment.

"Well," Angelina continued, "we can get into this later. For right now, let's stay on the line and see if we can reach Reggie. I spoke with him last week on another matter. We'll need to make plans to attend the funerals."

Rachel obliged and Angelina put the call on hold and dialed Reggie's cell. It was speed dial position number two; number one was her father's number. She should have been able to remember his number since she spoke with Reggie almost every day. Telling Rachel she spoke to Reggie last week about another matter was a little white lie. She had actually spoken with him for about an hour this same morning. They described how they were going to fulfill each other's sexual fantasies the next time they met. She put those thoughts aside as she waited for him to pick up. Reggie answered on the second ring.

"Hi Reggie, it's me," Angelina stated.

"I see that," he replied. He had noted the number of the incoming call on his phone. "How are you, babe? I know about Eddy and Candice. I let Rachel fill you in because she felt so strongly that she needed to be the one to tell you. I hope you don't mind."

"I'm fine with it, but I have Jack and Rachel on the line. We want to talk about plans to attend the funerals."

"I have some additional information regarding Candice," Reggie said. "I'll explain once we have the others on the line. Before you connect us, are you really okay?"

"Not really, but I'm a million miles from you now, and it's the best I can do."

What no one else in the group knew for certain was that Reggie and Angelina were lovers. There had been some speculation, mostly from Candice. Nothing was ever really confirmed. There was the issue with distance; however, they were dealing with it. In fact, Reggie had his ticket to Cairo booked for next week. To coincide with Angelina's parents' cruise of the Mediterranean. It would give Reggie and Angelina some alone time in the villa. At least, that was the plan.

"Let's talk," she replied and connected the group on the conference call.

Reggie informed the group that Candice's cremated remains had already been shipped back to her parents in Sweden. It was understood that there had been a simple ceremony and cremation in Mexico. Both of her parents suffered from Alzheimer's and knew nothing about her friends from Mensa or even that their daughter had been killed. The extended family had decided it would be best not to tell them. They held a private service in Sweden, for family only.

The details about Eddy's funeral, as relayed by Reggie, were simple. Eddy was to be buried in his hometown of Kingston, Ontario. The plan was for everyone to meet there. This would mean flying into Toronto and renting a car for the three-hour drive to the small town to the east. Reggie had the name of a good hotel in the area which he had obtained from Eddy's sister. He would make the hotel reservations. The group agreed to meet up with each other at the hotel.

CHAPTER TWENTY-SEVEN

June 6, 11:00 am EDT – Toronto, Canada

Reggie had a short trip from New York to Toronto. He timed his arrival to coincide with Angelina's. Their plan was to drive to Reggie's home town together and use that time to discuss what had happened to their friends. It would also give them an opportunity to talk and spend time with each other. Rachel and Jack made their own separate flight arrangements. Reggie and Angelina met in Toronto and rented a car. On the trip to Kingston, they spoke about their friends' deaths. They both seemed somewhat confused by the lack of details concerning the so-called robbery or hijacking. There wasn't anything they could do about Candice's funeral. The best they could do was to help Eddy's mother and sister.

They were just beyond the eastern-most boundary of Toronto before the traffic began thinning out and they settled in for the remaining drive. They had been warned that Toronto was a big city and the traffic was going to be awful but when you come from New York or Cairo,

Toronto traffic is a piece of cake. There had been a few delays due to the volume of traffic. They could now see nothing but clear driving ahead. It would be an additional two hours from this point on according to the GPS.

"Do you find it odd that they went back to Mexico?" Angelina asked.

"There are a lot of things I find odd. Going back to Mexico. The details or lack of details about what actually transpired and why Candice's body was dealt with so quickly, to name a few."

"Rachel thought that Candice may have been on a photo shoot. Perhaps on the beaches of Mexico. You know, a Playboy or Victoria's Secret shoot."

"Maybe. I hadn't heard that one. It could make sense. That's something Eddy would be only too anxious to see," Reggie quipped.

"Just Eddy? Any of you guys would want to be there for that kind of a photo shoot. Don't make Eddy out to be the only one of your gang of merry men interested." She had him on that one and she knew it.

"Where's the merry men coming from?"

"You know, Robin Hood and his band of merry men."

"Can we let that go? I was a teenager and shooting anything was a thrill. The bow was a compound-bow, you know. The kind used to hunt big game animals."

"Did you ever hunt any big game animals?"

"I went on one deer hunt, with Mr. Menotti. It was as boring as hell. They sit up in a tree waiting for a deer to wander by them below. Then they try to hit it with their arrows."

"A deer is hardly big game." Angelina laughed.

"They can turn on you just the same as a lion or elephant." Reggie knew he was stretching his story as far as it could go. He was enjoying the banter with his beautiful girlfriend.

Angelina seemed to let it go for a few minutes as she watched the scenery go by.

"Who's Mr. Menotti?"

"Mary Margaret's dad."

"Right...your first," Angelina smiled. She recalled Mrs. Viscusi's reference to this girl when they first met at the Viscusi estate.

"No. Not my first. Can we stop talking about this now?"

"For now."

"Thank you. I was saying, there are a few things I find odd. Maybe none of them are connected in any way. Remember when we were at the dance?"

"Where I met Demetrious...?" Angelina said. She stared off into space as if she was in a dream.

"Yes, where you met Mr. D. I'm trying to be serious, here."

"Sorry, go on."

"As I was saying, we were at the dance and I happened to see two tough-looking guys start to approach Edward in the back hall. Like they were going to maybe rob him or something. I went up to them, actually both Jack and I walked towards them. You know, to help Eddy if he needed it."

"What did these other guys do?"

"They walked away once they saw us coming. I guess we could have read the situation wrong."

"Maybe. What else?" Angelina asked while she thought about what he had just told her. She too had seen several people hanging around in the back hallway that night. That was one of the reasons she called for security. She had a feeling they were trouble.

"The guy and girl who were killed in the hotel. They were very close to Edward's room. One floor up as I recall thinking at the time."

"Hm... What else?"

"How about Eddy's boss being killed? That happened when he was in Mexico."

"How's that connected? He was killed here in Canada," Angelina questioned.

"How's any of it connected? Maybe it's not. Perhaps they were just in the wrong place at the wrong time. I don't know."

"It is interesting," Angelina admitted. "We'll have to ask Jack and Rachel if they had any similar feelings. How much longer until we get there?"

"You sound like you're ten, *asking how much longer*. It'll be at least another hour."

"Do I look like I'm ten?" she said. She straightened her shoulders and sat back in the seat. Reggie looked across the car at her and smiled. She certainly didn't look ten to him.

CHAPTER TWENTY-EIGHT

June 6, 2:00 pm EDT - Loyalist Motel
Kingston, Ontario, Canada

After Reggie and Angelina arrived at the hotel, they quickly checked in and went to their room to drop off their luggage. Reggie had called Jack's cell and they'd agreed to meet Jack and Rachel at a restaurant not too far from the hotel at five pm. Jack and Rachel were still on route and about ninety minutes away. The plan was they would have dinner and then head over to Edward's mother's house to see how she and his sister were holding up.

As it was only two in the afternoon, there was plenty of time before dinner so Reggie decided to have a shower. He had been rushed during his morning in New York and didn't have time to shower before heading to the airport. Angelina decided she would have a short lay-down. She had been traveling for about twenty hours in order to arrive there from Cairo. She did fairly well with travel and jet lag, but she was feeling a little tired. Reggie was enjoying a hot, steamy shower when he felt a sudden draft of cool air move the shower curtain against his leg.

"Angelina," he said playfully, "is that you?" An obvious question. Who else would it have been? Meeting each other in the shower was how they often began their romantic interludes.

There was no response. He continued his shower and was in the midst of shampooing his hair, when he felt the most wonderful pair of arms slide around his waist. It took him by surprise, just for a moment. He knew he had just been joined by the most beautiful woman in the world. His eyes were still full of soap as he turned. Her arms released their hold around his waist. He held out his hands, as if he was blinded by the soap, and began searching for his mystery guest,

"Who is it?" he smiled.

There was silence. He could tell by her touch that she wanted to play. They had been through some rough days with their friends being killed, and there were going to be more ahead before this was over. There was a lot of tension that had built up. The best way to relieve that tension was to stay focused on other things.

"Who is it?" he asked again.

Still silence, but this time his hands were taken into her hands and guided to her breasts. He could feel their familiar firmness and size. Then she leaned over and whispered in his ear

"Guess who?"

Reggie could have held her breasts all day. He was anxious to see more. He turned to allow the water to rinse the shampoo from his hair and eyes. He turned back to face his shower mate and found himself gazing at a very sexy, very beautiful, and very wet Angelina. He took her into his arms and hugged her close. Then he held her shoulders and moved her at arm's length while he took her in fully. She blushed slightly as she stood naked and wet before her lover. The only thing he could think of to say was

"Fuck me, you're gorgeous."

"You always were a sweet-talker," was her reply as she smiled.

The shower was turned off and there was a long period of time spent drying each other with the warm fluffy towels. This was followed by two hours of satisfying each other's every sexual need. Finally collapsing on the bed, exhausted and satisfied. They would have to take another shower for certain to wash off the sweat they had worked up. It was a good sweat, the best kind.

******

Jack and Rachel had arrived in town. They would have to wait for a very long time in order to meet up with Angelina and Reggie. Jack hadn't been paying much attention to the time. He and Rachel were deep in conversation concerning the death of their friends. Once they realized they were almost two hours early, they decided to go directly to the hotel.

It was only about 3:30 pm when they arrived at the hotel. Jack went to the front desk.

"You should have a reservation under Daniels," he said to the young woman at the desk.

She typed the name in her computer, found the reservation and proceeded to register these new arrivals. There was an information package about the hotel as well as a key card in the small bundle of paperwork she handed back to Jack.

"Welcome to the Loyalist Motel. My name is Lacey. If you need anything dial eight for the front desk and I will look after it for you. I hope you will enjoy your stay with us."

"Thank you, Lacey," Jack replied. "Has Reggie Viscusi checked in yet?"

"I'm very sorry, Mr. Daniels but I'm not permitted to give out that information."

"I know but we are here to meet up with Mr. Viscusi. It would be helpful to know if he is here and what room he is staying in."

"I'm really sorry, Mr. Daniels, but it's against the rules. I could get into trouble."

Jack realized that the young woman was just doing her job. She looked like a college student of maybe twenty, and this was likely a summer job for her. Rachel thought she might take a different approach. She gently touched Jack's arm and nudged him sideways, so she could approach the front desk.

"Lacey, we know you're just doing your job and we certainly don't want to get you into any trouble, but we have traveled from New York City to attend a friend's funeral here in Kingston. We are supposed to meet up with our friends. It would be very helpful if we knew what room they were in, or even if they have arrived." Rachel was being as persuasive as she could be.

"Who's the funeral for?" Rachel thought it was a rather forward question but then the young woman explained further. "I have a friend being buried tomorrow."

Both Rachel and Jack's stomachs dropped.

"Edward Milton," Rachel replied.

The young woman paused. Then looked around the lobby, to be certain they were alone, before she discretely wrote a note on a slip of paper, and handed it to Rachel. Rachel looked at the note and handed it to Jack. On the note was written 347, and thanks for coming for Eddy's funeral.

Jack and Rachel took the elevator to the third floor; walked quietly along the hallway and stopped at room 347. Jack knocked softly on the door. Inside the room, Reggie got up from the bed to answer the door. He threw on a bathrobe. He had ordered room service, ten minutes earlier, and assumed it was the food. Angelina was still exhausted from their love making session and the twenty hours of travel it took to get here. She simply rolled slightly and pulled the top sheet over her naked body. As the door opened, Reggie saw two familiar faces flash past him as they walked through the open door. He was about to say "I thought you were room service," when he heard a loud squeal from Rachel.

"Oh, my god, I'm so sorry, oh my god, I am so sorry."

Rachel realized that she had just walked in on their friend with a girl. How embarrassing? There was a slight pause as Rachel continued to avert her eyes and apologize for walking in on Reggie and whomever.

Hearing Rachel's voice through her sleepy stupor and forgetting where she was or with whom, Angelina rolled over, still covered by the sheets, and said: "Is that you, Rachel?"

As soon as the words left Angelina's lips, she knew she was in trouble. There was a slight delay while Rachel's brain identified the woman's voice as that of her dear friend, Angelina. Rachel's eyes grew wide and she began to hop up and down.

"Oh my god, oh my god," she screamed. She was pointing at the bed.

Rachel now had confirmation what she had suspected for some time; that her best friends were lovers. She had caught them red-handed. She seldom had the opportunity to tease Angelina about matters of the heart. This time she wanted to make the most of this situation.

"What are you doing? What are you doing? Why are you in his bed? Where are your clothes? What's happening? I don't believe this." She pretended to be outraged.

The commotion Rachel was making brought Angelina out of her sleep deprived coma. She quickly covered her naked body with more covers and slipped her head under as well. A speedy recovery from this embarrassing situation was not going to be possible. She knew she was going to have to face the music.

"Too late for that," Rachel said primly. "What the hell are you doing in Reggie's bed? Explain yourself, Ms. Angelina Evangeline."

Angelina peaked out from under the covers, and simply said. "Hi Rach, what's happening?"

Angelina kept a big smile on her face, attempting to ease the tension.

"What's happening is that I have just found my best friend in bed with my other best friend. When, what, and why am I just finding out about this now?"

Before Angelina had an opportunity to respond, Rachel turned to Jack and asked.

"Did you know anything about this?"

He was quick to respond.

"No way. This is all news to me."

As he spoke, he glanced at Reggie. Rachel was certain she saw a look of triumph pass between the two men.

"Don't bother with the looks. Either of you."

Both men shrugged their shoulders.

"Come in and let's talk," Angelina said. She managed to stand with the bed covers held tightly around her body. She motioned to Rachel to follow her to the bathroom so they could talk privately. Angelina shuffled into the bathroom, dragging the covers, and Rachel followed. Once inside the room, Angelina quickly dropped the blankets and reached for the second bathrobe. She wasn't quite quick enough. Rachel caught a full frontal view of her friend's naked body.

"My god, woman, can you not keep your clothes on, even for a minute?" She pretended to cover her eyes. The two friends looked at each other for a split second and then burst into tears of laughter. The guys stood in the doorway to the hotel room, confused by the sound of laughter coming from the bathroom. Jack looked at Reggie and gave his friend a thumbs-up sign of approval and said:

"Get dressed; I'm going to buy you a drink. We'll leave those two to bond."

The only other statement Reggie heard Jack utter under his breath and intended for Reggie's ears was, "That went well."

CHAPTER TWENTY-NINE

June 6, 5:00 pm EDT- Kingston, Ontario, Canada

The local yellow pages had thirteen pages of restaurant advertisement. Everything from Chinese to Greek, fast food to formal dining, it was going to be difficult to choose. Jack decided to ask the young desk clerk, Lacey, for a recommendation. He stopped at the front desk before he exited the motel.

"Most of the guys I know like the Double R. It's just down the road from here. I think that one is part of a chain. Have you heard of it in the States? If you go there ask for Tammy to be your waitress. She's a friend of mine. Her name isn't really Tammy it's Elizabeth but at the Double R all the girls use fake names and they all end in Y or at least the e'" sound, you know like Debby, Tammy, Kitty and so on." Lacey had said her entire message without a break or even pausing to take in a breath of air. It was one long, connected statement and apparently there was more, as she continued. "Her boss is a creep. He says they insist on them using false names to protect their identity, you know from customers, but the real reason is it makes them sound perkier. They like the girls to be perky. They wouldn't even give me a job. Apparently I'm not perky enough, meaning small enough. They like tiny girls, like my friend Elizabeth with less up top, if you know what I mean. On second thought, don't go there, the food is lousy anyway and I don't think the ladies would appreciate the waitress uniforms. They take advantage of college age girls and make them wear those terrible outfits, because they know we need the jobs."

Jack's mind flashed back to the lousy restaurant he and the guys had lunch, in the first day they were in Mexico. That cute little waitress's name was Tiffany, now that he thought of it.

"Maybe we'll find a Red Lobster," Jack smiled. He caught up with the others outside the motel.

"That's good too," Lacey replied as the door to the lobby swung closed behind Jack.

The dinner conversation was not very lively. They knew they were going to have a difficult evening, visiting with Eddy's mom and sister. After dinner, the foursome headed to Eddy's mother's house. None of them had met Debbie Milton, however, they knew a little about her just from listening to their friend, Eddy. It was a little past eight when they arrived at the house. The house was small but quaint. It was starting to become dark outside as it was now a little passed eight. Although it was becoming dark outside, the lawns and gardens appeared to be as well maintained as the house. They parked on the street in front of the house, in case the two cars already in the driveway needed to be moved. As they walked up the driveway, they could see into the living room through a front window. There appeared to be six people in the house. For a brief moment, they thought perhaps they should come back later. They looked at each other for consensus.

"Let's do this now," Reggie suggested. "It's getting late and I'm sure his mom needs to get some sleep before tomorrow."

He knocked on the front door. It was immediately it was opened by a young woman who they presumed was Eddy's sister, Anna. Anna seemed to know who these new visitors were and it was obvious by her reaction that she had been looking forward to meeting her brother's friends.

"You must be Eddy's friends from the States?" We were hoping you would drop by tonight so we could spend some time with you." she said. She turned to tell her mother. "Hey Mom, Eddy's friends from the States are here," she yelled.

It was obvious that Anna was excited by their arrival. Mrs. Milton excused herself from a group of people currently assembled in her living room, and came to greet them at the front door.

"Come in, come in," she said, ushering the foursome into the front hall and motioning for them to take off their jackets. The other guests could see that there were new arrivals so they stood up to leave. It was a perfect time and opportunity to call it a night. As one group was entering, the others were making their way to the coat closet and preparing to leave.

"Oh please," Angelina said, "don't let us disturb your evening. Please stay."

"No, no," was the reply from one of the older women in the group. "We must be moving on and leave you young people to talk."

"We will see you tomorrow at Saint Martin's," Eddy's mother said as the other guests exited the house.

Debbie Milton was a tall woman in her mid to late fifties, with graying hair. It was clear, from the lines on her face that the loss of her son and the pressures of raising two children on her own had taken their toll. She had a figure typical of a fifty something mom, not slim but certainly not overweight either.

Anna appeared to be younger than her years. She would soon turn twenty according to what Eddy had told them. Anna was petite, not much more than 5-foot 1-inch tall. Her waist was tiny and her shapely legs seemed to be disproportionately long in relation to her actual height. She wore a short black skirt. She had a very nice figure which her older brother likely ignored because he didn't want to admit she was maturing when he thought of her. Her chestnut hair was cut short to frame her heart-shaped face. This also added to her youthful appearance. Eddy had described this pretty young woman as his "kid sister" and called her Bug. She certainly didn't look like a Bug as nicknamed by her older brother. It was clear that he chose not to acknowledge that she had grown into a very attractive young woman. Rachel understood that Anna was attending Carleton University, in Ottawa, and assumed that Eddy had been helping out with some of the cost for his kid sister.

"Come in, Come in", Mrs. Milton repeated.

The friends each took a seat in the living room. It was a small room but tastefully decorated. Rachel sat at the end of the sofa and was quick to notice two 8 x 10 pictures on the side table. One must have been Eddy's father and the other was a picture of Eddy in his university graduation gown. She wasn't sure if she should make a comment about the pictures or not, so she decided just to see where the discussion took them. The conversation was upbeat for the most part. Debbie and Anna were both very interested in hearing about Eddy's friends and how they connected to their Eddy. There wasn't much said about Candice, during these discussions. The group felt that perhaps Eddy hadn't filled his mother and sister in on who he was dating. The only comment his young sister made was she thought Candice was a stripper. Her mother was displeased with her for using those terms to describe Eddy's girlfriend and a woman neither of them had even met. Angelina was quick to correct her assumption.

"Candice was actually *Dr.* Candice Bergen. She had a doctorate in marine biology and was a Mensa member. She was also a successful model and our friend," she corrected.

It was obvious that Mrs. Milton was impressed by this information. Anna still looked skeptical.

There were times during the visit that they struggled to come up with appropriate conversation, yet the entire group seemed to be dealing fairly well with their grief. From time to time, Debbie appeared to be listening but it was clear her thoughts were somewhere else.

It was approaching 10 pm and Jack suggested that they call it an evening. "Tomorrow is a full day," he stated. "I'm sure we are all going to need our rest."

Debbie was first to stand. A certain indication that she was exhausted and ready for them to depart. She offered her thanks and asked Anna to see her guests to the door. Debbie then moved to the kitchen and started to tidy up. The click and clatter of dishes knocking together could be heard. It was the familiar sound of a dishwasher being loaded. Anna retrieved their jackets and motioned to group to gather around her. They all assumed she was going to tell them something about how her mother was really coping with her loss. Instead, she made a statement that caused all four of them to gasp.

"They killed him, you know."

The foursome looked from one to the other, with expressions of confusion on their faces. Jack wasn't certain if he had heard her correctly.

"*Who* killed him?" Angelina replied.

"His company killed him," was Anna's emotional response.

"What are you saying?" Jack whispered, not wanting to draw Debbie, who was still fussing in the kitchen, into the conversation. "Why would his company kill Eddy and Candice?"

"Because they knew too much."

There was a lengthy pause as the group digested what this young girl had just told them.

"We clearly need to talk," Jack said. "Not here, but we need to talk about this, Anna. Can you spend some time with us, now? We need to know what details you have about their deaths."

Anna thought for a moment and then walked to the kitchen, "Mom, will you be okay alone, if I hang out with these guys for an hour or so?"

Debbie didn't hesitate in her response, "By all means, that will be fine. I'm just going to tidy up and then I am off to bed, so go. Lock the door on your way out, sweetie."

"You can come in our car," Angelina told Anna.

They didn't take the time to put on their coats. They walked very quickly to the rental car that was parked on the street.

"Let's head back to the hotel where we can talk," Reggie suggested.

As Anna was getting into the back seat, Reggie could see that she was looking off into the distance. Something had caught her eye.

"What are you looking at?" he asked.

Anna hesitated for a few seconds and then pointed to the car parked down the street, on the opposite side of the road. "See that car? It has been there for several days. Someone watching the house."

As everyone turned to look, the headlights on the car in question turned on and it was driven off in the opposite direction.

"We really need to talk," Reggie repeated. He started the car and turned to head back to their motel.

Angelina thought to herself; *there is something seriously wrong going on here. I can feel it.*

CHAPTER THIRTY

June 6, 10:00 pm EDT - Loyalist Motel
Kingston, Ontario, Canada

There was little conversation during the short drive back to the motel. The group wanted a proper venue to have their very important discussion. All of them were recalling the various conversations they had with each other at different times regarding the deaths of Eddy and Candice. They were anxious to find out if any of their suspicions and / or thoughts were close to what Anna was about to tell them. The group settled quickly in the small hotel room. Jack pulled four chairs from all corners of the room and placed them around the small desk where Anna sat. They chose Jack and Rachel's room. The bed in the other room was still disheveled from Angelina and Reggie's afternoon romp. It would be just a little too obvious.

Anna sat, looked around at the room and its contents, and asked Jack. "Are you and Rachel lovers?"

There was an uncomfortable silence that came over the group. Angelina was glad they had decided not to use their room. The questions would have likely been a little more graphic if they had. This young girl was very observant.

"Yes, we are lovers as you so quaintly put it," Rachel replied on behalf of Jack. "We have been for some time."

This was the first time Rachel had said that out loud. She felt good about it as she looked at her friend for her reaction. Angelina had a big smile on her face; she approved. Jack seemed to be pleased with her response. He liked it when she declared her feelings for him and their relationship.

"Neat," was Anna's response. "Eddy never said anything about that."

Rachel didn't respond, but she did think to herself that it was too bad that Eddy and Candice didn't really know about her and Jack. Eddy and Candice were together, at least since they last saw them in May. She also glanced sideways at Angelina as if to say, *I wonder if we should tell Anna what you and Reggie were up to all afternoon.* Angelina shook her head slowly in a gesture to her friend not to blab all the news. Rachel smiled knowingly at her friend.

Once settled, Reggie asked Anna, "What makes you say Eddy and Candice were killed by his company, and why would you think someone is watching your house?"

Anna was very quick to respond.

"I say they were killed by his company because that's what Eddy had warned me might happen. There were several incidents that occurred which gave him the impression he was in danger. Mostly it was after his boss was killed. I believe there is someone watching our house because Eddy told me he had seen them too. You saw the car tonight; he drove away when we looked his way."

"What are you saying?" Reggie replied.

Anna took a deep breath and began her explanation.

"Before he died, Eddy and I had lunch one afternoon. It was maybe mid to late May. He had called me and seemed upset about something. We met for lunch. He never asks me to lunch. I thought it was about a girl and he was finally seeing me as a woman rather than a kid sister. He called me bug most of the time. I hate that nick name. But when he phoned, he called me Anna. I knew it was important. Like I said, I figured he needed some womanly advice. I was wrong." With each sentence of her explanation Anna became more excited. She was trying to get all of the information out at the same time and it was becoming difficult for the others to follow.

Rachel and Angelina looked at each other and smiled. They knew how important it was to a young person to be recognized as a woman. They'd been through it themselves.

Before Anna continued, Jack said, "Take your time, Anna. There's no rush. We have all night."

"Okay, I'm sorry," she replied. "Like I said, it was clear that he was worried. He started by telling me that he had an insurance policy through his company for a million dollars, and the beneficiary was Mom. He also explained that he had other small investments and gave me this list."

Anna handed the list to Angelina. She looked at it and passed it to the others. There were four names listed on the small slip of paper; all investment-type companies.

Anna continued. "I was getting scared and I told him so. He said that what he was about to tell me could not be repeated to anyone. He went on to say he loved Mom and me beyond anything and would not put us in harm's way for the world. By then I was really getting scared."

Anna's eyes were starting to tear up. It was obvious that the next part of her story was going to be difficult for her. She took a deep breath before she continued. "He told me that he was offered a promotion and that was great; but the new division he would be working with had ties to the military division of his company. I don't think he knew there was a military division when he started there; at least he never told Mom or me about it. He said that he would be working on a top secret, new product for military application. It was a very special position and he wasn't even sure if he wanted it but he had already stumbled onto some of the information about the project in the company computer system. That was some time ago, before he went to Mexico where he met you guys. He knew right away, that he wasn't supposed to see it – very serious and scary stuff. He said it had the acronym ODD and then told me to forget that reference and never repeat it to anyone. He told me that when he saw the information it was only a day or two after he started the new job in product development. We knew about that promotion, mom and me, but Eddy wasn't sure if he even wanted that one. Eddy really liked to work in the field and this new job was more of an office job. Anyway, as soon as he stumbled onto this secret information, he thought he should tell his new boss what had happened, in case someone was going to get in trouble. He told me he discussed it with his new boss and explained that he got into the file by accident. His boss told him not to worry; he would smooth it over with the big managers in the company. Eddy asked his boss a few general questions but he said he didn't know anything about it either. His boss said he would ask his own superior." Anna paused to gather her thoughts. She continued. "Then Eddy told me that less than a week after their conversation, his boss was killed in an automobile accident. A hit and run. Coincidence? I don't think so," she mimicked. "I could see that Eddy didn't think it was an accident either. He was very concerned about what might happen. I think he was in Mexico when he found out about his boss being killed."

"I knew he received some bad news when we were in Mexico," Reggie stated. "That must have been it."

"I bet you it was," Anna replied. "We didn't hear from Eddy for a few weeks. Anyway, it was a long time afterwards that we got a knock on the door and it's the police telling my mom and me that Eddy and someone named Candice had been killed in Mexico. Some robbery or something and they were sorry to have to tell us but they were dead. The police didn't know the details of how it happened. Just that they were dead and arrangements had been made to send his body back to us. That same day, we got a call from a funeral parlor in Kingston advising us that they had Eddy. Mom and I went to see him at the funeral parlor and all they had was an urn. He was cremated in Mexico. We didn't even have a chance to see him one last time," Anna cried as she sobbed into her handkerchief.

You could have heard a pin drop in the hotel room. The friends were looking at one another with expressions of disbelief, confusion, sadness and even some fear on their faces. Anna's story had ended and she was weeping softly into her hands. She took a deep breath. The friends could see she was trying to control her emotions.

"What do you think?" Anna sniffled.

The group was silent while everyone digested what they had been told. Rachel and Angelina had moved closer to Anna and put their arms around her shoulders. Angelina broke the silence.

"He and Candice went back to Mexico for some reason," Angelina stated. "Did he tell you he was going back to Mexico, Anna?"

"No."

There was another long pause and Angelina said softly as she held Anna. "We need to find out what happened. We will find out what happened to your brother and Candice. There's something serious going on and we owe it to Eddy and Candice to find out what it is."

As she surveyed the group visually, she could see that everyone was on the same page.

"Let's get through the funeral tomorrow and then start to work. Anna, we're going to find you something to eat, a late night snack at the coffee shop, and after that we'll take you home. You've done a great job telling us Eddy's story and we know that he would be proud of you."

The group waited a few moments until Anna had her emotions under control, then left the motel and walked across the street to a small coffee shop. There wasn't much conversation and they finished their drinks fairly quickly. As the others walked back to the motel, Reggie volunteered to drive Anna back to her mother's house.

It was obvious that the group wasn't going to find out a whole lot about their friends' deaths that particular weekend. This was going to take some time and they needed to exercise some caution as well. If what Anna had told them was true, their lives could be in danger. This group was determined to obtain all the facts concerning the death of their friends. It was just a matter of time. They stopped briefly in the lobby of the motel and sat by the bay window overlooking the street.

"I have to head back to Cairo tomorrow, almost immediately after Eddy's funeral, to take care of a couple of sales of some small commuter jets," Angelina explained to the group. "I think we all have to take care of some business before we can free ourselves up to concentrate on our latest challenge. I think this is going to take some time."

"Before we head back to our rooms, I have something to tell you," Jack said. "Unfortunately, Reggie's not here but you can fill him in, Angelina. Just so everyone knows and there are no surprises." He looked directly at Angelina who made a kind of "*who me*" expression back to him. "I have requested and been granted a transfer to our New York office. Not a particularly great job, but I'm looking at other career options. At least it gets me closer to Rachel."

Angelina smiled, "Is there anything more we should know? Do we hear wedding bells perhaps?"

"No wedding bells," Rachel replied. "We just want to spend some more time together and see where it goes."

"I expect that I may be working out of the New York office as early as next week," Jack stated as he smiled at Rachel.

"Or sooner?" she whispered. It was more of a question than a statement.

"I'm sure Reggie will have some witty and humorous comments for you tomorrow about this latest revelation so be prepared for that," Angelina warned.

"He always does," Rachel replied.

"Let's summarize what we know and what we need to find out by the time we next meet," Jack stated. "One, we know that Anna believes they were killed by Eddy's company for supposedly knowing something he shouldn't have. Something we know only as ODD, and we know this because Eddy told her so. Two, we have no idea what an ODD is or what the acronym stands for in this case. We know that OD means oxygen deprivation in the environmental world, because we discussed all that and included it in our Mensa dissertation. Three, we know we need to be very careful, because this has already cost two people their lives. Four, we know that I'm headed for NYC and the lady of my dreams."

Everyone laughed and Rachel blushed. She kissed Jack on the cheek as they walked to their room.

The plans were already in place for Reggie to travel to Cairo in a few weeks to coincide with Angelina's parents' annual cruise of the Mediterranean. He and Angelina expected to spend time naked and sweaty beside the pool. Angelina had Anton looking after the office and she was confident she could deal with anything else that came up from the villa. Reggie was bored out of his mind with actuarial tables and trying to figure out what it was he was supposed to be doing in his new position of Vice President. He was looking forward to some downtime. More specifically, he was looking forward to exploring *every inch* of his gorgeous girlfriend's body. Every inch he promised himself. He also felt that perhaps he should be out there looking for a more interesting vocation.

While Angelina waited for Reggie to return from taking Anna home, she thought about what she was going to do regarding what Anna had told them. What their first step was going to be to find out what happened to their friends. She was considering asking her father for advice. Anwar Evangeline was one of the most successful arms dealers in the Middle East. *They were now supposed to be able to partner in some matters, so why not ask him?* she thought. The secret Eddy had discovered may have military application. Eddy thought it might be part of the military division of the company of which he knew nothing about. She felt comfortable with the idea of asking her father, but not actually having the conversation with him about this mysterious ODD object.

CHAPTER THIRTY-ONE

June 7, 11:00 am EST - Holy Trinity Church
Kingston, Ontario, Canada

The church was full to overflowing. It was clear from the turn-out for his funeral that Eddy was a popular guy. As Angelina sat in the third-row pew, she looked around at the ornate building and wondered what the church she might be married in would look like. She never admitted to anyone, including Reggie, that she was planning to marry him but it was very likely she would. She had never known a man like Reggie. He was kind, funny, thoughtful, annoying from time-to-time, great to look at and all those other characteristics that were part of the man she most wanted to be with. They were a perfect match. She was certain he was the one. She never thought she would make such a decision so soon after meeting someone, however when it came to Reggie, snap decisions seemed to be the only kind she made. She slept with him after knowing him for only eighteen hours, she recalled, and that turned out to be a good decision. *Maybe the decisions one makes quickly turn out better than those you ponder over for long periods of time*, she thought.

Reggie came down the aisle, made the sign of the cross and genuflected before sitting beside Angelina.

"Are you Catholic?" Angelina whispered. She and Reggie had talked about many topics since coming together, yet religion wasn't one of them.

"Yes. I'm Italian. Most Italians are Catholic." He seemed surprised that she wouldn't have already known he was Catholic. He assumed everyone knew most Italians were Catholics.

"We've never discussed religion. Does it bother you that I'm not Catholic?"

"Doesn't bother me but you realize, in order to marry me, you'll likely have to convert."

"Who said anything about marrying you? I just wanted to know if you were Catholic. You have to stop making these snap-assumptions. And why would it be me converting? Maybe it's you who should convert."

"You slept with me on a snap-assumption," he smiled.

"What did I assume?"

"That I would go along with your plans to sleep with me."

"Are you kidding me? Do you expect me to believe you would have turned down the opportunity? This is hardly the place to bring that up. I don't think your mother would approve of her little boy talking like that in Church."

"Are we talking about marriage or sex?" Reggie asked. He had lost his train of thought.

"Neither. We're in Church. Now is not the time," Angelina replied. "I was simply informing you that I'm not Catholic. That's all I said and you got off on all this other stuff. Don't presume, because we enjoy you-know-what, that we're going to be married."

"Can't have a marriage based on you-know-what," Reggie replied. Angelina looked straight ahead. She didn't have a come-back comment. At least not one she could say in church.

"Please stop talking," was the best she could muster.

******

Rachel and Jack were seated two aisles over, and in the second row, immediately behind Eddy's family members. Anna was sitting in front of them with her mother on her left.

Jack leaned forward in his seat. "Eddy was a well liked guy," he whispered to Anna "This church is full and then some."

Anna simply nodded in reply. It was clear that she was on the verge of tears. Jack sat back in his seat as the service began.

The church service lasted about an hour. In the Catholic Church, a full mass is held for funerals. After mass was over, there were a few people who stepped to the podium to say a few words. Each of them spoke about being with Eddy at some point in his youth; at a school dance or during summer vacation. All stories had a humorous element to them. Everyone made a point to tell the group what a fun guy Eddy was to be with; always a joke or a prank and never a harsh word to say about anyone. By the time everyone had spoken, there wasn't a dry eye in the church.

Eddy's uncle spoke last. He thanked everyone for coming and for the countless messages of condolence his sister and niece had received. He announced that there was a small reception at the Knights of Columbus Hall, across the road from Holy Trinity.

It took awhile for the church to empty into the parking lot and for the friends to meet up with each other. They were all on a tight schedule and wouldn't be able to go to the reception, however, they wanted to say goodbye to Anna and Mrs. Milton. They saw the two women shaking hands with various people at the end of the sidewalk leading from the church.

They all shook Mrs. Milton's hand and gave her a hug. Angelina asked Anna if they could speak to her for a minute and motioned for her to take a walk to their car with them.

"Anna, we are so sorry we have to leave so soon but we want to speak with you first," Rachel explained.

"The matters we discussed last night need to be kept confidential," Angelina said. "At least for now."

"I was going to tell my uncle and have him confront Mr. Stanley, the company president, about how we know what he is up to and we know he had a hand in Eddy's death," Anna announced.

"Have you said anything to your uncle yet?" Jack asked.

"No, I plan to before he leaves tomorrow."

"Anna, I know it's difficult and I know you want to get to the bottom of what happened to your brother, but you can't tell anyone what you know. It's too dangerous," Angelina explained.

"I'm not going to let them get away with it," Anna proclaimed.

"And we will help you with that, but you have to be patient. If you tell someone else then you put them in danger,"

"I never thought of that."

"We have resources and contacts that we can call on to find out what happened and who was responsible. If you will trust us; we will uncover the truth," Angelina explained.

"Really?"

"Yes, really. Trust us and we will help you."

It took a few moments for Anna to respond.

"You're right. I can't put others at risk. I need you to promise that you will keep me informed about the investigation,"

"You have our word," Reggie said as he hugged her.

Anna spotted her mother, looking for her. She kissed and hugged the four friends goodbye and walked away.

"Now all we have to do is keep our word," Jack said. He shook Reggie's hand and kissed Angelina goodbye. He and Rachel walked to their car and headed off.

CHAPTER THIRTY-TWO

June 13, 11:00 am EET - Villa Evangeline
Cairo, Egypt

It was the weekend after Eddy's funeral. Angelina was spending the time at her parents' villa. Her parents were making final preparations for their annual cruise of the Mediterranean. There wasn't much to prepare for as the yacht they were going to be on belonged to them. All they had to do was have their secretary make the travel arrangements. Angelina decided that now was the time to ask her father some questions. She and the group had promised Anna they would investigate what happened to Eddy, and they needed to start somewhere. Her mother was lying down as she usually did in mid-afternoon. Angelina could see her dad enjoying some time beside the pool.

As Angelina approached, her father saw her and waved her on, energetically. The last time they were able to speak privately was in New York a few weeks ago. He wanted to take the opportunity to be alone with his daughter. She sat beside him on a chaise. A maid arrived immediately with Angelina's favorite cold beverage. Angelina was deep in thought about what she was going to say to her father. She stood and absently started to remove her robe to take in some rays, when her father called her name in a loud voice.

"What are you wearing?"

Angelina was startled by this sudden burst from her father, "It's my bathing suit," she replied calmly.

"It's more like your underwear! Does your mother know about this?" His voice was getting louder as the conversation continued.

"She was with me when I bought it last year and thought it was quite becoming." That wasn't exactly true. Her mother was with her on the shopping trip, but Angelina had gone to purchase a new bathing suit and some other personal items on her own.

"Hardly the adjective to describe the strings you have tied around your body." He couldn't say much more if his wife had already approved of the purchase. From his perspective, the suit wasn't anything he would have approved his daughter purchasing.

"It's just a bikini. I have a one-piece bathing suit that shows more than this one," she said. It was the heat of the moment and she hadn't meant to convey that particular piece of information. Before her father had a chance to respond to her outburst, she decided to move on.

"Can I talk to you about something, Daddy?"

Her father sat up straight. He remained perfectly still in his seat and immediately closed his eyes. He breathed deeply to quiet his worried thoughts. His mind went to every possible calamity. *She's getting married; is this guy after her money? Is she pregnant? Is she taking drugs and someone is after her for drug money?* There was too much to think about all at one time. As his mind slowed he simply replied, "By all means."

With some reluctance. She sat on the lounger next to him. She hesitated before speaking. She had originally not intended to tell him about the ODD. She changed her mind. If he was going to help them find who killed their friends; he had to know the whole story.

"Daddy, have you ever heard of a military related term called ODD?"

"A what?"

"ODD."

Angelina was watching her father's face when she asked the question, hoping to see a reaction. In most instances, her father had the perfect poker face. It was imperative in his line of business. This time, however, she could clearly see that he winced when she repeated the letters. Her father looked into her eyes and said, "Angelina, what have you gotten yourself into?"

He was visibly shaking at this point.

"I haven't gotten myself into anything," she protested.

"Where did you hear about the ODD?" His voice was growing louder, again.

"So you *do* know what it stands for."

"I know what it is. The question is, why are you asking me about it?"

"So tell me what it is then, Daddy."

"*Daddy,* won't work for this one, Angelina. Daddy is what you call me when you're telling me you have damaged the car or when you come home late after school. Daddy is not what you call me when we are about to have a serious conversation, because this is a very serious conversation we're about to have." As he was speaking, the maid came around the corner with more drinks. Her father didn't even look up, he simply yelled "Not now!!" She turned and literally ran back to the kitchen.

"You're scaring me."

"You're scaring me more than you can imagine," he replied in his same elevated tone.

There was a moment of complete silence as the pair gathered their emotions before they moved on. Her father took in several more deep breaths.

"Let's be calm about this," Angelina said. "Remember, we had the whole *let's work together* conversation in New

York? I want to tell you a story about my friends, Edward and Candice."

"The ones who died a few months ago?"

"Yes, how do you know about that?"

"My dear, I believed there was very little I didn't know about you, although I'm now finding out there is more."

"Are you spying on me?" she asked heatedly.

Realizing he may have already said too much, Anwar decided to take a different tact.

"This isn't about me, Angelina. Tell me what you know."

"This discussion isn't over yet, Mr. Evangeline," she stated.

He knew he was caught but at least now he had time to craft a plausible explanation. Angelina cleared her throat and relayed, almost word for word, what Anna had told them in the hotel room. With each sentence of explanation, the expression on her father's face became more solemn and concerned.

"How many people know about this?" he finally asked.

"Four, including me, and of course, Anna," she replied. She could see that her father was visibly upset by the number.

"They cannot say a word to anyone about this. Do you understand, Angelina?"

"Yes, but what's wrong, Dad?"

"Before we talk any further, let's go into my study. It's more private in there rather than beside the pool," he informed his daughter.

Angelina pulled on her robe and followed her father into the study. Once seated, he came and sat beside her on the couch. He normally sat behind his desk, so she knew this was big stuff.

"What I say here," he began, "never leaves this room."

Angelina nodded her agreement.

"ODD stands for Oxygen Deprivation Device. It is a well-known fact, that in the case of oil rig fire for instance, when the oxygen is removed from that atmosphere the fire goes out, even if it was absent for only a short time. No oxygen, no fire."

Angelina nodded. *So it is the same as Candice was talking about in the environment, an absence of oxygen,* she thought to herself.

"In commercial use, there are usually explosives used to create this *no oxygen environment*," he continued. "We create a big blast; it sucks all the oxygen out of the air around the fire, and the fire goes out. Unfortunately, most often there is also a fair amount of property damage which results from a big blast like this. The fire goes out, but the drill rig is usually damaged and it's very costly to repair." He paused and took a small drink from his glass of wine. "For a number of years, companies have been researching ways to remove oxygen from dangerous fires, like oil rig fires without damaging equipment. In the commercial world, this is considered normal research. Recently, the idea of such a device has also become desirable in a military application. In the military application, the performance of the device is very similar; to remove the oxygen while not damaging assets. By removing oxygen for a calculated period of time, the enemy dies and all assets are left in good order."

Angelina flinched when he said die. Her father continued. "Assets such as tanks, missile weapons, buildings etc. In years gone by, the efforts were placed on trying to make more powerful explosives. Nuclear weapons were developed which destroy everything in their path, and then some, while leaving contamination for years. Using an ODD would have the same result on your enemy; they are dead, but there is no loss of assets; the perfect weapon. We really have no idea if this technology is even feasible, let alone already exists. We aren't even certain if there is anyone currently working on the development of the technology. The problem with developing this equipment for military applications is keeping it out of the hands of the wrong people. There are some factions that believe research, any research and development of this type of device should be halted entirely.

It is simply too dangerous on a global scale. How to prevent or stop it is another matter. I happen to agree that any research into ODD for military use should be halted. You might be surprised by this, knowing what I do for a living, but this is bad news, a dooms-day weapon if they can perfect it, and it scares the hell out of me. Me and a lot of others as well, I'm sure. Anyone with any consideration for the continuation of the human race, at least. Humans are a unique species to our world, Angelina. We are the only animals, on the planet, who consciously develop strategies and techniques to destroy one another. Other animal species kill. They kill for food and survival, but humans kill for totally different reasons. Some say we kill for no reason, but that's not true. There is always a reason and almost always it's one of three reasons. Greed, power, or religious intolerance. We humans are a strange breed, Angelina."

There was another long pause in the conversation.

"You wanted to know what I knew about ODD. So what do you think?" he asked his daughter, while she sat beside him with a solemn look on her face. "How might we work together?"

CHAPTER THIRTY-THREE

June 15, 10:00 am EET - Airtec Offices
Cairo, Egypt

Angelina was in her Cairo office, awaiting a conference call from the U.S. She heard the phone ring and Anton tapped on her door to indicate it was the call she was waiting for.

"Put it through," Angelina instructed.

"Hi, babe." was the first voice she heard. It was Reggie. "Everyone's here. Let's get this done."

"Before we begin," Angelina explained to the group, "I want you all to know that I have had a conversation about this matter with my father."

There was silence on the air before Rachel asked.

"Why would you ask your father about something like this?"

"Because, he knows about things like this. I need everyone to just listen for a few minutes. I don't mean to be forceful with you guys, but this is very important and we all need to be on the same page here before we have any further discussions about what Anna told us a few weeks ago."

"Okay..." Rachel said. One could tell from her voice that she was still trying to make sense of why Angelina would have a conversation with her father about a subject such as this.

"Good." she replied. "After this call today and from this point on, we cannot have any conversations over the telephone, through e-mails, or text messages about the information Anna shared with us. I know that sounds strange and scary but please listen. My father was very upset when I asked him if he knew about it and what he knew. He actually yelled at me and that's not like him. He knows what it is and he has warned me that it is extremely dangerous, and we need to take great care in what we do. I have thought about this a lot. I think the best and safest way to proceed is for all of us to meet in person. The best place is here in Cairo. More correctly, at my parents Villa just outside the city."

"Cairo," Rachel said. "What's in Cairo that would relate to Eddy and Candice?"

"I can't say anymore over the phone. I am asking all of you to trust me on this. I need you to come to Cairo next week. Trust that I have your best interests at heart."

There was silence on the phone. Rachel broke it.

"The last time we were together we couldn't pull you and Reggie apart. This better not be an excuse to get into Reggie's pants and freak me out again. I still have recurring dreams about that traumatic disclosure in my life."

"I assure you Dr. Wi," Reggie said, "we don't need a special reason to get into each other's pants."

"Oh please," she replied, "let's keep it clean here. I don't need to hear every sordid detail."

This light hearted exchange seemed to break the tension of the call. It usually didn't take much for this group to settle into the normal dynamics of their relationships.

"If we are in agreement with," Angelina continued, "Anton has booked all of you on a flight out of New York for next Wednesday. Bring your bathing suits. It's very hot here. My parents are away, so we have the villa to ourselves."

"What villa and who the hell is Anton?" Rachel chirped. "Since when do you live in a villa and who is this Anton guy?"

"I don't live there. It's my parents' villa. I'm staying here while they're away. Anton is my assistant in the office. He's a great assistant and will look after everything you need for the trip."

"Another surprise like the one we got at Reggie's parents' estate? Between that babe of a limo driver and now you and your villa and your assistant," Rachel mused. "Who are you people anyway?"

"Hey, I told you guys, it is not my estate it's my parents'," Reggie protested. "And Sam is a great driver."

"I know. I know what you said," Rachel replied, "but there are a few too many surprises when it comes to parents. Be prepared to explain when we see you next week, Ms. Evangeline."

CHAPTER THIRTY-FOUR

June 16, 11:00 am EET - Airtec Offices
Cairo, Egypt

The day following the conference call, Angelina received an e-mail from Eddy's sister. It indicated that Anna had received a package and needed to speak to Angelina about it. A rather vague request but Angelina thought she would call her, if for no other reason, than to find out how she and her mother were doing. She placed the call to Canada.

"Hello Anna, this is Angelina Evangeline. How are you and your mom doing?"

"Hi, we're fine. Did you receive my e-mail?"

"Yes, that's why I'm calling; what exactly was in the package?"

"It's a disc and it came from Eddy. He must have sent it before he was killed. It took a long time to get here. I came home last night and it was sitting at our front door. I opened it. The only thing in the package is a disc with Eddy's name on it"

"What's on the disc?"

"I don't know. That's the problem. As soon as I put it in my computer to open it, there's a password prompt. I have no idea what the password is. I tried all the usual ones that Eddy used but none will open the file. Do you think it's important?"

"I can't be certain, but my guess is since he took the time to arrange to have it sent to you after his death, it's likely very important. Why don't we do this, Anna? As we speak, I have some friends heading over to Cairo. One of these people is a computer software genius. If anyone can open it he can. I'm confident that we can get it opened. Once we find out what's on it, I can let you know."

"Is that Jack who I met here?" Anna asked

"Yes, Jack is a master with computers."

"You promise you will let me know?"

"Absolutely."

"Okay. How do I send it to you?" Anna asked.

"Call Federal Express and give them this number," Angelina flipped up the desk calendar on the front of her desk to where she kept special notes. She read off the special courier-account number to Anna.

"You've got it?"

"Yes."

"Call Federal Express and tell them you need them to come to your house and pick up a letter. Give them the number I just gave you. They will have it here in two days. This is a special account number I use to ship legal documents for the purchase of aircraft. Do you have any questions?"

"I forgot you sell airplanes." Anna said. "That's cool."

"Yes, it is cool. Anna, do you understand the instructions?" Angelina asked, trying not to sound annoyed by the twenty questions. "This is important."

"Yes. I will call them right now. You will let me know what's on the disc, won't you?" she asked.

"Absolutely."

"I could fly there and bring it with me," Anna offered.

"You could. Do you have a passport?"

"No, I don't," Anna lamented. "I'll send it by Federal Express today. Bye, Angelina."

CHAPTER THIRTY- FIVE

June 18, 10:00 am EET - Villa Evangeline
Cairo, Egypt

Within two days, the team had arrived in Egypt. Anton arranged the taxi from the airport to the Villa Evangeline which was located at the crest of the highest hill outside Cairo. As the group taxied to their destination, they were greatly impressed by the beauty and ruggedness of the Egyptian countryside. They were overwhelmed by the intense heat. Stepping from the arrivals door at the airport to the air-conditioned taxi cab was enough to take your breath away. Anton had instructed the taxi company to take a route that would provide the guests with some beautiful views of Cairo, yet ensuring they avoid the more questionable areas. For the most part, the trip was traveled on paved roads not unlike those found in the United States. The taxi stopped at the main gate of the villa and the driver leaned out of his window to push the call button on the post located to the left side of the driveway. They could see the security cameras scanning the entire driveway area. The gates slowly opened and the taxi continued up the driveway to the main parking area. Angelina was there to greet them. Everyone got a big hug from her and when she came to Reggie, she kissed him passionately on the lips and held it for a very long time.

"Okay, okay get a room you two," Rachel joked.

"We have one," Angelina replied. "And so do you my girl. Best in the house, facing one of the loveliest views in the country. Not that you're going to be looking out the window at any time," she joked as she gave Rachel a friendly tap on her backside.

As the friends walked through the main house, they were amazed at the architecture of the villa. It was mid-century in some ways yet modern in others. Because the villa was situated on a large hill, the rooms located at the back of the building were partially underground which helped to cool the space. The windows overlooked the hillside and landscape beyond. It was almost like they were suspended in mid-air. Concrete was the predominant building material, chosen to keep the house as cool as possible in the Egyptian summer heat. In the main living room, there was an entire wall of glass overlooking the pool and surrounding courtyard. The floors were marble, again to keep the dwelling cooler in summer. It was an elegant house but not palatial.

The crew dropped their bags in their rooms and gathered in the living room for a cold drink. It was a scorching hot day and the air conditioned house and cool drinks were just what they needed.

"Listen," Angelina told the group, "I had a call from Anna the other day."

"Eddy's little sister?" Jack asked.

"She's hardly little my friend. She has a better figure than me," Rachel joked.

"I didn't notice."

"Not likely," she replied.

"Apparently..." Angelina continued. "Anna received a computer disc from Eddy. It arrived by mail and was on her front step when she arrived home a few nights ago. She couldn't open it because it's password protected. She has no clue as to the password. She's couriered it here and it should be arriving late this afternoon, or early evening. Jack, do you think you will be able to open it?" she asked.

"If it's shiny and round I can open it," he boasted in jest.

"I'm suggesting we hold off on our discussion about the investigation until we see what's on the disk, if that's okay with everyone. In the meantime, it's hot as hell outside; who wants to take a rest and who wants to take a swim? My parents have a beautiful pool just outside these doors. Anyone opting to rest is required to rest and not mess up the sheets this early in the day," Angelina said while staring at Rachel.

"I'm not the one who hides under bed sheets as you may recall. I certainly didn't come here to rest. Let's go for a swim."

It didn't take very long for everyone to change into their swim suits. Angelina and Reggie were first to arrive and were at pool-side when Jack and Rachel arrived. Jack and Reggie quickly slipped into blue water, after almost burning their feet standing still on the hot patio stones. Rachel and Angelina opted for a chaise lounge on the cooler grass surrounding the patio. The grassed area around the pools was watered frequently during the day and for most of each evening. This kept it both green and somewhat cooling to the bare feet.

The ladies applied a modest amount of sun block lotion. Enough to allow for some tanning yet protect their skin from the intensity of the Egyptian afternoon sun. Angelina required less lotion than Rachel because of her darker skin tone. They stretched out on their lounges to enjoy the relaxation. Angelina glanced over at her friend beside her.

"If you're going to catch some sun, you have to take off your robe."

Rachel hesitated before she untied the rope belt around the robe and let it drop next to her on the chaise.

"That's a really cute suit," Angelina said while examining her friend's attire.

"I bought it in New York and I really liked it in the store, but putting it on just now, I think it might show too much."

"Does Jack like it?"

"Yes, Jack likes it. What's not for him to like?" Rachel replied in a joking manner.

"I think it's perfect. Be careful you don't get too much sun on your lily white skin."

"I don't have lily white skin," Rachel protested. "I'll have you know, this is the first year I can actually say I have a tan. I'm quite proud of myself." Rachel slid the strap of her suit off her shoulder to prove there was a difference in her skin tone.

"I see. I'm impressed, but in my country you're still a snowball," Angelina smiled. She laid back down and closed her eyes.

"I'm far from a snowball. Nice way to describe your friend, Ms. Evangeline," Rachel joked as she laid back in her lounger. She was trying to sound insulted by her friend's comment but when she compared herself to Angelina beside her, she was a snowball. She would have given anything to have Angelina's exotic skin tone.

"I like my suit," Rachel announced in a confident tone. "I'm here to get a tan, so let the tanning begin," she said and she settled into her chaise. She was careful to make sure all her parts were covered – at least as much as her suit allowed.

The ladies chatted while the men cooled off in the pool. The level of conversation slowly faded as the afternoon progressed. The two women drifted in and out of sleep in the warm sun. Their peaceful slumber was broken by a stranger's voice.

"Who would be Angelina Evangeline?" the deep voice asked. It was the courier delivering the disk.

Both Angelina and Rachel were startled but Rachel even more so. She quickly checked herself to make certain everything important was covered. Angelina didn't move, other than to identify herself and sign for the package.

Rachel was discreetly trying to pull her robe over herself. Trying to cover at least some of her exposed body.

"That was embarrassing," Rachel announced as the courier walked away.

"I'm sure we made his day," Angelina replied with a smile. She stood and began to put her robe on. "We have the disk, gentlemen," she announced. "Let's get to work. I think you and I, my dear," she said to Rachel, "need to change. These guys need to concentrate on the task at hand and are easily distracted."

CHAPTER THIRTY-SIX

June 18, 2:00 pm EET - Villa Evangeline
Cairo, Egypt

Everyone quickly changed back into more appropriate clothing. Rachel felt far more comfortable in shorts and a top. As she walked through the hallways on the way to her room, she was impressed that Angelina's parents had such a beautiful estate. A far cry from the meager existence most of her family and relatives had in China. Once changed, everyone returned to the living room wearing shorts and tee shirts.

"We should go into the media room," Angelina suggested.

She led the group to a lower level. Once everyone was seated, Angelina picked up the disk and took a closer look at it. There were no distinguishing marks on the disk that Anna had sent. It was just a normal looking CD. Angelina loaded the disk into the computer and the big screen at the end of the room lit up. She stepped away from the computer and motioned Jack to take over.

"You are the computer wizard. We're going to need your expertise to see what it is Eddy sent."

Jack positioned himself at the keyboard and worked through the normal boot-up screens.

"We don't have a password for this, do we?" Jack realized quickly.

"That's the problem," Angelina explained. "Anna couldn't open the disk and has no clue what the password might be."

"Normally," Jack explained, "the passwords people use are in some way indicative of that person's nature. Ball fans might use a baseball phrase as an example; their favorite team or player is most common. In the case of Edward, what would we say was his main focus?"

Without a moment's hesitation the other three people in the room all said.

"Sex."

"I'm going with that," Jack said, smiling at their response. "We apparently all know Eddy was a pervert. What would he choose as a password?"

The group thought for a few seconds and started to call out words and phrases for Jack to try.

"Breasts, bottom, vagina, penis, love making, oral sex," Rachel suggested in rapid succession.

Jack stopped what he was doing to smile at Rachel's enthusiasm.

"Keep in mind that this is Eddy we're talking about. I would doubt that he would say, *vagina*," he explained. He returned to the keyboard and continued entering potential passwords.

"Okay then, tits, ass, pussy, boobs, and blowjob," were the suggestions from Reggie.

Rachel and Angelina looked at him. "Really," Rachel said in her most proper lady-like voice.

"No, it's actually Candy," Jack yelled. "I'm in, let's see what we have."

The disk fired up and the image they saw on the screen gave them pause. It was a full shot of both Eddy and Candice sitting at a table, making the video disk they were now watching. It was sad to think their friends were no longer with them. Jack pushed the next tab and Edward's voice filled the room.

"Hey guys. Well I guess if you're listening to this, I'm no longer alive. I sent this disk to a good friend of mine with the specific instructions to send it on to Anna if anything should ever happen to me. My friend was curious as to why, but agreed to do this for me. You have likely guessed already that I have gotten myself into some serious hot water. I'm hoping that I haven't put Candice in danger as well," he said while he leaned over and kissed Candice on the cheek.

"We're in Mexico, not far from Mexico City on a photo shoot. Actually the shoot is over and we're heading back tomorrow. Can you believe I would ever be on a Victoria's Secret photo shoot? This is what every man dreams of," he continued as Rachel and Angelina smiled. This was the Eddy they knew and loved. "Candice got the approval to allow me on the set as long as I behaved. I did although it took every ounce of self control I had," he smiled.

"I had to hose him down once in a while," Candice was heard to say off camera.

"Only twice? You ladies should consider some of this year's evening wear. It's really... nice. You guys can thank me later," Eddy joked. "Anyway, I'm here with Candice and we are both enjoying ourselves."

His expression became more serious.

"If I am gone, it's important to know that my death was no accident. That may be the way it's reported, but believe me, if I died it was no accident. First, it's important that my mom and sister know that I had several insurance policies. I explained all of this to my sister, Anna, a few weeks ago but in case she forgets, I have good documentation on all of this. I had a million-dollar life policy on my own and a five-hundred thousand dollar policy through work. The one through work should be tripled if they consider my death an accident or anything other than suicide, so it should be one and a half million. That should be a total of 2.5 million. Could you follow up to make sure that's what they receive and advocate for them, if it's otherwise. I don't expect you guys to take care of mom and Anna but I would really appreciate it if you could check in with them occasionally."

There was silence in the room. Rachel could feel the tears welling up as she made an effort not to give into her emotions. It was as though Eddy was speaking to them from across that table he was sitting at, it was so real.

"If something happens to Candice," Edward continued hesitantly, "You should know that her parents are both in ill-health. The less they know the better."

With that he looked at Candice and prompted her to speak.

"Hey guys, I know Eddy is over-blowing this whole thing," Candice said in her usual upbeat tone, "but just in case he isn't, I love you guys. Even in the short time we have known each other, I really love all of you. My parents have all my paperwork. They are both suffering from Alzheimer's like Eddy said. I doubt that a visit would do them much good so do what you think best."

She glanced at Eddy to pick up the conversation.

"Alright," he continued. "Here's the long and short of it. I discovered some frightening information and it's of real concern to a lot of very powerful people. My boss was killed, albeit in a hit and run accident, a few days after he asked some questions concerning what I am about to tell you, so we know this is serious shit. Keep your wits about you and take care."

The friends' attention was glued to the screen. Listening to every word Eddy was saying while trying not to be too emotional about the loss of their friends. Edward continued.

"I was working on my computer late one night, getting caught up so I could get away for the Mensa conference, and I stumbled onto a file that was password protected in the main office computer. I was curious so I decided to try to open the file. It turned out that I.T. had given me a higher security clearance than they should have. When I used my password, it opened the file. I looked at some of the data, but didn't recognize it as anything I had been briefed about that we were working on. I was curious about what it might be. I assumed I had the wrong clearance code and shouldn't be in there at all, so I shut it down. I got thinking about it later and thought maybe I or someone else could get into trouble. I decided to at least report it to my boss. The next morning I went to my boss, John Bentley, and explained to him what had happened. After a short discussion he agreed with me about how it had happened. He assured me it was fine and believed it was an IT error. A costly one as it turned out for me," Edward said almost under his breath. "John told me that he was meeting with the big guy, Mr. Stanley, and he would explain what happened, and let me know if there were any problems. When he didn't get back to me, I figured everything was okay and I left for the Mensa conference. I met the love of my life and you guys which were two of the best things that have ever happened to me. There were a few things that happened at the conference that struck me as strange. Then I received the call from Monica that John had been killed in an accident. When I got back to the office after the conference, I started to think about everything and some pieces of a puzzle began to fall into place. It really started to come together when old-man Stanley called me into his office and offered me John's job as Manager of the department. He went on about being a team player and how he and I could work closely on some of the more confidential projects. From his choice of words and his voice inflection, I was getting the feeling that being offered John's job was a kind of a do-it-or-else offer. Take the job or get out or whatever. I ask him a few questions; nothing too specific. They were about what I had seen in the secret files. I was trying to feel him out. I could see that really pissed him off, but he kept his cool during our meeting. His parting words were something to the effect of take the job and work with me in total secrecy or else. I didn't know what the or-else was but there was one implied for certain. I went home and thought about it. Candice and I talked about it a little on the phone. I even spoke to my friend, Monica, our office manager about it. I was careful not to give her any secret information, but I wanted her opinion on me taking on John's position."

Eddy stopped to take a sip of his beer before he continued.

"Monica was excited for me, being offered the job and all, but she had concerns about how some of the longer term employees were going to feel about it. She had even more concerns about why I was offered the job. Not that she didn't think I could do it, but it was a big move for someone so new to the company. Then she told me that she had concerns about the death of John Bentley. Nothing concrete, simply that there was something wrong, that his death was not an accident. She had no proof of any wrong doing, but it got me thinking. I thought about what had occurred while I was in Mexico. Remember the guys who hassled me in the hallway at the dance? Reggie and Jack stepped in and they took off, but I had the feeling they would have done something if you hadn't intervened. Thanks, by the way, for that," he joked. "Then there were the two people who were killed in the hotel. Their room wasn't on my floor. It was on the floor above mine, and prior to that was the hit and run accident that resulted in John Bentley's death. It was simply all too much. I made a decision to find out more about what I had seen in the secret files. I went back to my computer and backed up the drive and rebooted the hard drive so it would recover some of the old data and next thing I knew I had my higher security code back. Guess the IT guys aren't that bright a bunch because I had full access to the files and I opened them. There were several files and attachments, and a cover letter from the CEO of the company. The files, the letter, and every attachment I could find are on this disk.

What I discovered, was that there is a new device developed with the acronym ODD. It is a similar acronym to the one we highlighted in or Mensa paper, OD in the environment. For the life of me, I couldn't figure out the connection until I was talking to Candice. Apparently, this ODD is similar to the marine OD."

He paused to take a drink of his beer.

"It turns out that our company was working on a new implosive device to remove oxygen from the air. My guess is that the second *D* refers to device. We were looking at Oxygen Deprivation or Depriving Device, ODD. Because we are in the natural resources business and deal with mines and oil companies, my first thought was that this is a new way to extinguish oil rig fires or maybe something that could be used by fire departments to put out burning buildings and shit. With an oil rig, you want to pull out the oxygen to put the fire out, but that's typically done with explosive material. You usually end up with a damaged rig and a lot of costly repairs. I could not imagine what the hell kind of product we could have developed that would be an implosive. I have no idea but apparently it exists, or it's close to becoming a reality, and I believe it's not for the betterment of mankind."

Edward paused for another drink.

"I'm Canadian; my beer is very important to me," he joked with his audience. "From what I read and you guys can read the stuff, it looks to me like they want to use this to kill people, a military application. This is about somehow pulling the oxygen out of the area where your enemy is standing and they suffocate. No damage to equipment or the environment, just a bunch of dead bodies. This was scary stuff. The more I read, the more it looks like Chemico isn't the only and likely not the biggest partner in this scheme. It looks to me like we were just a small component of a much larger project."

While Edward was explaining, Angelina recalled the conversation she had with her father not too long ago. He said basically the same thing as Eddy. Almost word for word.

"Here's the kicker," Eddy continued. "Airtec is the company that's working on the delivery system for this doomsday device. They appear to be running most of the show while our company is working on the new type of explosive. But your outfit, Jack, is in on it as well. Softco is the main player on the software side. Airtec has contracted the work to your company. What do you make of that? What are the odds of us working for three of the key companies in on this horrible weapon, meeting at a Mensa conference in Mexico? I haven't figured that one out yet. It's as though someone put us all together in Mexico for some reason."

The four friends looked at one another with puzzled expressions on their faces.

"That's all I know, guys. I hope it's enough. I was first thinking that you could go to the authorities with this, but my gut tells me that might be dangerous. If you think about it, being able to kill people without doing any property damage has to be the ultimate weapon of mass destruction. Bush may have had it right ten years ago, after all. This is big so think carefully about how you want to proceed. I believe the objective should be to destroy the technology rather than eliminate this particular situation. If this technology works, the world is doomed."

He paused while he formulated his final comments in his mind.

"And one last thing," Eddy continued. "The most important is the password to the detailed attachments on this disk. It's very secretive. If others lay their hands on this stuff, everyone is in danger. Angelina, I chose the password to be as safe as Reggie's high school locker used to be. You will know what that means. I love you guys and I've loved our time together. Take care and work smart on this one," he smiled as the screen dimmed.

With that, the prompt moved to the next request for a password. The group sat silent as their friends' image faded from the screen. Everyone had tears in their eyes. They were trying to get their collective emotions under control.

Jack was first to break the silence. "Let's kick some ass here and save the world. Anyone got any ideas what the next password would be?"

Angelina appeared to be deep in thought before she blurted out: "38-24-36", that's the combination."

"What? 38-24-36 sound like your measurements," Jack joked.

"Nice try and I wish sicko," Angelina replied. "Remember you perverts were goggling Dr. Julia Peterson when we were in Mexico; you know the *Playboy* pin-up from 1987 who was a member of Mensa."

"Oh yeah... I do," Reggie said. "She had one kick-ass body if I recall when Jack was looking at the pictures."

"Right." Angelina said. "It was all of you with the cell phones below the table. The number that was on the paper you handed around was 38-24-36."

"Let's try that," Jack said as he used the keyboard. "We're in! Good work Angelina."

Everyone in the room had brought their own lap-tops on the trip. Having access to one's computer these days was a necessity, and in this case it made it easy for everyone to review the data. Jack quickly linked everyone's computer to a shared drive and they began their review. Each member of the team had a different area of expertise. Rachel spent a great deal of her time reviewing the numerous drawings that were in the file. Reggie mentally ran all the calculations, while Jack reviewed the control software strategy included in the package. Angelina was reading the background information, trying to determine who the main players in this scheme were. It appeared that Eddy was correct in his opinion that Airtec was the lead member. There was a great deal of data to deal with all at one time, and the friends were beginning to show fatigue from their trip and the inevitable jet lag.

Before they knew it, it was eleven o'clock. Angelina suggested they call it a day and get some sleep. The suggestion was welcomed by all and after a night-cap, everyone retired to their rooms for a well deserved night's sleep.

After lying awake for half an hour, Angelina turned to Reggie with her big green eyes penetrating his and said; "You know, I've never made love to anyone in my bed at home before."

Reggie thought about the obvious invitation for a moment before responding.

"That's likely because anyone making love to you, as you so quaintly put it, would end up dead, if your father found out."

"My father isn't here," she replied. She smiled and rolled on top of him. Reggie reached over and turned off the light on the nightstand next to the bed.

CHAPTER THIRTY-SEVEN

June 19, 1:00 am EET - Villa Evangeline
Cairo, Egypt

Reggie and Angelina had fallen asleep shortly after making love. It was one a.m. when the entire house began to tremble. Angelina was first to be woken. She listened to the noise and felt the tremors for a few seconds before waking Reggie. Once she had identified the noise, they shot out of bed; pulled on some clothes, and she and Reggie raced down the hall to Jack and Rachel's room.

Jack and Rachel were dead asleep and hadn't heard or felt a thing until Angelina burst into their room and woke both of them. She shook Rachel gently at first and then more firmly when she didn't respond. Jack was startled when his eyes opened to the darkened room. Reggie turned on the overhead lights causing both Rachel and Jack to shade their eyes from the sudden burst of light. They were groggy but awake. Rachel sat up in bed and remained very still. She was feeling the tremors and could barely hear a faint noise coming from down the hall.

"Get dressed and meet us in the living room, quickly," Angelina said. Both she and Reggie left their room and ran down the hall towards the front of the house.

Rachel and Jack dressed quickly and ran after them. They weren't sure what was going on but Angelina sounded pretty serious so they knew it must be important. Upon reaching the living room, Rachel walked straight towards the large front window.

"Is it an earthquake?" Rachel asked. She stepped in front of the window and began to pull back the draperies.

As the draperies opened, a bright light appeared through the glass and the window began to fracture with hundreds of star shaped marks. It was obvious that these were bullets. Obvious to Angelina, at least. Rachel, however, thought she had done something to damage the glass and jumped back as it continued to fracture.

"Stop, don't stand in front of the windows!" Angelina yelled. She dove to push Rachel away from the shattering glass. They both landed hard on the tile floor with Angelina covering Rachel's body. "Get down. Everyone get down behind the couch. Try to move as close to the back of the room as you can," she instructed.

As they crawled to the back of the room, Angelina was examining Rachel's body; looking for blood.

"Are you hit? Are you injured?" she asked in a panicked voice. "Is anyone hurt?" she yelled to the group. "Stay down and move back."

Since it didn't appear that anyone was hurt, Angelina quickly crawled to the far corner of the room. Once there, she reached her arm up to what looked like a wall thermostat; she punched in a series of numbers and immediately a metal blind began to lower over the outside of the windows. It took only a few seconds before the entire room was shielded from the outside view and hopefully from whoever was shooting at them. A helicopter could be heard passing by the windows. With each pass, it continued to spray the building with bullets. The sound of the impact had changed. It was no longer hitting glass; it was striking the heavy metal material shielding the window. The bullets did not seem to be penetrating the armor plates.

"No one panic," Angelina gasped as she gained her composure. "We're protected behind these blinds, unless they throw something heavier at us."

Jack held Rachel close to him to protect her. "What the fuck is going on?" he yelled.

"We're under attack," Angelina replied. "I know that sounds scary but I need all of you to stay calm and listen to me. Follow my instructions to the letter, and we'll be fine." Angelina paused to catch her breath. "This place is a fortress. It would take an army to break in, once these steel shields are down. We need to leave this room and go back to the media room where we were last night. That room is below ground. We will be perfectly safe down there," Angelina pointed toward the stairs leading to the lower rooms.

No one said a word as they followed her instructions. It took only a few moments for the group to gather in the viewing room. They could still hear the bullets striking the shield in the living room, but it seemed less frightening from a further distance away.

"Let's have it," Jack demanded. "What the hell is going on here? Who is shooting at us and why do you live in a house with armor plated shutters?"

"I'll explain later," Angelina said. She kissed both Jack and Rachel on the cheek, as a sign of happiness that neither one of them was injured. "Reggie, I need to return to the upper floor. There's a window up there that can't be seen from the outside. I need to reach that window. Can you stay with me? Jack, I need you to stay here with Rachel."

Jack protested. "I can help. Tell me what you need me to do. I have never been in the position of having a helicopter gunship shooting at me. I'm on a steep learning curve here."

"Thanks, sweetie," Angelina smiled, "but I need you to look after Rachel first. I couldn't live with myself if anything happened to her or you for that matter."

Jack reluctantly agreed.

"What are you planning to do?" Reggie asked.

"I'll explain on the way," Angelina replied. She led the way out and down the hall. "In short, I plan to shoot that chopper out of the sky if I can get to the correct vantage point."

Reggie looked at her with a sense of wonder in his eyes. "I'm good with that," he said. He collected his thoughts and followed Angelina to a side stairway. "No big deal; we shoot down choppers every weekend where I come from."

"I'll go up first," she said. Then she hesitated for a moment and turned back towards Reggie. "And no comments about how nice my ass looks, please. You can look and touch as much as you want, once we get out of this mess. Concentrate on the task at hand," she jokingly said with a smile and a quick kiss on his lips.

"Right, no ass touching," he repeated with disappointment as they started climbing the stairs.

At the top of the stairs, Reggie peered through the tiny window. He had a clear view of everything around the perimeter of the complex. There was a dramatic drop in the landscape, once you looked beyond the fence surrounding the compound. The villa had been built on the crest of the hill to provide the best views of the surrounding countryside. He could see the chopper as it flew past and circled around for another run. He could see the damage the heavy caliber bullets were doing to the surrounding landscape. *This small helicopter was chopping up the outside pretty good*, he thought. *Someone's going to be pissed.*

Angelina twisted the dial on the combination lock and opened a cabinet that was located against the back wall of the tiny room. She pulled out a very long, very shiny, and very lethal looking long rifle and began to affix it to a base that was set up in the window. Reggie was not a stranger to guns. His father had an impressive collection in the basement. He had looked at them quite often as an adolescent but he had never seen a weapon like this one.

"Nice gun," he said.

"Thanks," Angelina smiled. "It's no bow and arrow but I think it's going to do the job."

"Bows and arrows are powerful too, you know," Reggie quipped.

"I'll use this if you don't mind," she replied and she began to fasten the weapon to a mounting bracket that was on the sill of the window.

Angelina was set and ready to go. Her rifle was mounted and she was bringing the telescopic site into focus for the next fly-by. As Reggie watched, he saw a number of heavily armed men, dressed in military attire, starting to spread out around the compound. He pointed them out to Angelina.

"Looks like we have company," he said while looking at the ground below.

Angelina took a brief glance at the men and returned her attention to her rifle.

"They're with us. It took them long enough," she said in an angry tone.

The chopper could be seen in the distance. It was clearly making another run at the villa. By this time, the men on the ground were both shooting at the chopper and trying to stay under cover, away from the spray of bullets spewing from the side door where the shooter was clearly visible. He was secured by a safety harness which allowed him to hang a fair distance away from the inside. This gave him the best vantage point from which to assault his target. Angelina was focused on the shooter as her finger squeezed the trigger. The next sound heard was from her rifle firing a single shot that echoed through the tiny room. Reggie kept his eye on the chopper as it completed its fly-by. The gunman's lifeless body was hanging from the safety harness. A clear shot, one shot, and he was dead. The chopper pilot, realizing the shooter was dead, retreated off into the distance.

"Pretty good shooting there, Annie Oakley," Reggie remarked. "You're full of surprises."

Angelina leaned over and kissed him on the mouth and put her arms around him.

"No surprises, I told you I could shoot," she replied. She picked up several boxes of bullets off the shelf in the cabinet.

It wasn't very long before their pleasure was interrupted by the sound of the chopper headed back for another run.

"It's coming back!" Reggie yelled.

"I see that. My guess is that they will try to hit us with something larger than bullets."

"That doesn't sound good. Can we take a hit from something larger than bullets?"

"Not sure; but we're about to find out," Angelina said while she watched the approaching gunship. She began refocusing her gun in the window. "In the mean time, I'll see what I can do with this." she said as she took aim.

As the chopper was about to cross the air space close to the villa, a deep whooshing noise could be heard. It sounded like another helicopter, but at a far deeper pitch. Angelina took her sights off the chopper and stood back from the window. As Angelina and Reggie watched beyond the tiny window, a huge helicopter came into view. It appeared slowly from below the sight line of the hill. As if time stood still and then started again in one-quarter time, the massive machine rose into the air like a phoenix. Angelina smiled when she recognized the new player in this deadly game. It was the ATT 720 Panther helicopter. The same machine used by the friends to tour the skies over New York. This time it's full armament had been mounted making this the most deadly attack helicopter ever made.

"It's Wendy Moore," Angelina muttered under her breath.

Wendy and the chopper had been in this area for several weeks, providing training to the new owner of the bird. She was now in the air and prepared to protect the villa. Angelina began to explain to Reggie what was happening. She spoke softly. It was like calling the play-by-play in a football game in slow motion. Angelina first identified the chopper that was attacking them.

"That's a Mercury model machine that has been retrofitted."

"It's a lot smaller than the other one," Reggie observed.

"They brought a pea shooter to a gun fight," she replied as she smiled.

"Who's flying the big one?"

"Wendy," was Angelina`s only response. Her eyes were fixed on the sky surrounding the villa. "Watch this."

"They look like two dragonflies hovering over the pond in central park," Reggie said.

"This ain't Central Park," Angelina replied under her breath.

They continued to watch the choppers dance. The smaller, Mercury chopper slowed. Its flight-line was blocked by the Panther which slowly ascended and hovered over the villa's air space. One could only imagine what that pilot must have thought when his approach was blocked by this super-chopper. Then, as if he was challenging the Panther, the Mercury began to advance on the villa. It moved slowly yet it was clear that it was an offensive move. The Panther glided into a defensive position as effortlessly as it had risen from below. Time seemed to slow even more as the two machines hovered as if waiting for the puck to be dropped in a hockey game. Again the Mercury attempted an aggressive move only to be countered by the lumbering giant. It must have been frustration that prompted the Mercury chopper to release a short burst of small caliber fire towards the Panther. It had no affect on the Panther's protective armor.

"That's your last mistake," Angelina observed under her breath.

There was an eerie stillness as both pilots contemplated their next move. Then a bright flash of light came from the Panther; followed instantly by the accompanying stream of fire exiting the back of the craft. It was clear that it had just launched a missile. The Mercury chopper instantly exploded in a ball of flame and crashed to the ground, rolling down the hill and out of sight. The Panther maintained its position. It was waiting for another attack, perhaps from a second machine. After a few minutes, the Panther turned slowly; moved closer to the villa and descended to land near the pool. The engines were left running. Angelina's cell phone rang. She immediately flipped it open.

"Nice shot, girlfriend," Angelina said.

She listened for a few moments. It was clear it was the chopper pilot speaking to Angelina.

"Thanks again. We'll see you back in the States," Angelina replied and she disconnected the call.

"Wendy?" Reggie asked.

"Yes, the pilot who took us for a ride in New York. In fact that was the same chopper we flew in. I told you guys it was headed for overseas when we first boarded."

"That was the same helicopter? It looks a lot bigger."

"You'd look a lot bigger too if you had several million dollars worth of guns hanging off your belt," Angelina replied while she watched the helicopter disappear in the distant horizon.

"I love Wendy," Reggie replied in jest.

Yes, I think he would once he saw her, Angelina thought to herself. Wendy was a very beautiful woman. No one in the group had seen her without her coveralls and helmet but Angelina knew they would someday. Angelina simply smiled at Reggie as they headed back down the stairs.

CHAPTER THIRTY-EIGHT

June 19, 4:00 am EET - Villa Evangeline
Cairo, Egypt

Several hours had passed since the attack. The army of men that had appeared out of thin-air and in full combat gear was busy cleaning up the debris caused by the thousands of bullets that had been fired. The heavy metal curtains remained down on all windows as a precaution. Inside, Jack had made everyone a stiff drink, and they were sitting in the living room quietly thinking about what had occurred. Even though it was very early in the morning, the drink was appreciated by all. It was four o'clock in the morning, and Angelina suggested that they all try to get some sleep.

"We can regroup in the morning and start tomorrow with a clear head. I am so... sorry about what has happened. I know you and Jack have a million questions you want to ask," she said facing Rachel. "The best I can do right now is to say I will explain everything in the morning. Trust me, everything will be fine."

"I hope so," Rachel replied in her mock-indignant voice. "I don't need any more of this kind of excitement. These kinds of things can't keep happening."

With that, each couple retired to their respective room. Reggie had stayed back to talk to Jack about some of the precautions he felt they should be taking, starting tomorrow.

They concluded that the reason for the attack had been because of the disk Eddy had sent them. Eddy had been right; this was dangerous stuff. Jack and Rachel were now involved in it too. Reggie knew that he and Angelina had to provide their friends with more details both about themselves and their families.

As Reggie opened the door to their bedroom, he could see Angelina lying on the bed. He stood next to the bed expecting her to speak; but it was clear that she was in a sound sleep. He lay next to her and pulled the top sheet over her. He put his arm around her body as he snuggled against her back, and as was his habit, he held her left breast in his hand as they slept. Angelina had told him that she felt quite safe when they were in this position. He too drifted off to sleep.

******

Reggie was in a deep sleep when Angelina started to shake him. It was now five am.

"Get up, get up, you have to get up and get out of here!" she yelled while she tried to wake him.

"What's the matter? Are we being attacked again?" he asked. He was trying to clear his head and get his brain to function.

Angelina peered outside through a tiny opening at the very edge of the steel shutters that covered the windows. "Worse than that, it's Daddy," she replied. Reggie could hear the now-familiar sound of a helicopter outside their window. "It's my father and if he finds you in my bed, he will kill you," Angelina pleaded with Reggie.

"You mean he's going to be really pissed, don't you? He wouldn't actually kill me, would he?"

"I mean he is going to kill you if he finds you here with Mr. Stiffy there," she said as she pointed to Reggie's erection. "He will first cut it off and nail it to a tree, and then he will kill you. You need to get out. Go to the guest room.

We have to change places with Jack and Rachel. We have no time, so move or die!" she yelled. Angelina rose and pulled Reggie's arms to get out of the bed. She grabbed his suitcase and threw everything that looked like his into the bag. As they ran down the hall, Angelina turned and pointed to Reggie's stiff penis,

"Does that ever go down?"

"Not when you're around," he replied.

They burst into Jack and Rachel's room. Rachel and Jack were both asleep. Rachel woke immediately when they entered the room.

"Rachel, I need you in my bed! Right now, come on. You need to move into my bed!" Angelina yelled and she started to pull her friend out of bed.

Jack, who was still half-asleep, rolled over when he heard what she had said. He mumbled, "It's not a dream; there really are two chicks in a bed. It's real, and my dream is real."

"It's a dream in your head, sicko." Both Rachel and Angelina yelled at the same time.

"Rachel, my father is landing outside. If he finds me with a man in my bed, there will be one less person for breakfast."

Rachel jumped out of bed forgetting that she was wearing a very sheer negligee. Her entire body was clearly visible. She attempted to cover herself. Her arms went up to cover her breasts and her hand was held between her legs.

"Don't look, don't look!" she screamed and turned her back to Reggie. She knew he could still see her nearly naked ass but *it's better than the alternative,* she thought.

"Where did you get that?" Angelina screamed as they ran down the hall.

"From Candice. Remember New York?"

"Oh yeah. Mine is black but it looks very similar. Nice outfit," she recalled. The men each took one of the beds in the guest room and got under the covers, pretending to be asleep. The women both jumped into Angelina's bed and pulled the covers up. They had just made it in time. As they settled into their respective beds, Anwar Evangeline was rushing to exit the helicopter for the short walk to the house. He used a remote control device to raise the steel shields from the doors and windows, and burst into the main house. His first concern was for his daughter. He rushed down the hall, calling her name and burst into Angelina's room. The two girls, pretending to have been awakened, rubbed their eyes.

"Is that you, Daddy?" Angelina asked in a baby-like voice. "This is my friend Rachel and the guys are all the way down the hall in the guest room."

"Why are there "guys" down the hall?" Who are they and what do they want?"

"Reggie Viscusi is one of them. You remember Reggie, Joseph's son. The other one is Rachel's boyfriend, Jack. By the way, this is Rachel Wi," Angelina said pointing to her bedmate.

"You already told me who she is. You didn't tell me that Reggie is your boyfriend."

"Daddy," she replied with a more adult tone to her voice. "I'm not sixteen any more. They are our boyfriends and we are here to work on that problem I spoke to you about. Remember, the ODD."

"You are still my daughter. We can talk about this later. Does my house being shot to hell and your life threatened have anything to do with the ODD? I told you this was serious business. What have you done, Angelina?"

"We haven't done anything," she protested. "Can you just give me an opportunity to explain? We're in trouble, I admit, and we need your help. Let us get up, and dressed, and we can all sit down to an early breakfast. It's only half past five," she said glancing at the bedside alarm clock. "We will tell you what we know."

"Don't take too long, and bring your boyfriends with you," Anwar shouted. He left her room.

Angelina watched her father outside her window giving instructions to the clean-up crews. He was pointing to all of the damaged furniture and broken patio stones and instructing them to repair them immediately. His foreman was instructed to replace the damaged glass and to make sure this time that it was thick enough to handle the heavier caliber bullets. Her father sounded angry that the glass that was installed hadn't withstood the gunfire. After fifteen minutes or so, the young people were dressed and assembled in the kitchen. Angelina's father was beginning to prepare a full breakfast. They sat in silence. Mr. Evangeline's mood seemed to have mellowed from when he first arrived.

"Mr. Viscusi," Anwar addressed Reggie. "It would seem that you and my daughter are more than teammates on a Mensa project."

Reggie didn't know where this was going. He looked to Angelina for support.

"Yes father, Reggie and I are a couple," Angelina replied on Reggie's behalf. "We didn't want to tell anyone until we were sure."

"You didn't want to tell your father?"

"You or mother, or Reggie's mother or father. If you all knew, you would have tried to move our relationship along faster. We wanted time on our own."

"Are you certain, young man? You know my daughter is very precious to me. Her affections are not to be toyed with."

Anwar continued to prepare breakfast as he spoke. There was a heavy frying pan on the stove with bacon already starting to sizzle. He had eggs in bowl and began to whip them with a fork. He had even managed to place six slices of bread into the toaster. It was like he was a short-order cook in a diner.

"I assure you, Mr. Evangeline, I would never toy with her affections. We are very serious," Reggie confirmed. He also thought to himself that if her father ever knew what they had been doing earlier in Angelina's bedroom, he would be more than displeased. Anwar seemed to be accepting what they were telling him, for now at least. Angelina's expression had turned from concerned to happy when Reggie told her father they were serious.

"We need to talk, but before we do, I am expecting another person who is due to arrive at any moment. We will wait for him," her father stated with certainty as the faint sound of another helicopter could be heard outside beyond the open patio doors.

Jack and Rachel were already seated at the breakfast table. Rachel was visibly upset upon hearing the same noise as she had the past evening. She moved closer to Jack. He placed his hand on her knee to assure her that everything was going to be alright.

"Don't be afraid, my dear," Anwar directed to Rachel. He could see the fear in her eyes as a result of hearing the familiar sounds. "This is a friendly visit. I promise you, there will not be a repeat of the events of last night."

Rachel seemed to be reassured by his words. She reached under the table and placed her hand on Jack's hand to be certain she didn't lose that sense of safety. Anwar, Angelina and Reggie moved to the window to watch the chopper land. Once on the ground, several large men exited the side door followed by a heavy-set and somewhat shorter man, dressed in a dark business suit. Reggie didn't look closely at the man's face until he was very close to the house.

"That's my father," Reggie said in a confused tone. "What's my father doing here?"

Anwar didn't reply to his question. Their visitor had just crossed the threshold and was being greeted by a warm handshake.

"Welcome Don Viscusi," Anwar said while he shook his guest's hand. He placed his left hand on Mr. Viscusi's lower arm as an additional sign of welcome and respect.

As soon as the word "Don" left Anwar's lips, Angelina looked directly at Reggie. "See, your dad *is* a Mafia guy," she mouthed silently to Reggie.

Reggie pretended he didn't understand what she was saying, which only frustrated Angelina. She shook her head.

"Welcome to Villa Evangeline. I trust your flight was comfortable. You look well," Anwar finished while glancing around the room. "I must apologize for the state of my home," he said gesturing to the damaged area beyond the door. "As you know, we had some problems last night. I am pleased to advise you that restitution for this violation of my personal property and endangerment of my daughter and her guests is underway."

"I'm pleased to hear this," Joseph replied as he glanced at the group. He fixed his eyes on his son. "How are you my son?"

"I'm well, Father, but why are you here?"

"You have a very short memory, my son. We discussed this possibility in New York when we last met. Working together on some special projects was the term I believe you and Angelina used," he said.

He turned to Angelina and kissed her on one cheek and then the other. "How are you, my dear?"

"I'm very well, Mr. Viscusi. Have you been introduced to our friends? This is Rachel Wi and Jack Daniels."

"The other half of the team. I remember them from our dinner," Joseph stated. He shook Jack's hand and kissed Rachel on each cheek.

"Yes, of course. I'm sorry," Angelina apologized. "Things have been a little hectic around here. I forgot."

"Yes, the other half," Reggie confirmed.

"How did you get here so quickly, father?" Reggie asked. "All of this happened only a few hours ago."

"Our good fortune, I expect. Coincidentally, I was scheduled to have a meeting with Mr. Evangeline later this afternoon. I received a call early this morning and a helicopter was sent to my hotel, and here I am."

"Why were you scheduled for a meeting with Mr. Evangeline?"

"So many questions, my son. It will all become clear when we begin our discussion after breakfast. This smells wonderful, Anwar," Joseph said looking at the plates of food on the counter top beside the stove.

"Joseph, before we begin, I must tell you of a recent revelation concerning our two families," Anwar stated.

Reggie and Angelina both had a look of concern come across their faces, as he spoke.

"It would seem that our children have decided to become a couple, boyfriend and girlfriend," he finished.

"Well, I am pleased and I am certain your mother will be as well. Almost all she talks about these days is becoming a grandmother. She will be pleased that there is some movement in that regard," Joseph stated.

"We're a long way from getting married and having children," Angelina quickly pointed out. She did it as much to appease her father as to inform Joseph.

"Oh, once that Viscusi charm sets in my dear, you will be butter in his hands," Joseph joked.

Angelina looked at her father's face and to her surprise, he didn't look angry about where the conversation was going.

"He is a charming one," Rachel interjected with a smile. "That Viscusi charm is difficult to resist."

"We would also be very pleased if these two were to marry and present us with a grandchild or two," Anwar stated. He was ready to move on in the conversation as were Angelina and Reggie. "We have a very serious situation developing and we need many kinds of problem solving skills. Your father brings many talents to this issue. I asked him to come to Egypt so we could discuss what appears to be a hornet's nest you young people have disturbed. Why don't you help yourselves to a quick breakfast? Then we need to take a seat in the viewing room and review the contents of the disk you received."

Reggie was about to ask the next obvious question, *how did they know about the disk?* , when Angelina reached out and touched his arm,

"Don't say anything," she whispered. "Trust me, it's best to listen at this point," she paused for a moment. "And what about the "Don" Viscusi? You ignored me earlier. I saw it. This is more proof that your father is Mafia."

"It's best to listen," he repeated, trying to ignore her last comment as they walked off to join the others. "Think about how many grandchildren you are going to bear in your prime child bearing years," he joked. *That will take her mind off the Mafia*, he thought to himself.

CHAPTER THIRTY-NINE

June 19, 7:30 am EET - Villa Evangeline
Cairo, Egypt

Once everyone had settled in the viewing room, Jack moved to his seat next to the control panel.

"I've loaded the disk. Do you want to see everything?"

Anwar replied to the affirmative by a nod of his head. Jack clicked the next button on the presentation. The first part of the film was very difficult for the group to watch. They saw, for a second time, Eddy and Candice explaining what they had found. They were all affected by the review, but Rachel was visibly saddened by seeing their friends' images, again.

"Well that's the explanation," Jack stated as Edward's picture faded from the screen. "The rest are attachments, drawings, mathematical calculations, and the like."

"We need to see it all," Joseph said. Jack complied and pulled up the attachments, one by one, for everyone to view. The details seemed endless and the various screens of data and drawings moved over the screen. Once completed, the screen went black and there was silence in the room.

Anwar broke the silence. "We certainly have a situation here; a very serious situation. I will explain what I know about this matter; but let me first tell you that I am sorry that it was necessary for you to watch your friend's explanation for a second time. It was necessary to do so. I appreciate that they were your friends and it saddens you to review this once again. I also want to tell you that their deaths were not accidental. I think you already know this, however I wanted to make this clear to you. I am going to ask Mr. Viscusi to explain what he knows about the incident."

The missing reference to "Don" was noticed by both Reggie and Angelina. Was this Don as in the *godfather* Don? Reggie knew his dad was in the mafia. He tried to deny it to himself and others; but he knew it was true. This latest revelation confirmed it once-and-for-all, however, he had no idea he was the top man.

Joseph began. "We know that the knowledge of this weapon, at least the details on how it works and the progress being made in perfecting the technology, is known to a very few people. The presidents of both Airtec and Softco for two, perhaps. Chemico's president is involved as well. We believe his involvement is as a supplier of the blasting material itself. We are still looking into that company's involvement. We have determined that two others are deeply involved. The Under Secretary of Defense and the Assistant Deputy of Homeland Security. As far as we can tell, these are the only two government people. It appears that these four want to be the heroes in the arms game by giving the U.S. this technology first." He looked at the four young people as he spoke. He could see the serious expressions on their faces. It was clear they were beginning to grasp the severity of the situation. "Your friends were murdered, and it was done either by others working for one or all of these people."

Rachel gasped when Reggie's father said murdered. She brought herself quickly under control again and continued listening. "There were no burglars. This wasn't a robbery gone wrong. Your friends stumbled onto something. They were considered to be security risks, so they were eliminated. I have looked at these drawings and calculations. I don't have the technical knowledge to decipher them. You four, however," Joseph said as he moved his hands in a circular motion including all of them, "have the knowhow."

"Was the episode in Mexico at the Mensa Conference associated with this same issue?" Reggie asked. He directed the question to his father.

"What incident at the conference?" both Jack and Rachel asked almost in unison.

"There was the accident behind our limo, remember?" Reggie answered.

"Yes, there was a car accident behind our car. What's the significance of that?" Rachel asked.

"It was no accident. That car was following us and someone took it out by slamming it broadside." Reggie replied. He looked to Angelina's father for his response.

"We thought at the time that it was an attempt on Angelina," Anwar responded.

"Why would anyone want to hurt Angelina?" Rachel asked in a confused tone.

There was a hesitation in the conversation for a few moments.

"Rachel and Jack, there are some pieces of this puzzle of which you are unaware. There are times, however, when not knowing is better than being in the loop, so to speak," Joseph stated. "In this situation, I believe you deserve to and need to know everything that's going on in this dynamic. Before we proceed further, we need to have a discussion."

"Why not let us tell them?" Reggie asked. "Angelina and me."

Both Joseph and Anwar hesitated.

"Fine. Agreed. We will remain should there be any questions for us. I suggest you begin immediately. Rachel and Jack have some decisions to make with respect to their future involvement," Joseph replied.

"If I may say a word," Anwar interrupted. "This weapon, or potential weapon, is a doomsday device. I hope everyone realizes that. Those who possess this technology will have ultimate control over their enemies and perhaps all global governments. This unit kills people and leaves the assets unharmed. The cost of military action is calculated in direct cost, such as equipment and men. The ultimate cost and the ultimate deterrent to total destruction is the cost to rebuild. Money to these people is more important than innocent lives, ladies and gentleman, and we need to understand this. People sniffle and cry foul when civilians and soldiers die in these conflicts. The real issue for those making the decision to fight is the cost to replace the infrastructure. The lost revenue from loss of oil or other natural resources."

"Are you saying that all the propaganda about loss of life and how terrible the other guys are to kill our people is simply political posturing?" Angelina asked.

"Nail on the head," Anwar replied. "You have hit the nail on the head, my girl."

Joseph took the floor. "We know what this looks like and we know how dangerous it is. We should also know that we can't just stop this one incident from occurring. There will be others who will follow in these terrifying footsteps. Your friend, Edward, was correct when he said it on the tape. We need to destroy even the idea that this will work at all and put the possible use of ODD out of everyone's mind. A pipe dream that will never become a reality." He stopped and looked at his audience. "Well, how do you clever young people propose we stop this thing once and for all?"

CHAPTER FORTY

June 19, 9:30 am EET - Villa Evangeline
Cairo, Egypt

As decided, it was time to bring Jack and Rachel fully into the fold. Angelina and Reggie agreed that before any progress was going to be made on the problem at hand, Jack and Rachel deserved an explanation. They were never part of the discussion between Angelina and Reggie and their fathers about joining forces for some possible work. Since there was an element of danger and possibly legal issues as well, they needed to be told. Nor were they aware of the true nature of Anwar's and Joseph's family businesses. All of this information was important for them to know. The two older men left the young people to talk in the viewing room.

Angelina began. "Guys. First off, you know Reggie and I love you both. We would never intentionally do anything to put you in harm's way. We are going to fill you in on some very important and sensitive information about ourselves. You two are the only ones we trust with this information which demonstrate how much we love and trust you. If, after we have explained everything to you, you feel that you don't want to or can't join us in our exploits, we will totally understand. We will still love you and we will remain best friends, however, we will respect your wishes."

"Does this have anything to do with you getting pregnant and giving Reggie's mom grandchildren?" Rachel asked in an attempt to break the tension in the room. Angelina's mind flashed back to an earlier conversation she had with Reggie at his parents' home. And how his mother thought she looked bosomy?" *I am a bosomy woman in my prime child bearing years* raced through Angelina's mind.

"You know," Reggie said with a smirk on his face, "Angelina is in her prime, child bearing years, according to my mom. She said so."

"Yes," Angelina said, "There has actually been a conversation about me having big boobs and being in my prime child bearing years. And this conversation did not include me."

"You were included. You're the one with big boobs and giving birth to all their grandchildren," Reggie joked.

"Can we get on with this?" Angelina asked. She knew she was the brunt of the joke and she was being a good sport about it.

"Yes, fine," Reggie said. He entered into the discussion. "Angelina's dad is an arms dealer."

Angelina's eyes almost popped out of her head.

"You don't just jump in and make a statement like that," Angelina protested. "You have to work it into the conversation. How would it sound if I just blurted out that your dad's in the Mafia?"

"Your dad's in the Mafia?" Jack asked. This was news to him, and he wasn't certain how he felt about being involved with someone linked to organized crime. He was pretty sure Rachel would feel the same.

"That's yet to be confirmed for certain. Well yes, I guess," Reggie stammered as Angelina nodded her head in confirmation and pushed her nose to the side. "The point is that our fathers both have jobs that, shall we say, are unconventional. Selling weapons and being in business that some might define as organized crime, is unconventional. Angelina and I have asked our fathers if we could play a role in their activities."

"You want to be a Mafia guy and sell weapons?" Jack asked in disbelief.

"No, not directly," Angelina interjected seeing that Reggie wasn't managing to get the information out in the right framework. "We think we have some special talents, as do you two. We think there may be projects from time to time where we could collaborate. For instance, this matter before us. Our fathers are well connected, and both wield a significant amount of influence in many areas. We are going to need to tap their resources if we hope to find who killed our friends. There may be a situation down the road where the roles are reversed. It's a mutual sharing thing."

"And you think we can bring something to the table?" Jack asked.

"Absolutely. You're a gifted computer specialist and Rachel is one of the best engineers I have ever seen," Angelina added. "We would love to have you on the team."

"And what about our existing jobs?" Rachel asked.

"I think we are all looking for a change. This may work into something bigger for us all," Angelina said in a hopeful tone.

Rachel was looking directly at Jack as she considered the situation at hand. "This might be fun. It could also be dangerous, but I'm in if you are," she agreed.

"Let's make it a double with Jack Daniels," he agreed without hesitation.

"That's it then," Reggie said. "A new team is born. If I had a drink I would toast to our future adventures," he finished. They rose to find their senior partners.

CHAPTER FORTY-ONE

June 19, 11:00 am EET - Villa Evangeline
Cairo, Egypt

It had been a long morning already, but the discussions were progressing. There were several glimpses of ideas kicked around and discussed. Jack was first to suggest an actual next step.

"We have a lot of information, however what we really need is access to both Softco and Airtec's main computer systems. I can get into Softco, no problem, but I'll need some time to break the security at Airtec. In order to do that, I am going to need a little more computer power than my laptop provides."

Anwar stood and motioned for the group to follow him. Without saying a word, he led them to the basement of the villa. He stood in front of what appeared to be an ordinary door; inserted a key-card and the door opened. As the group entered the room, they were amazed by what they saw. At one end of the room, there were a number of very large screens; very large one, in the center, flanked by two smaller screens. A console was set up towards the back of the room.

The console was a mass of flickering lights, meters and gauges. It looked much the same as a control panel for a major rock concert or perhaps even NASA.

"Shit." Was Jack's initial reaction.

"What do you think, Mr. Daniels?" Anwar asked. He was obviously proud of his private, state of the art computer lab.

"I think it'll do," Jack responded, as he began to review the control panel.

"When was this built?" Angelina asked her father, in an irritated tone.

"Some parents redecorate a child's room when they leave the nest. In my case, I built a new play-room."

"You could launch a missile from this room," Jack interrupted in a loud and excited voice.

"Yes, actually you can," Anwar replied as he smiled.

The team gathered around the console and watched Jack work his computer magic. After what seemed like a lifetime, but was in reality only twenty minutes or so, Jack was into the Softco main frame.

"I'm in, now let me get Airtec running in the background." As he spoke, the logo for Airtec appeared on the second screen. *Now a password.* Jack thought for a few moments. He keyed in a series of letters. The Airtec screen lit up again. The password was Airtec spelled backwards. This time the company logo and watermark "Top Secret" appeared across the bottom of the screen. "Not anymore," Jack uttered, in direct response to the top secret notification. "Your ass is grass, Mr. Airtec."

After a short time of viewing a number of technical drawings, Rachel stood up to speak.

"This is brilliant," she said, breaking the silence. "It's scary as hell; but it's brilliant. This is a flying machine that uses, what can best be described as pulse drive. Like they pretended in the Star Trek movies. Apparently, pulse drive actually exists. To boot, this is capable of operating in stealth mode. It can't be detected by any conventional radar or other tracking device. This ring of machinery can go anywhere, anytime, and no one would ever know."

"There's more," Jack added. "From what I can see, Softco may have kept details on the entire package. They were really bad for that. They liked to have everything, even if it didn't have any impact on the programming. Using the disk over there," he said pointing to the main screen, "you can hover above a target without detection. The details of the active ingredient, so to speak, for the explosion part of it are not here. However, from this computer simulation, we see how it works." He pushed a key and the second small screen lit up.

The group watched as the simulation showed the circular device hovering above a group of fifteen or twenty mock-soldiers. There was a bright flash and the device vanished from the screen. It disintegrated into tiny pieces and drifted away in the wind. A few moments later, there was a camera pan of the ground under the device. All the soldiers were lying on the ground, presumably dead. There was a slow motion rerun of what had just occurred. A flash could be seen which destroyed the device. At the same time, the simulated air below the device suddenly shot straight up into the atmosphere.

"See how it works?" Rachel said. "First, there is an explosion or actually an *implosion.* It destroys the delivery sphere while setting off a chain of events that result in the air from everything below it. There's no damage from any vacuum being created because there doesn't appear to be a vacuum, even though the air shoots up. The good air must be replaced by bad air, like carbon dioxide, if there is no vacuum created," she thought out loud. "The loss of air seems to last long enough to suffocate people, as the demo shows. There is no damage to anything other than the people. From the angle of repose I see from this device, it appears that the area affected is a factor of maybe 1000 of the diameter of the device. If the sphere is one foot in diameter the affected area below is 1000 feet in diameter.

Imagine what would happen if there was a device ten feet in diameter? You could wipe out the population of an entire city block without disturbing a leaf on the ground."

There was a silence that came over the room. It was clear that everyone was contemplating the devastation the ODD could cause.

"How do we prevent this?" Anwar asked.

"The only way," responded Joseph, "is to foil the plan. Cause the device to malfunction. Destroy all plans and documentation of the device, and people will lose interest. Is there any way you young folks can modify the plans that will cause this to fail? Fail so miserably that it will be abandoned for a very long time?"

"What about the few people who know it does work, the government officials and the heads of these companies? How do you prevent them from starting it up again?" Rachel asked.

"There are ways to deal with them," Anwar added. "Let Mr. Viscusi and I assist you with silencing the existing people. You, clever people do whatever you can to screw this thing up enough to blow up in their faces."

CHAPTER FORTY-TWO

June 20, 2:00 am EET - Villa Evangeline
Cairo, Egypt

It was fifteen hours of concentrated and detailed work. The group had a plan they could present to the two senior people on the team. Angelina found her father and Don or Mister Viscusi, whichever salutation was appropriate, and asked them to join the others in the control room. As the everyone took their seats, the large screen lit up with a detailed drawing of the delivery saucer.

Rachel was first to speak. "I think I have found a weakness in this design," she said with a tone of exhaustion. "This was obviously designed as separate components, with no two designers being aware of what the totality of the project entailed. I can see that in the different method of applying some of the basic CAD techniques, "Computer Assisted Design." There seems to be an abundance of acronyms floating around. Some drawings were even in a different version of the CAD program which made it easy to spot. According to what I have seen so far, it appears that I can institute a design change anywhere without the original designer being aware of the changes I have made. This is a very poor technique and one I would never use. Although in this circumstance and the need for secrecy, I can see why they did it. The design changes I make will render it inoperable."

"You're saying, no one person really knows or has access to the total design of this ODD weapon?" Anwar asked.

"Almost correct," Rachel continued. "The only one who would likely have everything would be the CEO of Airtec, Mr. Dennis Wirth. I have only met Wirth once, when I first joined the company. I hear he is a bit of a recluse. He stays in his office quite a bit of the time. Jack, I don't think the Softco people have the entire picture. Not from what I see."

"I know him," Jack stated. "I've met Dennis Wirth in our offices three times. He must have been there discussing this programming. From what I understand, he spends most of the day in his office because he's screwing his twenty-something year old secretary. Rumor has it that the duties she performs have nothing to do with her secretarial skills."

"Nice," Angelina responded under her breath. "A real charming sleaze bag."

"I can make some changes, as I said," Rachel continued. "I am certain it will render this machine inoperable, however, at some point in time, someone will be able to reengineer the design. The only way to deal with this in the long term is to eliminate the design from all files that reference even a portion of the total picture."

"What makes this thing fly?" Anwar asked.

"I really don't have a definitive answer on that," Rachel admitted. "From what I see, it shouldn't be able to fly, but it appears to use some sort of a pulse type system. A pulse is created by a series of mechanical activities from within the machine itself. Kind of an action-reaction set up. This is a basic law of physics. Remember "for every action there is a reaction"? This is it."

"And what sets it off?" Mr. Viscusi asked.

"I will speak to that," Jack said. "Again, we can't be certain and we don't have every detail. It looks like the energy comes from within the control strategy software. There is a simple detonation of what appears to be a device similar to a blasting cap. There are quite a number of controlled delays built into each small explosion. The end result sets off what appears to be not much more than typical explosive material. The most common form of explosive is made from ammonium nitrate, more commonly known as lawn fertilizer, soaked in diesel fuel; little beads of it. It's the sequencing of the delays in the detonation, almost a particle at a time, that seems to give it such a vertical velocity. There must be an additive, other than diesel fuel, added to the ammonium nitrate to create this particular product but I can't find a reference to it. What occurs is that the vertical velocity sucks the air or oxygen from below. At the same time it draws in ambient air from outside of the affected area. This air is almost entirely toxins and or carbon dioxide. It replaces the missing air, so there is no vacuum created. Just as Rachel described. It's really rather simple yet ingenious. When I look at it, this has really been done with not much more technology than has existed for a very long time. It appears to be the timing of the implosions which are controlled by the software that seems to be the key and maybe this other elusive additive as well; but I'm not seeing it."

"So," Angelina interjected, "Rachel scuttles the circular delivery component. Jack programs the software so it fizzles out. What do we do about someone bringing this back to life at some time down the line?"

Anwar stood and walked over to the senior Viscusi. "I believe we can take care of that," he said.

"No problem," Joseph agreed.

"I'm not going to ask how you are going to do that. The key to making this all come together is to have access to the server," Jack stated. "I can make some changes remotely, but for the bulk of them, I need to be able to put this key," he said as he held up a memory stick, "into the main frame and dump the files. The same issue for Rachel. We will need to gain access for her purposes as well. I'm guessing that both of these systems will be loaded on that computer in Wirth's office."

"So how do we do that?" Reggie asked.

"We need to disable or reroute the building security system. Then we have to get into his office and gain access to his computer, and dump the file," Jack said. "I can do some of that from here but we need to see the layout of the offices to determine how we are going to get in. I can't dump the file remotely. I need to use the memory stick. I suggest we head back to the States and regroup after we have that information."

"You are welcome to use my home," Joseph offered. "I do not have as elaborate a computer system as Mr. Evangeline, however, it's a secure place."

"Great. We'll set up there," Reggie replied. He was pleased that the Viscusi home was going to be a key part of this operation.

As the meeting broke up, everyone returned to their rooms to pack for the return trip. Rachel took Jack aside and whispered. "I'm not really comfortable with going back to the Munster's house," referring to the Viscusi estate. "It's creepy and no one there seems to have a neck." She said as she pulled her shoulder up towards her ears to demonstrate the loss of her neck. "They all look like gangsters."

"Reggie is in some kind of denial if he doesn't see that his father is connected to organized crime. Sam, the limo driver has a neck though. I'm sure she does," he joked.

Rachel, thinking about that last statement, tsked. "I doubt you were looking at her neck, so how would you know? Maybe a few inches below that but her neck wasn't her most noticeable feature."

"It'll be fine," Jack assured her. "I'll be with you all the way and we can check out Sam's neck together. We only need to be there long enough to set the plan. Then we have to head for California. Maybe we could work out of Angelina's place."

CHAPTER FORTY-THREE

June 22, 2:00 pm EDT - Viscusi Estate
New Canaan, CT

By the time the group made it back to Connecticut, from Cairo, they had lost two more days in their tight schedule. The next step was to gain access into Wirth's office and make the changes to his computer. The prelude to that was to obtain the layout of the office and the security system. That portion of the plan had yet to be developed, or so the guys thought.

"We need to see Wirth's office and take some pictures of the layout. Then we can formalize how we are going to gain access to the main server." Jack said.

Angelina took over. "We know that Wirth is a skirt-chaser. His secretary looks like a high-class prostitute. Almost everyone is aware that she has an apartment in a very expensive building, most assuredly paid for by Wirth. We have to use his lust to achieve what we need. Rachel and I are going to set up a meeting with Wirth."

"How, exactly, are you going to do that?"Jack asked.

"I'll tell my boss that I'm hearing complaints about sexual harassment issues occurring at some of our locations. As one of the more high-profile females in the company, I have been asked to address the situation with the big man. That's not far from the truth. Under the circumstances, he will most likely want to shed suspicion from himself. When you're dealing with a low-life like Wirth, you have to play the cards you're dealt. I will say that Rachel is the representative from the New York office because it's been reported there as well. Human Resources will have no choice but to call for the meeting and Wirth will want to take it to divert attention away from himself."

"That gets you a meeting and into his office. How exactly are you going to manage to take pictures when you're sitting in a meeting? Jack asked. "Without pictures of the office layout, we risk setting off an alarm when we go in and actually change the working drawings. The building drawings I have used to set up the alarm interface are old. They've never been updated to reflect the new office configuration."

"We'll get the pictures, Jack." Rachel assured with a subtle smile.

"How... are you going to do that? We can't send you into a dangerous situation without safeguards. Remember, these are the same people who killed Eddy and Candice. I'm not getting the entire story here. What aren't you telling us?"

Rachel glanced towards Angelina. She was counting on her for some backup on her explanation of what they had planned.

"There is an element of danger, we'll admit that," Angelina conceded. "But we think we can distract his attention sufficiently during the meeting to allow us to take the pictures you need."

"I'm with Jack on this one," Reggie added. "How exactly are you going to distract him? We need to know before we go one step further in the plan."

"You sound like we need your permission. Are you saying you won't allow us to do what we are planning to do?

Because I hope that's not what I'm hearing," Angelina replied.

"I don't know what it is you're planning to do."

"So you are saying we need your permission? You're not my father, and even if you were, I don't need his permission either," Angelina argued.

"Okay then, let's include him in on this discussion. Tell us what your plan is and we'll see what he thinks." Reggie had called her bluff. He knew there was no way she would want to discuss this with her father.

Angelina was silent. She knew if her father heard what they were planning he would object. She also knew that even though she talked tough, when it came right down to it her father did have a tremendous influence.

"Rachel, can you bring in what we purchased this morning in New York?" Angelina asked.

"What did you buy this morning? You said you needed to make a stop at Rachel's place. We took a shuttle out here so you could have Sam and the car. We assumed you were picking up some clothes or whatever, not shopping."

"We also don't need your permission to shop," Angelina said. "Do you want to see what we bought and hear our plan, or not?"

Rachel had arrived back in the room with an arm-full of garment bags.

"I have already called Human Resources and had a conversation with my boss. The meeting is set," Angelina admitted. Reggie appeared to be ready to speak. "You said you would listen, so listen," she warned.

Reggie sat back in his chair.

"We have a meeting with Wirth, tomorrow at three," Angelina said. "That`s already done and we can't change it now, like or not."

"All that you said earlier is already in place? You've made the calls and the meeting is to be about alleged sexual harassment issues. I thought we were rolling that around as one possible scenario and now you tell us the meeting is set for tomorrow," Reggie stated. He sounded more annoyed than angry. Annoyed, perhaps, because the women went ahead with their plans without discussing them with the two men first.

"Are we listening.., only?" Angelina reminded Reggie.

"Go ahead. I'm sorry," Reggie said quietly.

"The sexual harassment excuse is a good one. We did agree that Wirth is a letch. He chases every skirt he sees so we can use that to our benefit. With what we have purchased, we will distract him from the conversation enough that we can take the pictures you need, Jack."

Rachel started to display the clothing she and Angelina had purchased. She laid out each outfit on the sofa for the guys to see.

"If I'm right, he's going to be busy ogling us. We should be able to get some discreet shots of the office layout. That's what the letch likes, a lot of boobs and leg. As much as I would like to punch him in the face for being such a low-life, we have to pander to what he wants or this isn't going to work. We can't go in there dressed in a Pollyanna outfit. He won't give us a second look. He needs to have the real-deal so he will lose focus during the meeting," Angelina said.

"I'm wearing an overcoat when I'm on the street. I don't want guys stopping their cars and asking me how much?" Rachel stated emphatically and smiled slightly to show her agreement with the plan.

Jack and Reggie were silent. They were trying to come up with a plausible reason for not using this part of the plan. Reggie glanced at Jack, hoping he had a good reason. It was clear that he didn't.

"Good plan," Reggie relented. "I would suggest you not discuss this with your father, Angelina."

Both Angelina and Rachel smiled. They were pleased.

"Nice outfits, by the way," Jack noted. "What little there is of them."

"Any chance I can have a preview?" Reggie whispered as he hugged Angelina.

"We'll see," she replied as she kissed his cheek.

"Since the meeting is set for three, we'll have to catch the earliest flight we can, tomorrow," Jack said. "I'll access the internet and book the flights."

"We can use my place as ground zero and stage the plan from there," Angelina suggested.

******

This was their first visit back to the Viscusi estate since Reggie and Angelina informed Joseph they were a couple. It was clear to them that he had told Mrs. Viscusi in the way she greeted them when they arrived. She was upbeat and full of excitement. Angelina knew there would be increased pressure on both she and Reggie to move it along to marriage and children. This was one of the reasons they hadn't said anything before now.

Angelina had thought a lot about the discussion regarding grandchildren. She knew that she wanted children, as did Reggie, but she wanted them to be allowed to make the decision of when by themselves. She wanted Reggie to say something to his mother. Something that would move her off the grandchildren track.

"Reggie, I need you to talk to your mother about her immediate desire to have grandchildren," Angelina said.

"She's just excited. Your mother's not much better."

"My mother is a lot better and I have already spoken to her about it. She has agreed to let up on the subject of grandchildren."

"I find it hard to believe she gave in so easily. After one conversation? You obviously have the power of persuasion, the magic touch. Why don't you use it on my mother as well?"

"No way. She's you're mother and you're her little boy scout. You must do it. Hopefully, she'll listen to you."

"You can't let the boy scout thing go, can you? Reggie smiled. "I'll talk to her but she won't like it. You take a chance of making it worse," he warned.

"How can it be any worse? I'll take that chance."

"I'll speak to her before dinner," Reggie relented. He knew it could backfire on them.

"I love you," Angelina whispered as she kissed his cheek and left to join up with the others.

******

Shortly after his conversation with Angelina, Reggie found himself alone with his mother in the dining room. She had taken over setting the table from the maid. She often complained to Joseph that Maria wasn't the best maid they had ever employed. Joseph maintained that she was the daughter of a friend of their cook and no one else would give her a job. Joseph liked Maria. She was polite and worked hard. She was one of the few people he could have a conversation with in Italian. Maria didn't speak English so it was a true and pure Italian conversation, which Joseph enjoyed.

Reggie walked up behind his mother and hugged her.

"Mom, you know how you have mentioned that you think Angelina and I can give you grandchildren, and so on?"

"Yes, I think the two of you will produce very beautiful children."

"You see, that's just it mom," he said. "I have no doubt that I will ask Angelina to marry me, but we have only been together for a short time. It's best to strengthen a relationship before marriage. She is absolutely the most beautiful woman I have ever seen and she has a brilliant mind but matters of the heart take time to nurture," he smiled.

"Matters of the heart? she smiled. "I don't feel that I am overstepping my bounds in discussing these matters with my future daughter in law."

Can you just cut back a little?" Reggie begged. He wasn't getting anywhere with this conversation so he played his last card, begging. This turned out not to be the best decision. He could see his mother was not pleased that he refused to see her side. She looked at his face before she turned away.

"I see. I won't say another word about it," she said and she walked out of the room. It was clear from her tone that she was unhappy about being asked not to comment on a matter as important as this was to her.

That didn't go well he thought to himself.

The group was seated for an early dinner. It was obvious that Reggie's mother was upset about something. She was fidgeting with silverware and the linen napkin at her place at the table while she waited for the others to arrive and take their seats.

"Did you talk to her?" Angelina whispered to Reggie outside the entrance to the dining room.

"Yes, but I don't think she was real happy about it."

"What did you say to her?" She was concerned that he might not have handled it in the best way. She knew it would be a delicate matter to discuss with his mother.

"I don't remember, word for word, but something like lay off the baby stuff and she said okay," he replied.

Angelina was stunned. She stopped in her tracks and looked into Reggie's face. She could not believe he had handled this delicate matter with such directness.

"*Lay off the baby stuff?* Is that how you phrased it?"

"I didn't say those exact words, but it worked. She agreed to lay-off."

Angelina didn't know how to respond. She was concerned that he may have handled it poorly, and upset his mother, but at least he handled it.

"Well, happy or not, at least it will stop."

Everyone at the dinner table had a lot on their minds. There was little conversation but that was to be expected. Mrs. Viscusi had no idea what the others were about to embark upon. She was still fixated on her earlier discussion with her son. Mrs. Viscusi cleared her throat, she had something to say.

"So Rachel," she said. "Isn't it nice that you and Jack are together? How long do you expect it will be before you have children?"

Rachel and Angelina stopped eating in mid-chew. Angelina focused on her plate. To glance at Rachel at this time would not be a wise move. Rachel took a moment to formulate her reply. She knew this was likely related to Angelina and Reggie so she had to answer correctly to get herself off the hot seat as well as help her best friend. On the other hand, she found it quite amusing that Angelina was being pressed to have children. Rachel seldom had the upper hand, when Angelina was involved. She chose to have some fun. She slowly folded her napkin and placed it beside her plate.

"Mrs. Viscusi, in my country it is customary for a woman to wait for at least a few years after marriage before having children," she lied. "I will say, however, that this has been a topic of discussion among us. I would fully expect to see Reggie and Angelina have children before us," she smiled.

Angelina hung her head and stared down at her plate. Rachel had one over on her and she chose to take the opportunity to have some fun at her expense. She had to admit that had the roles been reversed, she would have done exactly the same thing. She had no doubt that Rachel would do anything for her, but when it came to the jibs and jabs of their relationship, Angelina gave as good as she just got and she just got it good. It was rather humorous to those not directly in the line of fire. She looked up, and gave Rachel one of her "I'll pay you back for that" smiles.

"I wouldn't count on that, my dear," Mrs. Viscusi replied almost under her breath. "Hopefully it won't be too late, if and when they decide to become parents."

This was exactly what Reggie had warned her might, and in addition her friend sold her down the river.

No one uttered a word. Angelina finished her meal in silence.

CHAPTER FORTY-FOUR

June 23, 1:30 pm PDT - Angelina's Apartment
Los Angeles, California

The flight from New York took off at six am, and due to the time difference, they arrived in Los Angeles early in the morning. They quickly settled in Angelina's apartment to prepare for their mission. They were cutting it close. The meeting with Wirth was set for three o'clock.

As planned, the two women put on the sexy clothing they had purchased for the occasion. They took one last look at themselves in the floor length mirror in Angelina's bedroom. They did look like high-class prostitutes, but they had a job to do and they were going to do it. They stepped out of Angelina's bedroom and into the kitchen where the guys had set up Jack's computer.

"Now that's what I call eye-catching," Jack gasped as he caught his first look at the women.

The women were stunning. Angelina wore a fitted white suit jacket over a neckline-plunging red silk camisole. Her pencil skirt hugged her curves and ended a few inches above her knee. She finished the outfit off with a pair of black 6 inch Jimmy Chu shoes. Rachel, who was considerably shorter and less well proportioned than her exotic friend, took a different approach. She wore a short pleated kilt-type shirt and a clean-white blouse over a tiny white tee shirt with spaghetti straps. Her silk stockings were held in place by a garter belt and she wore a pair of black platform Mary Janes. Everything she wore accentuated as much of her petite figure as she could. Rachel thought she looked more like a school girl than a business woman. Angelina was at least wearing a suit jacket. Both she and Angelina knew that Asian school girl was a favorite fantasy for men like Wirth, and they were determined to play to his weakness.

"Maybe you could take a few moments before you go," Reggie joked as he stepped up behind her and slid his arms around Angelina's waist.

"You like?" Angelina asked in jest.

"I can see everything from here," Reggie replied. He was looking down her front. From his vantage point there wasn't much he couldn't see.

"Save it for later," Angelina replied. She wiggled out of his arms. "We have a job to do."

"I love your working girls clothes, "Jack quipped as Rachel put on her overcoat.

"It's eighty-five degrees outside," Reggie said.

"I'm wearing a coat," Rachel asserted.

The ladies left. Jack and Reggie remained in the apartment. It was a twenty-minute taxi ride to the Airtec office. The cab driver nearly got into a minor collision while looking at his passengers in the rearview mirror. It was the exact response the women were hoping for, but not from their driver.

******

The reception room door was heavy when Rachel pushed through it. There were a number of chairs lining the perimeter of the room, and a desk was located at one end. One office door was closed behind the receptionist. At the desk there was a blonde woman, likely in her late twenties, with her hair pulled up in a pony tail. As Rachel and Angelina moved closer, they noticed that she wore a sheer white blouse. Her red lace bra was easily visible through the fabric. They also notice that her breasts were overflowing her bra. Rachel leaned to Angelina and said. "Why do these guys always go for the blonde bimbos?" Angelina simply smiled in response.

The receptionist eyed the women, head to toe, when they approached her desk. They introduced themselves and were asked to take a seat. It wasn't very long before they were approached by a different woman, presumably Wirth's secretary. She too was blonde and curvaceous. As Rachel and Angelina walked through the small outer office it appeared that all of the women were young, blonde and shapely. Curious but not surprising given who the boss-man was.

"Mr. Wirth will see you now," the secretary announced directing the women through the now-opened office door.

Dennis Wirth sat behind a very large desk. He was tall, perhaps six-foot-two, they noted when he rose to shake their hands. He was slightly balding and his remaining hair was combed over and died black. He appeared to be forty-something, the women thought.

"Please have a seat, ladies," he said. He motioned for them to sit. "I understand that you are here to discuss some sexual harassment complaints. I want to assure you that we at Airtec take these complaints very seriously. I am here to get to the bottom of whatever it is."

He was quick to get down to business, likely because he was concerned about the allegations being linked to him. The board of directors of Airtec knew Wirth's reputation, with respect to him being a womanizer. They looked the other way because he was a performer. The company was extremely profitable and a great deal of the credit for that was due to Wirth's leadership.

A nice speech, Angelina thought to herself. *Too bad he hasn't looked either of us in the eyes since we got here. I'd bet he hasn't even noticed the color of our hair or eyes. In all fairness,* she thought, *we are playing him by dressing as we are.*

Angelina began to describe some of the fictitious situations that were occurring in the company. "Do you mind if I stand and use the white board to write some of these points down?" Angelina asked. As she spoke, she made every effort to move in such a way as to allow the front of her jacket to open just enough to show her partially covered breasts. She also used her best Marilyn Monroe voice, although she found it difficult not to laugh out loud when she did.

"Not at all," was the response. Wirth watched her walk to the white board. Rachel also stood. She walked around behind the chairs they were sitting in. Rachel had struggled with her short skirt. It was almost impossible to retain any sense of modesty when the skirt she wore barely covered her butt, when she was standing. Sitting was a whole other matter.

Their choice of wardrobe seemed to be working. Wirth had a varied menu to look at; his eyes were going back and forth between the two beautiful women. It was rather humorous for the women to see how much they could manipulate this skuzz. With each example Angelina gave, she would reach towards the top of the board to write it down. Her short skirt would rise, and although there was not a clear view of her bottom, the tops of those infamous sheer stockings could clearly be seen. Rachel wondered how Angelina had mastered that trick. Rachel never could do that. If she had been in Angelina's place, her butt would be in clear view, making the same moves Angelina was making. Angelina's efforts drew Wirth's attention away from Rachel and allowed her to record a few more feet of film. Rachel stood behind the chairs and leaned forward to give Wirth a peek at her breasts, without actually pulling her blouse open and exposing them. She knew the view of her from behind would show everything she had. She stayed facing forward as much as she could. Rachel couldn`t believe she was actually doing this. She had changed a lot since she met the group in Mexico.

Angelina took advantage of these diversions and captured even more on film from her vantage point in the room. Wirth had no idea what either of them were saying. Rachel roamed the room as the tiny movie camera in the jeweled pin she wore on her blouse, silently captured the required footage of the office layout. She was careful to include a shot of the computer on his desk. The meeting was short, lasting twenty minutes, and concluded with Wirth promising to look into the complaints that were discussed. As he escorted the women through his door to the outer office he asked.

"Why don't we discuss this further, say at dinner tonight?" He addressed his question to both women, hoping one, or better both would take the bait.

"We would love to," Angelina said as she squeezed his arm, "but we both have flights out tonight. I need to get back to Egypt and Rachel back to her drawing board."

While she was replying to Wirth, she looked over at his blonde secretary sitting behind her desk. She seemed upset at hearing her so-called boyfriend hitting on every skirt that came into the office. The women left and hailed a cab for the ride back to Angelina's apartment. As soon as the cab left the curb, they both broke out in laughter. They had pulled it off. Rachel had been in such a hurry to get out of the office, she had neglected to put her overcoat back on. An oversight not missed by the watchful eyes of their cabbie. He was enjoying the view through his rearview mirror.

The computers were on when they arrived back at the apartment. Jack was looking at a schematic drawing of the security system in the Airtec office, and laying out the procedure to bypass the system.

"How'd you do?" both men asked in unison, as the girls entered the apartment.

Reggie took a closer look at the women's clothes as they walked into the kitchen.

"You didn't have to sleep with him did you?" he said while giving them the full up and down viewing.

Rachel responded by buttoning her blouse to the second top button as she spoke. She had forgotten to do that when they left the office, they were so excited by what had just occurred in the office.

"No I didn't sleep with him, but I could use a shower. I have to wash the creepy off me." she teased.

Jack and Reggie looked at each other as the girls started to laugh. They were pumped that they pulled off the caper.

"What have we got?" Angelina asked trying to draw them back on task.

Rachel plugged her camera into his computer and downloaded the twenty minutes of footage she had taken. For Reggie and Jack's pleasure, she included a discreet shot of the blonde secretary leaning over her desk. Her breasts were almost entirely out of the support cup. The boys looked but wisely did not comment. Angelina downloaded the footage she had taken as well. After viewing the films of the layout, Jack pulled up the CAD program and plotted out the final details of the building layout. He had already downloaded a copy of the original building drawing. There had been significant changes made over the years that apparently, had not been updated on the drawings. After twenty minutes or so, there was a printed drawing with the details of the office overlaid onto the paper.

"Alright," Jack summarized. "We need to go through the front door and the main lobby. Then on to the elevator which appears to require a key code after normal business hours, or we could take the staircase. Since the office is only four floors up, I'm thinking we should avoid possible detection by breaking into the elevator system, and instead take the stairs. Then we access the outer office and into his private office. All of these are key-pad activated and I just happen to have the list of number sequences printing, as we speak." As Jack finished his statement, a second paper emerged from the printer. This one was a copy of the previous schematic and included all of the codes for the various doors. "So who goes in?" he finished.

"You and me, Jack, I think it would be best," Reggie volunteered.

"Why not us?" Rachel asked pointing to her female partner-in-crime.

"It's best if Jack and I take this one. You ladies can stay at the main entrance and let us know if anyone comes. We have already rented a car for the night. You've gotten us this far. It's our turn to have an adventure. Besides, Jack's our computer guy."

After some continued resistance to the idea, the ladies gave in. The fact that Jack was the computer guy tipped the decision in their favor. It was settled; 3:00 a.m. the following morning, there would be an assault on the Airtec offices.

CHAPTER FORTY-FIVE

June 24, 3:00 am PDT - Airtec Office
Los Angeles, California

As the women waited in the car parked near the front entrance, they watched the guys enter the building.

"No alarms yet," Angelina pointed out. "So far so good."

They watched their progress through a G.P.S. and an iPad. They could see the two dots representing the men, as they progressed through the office complex. After a short time, they were into Wirth's office.

"That wasn't so hard," Rachel said. "Let's hope Jack can upload the design changes onto Wirth's computer."

Jack had secured the passwords required to access the CEO's personal system. He began by reviewing the file set up. He noticed that two files were marked differently from the others. He opened the files to see the all-too-familiar drawing they had seen back at the villa in Egypt.

"Bingo," he stated. He inserted the prepared memory stick into the side of the monitor and punched the required keys. The memory stick contained all the changes that he and Rachel had made to the engineered drawings. The changes that they hoped would render the ODD ineffective. It took only twenty-seconds for the file to be uploaded into the system. "Christ," Jack exclaimed. "This system has some balls. I expected it to take at least ten minutes to upload such a large file," he said as he removed the key. "Let's get the hell out of here."

As soon as those words left his lips, they heard a noise. It was coming from the other side of the wall in the office. Jack held his finger to his mouth, signaling the need for silence. They heard a man and a woman arguing. As they stood frozen in place, they could hear more clearly. It was Wirth and an unidentified woman. She was complaining loudly about him looking at every pretty girl that walked past him and how she was tired of it all. She was supposed to be his girl, she shouted, and if he didn't knock it off, she was going to move on. They heard Wirth pleading with her to stay. The voices softened and the volume lowered. Jack and Reggie stood for a few minutes until the sounds coming from the hidden room changed from an argument to the unmistakable sounds of make-up sex.

"Like I said," Jack repeated, "let's get the hell out of here."

They began backtracking the route they had used to access the office. They left the building through the front door and the women pulled up alongside them. Reggie walked to the driver-side door, opened it and motioned for Angelina to step out of the driver's seat. Jack hopped into the back seat of the car with Rachel.

"What are you doing?" Angelina asked.

"I'm driving back."

"No you're not, I'm perfectly capable of driving back to my apartment. I'll have you know I drive in this city all the time."

"You drive like a crazy person. Much too fast."

"It's three-o'clock in the morning. You can drive more quickly at three in the morning. There's hardly anyone else on the road. Get in the other side, please."

Reggie knew he wasn't going to win this argument. Angelina did drive too fast and it was something he needed to speak to her about, but not right now. As soon as he had closed the passenger-side door, she squealed the tires as she drove away. She quickly reduced her speed to the posted limit. She knew Reggie was right. She did drive too fast but she liked it fast. That's why she loved to fly so much. She was addicted to speed. Reggie didn't comment on her little defiant episode with the tires.

Jack wanted to get back on task.

"That was close," Jack said from the back seat. "Wirth was banging someone in the back room. From what we heard, it was pretty tense in there. There must be a secret love nest concealed behind the bookshelves."

"Why doesn't that surprise me?" Angelina stated.

The foursome headed back to her apartment. As they drove, they kept a close watch on any cars sharing the road. They were concerned about being followed, but it didn't appear that they were. They entered Angelina's apartment, and to their surprise, they found both Anwar and Joseph sitting in the kitchen enjoying Reggie's beers.

"How did you get in here, Daddy?" Angelina asked her father. Her tone reflected her displeasure that he was in her space without permission.

He leaned over and kissed her on the forehead. "I have my ways," he replied.

"Well in the future, I would appreciate you letting me know when you are going to break into my apartment. I have personal stuff here."

"I see that," he replied. "I saw some of your personal "stuff" on the bed when I used the washroom. Does your personal stuff also include some of the men's clothing I see strewn around the apartment?" He asked as he gingerly picked up a shirt that Reggie had tossed on the floor. "Who does this belong to?"

"That's mine," Reggie volunteered. He took it from Anwar and threw it on the couch. "We have been here for some time and I had to change my shirt."

"From what I see, this is neither the first time nor the longest duration that you have visited my daughter's residence," her father responded.

Angelina feared that if her father were to take a look inside her closet, he would see a number of Reggie's shirts and pants, not to mention his underwear in her dresser. He knew about them being together, but he would never approve of them cohabitating. Wanting to stop this line of dialog she interjected.

"We got in and we have downloaded the files that will change the design. Jack found all the files on this one computer. We don't have a need to do this again with Softco. Apparently this Wirth guy has such a big ego about this project, he kept it all to himself," Angelina explained.

"Good for us," Jack explained. "The next time they try to use the ODD what's going to happen?" he asked Rachel.

"It's going to blow up. I mean literally blow up in their faces. I have changed the design enough so it will act almost in a complete reverse of how it was originally designed. At least I'm pretty sure I have. Not being familiar with the pulse-drive technology is a real disadvantage when you're trying to screw things up. I still don't really see that the technology is based on sound engineering but apparently it works. No longer though if my changes are correct. They will change the parameters just before they launch the device, according to the procedure written on the drawings."

"And coupled with the sequence changes I made to the detonation software," Jack continued, "the device is never going to work. How are we doing with the political bigwigs?" he asked the two older gentlemen.

There was a hesitation before either of them responded.

"We haven't had as much success as you young folks," Anwar explained. "By the end of the week," he said. He looked to Joseph for confirmation of the timing, "the problem should be solved."

"Yes, by June 30," Joseph confirmed.

The foursome looked one to another. They had expected more from these gentlemen than the short answer they got. Perhaps some additional details or review of the plan might be in order.

"Great." was all that Reggie replied. He knew his father was unaccustomed to being questioned concerning his actions. He suspected Anwar would feel the same way.

"Let's get out of here and let these guys, I mean, let *Angelina* get some rest," Jack said. He realized instantly that he had made a mistake by implying that more than Angelina would be staying here. No one seemed to have noticed.

The two older gentlemen were first to leave. Angelina watched from her front window as their individual limos left the front of the apartment complex. Jack and Rachel took off for their hotel in the rental car. Reggie and Angelina were left alone in her apartment.

"Well," Reggie exclaimed once the last of their visitors cleared the door way. "That certainly was exhilarating and an adrenaline rush. You looked especially hot earlier in your short skirt and tight jacket."

Angelina disappeared into her bedroom before Reggie finished speaking. He thought perhaps she hadn't heard him speak. He waited for a few moments before he followed her. He was concerned that she may still be angry about the whole driving incident. He entered the bedroom. The room was in darkness. He walked over to the side of the bed and turned the lamp on. Angelina was lying naked on the bed in a very provocative pose. She looked into Reggie's eyes and purred.

"I hate it when there is an adrenaline rush, don't you?

CHAPTER FORTY-SIX

June 30, 12:00 am CST – Cancun, Mexico

Maxwell Wesley, Under Secretary of Defense and Jason Being, Assistant Deputy for Homeland Security, boarded the sleek 120 foot yacht moored in the bay. It was a picture-perfect day with full sunshine and mid-eighty degrees temperature. The seas were calm. The men could see upon their arrival at the ship that the crew accompanying them on this trip was as they ordered: beautiful, shapely young women, six in total- two fair skinned blondes, two raven haired Asians, and two stunning African Americans. The tops of their bikinis barely covered their ample breasts while the g-string bottoms provided the men with a view of their firm round asses.

The captain was an older man, likely in his mid-sixties. He was accustomed to this kind of a pleasure cruise. The cruise had been arranged by none other than Dennis Wirth of Airtec. It was an early gift of appreciation for the business deal they were about to finalize. Wirth was not in attendance.

He was organizing a demonstration of the new weapon in order to seal the deal. As the men boarded, they were informed by the captain that Wirth was on the video phone in the lower cabin and wanted to speak with them before they launched. Entering the lower cabin, two of the "crew" were preparing lunch and drinks for the guests. The men gave them each a pat on their asses and sent them to the upper deck while they took care of the phone call.

On the large screen at the end of the cabin the two men could see Wirth sitting in his office at Airtec.

"Good morning, gentlemen," he stated. "I trust you find your accommodations and the company acceptable?"

"So far so good," both men echoed.

"Let's begin. I am, as you know, arranging for a demonstration of the ODD. Everything should be in place and ready to proceed by later this afternoon. I'm currently connected to my Swiss account, and I see that there has been a recent tentative deposit of the $40 million we agreed to earlier. The funds are currently on hold until the final password releases them to permanent deposit. It is agreed that this final transfer will be done once you have confirmation that there is a working model of the device. I trust this is still an acceptable arrangement for both of you."

"It is," they stated.

"I will call you again once I have confirmed an exact time for the demonstration. You need to take precautions to make certain the women I have provided for you are not witness to this event. Until then, enjoy the ladies. They are, each and every one, the ultimate professional and will do whatever you ask of them."

With that, the screen went dark.

"Let's get the party started," Being said. He picked up the phone and called through to the captain to have the women sent to the lower deck. The men watched in anticipation as their play toys descended the stairs.

With the ladies all below deck and the yacht preparing to launch, the captain stepped from the ship's deck to the dock and changed places with another man. The new captain was dressed in a black suit. He stood over six feet in height and weighed in excess of 300 pounds. It was Vincent Carpello. The body guard known as Uncle Vincent.. No one below deck was aware of this change in navigators for their voyage. The ship took to the seas.

Wesley and Being spent the afternoon enjoying the many pleasures afforded them by the women. The sound of the music and laughter coming from below was loud as the ladies entertained the men. At four p.m., Vincent stopped the engines and descended to the lower level. The two men were both heavily entangled with naked women in various positions and didn't notice his presence until he cleared his throat several times. Once realizing he was there, they both sat up and took notice.

"Ladies," Vincent said, "Gather your clothing and move to the upper deck."

The women hesitated and looked to their two male companions for instructions.

"Ladies, I would suggest that you follow my instructions if you hope to enjoy the rest of your day," Vincent repeated.

The women gathered up their clothing and scampered up the stairs. Vincent kept his eyes on the two male passengers they left behind. Once on deck, the women were assisted onto a smaller boat that was moored alongside. Some were still naked and carried what clothing they had. The second boat then turned toward shore and accelerated. Both Wesley and Being were dumbfounded by what had just occurred.

"Who are you?" Wesley asked Vincent. "Do you have you any idea who we are?"

Vincent was silent.

As Jason Being was about to take a shot at asking Vincent some questions, the big screen at the end of the room flickered. Dennis Wirth could be seen sitting at his desk. He had a worried look on his face as he spoke.

"Gentlemen, there has been a change in plans. The demonstration has been cancelled. In fact, the entire project has been cancelled," he stated.

"What are you talking about?" Wesley yelled. "I have my neck on the line on this one. We have both put $20 million into your pockets to have an exclusive rights to this new technology. We have our own as well as many other investors' money on the line with this deal. We *both* have," he said as he looked at Being, "and now you're telling us it's a no go. That's simply unacceptable. You will certainly never see any of that money in your hands. And you can fully expect to be prosecuted for deceiving us and our investors."

"If you recall," Wirth interrupted, "none of that money has been permanently transferred to my Swiss account. In fact, it has been recently transferred out of the current Swiss account entirely. It seems to have disappeared. The only trace of this money is coming from you two with your approvals to move it to who-knows-where. I'm sure a lot of people will be interested in how that works."

There was silence as the two men contemplated their next move.

"Gentlemen, I want you to understand that the technology we spoke of does not exist. It never has and it never will. To prove it to you, I ask you to take a position on the upper deck. I will show you the extent to which I am telling you the truth," Wirth stated.

"What do you mean it doesn't exist? We saw the demonstration on film," Being stated.

"It's all smoke and mirrors. Some good science fiction for sure, but it's not real," Wirth repeated.

"You're a dead man," Wesley yelled as the news was sinking in. "You're dead. Do you hear me?"

"That very well may be, Maxwell; but you two are not out of the woods yet, either. I suggest you take a few moments and have a look at the confirmation demonstration I am about to show you. It will convince you that this is an imaginary technology."

"You gentlemen need to come to the upper deck, now," Vincent insisted. He motioned his arm towards the stairway leading to the upper deck. "I won't ask you twice."

The two ascended the stairs and stood on the deck which was now almost in total darkness. The sun had set. There was nothing to be seen for miles around the ship. They were instructed to take a seat. After a few moments of silence, a streak of light was seen moving though the sky. It stopped and hovered above their boat. Both men began to panic. They were anticipating the device going off and killing them.

"What the hell are you doing?" Being screamed at Vincent. "We'll all be killed."

Without warning, there was a thundering explosion overhead. The ship's deck was covered in a very fine dust-like material as the sphere disappeared from sight. Then there was total darkness again. The men waited for what seemed like an hour, but was in fact only a few minutes, to digest what they had witnessed. They were confused to say the least. They were spared from death but confused by the device not working as they had seen it demonstrated previously. They were directed back to the lower cabin. Wirth could still be seen on the screen.

"You see gentlemen, it's a hoax, a myth. It doesn't exist," Wirth stated.

"We viewed the classified film where it worked perfectly," Wesley said as he looked at the screen.

"A clever ruse created by computer animation."

"Where's the money?" Being interjected,

"As I said, the money is gone. It is no longer in any of our Swiss accounts. It seems to have vanished."

"Forty million dollars does not vanish into thin air," Being insisted.

"You're welcome to see if you can find it. As much as you were duped into believing the technology existed, we were all taken by the transfer of the money to an unknown benefactor."

"We will have you behind bars!" Being yelled.

"I doubt that will be the case."

The statement came from someone who was in the room with Wirth.

"Who else is there with you, Wirth? Why didn't you tell us we had an audience? What kind of a scam are you pulling here?" Being questioned.

"A pretty good one," the mystery voice said. "You gentlemen in your weak effort to be the American heroes and make your fortunes have spent forty million dollars of other people's money for nothing. As well we have some pretty telling film footage of one of the lamest orgies I have ever seen. It's sure to be of interest to a few others on Capitol Hill, not to mention your wives. The women were beautiful and I commend Mr. Wirth for his selection, but you were both less than impressive. You, Mr. Wesley, have the smallest dick I have ever seen. Do you really think women like these are impressed by a little slap and tickle? They were toying with you and the film clearly makes you look like the none-performers you are."

"This is blackmail," Wesley screamed, "and you won't get away with it."

"We already have, my greedy friends," the voice said. "Now listen carefully. What I am about to tell you is life-altering information for you as well as for your immediate families and your extended families and friends. The large man standing in front of you will take the ship back to shore. You will be picked up and driven to a private airport. You will board a private plane and returned to the U.S. Upon arrival in the States, you will be picked up and delivered here to this office. I will see you in person tomorrow," the voice informed them as the screen went dark.

"I'm not going anywhere," Being bluffed.

Vincent pulled his gun and aimed it at Being's head.

"You don't have the nerve," he said just as the loud bang was heard from the revolver. Being grabbed the side of his head. The bullet had just whistled past his ear, removing a small piece and creating a gush of blood.

"You shot me!" he screamed at Vincent.

"Actually, I believe I have simply convinced you that we are serious," Vincent replied. "Now, unless you want to lose some of your other ear, I suggest you join me on deck and prepare for the boat and plane rides ahead for the next few hours." He threw a first-aid kit to Being as he finished speaking and climbed the stairs leading to the upper deck.

The men complied. They both sat in seats at the stern of the yacht. Vincent put the vessel to full throttle and headed for shore. Being was holding a handkerchief firmly against his wounded ear. It appeared that he had stopped the bleeding. Wesley sat still and offered him no assistance in his hour of need.

CHAPTER FORTY-SEVEN

July 1, 2:00 am PDT - Airtec Office
Los Angeles, California

The flight and the subsequent limo ride were uneventful. Neither of the men spoke a word. It was clear from the looks on their faces, they were both frightened and pondering how they were going to get out of this mess. As planned, they were met at the airport by a limo and a short time later arrived at the head office of Airtec under cover of darkness. The three men took the elevator to the executive floor. They entered the main office to be greeted by a very lovely young woman. She introduced herself simply as Mary Elizabeth and explained that Miss Wentworth, Mr. Wirth's secretary, had the evening off and she was filling in for this late night meeting. The truth was that the regular secretary had no idea what was happening in the office. She was in her apartment, likely asleep at this late hour. Mary Elizabeth picked up the phone and dialed the adjacent office. She had made the trip from New York to provide secretarial services to Joseph Viscusi.

"Your two o'clock is here, sir."

She stood and ushered the three men to the office door, quietly knocking before opening the door to provide access to the inner office. The men were instructed to take a seat by a man they didn't recognize. Next to the stranger sat a second unfamiliar face, and a very frightened looking Mr. Wirth.

Jason Being was first to speak. "Do you clowns have any idea who we are? How much trouble you're in? Kidnapping us; wounding me. We will have you in jail by sunrise," he threatened.

"Are you finished, Mr. Being, or is there something else you want to get off your bloated chest before we explain how this is going to work?" Anwar stated in a very calm and monotone manner.

There was silence from the two politicians. They were unaccustomed to being spoken to in that way and didn't know how to respond, or even if they should respond at all.

"Ah, we seem to be getting somewhere," Anwar continued. "As you now know, the technology you were in the process of purchasing does not exist. There is no ODD and the sooner you accept that fact the better."

He paused while the men considered the information. It looked like Being wanted to respond, but he remained silent.

"As far as the 40 million dollars, it's gone," Anwar continued. "It also no longer exists as far as you are concerned. You can chalk that up to bad judgment on your part. In both cases, we know that this amount of money comes from both of you and a number of silent investors. There are going to be a great many questions asked by these investors about their money you lost. I assure you, the trail of all that money leads to you. There is sufficient documentation that can easily be uncovered, if we so desire, to put you behind bars for a very long time. In this country, there is more emphasis on money than people. You receive more jail time if you copy a video movie than if you beat your wife. It's the money that is important. They will be forced to nail your asses to the wall, or worse, depending on who you convinced to be your silent partners in this endeavor. Is there any doubt in your minds?" he asked.

Both men nodded their heads in agreement.

"Good," Anwar responded.

Joseph Viscusi took over. "I want to be certain that you both understand, should there be the slightest hint, rumor, or indication of any kind of retribution against me, my family or Mr. Evangeline, or his family, the consequences will be swift and without mercy. You, your wife, your children, your grandchildren, your in-laws and your cousins will all be removed from this earth within 24 hours of a situation that puts us at risk. You had best hope we don't stub our toes getting out of the shower tomorrow as we could consider it a threat. Do you understand and do you acknowledge that we have the power, the resources, and the will to fulfill this promise to you as well?" He finished and looked at the two politicians sitting quietly.

"Yes. Yes," each man responded.

"Louder. I want to be certain you both have a firm commitment to your response."

"We agree," they both stated in very loud voices.

"Good," Joseph replied. "You must understand that we make the rules. There are no laws or precedent setting the agenda here. If we say you're ended, you're ended. We do not hide behind any secrecy and that is why we sit here before you this evening. You see our faces. You hear our words and hopefully you believe our commitment to this situation. We wish no harm to befall your families as a result of your poor judgment."

There was a period of silence as the two waited for the next axe to fall on them.

"Gentlemen, we have an understanding. I don't think we need to prolong this discussion. I will have Vincent show you the way out. Mr. Wirth has some additional issues to deal with. He won't be joining you at this time," Joseph concluded.

The two looked at Wirth. They could see that he was very concerned about what those other issues may be. They rose and headed out the door as quickly as they could. Vincent escorted them down the elevator and ushered them into a waiting limo.

"Let the driver know where you want to go and you will be dropped off, gentlemen," Vincent explained.

The limo slowly pulled out of the entranceway and headed into the dark streets. Vincent returned to the upper level office for the continuation of the meeting. He entered the office, Anwar was in the midst of his explanation of the remaining issues.

"Mr. Wirth, we all know that there is some credibility in the technology you have created here. We hope that we have convinced your fellow conspirators that the technology does not exist, however, you know better. For the life of me, I do not understand where your thought process was to precipitate such a deadly weapon, knowing the world's political situation. In years gone by the U.S. had to deal with Russia and China as far as trade embargos and concerns with nuclear proliferation but today many, many countries in the world are in political turmoil. I have only to look to my country of Egypt to see that. There are radicals around every corner whose sole purpose in life is to end your life and the lives of everyone in the U.S. America has learned nothing from 911, unfortunately. It took years to find the one man you believed responsible. All of your wealth and all of your armies could not find and kill one man living in a cave. This new technology cannot exist in today's world, and we need to make certain of it."

Wirth was clearly sweating as he listened to Anwar.

"We also know that at least two young people have been killed in the attempt by others to cover this up," he continued.

Wirth was visibly shaken that he was being linked to the deaths of Candice and Edward.

"I see from your expression," Anwar continued, " that you were already aware of this. We will find the culprit in these murders, and we will deal with that at a different time. Suffice it to say, we believe your actions precipitated, or were directly the cause of the death of those promising and very bright, young people. If we find this to be true, you and all involved will pay the ultimate price for that."

"I had nothing to do with anything like that," Wirth lied.

"Sit and listen," Anwar responded in a firm and threatening voice.

"I am also as concerned that as a result of your actions, my villa where my daughter and several of her friends were staying was attacked by a helicopter gunship only a few weeks ago. They destroyed my personal property and made an attempt on my daughter's life. You may have read about several persons who have met untimely deaths in recent weeks. This is a further example of how seriously we take these matters in my world." With that Anwar sat behind Wirth's desk.

There was a continued pause as Joseph Viscusi took his position facing Wirth in his chair.

"So how do we ensure that this technology never rears its ugly head again?" Joseph asked. "How many copies of the plans are there in existence? Be cautious about your answer. We tolerate no deception."

Wirth paused before answering. "*To tell you the truth* gentlemen, I am the only one who has a copy of the file and who knows the complete system set up. No other copies exist."

Anwar and Joseph looked at one another knowingly while they thought about his reply to their question. Joseph decided to continue his line of questioning.

"And how can we be certain, if we destroy your copy of the data, you will not try to recreate the system at some future point in time?" Joseph asked.

"You have my word on that gentlemen. My word is my bond. *To be honest with you*, I have always been a man of my word. A great many business deals are sealed with a simple hand- shake." Wirth replied with a sense of pride.

Once again Anwar and Joseph glanced at each other in response to his reply.

"Alright then," Anwar took over the conversation. "We are going to have you go into the next room," as he motioned to the secret room located behind the book case, "and we are going to have our computer expert come in and erase all of the computer files referencing this most deadly device."

Wirth rose from his seat and was ushered into the secret room.

"How did you know about this room?" he asked Joseph as he passed him in the entrance to the hide-away.

"Mr. Wirth, there is very little we don't know about you. This little love nest you have here is typical of a great many people in your position."

Once Wirth was locked in the room, Joseph opened the office door and motioned for Jack to come in. Three of the four young people had been waiting in the outer office while the interrogation was taking place. Just as they were seating themselves in Wirth's office, Reggie rushed in the door as well.

"Hi," he said to the young woman at the reception desk. He hadn't recognized Mary Elizabeth. "I'm Reggie Viscusi and I'm supposed to be in this meeting," he motioned towards the now closed office door.

"Yes," the young receptionist replied.

"I know you," he realized. He stopped beside the desk. "I'm sorry, Mary Elizabeth. There has been so much going on today, I was in a fog."

"Go right in," she replied smiling.

"Mr. Daniels, we need you to permanently erase each and every reference, drawing and piece of correspondence referring to the ODD project," Anwar instructed.

"Everything must be gone and be permanently unrecoverable."

Jack turned on the computer and proceeded with the total file erase. He had brought a special memory stick on which he had prepared a specific software process to achieve the results he knew they were going to need. While this was being done, he also dialed into the video camera that was located in the back room of Wirth's office. The group could see him pacing the room as he waited alone.

No one commented. They simply watched as Jack ran the system clean-out. It seemed to be taking a longer than expected amount of time.

"Are you having some difficulty?" Anwar asked Jack.

"No problem, there's simply a lot of data in a great many places that has to be found and erased. Then the backup or trash-can section needs to be cleaned as well. I have written the software to be very precise and exacting. We don't want to miss a letter of correspondence, nor a digit of calculation," Jack replied.

"Very well. I'm not criticizing your work, Mr. Daniels. I'm simply curious about the process itself," Anwar assured.

After twenty minutes had passed, Jack announced his success.

"All done," he exclaimed. "Every bit of ODD is gone, forever." He leaned back in the executive chair he was sitting in, pleased with his results.

"Thank you, ladies and gentlemen," Joseph replied. He directed at the young people in the group towards the office door. "Why don't you go and have some late dinner and leave us to finish our work with Mr. Wirth?"

As they left Reggie made a point to introduce Mary Elizabeth to the group.

"Mary Elizabeth, how do you like the weather here in California? It's certainly nicer than New York at this time of year," Angelina joked.

"I love California at any time of year," she replied.

The group exited the office and entered the elevator."What was that all about?" Reggie asked.

"Oh nothing," Angelina replied. "I was just thinking about what you might look for in an assistant if you should ever need one. Follow in your father's footsteps, if you know what I mean."

"I don't think I will ever have an assistant but if I ever did, Mary Elizabeth is certainly a very loyal employee. That is her most significant trait," Reggie replied.

"I think she maybe has one or two other pretty significant traits," she said in obvious reference to Mary Elizabeth's figure. "She is very pretty," Angelina continued. She knew it would elicit a response from Reggie. "She reminds me of your limo driver, Sam, only younger, don't you think?"

Reggie thought about her question and realized this was another smart-ass attempt to tease him about the exotic women that seemed to be in his father's life.

"No comment, I'm not having this conversation," was Reggie's only reply. They left the building and entered the limo to head out for their late dinner.

Vincent passed them at the entrance to the building. He was returning to the upper floor as the young people were exiting the office.

"See you later," Reggie said.

Vincent did not respond.

"Boy, your uncle is a quiet one, isn't he?" Rachel joked.

"Yes, he is," Reggie said not wanting to be the brunt of more teasing about how many uncles he had who all looked like enforcers.

The foursome went to a small coffee shop to enjoy a late night snack. No one really felt like a large meal; just a few baked goods and a latté were required.

******

Wirth was brought back into his private office. "Well, Mr. Wirth, I believe we have an understanding. I am convinced that you take our concerns seriously," Anwar stated.

"Yes, I do."

"Vincent, "Joseph instructed. "Escort Mr. Wirth to the lobby and get him a limo for the ride home?"

"No need," Wirth interjected. "I have my car. It's parked in the underground parking."

"Then by all means escort Mr. Wirth to his car, Vincent."

When they exited the elevator and entered the parking area, the security guard could be seen snoozing on a pile of cardboard stacked in the corner of the lot. Wirth took notice.

"I'll have to deal with that tomorrow," he stated to Vincent.

Vincent remained silent.

Wirth got into his Lamborghini sports car and revved it up as he maneuvered his way from the underground lot. Vincent was not impressed by his boastful display of wealth.

******

The four young people were exhausted from their day's activities and the tension and drama of the situation. Reggie and Angelina returned to her apartment. Jack and Rachel spent the night at one of the finer hotels, close to Angelina's place. This had been pre-arranged. Angelina and Reggie woke early and spent some quality time showering and enjoying each other's company before Jack and Rachel appeared at the door, precisely on time. They had planned to have breakfast together at a little spot that Angelina enjoyed, when she was staying at her apartment in California.

As they were about to leave, both Angelina's and Rachel's cell phones chimed to signal that they had an e-mail message. They took their cell phones from their purses and opened the e-mails. It was addressed to all employees of Airtec Engineering, and it was from the Vice President of Global Operations. Angelina looked briefly at the e-mail and decided to read it aloud. Rachel stopped reading and listened.

"Hear this," Angelina stated. "This is from the VP of Global Operations to all Airtec employees. Ladies and gentlemen, it is with tremendous regret that I must inform you that Mr. Dennis Wirth, CEO of Airtec Engineering, was killed in an automobile accident last evening. The details are not as yet available; but from what we know he was driving down the coast highway and lost control of his car; went through a guard rail landing in the ocean below. The rescue crews were quick to respond; but unfortunately, he was pronounced dead at the scene. I know you all join me in conveying our deepest sympathies to his wife, Margret, and daughter, Susan. This is a tremendous loss of a great man who moved this company from humble beginnings to be the leader in the industry we are today. At this time, there have been no details released about funeral arrangements. You will be notified once these plans are confirmed. In the interim, I have been appointed as temporary CEO of Airtec, pending a review by the board. The board will convene as soon as it can be arranged. I ask all of you for your continued support and assistance to get the company through this most difficult time."

When Angelina finished reading the statement, the group stood in the hallway of her apartment in silence.

CHAPTER FORTY-EIGHT

July 3, 12:00 am EDT - Viscusi Estate
New Canaan, CT

The entire team had returned to New York. They all decided they needed to obtain more details about the demise of Mr. Wirth. It was too much of a coincidence that he just happened to have car accident, twenty-minutes after having, what must have been a very serious conversation with Joseph Viscusi and Anwar Evangeline. If the group was going to become involved in this side of the new business, then they needed to know everything, regardless of how ugly it got.

Joseph had mentioned to Reggie that Anwar was going to be his guest at the Viscusi estate in Connecticut for the weekend and would be returning to Egypt on Monday. As they approached the gate to the estate, it swung open. Passing by the guard house, they could see Vincent sitting in the chair by the window and waved as they passed. Vincent nodded. As they entered the house, Reggie called for his mother. He was quickly met by the maid explaining that Mrs. Viscusi and Mrs. Evangeline had gone into New York for some shopping. He and Angelina were surprised to learn that Mrs. Evangeline was also visiting. They could hear two men talking in his father's office as they approached. Joseph had spotted Reggie and walked to the office door to greet the group who followed Reggie into the house.

"Come in, come in," he gestured to them. "We were just having a pleasant conversation about the world in general. It's nice that you have come for a visit. This is an unexpected pleasure," Joseph stated.

"I wasn't aware that mother had accompanied you on this trip," Angelina said as she hugged her father. "If I had known, I would have made arrangements to go with the ladies on their shopping trip. Both Rachel and I could have gone."

"It was decided at the last minute," Anwar explained. "Your mother hasn't been to the U.S. for a few years. She felt it was time to do a little shopping in some of her favorite stores. I also wanted her to meet Mr. and Mrs. Viscusi as we seem to be connected through you two." He pointed to his daughter and Reggie. "Your mothers seem to feel that there is a little more encouragement required to move things along between you two. I wouldn't know about that. Apparently I'm not in the loop on a lot of the fine details. I don't suppose there is anything you wish to tell your father about your relationship, is there Angelina?"

Anwar looked at Rachel. He felt she might divulge some secrets yet to be shared. She said nothing; yet there was the tiniest of smiles that could be seen on her face.

"Daddy, you know you will be the first to know if we have anything to say," Angelina replied in a playful voice.

"Perhaps third, forth, or fifth to know might be more accurate," was Anwar's only reply. He kissed his daughter on the cheeks.

"Reggie, we haven't heard from you on this subject," Joseph interjected.

Reggie held up his hands, in a sign-of-surrender, and said nothing.

"Dad," Reggie began after everyone had finished their casual conversation about the weather and the ladies' shopping trip, "I suppose you've heard that Mr. Wirth had an unfortunate car accident last evening?"

Joseph and Anwar glanced at each other. It was almost as if they were surprised by Reggie's question.

"Yes, we did hear about the accident. I understand he drives a very powerful sports car. These things sometimes happen when people drive too fast," was Joseph's response.

The group had discussed this, on the way here this morning. They all agreed that they were going to be upfront in questioning the two fathers. If they were going to be connected with Joseph and Anwar, even if it wasn't a direct connection, they felt they needed to know the truth about what had occurred. Reggie took a more direct approach with his next question.

"Did you have anything to do with it?" he asked in a more sheepish tone than he had intended.

Joseph hesitated before answering. Again, both he and Anwar seemed puzzled by being asked the question. Of course, they had something to do with it. They had everything to do with it; however it wasn't a subject to be discussed, openly. In their businesses, one could never assume that one's conversations were totally private. There was always the possibility that someone else was listening. The entire Viscusi house was swept twice daily for listening devices. It was a practice Joseph put in place from the day they moved in. I addition, there were also detectors located in various positions throughout the grounds to detect any presence of listening devices outside the main house. Joseph felt the preamble to his answer was to explain what they had learned from some of their people.

"There is some information we have uncovered, concerning your friends' deaths," Joseph said.

"Information from where?" Reggie asked.

"Let me finish, please. We sent two of our men to Mexico to investigate the murders of Mr. Milton and Dr. Bergen. The authorities were, shall we say, less than forthcoming with any information concerning the incident, however, we have other connections. We have determined that there were three, possibly four agents who visited Mexico City at the time of their death."

"What kind of agents?" Angelina asked.

"Our own Homeland Security, we were told. It's seems that some agents from Homeland Security orchestrated the murders through a third party organization that operates in Mexico City. Their leader owns a number of strip clubs and bordellos throughout the city. They also deal drugs and provide deadly services such as they did with Mr. Milton and Dr. Bergen. There was a coined phrase at one time, Murder-for-hire, I believe it was. They were hired to murder your friends."

Rachel gasped quietly.

"This ODD matter may not be entirely over. There could be some loose ends yet to be snipped," Anwar added.

"We believe that Mr. Wirth's involvement was pivotal to the entire scheme. His company was providing the delivery device. He seemed to be the only one who had all of the plans and specifications in one location," Joseph continued. "We know Homeland Security is implicated in the scheme, or at lease someone at Homeland. Certainly, Jason Being is one; there may be others. How much Being really knows is uncertain. He and Mr. Wesley were major fundraisers. They solicited the investors and raised the money to finance the project. If Wesley was involved with knowledge of the Department of Defense, then we have a problem. We don't believe that to be the case. He appears to be simply a money-man. We don't believe Jason Being is working with the full knowledge of Homeland Security, either. It's the Homeland connection we are most uncertain about. We can't put our finger on the level of involvement by Homeland; if there is any at all. There may be agents working on their own. We don't know."

"What we do know, for certain, is that Mr. Wirth could not be trusted. It was clear that there would be another attempt to resurrect the ODD project," Anwar added.

"After you left the office last evening, we had a final discussion with Mr. Wirth about ending this terrifying technology. He assured us that he was the only one with a copy of the detailed drawings and specifications, however, we were concerned about the honesty of some of his responses," Joseph said.

"You are all intelligent, young people," Anwar interrupted, "Here is a tip that Joseph and I both have used over the years in some pretty high-level negotiations. It is always best to ask your opponent a direct question, is rule number one. This is especially true if you have just met them and have no history with their trustworthiness. Rule number two, and the final rule you need to know; if the response from your opponent begins with a preamble such as 'to be honest with you, or to tell you the truth'; you must assume that everything that follows either of those two statements is untrue. It's a simple rule but it's a very important one to remember. This is particularly relevant if the person you are asking is in a state of upset or nervousness about the situation."

"If they are under pressure of some kind," Joseph added.

"Yes," Anwar continued, "that is very true, Joseph. In our discussion last evening, Mr. Wirth used both forms of preamble in answering our questions. We knew he was not being truthful in his responses."

"So you caused the accident?" Reggie spoke more forcefully.

"Let us simply say that we were not surprised when Mr. Wirth's tendency to drive too quickly, in his super-fast sports car, was the cause of his demise," Anwar stated. He looked towards Joseph for confirmation.

"We can tell you, during our discussion with Mr. Wirth, we determined that he was directly involved in the death of your friends. We are confident that either he ordered it himself, or was at least involved in the decision to take those tragic measures," Joseph confirmed.

There was silence in the room. The young people thought about their next question. It was clear by their expressions that they were in agreement with the demise of Wirth. Since he was connected to the death of their friends and was a risk for renewing the interest in the ODD, then he had to go.

Joseph and Anwar seemed reluctant to provide any additional details with Jack and Rachel in the room. It took Angelina a few moments to realize that they had not specifically advised their fathers that the foursome was now a team, without secrets. During their time together, they had all realized that they weren't happy in their respective careers. None of them were. They had missed so much time from work investigating the murders that their employers were asking questions. Both Rachel and Angelina had received phone calls from their immediate bosses. Jack was also informed that there was a backlog of programming which required his attention. The president of Reggie's company had left numerous messages for his newest and youngest Vice President. The foursome hadn't worked out any of the details of what they wanted to do, or how they would do it; but they knew it wasn't what they were doing now. They felt obligated to notify their respective employers that they were leaving.

"Dad," Angelina began as she pointed to each of the young people, "we have all decided to join forces and create a team. Outside of Mensa we mean. We work so well together, Angelina said."

"And what would this team be doing?" Joseph asked

"Well, just what we are doing now," Reggie interjected. "Jack and Rachel are equal partners. We have told them about our connection with you and Mr. Evangeline and how we can mesh our talents with your talents, contacts, and resources."

"I see," Joseph replied. "Are they fully aware of the danger associated with our new relationship?"

"We are fully aware there may be danger, or more likely, there will be danger and we accept that," Rachel said.

"Once we have made this bond, it can never be undone," Anwar stated.

"These types of relationships are permanent," Joseph added.

"We understand," Reggie said. "We are all looking for other careers than what we currently have. We are all free-thinkers and working for a large company is not best suited to us. We want to find our own way in our own company. We don't know if there will ever be another situation like the ODD, but we have an idea there may be. Trouble seems to follow us around," he joked as he looked at his friends and smiled. "You just said this isn't over yet. There's one possibility, right there. If it doesn't turn out to be the case then we will work on our own projects and follow our own careers."

"Do you all have the same career objectives?" Joseph asked.

"No, and that's the point," Rachel said. "We all have different career desires. We need to have a relationship where we can work together when we need to, and yet allow each other time and space to do our own thing. We admit that we haven't worked out all the details of how that's going to work; but we feel it can work."

"A noble and difficult objective," Anwar stated.

"Yes, but one we can achieve with your help," Angelina said to her father.

"And do you trust each other sufficiently that your father and I can be assured of confidentiality?" Joseph asked.

"We trust each other with our lives," Rachel said. "And you can be assured, whatever we discuss as a team, stays with the team."

"I'm glad to hear that. There will be times when we will all need that level of trust. We will take you at your word," Anwar said. "A new team is born."

There was a period of general discussion and a few extra hugs and handshakes to solidify their new bond. Reggie felt, it was one of the first orders of business was to find out, once and for all, if his father was a Mafia guy, as Angelina had so-named him. If the new group was going to be linked, they needed to know everything.

"Dad," Reggie interjected, "I'm going to ask a blunt question. Keep in mind that it is with the greatest respect that I ask you. Are you in the Mafia?"

The others in the group were silent, awaiting his response to this very direct question. Joseph could be seen formulating his reply. What Reggie didn't know about the rules associated with the mafia, were that the organization always came first, ahead of yourself and your family, if need be. And you never admit *to anyone* that you belong to the organization, or even that it exists. Joseph's reply to his son's specific question had to be crafted with this in mind. It was sometimes necessary to lie to protect one's family.

"Son, I am going to reply to your question keeping, everyone's personal well-being as a prime concern. The word Mafia is a myth. Some call it the mob and any number of other names, but it does not exist. If it did exist," he continued, "it would be a relationship that would transcend any other. A relationship to a family that could not be discussed. Do you understand what I'm saying?"

"Why did Mr. Evangeline refer to you as "Don" when you first arrived in Cairo, after the gunship incident? Reggie continued.

"The term "Don" has occasionally been used with my name as a gesture of respect. I am involved in some dealings that would best be described as less-than-forthright in the eyes of the law. I know in your heart, you know this is the case. You don't have to agree with everything it entails but you can't continue to be in denial. "Don" is a term Italians and others often use when addressing people who have given back to the community. You know that your mother and I have been most generous over the years with various charities. In particular those dealing directly with people originating from Italy. I am often called upon to use my negotiating skills to resolve an issue, perhaps, concerning an old woman renting an apartment and a rent increase. These are things I am asked and I do for the betterment of our people. Let's accept this as the answer to your question, and let it be."

"Father," Angelina began once Joseph had finished his statement. She knew the answer to her question, but it was important that her other friends hear it first-hand. They had to know everything about the situation they were getting into. "Are you also involved with less than forthright dealings, as is Mr. Viscusi?"

"My dear, you know the business I am in deals with weapons. Although I have never explained it to you in detail, I have also never tried to hold that information as a complete secret. You only have to look at the security at our villa to realize we deal with some pretty unsavory people. How many people do you know have amour plated coverings on the windows and an armed militia at their disposal should difficulties arise? Let's not be naive about these things, my dear."

"Father," Angelina continued, "it's true that I did know a little of what you do but not in any great detail. My point is that it's important that all members of this team are aware of the potential dangers of being a member of our new team."

"We understand," Joseph replied, "and we respect that. I think you all know the answers to your last questions. Assume you are correct and we can move on."

"One thing," Anwar interjected. "Regardless of what it is you end up doing, your mothers cannot be made aware in any way that you are associated with our respective businesses. I, for one, would rather deal with an army of terrorists than your mother, Angelina, if she was ever to find out."

They all smiled at the thought. Both men knew, whatever the relationship with their children was, if they were linked to them, it would bring an element of danger. Anwar and Joseph acknowledged there were some definite advantages to having access to the skills these young people possessed. They were confident the required level of confidentiality would exist.

"Agreed. Let's spend some time over the next several weeks discussing how this all might work." Reggie said to his father and Anwar. "We will likely have many questions. We hope you will bear with us during this transition period. Now that we have a plan in place, the time is right for me to give my notice at work."

"I will, too," Angelina added.

"Us as well," chimed in Rachel and Jack.

"That's the first step in the plan," Reggie finished, then hesitated."Our only issue now is money," he said looking at the two older gentlemen. "We have talked and we all have put some money aside. In additional, we have 401K's. We can borrow against them as well. Whether or not it's enough to carry us through the start-up phase of our businesses remains to be seen; but it's a start."

There was a pause in the conversation. The group was surprised to see smiles appear on both of the elder gentlemen's faces. Anwar was first to reply.

"Children. We have some good news for you. First off, you need to form a company of your own. One each individually, under another larger umbrella company, would likely be best from a tax perspective. We can look after that in the near term. This would be the best way for your father and I to participate; on a contract basis. In this way, you could also use the newly formed company to pursue other interests, in addition to those of which we now speak. "

"I will help you find an appropriate office space," Joseph offered.

"Terrific," Reggie replied. "We can't afford much. Please keep that in mind when you're looking."

"Now, Angelina, you will have to move to New York. We will have to find you an apartment, close to the office," Anwar said. "You can move out of your office and apartment in Cairo. I never liked that set up."

Angelina knew this was going to be an issue. She and Reggie had already decided that once they left their respective jobs, they were going to get an apartment together. She knew her father would freak at this news, so she left that announcement for another conversation.

Anwar continued, "The really good news is that you will definitely not have money issues."

"Are you going to finance us?" Angelina asked. "We really want to do this on our own. If we run into trouble, we know we have you as a back-up, and that's great..."

"Let me finish, my dear," Anwar interrupted. "As a result of the most recent business venture, there is an excess of money remaining in a Swiss bank account. Money that no one has claimed. Quite a lot of money. This money was raised by our political acquaintances from a number of their wealthy investors. I'm certain all of them know by now that this investment has gone wrong and they have lost their money. This is not an uncommon event when wealthy people invest in non-conventional projects. Losing money is the risk they accept. This money can be used to finance your new company. Think of it as a *contract fee* for your most recent and valuable work."

"Fantastic", Angelina said. "Your suggestion to form a new company which would allow all of us to pursue other interests is a great one. I know that both Rachel and Jack are of the same mind as we are with respect to their working careers. We can start up a company with all four of us. That would be great. We like that idea. See, we are helping each other already," she laughed.

Reggie interjected, "Each of us could do what he or she wanted as far as work; but we would keep it under one umbrella. We could cut costs by having one office with shared staff. How much money are we talking, Dad?"

Before he answered, Angelina interrupted.

"Anton," Angelina said. "I bet you Anton would be more than willing to move here and look after the office. If I close down my Cairo office, he's going to need a job. He and I have had numerous discussions about America. He's interested in immigrating."

"Son, to answer your question, there is forty million in the account," Joseph stated as if it were nothing.

The young people couldn't believe their ears. They were momentarily stunned by the news.

"Dollars? U.S. dollars? Forty million U.S. dollars?" Angelina asked. The two men nodded in the affirmative. Both she and Reggie sat down to ponder how much money that was before continuing the conversation. Rachel and Jack held each other's hand. There was an air of excitement in the room, while they considered all of the possibilities afforded by this new venture.

Just as the discussion was getting more involved, Vincent walked into the room and whispered something in Joseph's ear. Joseph's face went solemn. He moved closer to Anwar and relayed the message very quietly.

"What's wrong?"Reggie asked.

Both men hesitated and then Joseph spoke.

"You want to be involved in the business. The business has an immediate problem. It seems that either Maxwell Wesley or Jason Being is making some noise about some missing funding."

"Which one is it?" Anwar asked in a menacing voice. Unaccustomed to hearing her father speak in this manner, it caused Angelina to turn to him with a serious look on her face.

"I believe it's Wesley," Joseph replied, "but we need to deal with both men."

"How are we going to deal with them?" Reggie asked. He knew the answer, but the group needed to hear it.

"We need to have a sit-down meeting with both of these morons. I don't think they heard what was said earlier in our dealings. They need to be reminded," Anwar stated. "You want to be in on the family businesses. This is as good a time as any to hear your input. Perhaps, you may have a solution to reduce the risk of these people meeting the same fate as Mr. Wirth."

Joseph walked to the study door and closed it.

Angelina and Reggie were seated on a couch at the far end of the office. Rachel and Jack found chairs to sit in as the elder men discussed the situation. They were concerned about having either one of these two politicians meet the same fate as Wirth. Anything such as that was certain to draw attention from law enforcement. They also knew that because of the greed and ambition of these men, and the risk they placed all of society in, they were the bad guys.

Reggie was first to speak.

"It needs to be confirmed for certain which one, or if both are the risk. There's simply too much at stake to be anything other than absolutely certain. We are talking about a potential catastrophic consequence if we make the wrong decision," Reggie said.

"You don't want to give them a second chance?" Anwar asked.

"I agree with Reggie," Angelina replied, "I think everyone deserves an opportunity to reverse a bad decision they may have made, but these guys have already had a second-chance. I believe they have played their final hand. We must be certain we don't have a recurring problem."

"I think one or both of these men are in trouble with their investors. We must make certain they take the hit for their actions," Joseph added.

"No doubt, they are under tremendous pressure from some pretty heavy-hitters for losing money like this," Anwar added. "This amount of money makes people make bad decisions. We can't afford to let it happen. We must determine who it is and deal with it once and for all."

"Good," both Angelina and Reggie said in unison.

"Are you and Jack okay with this?" Angelina asked her friends.

"We don't have a choice. As much as we would all like to see a different resolution to this problem, there isn't one. We didn't create this dilemma," Jack said. Rachel nodded her agreement.

Joseph took a seat behind his desk. "We have our answer," he said. "Why don't we take a break and discuss what you're going to do with all that money?" Joseph suggested. He wanted to be alone to make the final arrangements.

The young people left the office feeling both conflicted and anxious because of the decision they believed necessary to make, and yet excited about their new adventure. They were starting a new business. They had more money than they ever expected to have and they seemed to have been given credibility by some very important people. They spent the afternoon talking and planning. Joseph and Anwar joined them towards the end of the day. They had confirmed that it was Wesley who was leaking information concerning the ODD. It had been decided that the leak had to be dealt with permanently. The young people were in agreement with the action required. They returned to the city.

CHAPTER FORTY-NINE

July 5, 4:30 pm PDT- Las Vegas, Nevada

In Las Vegas, the convention had ended. Maxwell Wesley had taken his seat in the back of the limo, to return to his hotel. He was at the convention to raise money for the party and it looked like they had done very well that afternoon.

He was receiving some threatening phone calls from some of his investors. For the time being at least, it appeared there were no immediate consequences for the loss of the money. Wesley had also been in contact with Jason Being, at Homeland Security. He too was being pressured by his investors for a return on their investment. Everyone involved had been told that the deal was off and the money was gone. A risky investment gone bad was not unusual. Both Being and Wesley feeling pretty smug about how they had side-stepped the consequences for their failed attempt in the arms race. There remained a few persistent investors looking for their money, but Wesley and Being felt they could handle them. There were also rumors floating about regarding the development of some sort of a new super weapon, however, the details were unknown. As Wesley sat in the limo, the door locks could be heard to engage, and the limo started down the road. At what should have been the turn to the hotel, the driver kept on a straight path.

"I think you missed our turn there, buddy," Wesley said through the glass separating the front and back seats. There was no reply. "You missed the turn back there. You need to turn around and head to the hotel," he repeated in a more forceful manner. After waiting for a response and getting none, "Listen asshole, you need to stop this car and turn it around right now."

With that, the car turned but not in the direction he expected. They passed several buildings that appeared to be warehouses and pulled into an open bay-door. The door closed and the locks on the car doors were disengaged. The glass partition was lowered, and the driver said. "You need to step out of the vehicle."

"Fuck you," Wesley replied, "I'm not stepping out anywhere. You need to start this car and head back to the hotel before you find yourself in jail for the rest of your life. Kidnapping a federal politician is a federal offense, even in Nevada."

The side door opened. Wesley saw what was now a familiar face. It was Vincent.

"Get out of the fucking car before I turn you inside out, you little fuck," he said in a most convincing tone. Wesley exited the car. He was shown into an office located towards the back of the warehouse and took a seat. It was only a few moments before the door opened and two more people he recognized entered the room. His heart dropped when he recognized Evangeline and Viscusi. He didn't say a word.

"Mr. Under Secretary," Anwar started, "we are hearing rumors that someone is attempting to regenerate interest in the new technology we had discussed several weeks ago. Would you know anything about that? We have already had a conversation with your friend at Homeland Security, and he assures us that it's not coming from him. In fact his exact words were, "To tell you the truth, I think the leak is coming from Wesley". What would you say about that?"

"He's lying. To be honest with you, he's a liar and has been known to be many times before. I wouldn't believe a word he says."

"I would tend to agree with you, sir," was Joseph's reply. "If it's not coming from you, then all we really need to do is reinforce in your mind the importance of candor in this situation and have your assurance that you have put this behind you."

"You have my word on that," Wesley replied.

"I'm sure we do," Joseph said. "Vincent, if you would be so kind as to drive this gentleman back to his hotel, it would be appreciated."

Wesley and Vincent left the small office, got back into the car, and drove off into the darkness.

"Well, well," Anwar said to Joseph, "we have two politicians to deal with from what I hear. I would not recommend we deal with both of them at one time. It may bring a great many questions. I believe that Mr. Wesley is the first on our list. I am confident that Mr. Being will remain silent, once his cohort is gone."

"I agree. You are absolutely correct," was Joseph's reply.

******

It was Monday morning when Angelina opened the newspaper and read the headlines. Maxwell Wesley – Under Secretary of Defense has died in a private airplane accident on his return from the republican convention in Las Vegas. She yelled to Reggie who was brushing his teeth in the bathroom.

"Listen to this, Maxwell Wesley – Under Secretary of Defense has been killed in a private plane crash. Apparently, he was an avid flyer and had taken his own four-seat aircraft to Las Vegas to attend the Republican Party convention. On the return flight, there was some yet to be determined mechanical difficulty and the plane went down shortly after takeoff. He was the only one on the plane." she finished. She closed the paper and folded it in its original form.

"My guess is that Mr. Wesley needed to take a few more flying lessons," Reggie replied.

They looked at each other in a knowing way and said nothing.

Both Anwar and Joseph had also read the news about the demise of Wesley. Anwar called Joseph.

"I see that the plan is complete, Joseph."

There was a slight hesitation before Joseph replied.

"There was a plan but someone beat us to it," Joseph replied in a worried tone. "Someone else took care of this before we had the opportunity."

"Any idea of who that may have been?"

"None," Joseph replied.

There was another hesitation while both men considered what had occurred. They had planned to dispose of Wesley, but before they could execute their plan he was dead by another's hand.

"End result accomplished," Anwar said as he hung up the phone.

******

Meanwhile in Washington, Jason Being was picking up his paper from the step in front of his house. He read the headline and slowly folded his copy back to its original form. He walked to his office and placed a call. The message he relayed to the person at the other end of the call was crisp and succinct, "The deal is off. The technology doesn't exist. The issue is dead." He hung up the phone.

CHAPTER FIFTY

August 15, 5:00 pm EDT - Office Building
New York City, New York

It had been six weeks since the group had given their respective notices to their employers. They had spent this time making plans and getting the groundwork laid for their new businesses in New York. Reggie and Rachel had both moved to much larger condos downtown. They were now living with their significant others.

Reggie was reluctant to leave his old apartment behind. Despite it being in a questionable neighborhood, above a pizza and message parlor, he really liked the people. He had an idea in the back of his mind about rejuvenating the old neighborhood. Trying to bring in new investment. Have people spend some money fixing up the houses and businesses. He knew Angelina was not keen on being in that area. He agreed, for now at least, to move to this newer place.

Angelina had yet to disclose the new living arrangement to her father, however, she felt that it wasn't going to be much of a surprise. She had discussed her intentions with her mother and her mother had promised Angelina that she would work the information into a conversation with her father. Angelina felt comfortable that Reggie's life would not be in danger from her father.

As promised, Joseph had secured a prime office in a small office building in Manhattan. It was a unique building, one that had been overlooked by progress. It was wedged between two towering office structures. Despite the acute shortage of office space in New York, Joseph managed to secure this prime location. Apparently, the existing tenant had a sudden need to move locations. At least that was the explanation given for the space being available. Anwar and Angelina had been on the phone for three weeks trying to facilitate the emigration of Anton. They had just received formal approval. It took some significant money and many favors to expedite this as quickly as they did. Anton had only been in New York for three weeks and already he had managed to find his way around as well as have the offices painted and all the furniture in place.

It was late Sunday afternoon when the group gathered for their first look at the new offices. As they approached the front door of the building, they were impressed that a building from this era still existed in New York. It was a textbook snapshot of 1920's- architecture. As perfect as the day it was built. As if time had simply passed it by. Every art-deco detail was gleaming and original, they noted, as the group made their way through the small lobby. The original elevator was still in use. It barely fit all six occupants. They had to stand to the side to make room for each other. The iron safety gate was pulled across the brass and black-iron door, and the elevator creaked its way up the four floors to the top floor of the building. As they pulled the elevator doors aside, the same decor appeared in the narrow hallway leading to their new offices. None of the four young people had seen the building, let alone been in the any of the offices. Between Joseph, Anwar, and Anton, everything had been taken care of. Mrs. Evangeline and Mrs. Viscusi had also added some of their own decorative touches to the space. Both women were ecstatic at the news that their children seemed to be progressing in their relationship. *Surely marriage and children were just around the corner;* they thought; they hoped.

As the group approached their office, they noticed that the window in the main door was covered with brown paper and painter's tape. They assumed it was a last minute detail, a slight oversight that could be easily fixed. As they stopped at the entrance to the office, Anwar, Joseph, and Anton were all waiting for them at the door.

"Come into your new space," Anton said. He swung the heavy door open.

The group entered and stopped just inside the door to take it all in. The outer office was large. There was a period-desk for Anton at the far side of the main foyer and four chairs for visitors were placed against the wall to the left. Tasteful artwork, including an original Andy Warhol was hanging on the freshly painted walls. The faint smell of paint lingered. There were five office doors located around the perimeter of the main office, one read "conference room" on the glass in the door.

On each private office door, was the name of one of the partners, and their company name, printed neatly in black and gold lettering on the glass. Rachel Wi, Wi Exclusives; Angelina Evangeline, Angel Air; Reggie Viscusi, Math Counts; and Jack Daniels, Software Solutions. The four were very excited to finally see their dreams starting to take shape.

The outer office, and indeed the entire building, featured 1920's art-deco style in its beautiful millwork framing on the windows and every door. The entire building was a picture from the past. Most, if not all of the tenants had made great efforts to retain the original décor of the building. This office gave one the feeling of being in a silent, or early-talky movie.

A movie where the women were called dames and the men wore fedoras and smoked cigarettes. One expected Bogy himself to come through the door at any moment. It was fun to be a part of the culture that had been New York City, so many years before. Before they were born. In fact before their parents were born.

As they entered their respective offices, there was a sound of awe coming from each of them.

"I *cannot* believe this," Angelina said. "You have outdone yourself, Anton. This furniture and the color is exactly as I would have chosen."

"Me too," Rachel called, from inside her office. "It's perfect."

"How did you get it so right?" Angelina asked Anton.

"That's what I do," was his only reply. Anton was always the modest one. He didn't like the attention being directed towards himself.

Reggie took a seat behind his new desk and gazed at his surroundings. He first noticed the wet-bar at the side of his office. In an 8 x 10 black picture frame, he saw a picture on the wall next to the bar. He rose to look more closely, and as he approached, he saw that it was a picture of Edward and Candice. A picture that had been taken at their first meeting in Mexico City, he recalled. He took the picture off the wall and placed it on the corner of his desk. He returned to his chair. As he gazed at the picture, his memory went back to the time it was taken. The memories of everything he and the rest of his friends had experienced since that day came rushing back.

They had met just this past March, not quite five months ago. In that short time he had fallen in love with the most beautiful woman in the world; the day they met. The entire group had bonded, at the Mensa meeting. As if they were intended to be together. They lost two of their newfound friends when they were murdered. Murdered, because they accidently discovered information concerning the most deadly weapon that had ever been conceived.

The group had unraveled the mystery surrounding the development of the deadly ODD device, and they had put an end to this dreadful technology, or so they hoped. Reggie knew there were more conspirators to be dealt with. His father and Anwar had discovered there were at least three, possibly four, Homeland Agents who likely had a hand in their friends' deaths. Jason Being remained a threat, although they were reasonably certain they had secured his silence when his partner in crime, Maxwell Wesley, was tragically killed in a private plane crash. Dennis Wirth, the CEO of Airtec, and the individual everyone believed was the king pin of this entire operation, had also met his maker when he drove his Lamborghini off the coast highway late one night. All of this, all the good and the bad of it, had brought them to where they were today. Standing in their new office, ready to start their new careers, and working with the people they most loved.

Reggie got up from his desk and walked to his office door with the picture in his hands, just as the other three friends were doing the same thing. They each had a tear in their eye upon discovering this thoughtful gesture from Anton.

"It couldn't get any better than this," Reggie thought as he gazed at his friends.

They excitedly toured each other's offices and were overwhelmed by Anton's thoughtful touches. There was not one thing that any of them would change. It was perfection.

After a long afternoon of discussing plans for their future in their new conference room, they decided it was time to head out for a celebratory dinner. Tomorrow was going to be the first day of the next phase of their lives and they couldn't wait.

"My treat," Mr. Viscusi announced, "the Waldorf serves the most succulent duck on Sunday evenings, and you're all invited. Mrs. Viscusi and Mrs. Evangeline will be joining us for dinner."

As reluctant as the young people were to leave their new surrounding, they were excited about the family meal. Rachel and Jack were now family too.

Upon leaving, the main office door was closed and locked. Anton then pulled off the brown paper and painters' tape that had been covering the window. The group hadn't yet decided on their company name. They had come up with several potential names that everyone liked, but they couldn't decide on one. It was agreed that Joseph, Anwar, and Anton would review the list and make the final decision. The group was excited to see the name they had chosen. Anton stepped back from the door to reveal the new company name. In large black and gold letters it read, **Think Inc.**

The second volume in the Think Inc. Mysteries will be available soon. *Second Chance* continues our saga as the Think Inc. Team saves the world from yet another catastrophic circumstance. Be prepared for some twists and turns as the team hones its problem solving skills.

The Story Continues…

ABOUT THE AUTHOR

I recently retired from my business career.

Many people asked me what I planned to do with all of my free time. I have many interests, however, it has long been a dream of mine to write. That may or may not surprise some, but that's what I intended to do and have been doing. What you see in this volume is the first of what I expect to be a long list of books as yet to be penned.

Last Breath is the first book in the Think Inc. Mysteries series, which chronicles the exploits of a team of highly intelligent and uniquely talented twenty-somethings as they attempt to save the world from certain destruction. Follow the exploits of a sexy and seductive Egyptian beauty, her sultry *Playboy* model friend from Sweden and the China doll just uncovering her hidden sexuality. Together with their closest friends and lovers, they put their collective genius to work to save us all.

I hope you enjoy the read as much as I enjoyed creating it for you.

H.P. BARNETT

26387049R00195

Made in the USA
Charleston, SC
05 February 2014